Perfect Little Ome

Perfect Little Omega: Part Two

An Omegaverse Romance Duology

Leigha Madison

This is a work of fiction. Names, characters, places, and incidents either are the product of the author's imagination or are used fictitiously. Any resemblance to actual persons, living or dead, events, or locales is entirely coincidental.

Copyright © 2023 by Leigha Madison

All rights reserved. No part of this book may be reproduced or used in any manner without written permission of the copyright owner except for the use of quotations in a book review. For more information, address:

First paperback edition March, 2023

Book design by Leigha Madison
ISBN

DEDICATION

TABLE OF CONTENTS

CHAPTER ONE

Brooks

The muffled sound of gunfire from outside grabs my attention, as we ascend the stairs back to the main storage area. The basement where Ricci supposedly had his tech girl set up is completely empty, so we came back here to reconvene.

At the sound of more shots being fired, we race to the door together, slamming outside to hear screeching tires and loud swearing. It sounds like Remi and Dmitri, but what the fuck are they doing here?

I look at each of the guys, communicating silently with hand gestures. Still not sure what exactly is going on, we approach the corner of the building cautiously, guns still drawn.

I lean around the corner, trying to get an idea of what's going on. All I can see are outlines in the dark. It looks like two men and they're crouched around a body; one of them is performing CPR while the other is on the phone.

It's definitely Remi talking, "The Sylvan building, east alleyway, gunshot to the chest. Dmitri is performing CPR but it doesn't look good. I need you to get an ambulance down here now. NOW!"

I immediately round the corner, cocking my head to get the others to follow me, "Remi? What the fuck are you doing here?"

"Conti? Fuck man, shit. They got Sloane. Simon…we tried to stop them, but we couldn't leave Simon," he said, dropping down next to Dmitri and taking over chest compressions so Dmitri can start giving breaths.

"Simon?" Kaiser says, bewildered.

"The ambulance is coming. I called my best guy on the force, they're going to escort EMS here immediately. I don't know man, it's fucked…I don't know…" Remi trails off, continuing chest compressions.

My stomach sinks as what he's saying finally clicks somewhere in my brain and I race across the twenty feet separating us, Hudson and Kaiser on my heels. My heart shatters at the mournful howl Kaiser belts out, seeing Simon prone on the ground and coated in blood.

"No, NO! What the fuck. This is not how this goes. Fuck man. Do something!" Hudson yells at Remi and Dmitri, already doing all they can for Simon.

I drop to my knees next to them, the pooled blood coating my chaps. Kaiser collapses against me, tears streaking down his face as we watch Remi and Dmitri work to keep Simon alive despite the blood loss.

I count along in my head; thirty chest compressions, two breaths and repeat. Somewhere during the second round of counting, I tear my gaze away from Remi's hands, "Sloane. Remi, you said they got Sloane? What does that mean?"

"What? What the fuck, Remi?" Hudson echoes from further up the alley, waiting to direct EMS down to us.

"Someone. I don't know. I heard her screaming, then Otto I think and Ben…" he trails off, starting the third round of counts before they switch off again.

"Otto and Ben?" Hudson yells, "OTTO AND BEN? What the fuck are you talking about?"

"Shut up, Hudson," I bark, making Kaiser shudder against me with the force of dominance, "we have to take care of Simon first. She wouldn't forgive us if he died."

Kaiser chokes on a sob next to me and I squeeze him tight, grounding him as best I can in the moment. I finally hear sirens approaching as Remi and Dmitri switch positions and I drag Kaiser away from them to give EMS room to approach.

Several cops and EMS arrive on the scene, dropping down around Simon while Remi relays all the information they have. The EMTs take over, cutting up the center of his shirt and strapping pads to his chest.

"Bradycardia with acute hemorrhage, start a central line and hang saline. We need to stabilize him for transfer," the first one says, pulling packages and tubing out of his kit and passing it to his partner.

He grabs a large pressure bandage, pressing directly into the wound on his chest before wrapping it around his upper body. His partner works with him to basically tilt Simon back and forth, getting the bandage around him once before tightening it down by twisting a small bar at the end.

Once that's done, his partner starts an IV in Simon's arm, attaching a clear bag and squeezing it while the first one grabs the walkie talkie on his shoulder.

"Get ready to transport to St. Ann's," he tells his partner, "This is unit 306 delta, we have incoming trauma, GSW to the chest, will need blood product and immediate OR clearance. Let's move him!"

We stand back and watch as they roll Simon onto the stretcher and hustle him to the ambulance. I push Kaiser to follow them, "We'll meet you there, but you should ride with."

He hands me both his weapons before catching up to them and climbing in.

I turn to Remi and Dmitri, Hudson coming to stand at my side after watching the ambulance leave with Simon and Kaiser safely inside.

"Please tell me what the fuck just happened here," I grit out.

"Where the fuck is Sloane?" Hudson questions.

"Okay, listen. I'll tell you what I know. Dmitri and I were at Finesse trying to get some more information about Iris being there. Sloane calls me wanting the door codes, I tell her no, she tells me what's going down, I tell her to go back to wherever she's supposed to be, that me and Dmitri are on our way."

"Why the fuck was she asking for door codes?" Hudson growls.

"She said she was worried and wanted to follow you guys in," Remi shrugs, "Dmitri and I pull up, we hear her screaming and follow the sound. It's dark back here, so I can't be sure, but it looked like Otto. He was standing over Simon, pointing the gun at him. We fired at him, one of us hit him, hit the van, but it didn't stop them. He got into the back of the van and then shot Simon before closing the door."

"You said Ben, earlier, Otto and Ben," I question.

"I think Ben was yelling at Otto to get in the van. I think it was Ben and Otto, they took her. It was a blacked out cargo van, like the ones back here, but newer. All tinted. No plate. Lots of bullet holes now though."

"You were firing at a fucking van that you know Sloane was inside of," Hudson snarls at him, stepping into his chest and pushing him back.

"You wanted me to just let them fucking go without a fight," he yells back, shoving Hudson away from him.

"If she's fucking hurt because of you," Hudson threatens, gripping his shirt and getting in his face.

"She's fucking hurt because of you fucking idiots. She's gone because you fucks decided to bring her to an obvious fucking set up. FUCK," Remi screams into Hudson's face before pushing him away again, then yanking at his own hair, smearing Simon's blood through the strands.

"This is serious, we need to report back to Morris, now. I don't give a fuck who wants to take the blame, but we need to let the old man know what's going on," Dmitri tells his brother, wiping his hands on his jeans.

The sight of all the blood on them and the ground around us, brings me back to the harshness of my current reality. Sloane is gone. Simon is shot. We don't know where she is. We don't know if he's going to make it.

"Fuck. Okay. We have to…you two report to Ricci. We're going to the hospital. Simon is our tech guy so we're not going to be able to track anything down without him. You need to let Morris know that this building is empty, so I don't think his tech girl is going to be a help, either. Wherever she is."

"Sloane had the keys," Hudson rasps, his voice betraying his inner turmoil.

"The Vyrus won't fit us both. I'll call and have them taken back to the warehouse, get a car delivered to the hospital. Can you give us a ride before you head back to Morris?"

Dmitri nods grudgingly, his lip curling as he turns toward the back of the building and pulls Remi along with him. Hudson and I follow, while I pull out my phone to direct pick up of the SQ5 and Vyrus.

Next, I send a mass text, directing every one of my soldiers across the city to be on the lookout for Sloane, Ben, and Otto. I make sure they know to connect with all of the packs around us, to get the information out to every person they can.

I'm torn between the hospital and hunting Sloane down myself. I can't leave Kai hanging on his own, but I can't leave Sloane to think we're not looking for her. I know that Ricci is going to get people out just as soon as he can, too.

I know Sloane would never forgive me if something happened to Simon and I wasn't there for Kaiser. I know that Kaiser needs us right now, too. Not to mention the fact that I don't have anyone on payroll nearly as good as Simon. Any hunting for Sloane we do is going to be the most basic, boots on the ground version.

The ride to the hospital is short and silent, Remi pulls up directly to the ER entrance and drops us off before speeding away to report to Morris that we lost his only daughter. That we deliberately took her into a hostile situation only for her to be kidnapped and taken to God knows where.

Hudson and I don't talk, don't even look at each other. We trudge through to the triage desk and are informed that Simon's already been taken to surgery. Third floor waiting room. More silence as we head to the elevator and ride up, finding Kaiser staring blankly out the window in the waiting room, his hands covered in dry blood.

Hudson and I post up on either side of him, lending as much support as we can, knowing that the pain we're feeling isn't the same as his. So we stand with him, surrounding him with the comfort of pack and family and we wait.

Eventually we coax Kaiser down into the chairs, Hudson going to the vending machines for the most god awful coffee. Nurses check in from time to time, reminding us that it's good he's still in surgery.

He's fighting.

They're doing the best they can.

He's lost a lot of blood, but they're the best surgeons in the tristate area.

None of it seems to penetrate the fog around Kaiser. As the sun begins to peek over the horizon, bruising the sky with its arrival, Hudson finally convinces Kai to wash up in the bathroom. He even manages to find a scrub shirt big enough to fit him.

While they're out of the room, I take the opportunity to call Morris.

"Conti," Marco answers, even though I called Morris' cell directly, "you better have a damn good excuse for what the hell happened last night."

"An excuse for why your pack kidnapped my mate and tried to kill my beta? Maybe it's you who should have the explanation. Why are you even on this fucking phone right now?"

"As you can imagine, Morris is dealing with quite a bit right now. I'm choosing to play secretary for him so he can focus on more important things. Like getting his fucking daughter back," he snarls.

"If his house wasn't full of rats, we wouldn't be in this situation right now," I growl back, posturing through the phone even though I know I should be handling this differently. The anger and frustration has been building overnight, every hour staring at the clock waiting for the surgeon, no word on where Sloane could be, is finally coming to a head.

"Fuck you, boy. You think you're so tough, but you're the one who lost her. In the end, that's what matters here. You couldn't protect her. Because of your failure, she's gone."

Growls rip from my throat as he continues to taunt me, dropping truth after truth that I don't want to hear.

"Anyone who really knows Sloane, would know that she wouldn't stay in that fucking car. Someone who actually fucking cared about her, would have made her stay home, where she would have been safe. You rant and rave about your mate being taken, but you don't even fucking know her well enough to keep her safe."

"Marco," Morris' bark reverberates through the phone, causing me to flinch slightly but regain my composure quickly.

"Brooks, I'm assuming," Morris' voice comes through the phone.

"Yeah," I pause, suddenly at a loss for what to say. Anger was easy when it was Marco, but this is Sloane's father, his pain must rival mine right now.

"I understand you're at the hospital right now. Once you get a report on Simon's condition, I want you to meet me downtown. We need to work together if we're going to get her back. Text Remi when you're done and he'll pick you up. It's not your fault, Brooks."

"I'll be there," I choke out before ending the call.

The emotional crash is happening. Everything hitting me at once. Simon bleeding out in the alleyway. Sloane gone, kidnapped by the very people who were supposed to protect her. Kaiser a broken shell of a man, the two people he loves in imminent danger. And Morris Ricci being understanding, telling me we need to work together, is enough to break the fragile hold I have.

I bury my face in my hands, sob after wracking sob echoing through the waiting room. It's not long before I feel Hudson and Kaiser sit down with me. Each throwing an arm across my back and huddling together.

The scent of their tears mingles with mine and it takes everything I have to get myself back under control. I'm not the only one suffering here. We're all processing the pain of this situation and we need each other now more than ever.

I clear my throat, "Ricci wants me to meet him downtown once we've got an update on Simon. Wants us to work together to get her back."

Kaiser nods, his focus on his now clean hands. "I want to stay here. Wait for him to wake up."

"Of course. One of us needs to be here with him at all times," I reply, squeezing his shoulder, letting him know that I support whatever he needs.

"I'm with you. We need to find her, Brooks," Hudson says, his voice thick with emotion and unshed tears, "I can't live without her, man. I know that sounds so fucked, but it's true. There's like this hole," he says, grasping at his chest.

"We all feel it," Kai tells him, leaning over to press his hand overtop Hudson's on his chest, "I just wish we had told her. Simon knows we love him, but does Sloane?"

"Fuck, dude, we have to get her back," Hudson practically whines; a sound I've never heard him make before.

"We're going to find her. If it takes everything I am and everything I own, we will find her and bring her home," I vow to them.

As we lapse back into silence, it isn't much longer before a surgeon pushes through the waiting room doors.

"Brooks Conti?"

"That's me," I stand, Hudson and Kaiser rising with me.

"He's alive," the surgeon doesn't waste any time giving us his report, "he lost a lot of blood and the bullet was lodged incredibly close to his spine. We were able to remove it, but there's a lot of damage and swelling in the area. We've got him in a medically induced coma that we'll be keeping him in for at least 24 hours to ensure he has optimal time to recuperate before assessing his brain function."

"Brain function," Kaiser whispers, horrified.

"He lost a lot of blood, which we've replaced as best we could, but he coded several times, so his brain was deprived of oxygen for a period of time. We're hoping there was no lasting damage, but we can't be sure until we can fully assess him. Twenty four hours will give his brain time to heal and time for the swelling to go down along his spinal column. We'll be able to assess both when we bring him out tomorrow afternoon."

"There's swelling around his spine," Hudson repeats, tentatively, "that's…not good."

"No, it's not. There was extensive damage, as you can imagine. We'll need the swelling to go down before we can determine what, if any, permanent damage he has."

"Permanent spinal damage," I say, "You mean he might be paralyzed?"

"It's hard to say, this early in recovery, but there is a small possibility of paralysis."

Kaiser sits down heavily, his upper body slumping over as he hugs himself. Hudson drops down next to him, rubbing his face against his shoulder and neck, comforting him the only way he knows how.

"Okay, just so I have everything straight, doc. You're going to keep him in a coma for the next 24 hours, so no chance of him waking up?"

"Correct."

"And once you wake him up, you're going to do some tests to see if he has any permanent brain damage or paralysis?"

He nods.

"I don't suppose you can provide odds on the likelihood of either?"

"I really can't. Every patient is different, what their body can handle is different. He's a fighter, he has a strong pack behind him and he's in a state of the art facility. I can't give specifics, but I think he's going to pull through okay."

Kaiser looks up at him, "Truth, doc?"

"I can't guarantee anything, but I have a good feeling that everything will be okay."

"Thanks, doc. Will one of us be able to stay with him?"

"Once he's out of recovery, we'll get him transferred to the ICU and one of you will be able to stay, yes."

I nod and shake his hand, emotions overwhelming again and I don't trust myself to speak.

"I'll have a nurse show you to the ICU once we get him transferred," he tells us as he walks out the door.

I sit down on the other side of Kaiser, wrapping my arms over Hudson's so we're all huddled together again. Now we know where Simon's recovery is at, Hudson and I are free to go join Ricci in the hunt for Sloane, but we don't move. We're not going to leave Kaiser like this. Until Simon is moved into a room and Kaiser can join him, we'll be here, comforting him the only way we know how.

CHAPTER TWO

Sloane

"Ugh, shit," I groan, the taste in my mouth combined with a weird rocking motion causing my stomach to lurch. I swallow rapidly, trying in vain to prevent myself from vomiting, but it doesn't work. I just barely manage to get my head over the edge of whatever I'm laying on before my stomach empties itself.

My throat burns with each heave. It's been awhile since I've eaten anything, so it's mostly bile. By the time it finally stops, my head is pounding and I can barely move with the pain. I take a moment to lay back and rest.

The last thing I remember was being hauled out of the van at a shipping dock. Ben held me at gunpoint while Iris took my gun and ammo, phone, bracelet and toe ring. Then, they drugged me, holding a sickly sweet smelling rag over my nose and mouth until I felt my body give out. They must have moved me here once I was out.

As my head pain dulls down to a low throb, I squint my eyes and take a look around. It takes a few moments for my eyes to adjust to the brightness in the small room. There's a tiny window in one corner which gives me enough light to see that I'm on a small bed. There's a bench to one side of the room with a small table, counter, and sink.

I realize, by the shape of the room and the strange rocking motion, that I'm on a boat. There's a door hatch at the opposite wall. I can hear footsteps out on deck, so I know someone is out there moving around. Not that I thought they would leave me alone, but I know my mother isn't the brightest bulb, so it wouldn't surprise me.

The room is so small, the smell of vomit is overwhelming and it's making my stomach roil. I have to get out of this room or I'm going to be throwing up again and I don't think my body can handle that right now.

I slide off the side of the bed, as far away from my vomit pool as I can get and shuffle the two steps it takes to get to the door.

Locked. Of course.

I knock on the door as hard as I can, which it turns out, is not hard at all. The lingering effects of the drug makes my body feel weighted and awkward, my muscles don't want to cooperate. I can barely raise my arm above my waist.

I lean against the wall and kick at the door, thinking I can generate more noise with my foot than my fist. Even though it still doesn't sound that loud to me, after a few good thumps, I hear footsteps approach from the other side.

The door swings out and up, the brightness of the daylight blinding me and causing me to stumble back. I barely miss stepping in my puke before tumbling back onto the bed, my arm flung across my eyes.

"I'm so sorry, sweetheart," my mother coos, "let's get you out of there."

I blink rapidly, my eyes watering from the brightness and the lingering pain from vomiting. I don't want to go near her, but I also don't want to stay in this tiny room. She's standing in the doorway, holding a handkerchief to her nose. As if the smell isn't her fault to begin with. I certainly wouldn't have vomited everywhere if they hadn't drugged me.

Once I feel like I can see, I slide off the bed again and move to the door, trying my best to slide out without touching her. I turn to the side and try to scooch out.

No such luck.

She wraps her arm around my shoulders and guides me to the bench seats on the deck. She tugs me down next to her, wrapping a blanket around my shoulders and holding me close as if she actually cares about me.

"I'm so sorry for how things have unfolded, dear, I truly wish things had been different," she tells me, rubbing circles on my back.

"Where are we? What's going on," I manage to choke out the questions past the swelling and burning in my throat from my unsavory vomiting session.

"We're on our way to a little meeting, that's all. How are you feeling?"

"Like shit. Now tell me what's going on," I grit out, putting as much authority into my voice as the pain will allow me.

"We're on a boat, as you can see, we're on our way to a very important little tête-à-tête. One that you need to be prepared for. You've been out for a little over a day already, I was worried we gave you too much."

"A full day," I squawk, the horrific sound not conveying my distress at having lost so much time already. No wonder I feel like such garbage.

"Yes, as I said, I was worried about you, but now you're awake so we can get you feeling better," she smiles at me, as if being kidnapped and drugged to the point where you lose an entire day is totally fine.

"You've lost your mind, truly," I rasp, staring at her in shock.

"Nonsense. Otto! Bring Sloane a bottled water, darling," she calls, waving toward the front of the boat.

I look toward the front of the boat and see Otto and Ben standing at the wheel, hunched together and conversing quietly. Otto's arm is in a sling, his shoulder under his shirt bulging with what I assume are thick bandages, his coat draped over him like a cape. My stomach lurches again, processing the absolute betrayal of my father's most loyal men.

Seeing Otto brings back more memories from when they abducted me. Otto leaning out the door, his gun going off, the blood on Simon's lips. I can't stop myself from heaving again, turning toward my mother, hoping something comes up just for her. Unfortunately, my stomach is indeed empty and I'm only able to retch a few times before getting it under control again.

"Fuck all of you," I swear, the anger boiling inside of me giving me the strength to shove my mother away from me. I lurch to my feet, intending to go after Otto, but Ben brings the wheel around quickly, the deck seeming to move under me and I fall to my knees.

"Don't think you'll be getting too far without your sea legs, Sloane. Best for you to just sit back down and drink some water like your mommy says," Ben tells me, not even bothering to look over his shoulder at me.

"Fuck. You," I scream with everything I can muster, not caring how raw my throat is or the fact that I can barely raise my voice. I need a way to get this pain out of me.

I scream until the screams turn into sobs. The sobs fade away into silent tears streaking down my face and pooling on the deck. I curl myself into a ball, desperate to escape the pain, knowing there's nothing I can do. Shallow whines escape as I remember.

So much blood. I know Otto shot him in the chest. I remember watching the red spread across his shirt and the blood staining his lips before they took me away. The screams. My own screams echoing back to me through the inside of the van. There's no way he survived that.

I begin sobbing again; my beautiful beta taken from me. How can I survive without him? How can *they* survive without him? My poor Kaiser, his lover is gone. And Hudson and Brooks. Their best friend, cold in the ground by now.

"Are you quite done, dear? You're overtaxing yourself and we really need to get you in better shape before the rendezvous," my mother states matter of factly, kneeling down beside me and offering an opened bottle of water.

I try to slap the water out of her hands, but Otto grabs my wrist. I didn't process the fact that he was kneeling at my back. He uses the grip on my wrist to pull my arm behind my back, pushing my hand up between my shoulder blades until I cry out in pain. Even with him injured, I don't stand a chance at overpowering him.

When I plan my escape, it will definitely hinge on catching them off guard.

"I don't want to hurt you, Sloane, but I will if you don't cooperate. We're trying to be nice, the least you can do is return that nicety with politeness."

"Nice? You're being nice?! You kidnapped me. You drugged me. You stole me away from my mates - you killed one of them! You've betrayed the pack! If you think I'm going to be polite to you, you are seriously delusional, asshole."

"Sloane, baby, there's no reason to be like that. You're much better off with us. We're doing what's best for you," my mother exclaims, reaching out and trying to brush the remaining tears off my face.

"Don't talk to me, Iris," I stress her name, pulling myself into a sitting position once Otto eases up on my arm "you are nothing to me. Less than nothing. The fact that you're behind all of this…I don't know whether to be surprised or disgusted."

"You don't know anything, Sloane," Ben tells me, still facing away, "Now, I suggest you listen to your mother, drink some water, and keep your shit together. We're almost at the rendezvous point and I will drug you again if you keep this up."

I stare daggers at Ben's back, wanting to unleash a torrent of verbal abuse on him, but also not wanting to be drugged again. I already feel like absolute shit and I know I need to try to keep my head together if I am going to find a way out of this. Begrudgingly, I heave myself off the deck and grab the bottle of water from my mother before sitting back down on the bench seat.

I know my father will come for me. Brooks and the others…I don't know what to expect. I would assume they would come for me, too, but the pain Kaiser must be feeling. And it's because of me. They were using Simon to get to me and now Simon…God…Simon.

It takes everything inside of me not to break down again just thinking about my handsome beta. The fact that we'll never be able to explore what could have been between us. I can feel my heart crack, surprised the sound isn't audible given how much it hurts.

I know I need to be strong right now, to try to find a way out of this, but I just can't. Between the residual drugging, the pain in my head and now my breaking heart, I don't know what I'm going to do. I know I have to stay alive until they can rescue me, but right now all I want to do is roll myself up and cry until I pass out.

I focus on bringing the bottle to my mouth and taking small sips of water. I know I need to rehydrate and focusing on small sips will hopefully keep my stomach from rebelling too much.

My mother and Otto sit together on the opposite bench from me, Iris watching like a hawk, each sip of water I take. I can't believe that she really was behind all of this. Hudson was right about her, I muse to myself, though wrong about the rat. Or I should say, rats.

I wonder if Leone has been pulling strings in the background all along. Once he realized the stories he told me about Brooks wouldn't work, he just decided to have them kidnap me? To what end, though?

And if Leone is orchestrating all of this, like Hudson suspects, what is his end game? All of this just to have me? That doesn't make sense. There has to be more going on here. I wish that I was more informed about everything that went on with dad's business. Maybe if I knew more I would be able to pinpoint why Ben and Otto have betrayed him.

I'm so confused about everything right now and even though I want to try to get more information, the pounding in my head is making it harder for me to focus. Hopefully I'll be able to overhear something helpful once we reach the rendezvous point and whoever we're rendezvousing with.

I need to figure something out and be ready to escape if the opportunity comes up. First thing, I need to get rid of this head pain.

"Can I get something for my head," I ask through gritted teeth, "if I can't get rid of this pain, I'm just going to keep throwing up."

"We don't really have a lot of supplies on board, I'm afraid," Iris replies, "but I might have something in my purse. Let me check for you, dear."

She gets up and moves toward the cockpit where Ben is at the wheel, pulling her purse from under a shelf and rummaging through it. I glare at Otto, wishing that I had the ability to light him on fire with my anger alone.

"Hating me isn't going to change anything, *bimba*. You're better off focusing on getting hydrated and navigating your new life."

"What does that mean," I ask.

"It means, you're going to be a perfect little omega for our business associates. And once we hand you over, no one is going to find you," Otto says chillingly.

I stare at him in horror. I can barely breathe with the shock and despair rushing through me. They're going to give me to another pack and expect me to mate with them?

Seeing the dumbstruck look on my face, Otto smirks, "Business is business, Sloane. Unfortunately, you're in the way of our business right now and we can't have that. You just keep making things difficult for us, so you see, we didn't really have a choice at this point."

"I don't even know what that means," I hiss at him.

"See Sloane, we've been trying for years to get your father to expand into other, more lucrative avenues, but he's always refused. Certain things were orchestrated in an effort to get him to comply."

"Still not getting it," I reply.

"Of course you aren't," Ben interjects, "you've never paid enough attention to the business to even begin to understand what we're doing. Just a pretty princess living off the profits and waiting to be married off like a little trophy wife."

Otto glances at Ben's back reprovingly, "As true as that might be, it would help if you just let me tell the story, Ben. Anyway, Sloane, your new designation changed a lot of things for us. Namely the fact that your father became even more adamant against our business proposal."

"Must not have been a very good one, if papa wouldn't agree to it," I sniff with disdain, broken down and aching on the inside but trying to maintain a facade of 'don't give a fuck'.

Continuing with his explanation, ignoring the fact that I've spoken, "Using some soldiers we knew were loyal to us, not your father, we worked up a few minor issues, sabotaging him from the inside. A few shipments go missing, angry phone calls from drug lords, the whole shebang. If he would have just listened to us, we could have gotten out of the drug trade for good."

I make it a point to look down at my nails, holding each hand up and turning them side to side. I need him to get on with this story so I can figure out where we are headed and what I need to do to get out of this.

"Instead of taking the bait and agreeing to alternative options, forgoing the drug trade all together, he opted to make an alliance, thinking we were going to war with some imaginary rival family," Ben's voice drips with disdain.

"After that," Otto huffs, "we figured we could push to get you mated to someone and out of the picture, then he would have his alliance and we could continue to operate behind his back, but stop sabotaging shipments. Everything would go back to semi-normal."

"Unfortunately, you have not been cooperative," Ben adds.

Otto glares at him for a brief moment before continuing, "Yes, well, that has definitely put a kink into our plans. You choosing Brooks Conti created quite the conundrum. Too big of a fish, too close to your father, too much at stake for you to go through with that."

"You supported them," I screech, my throat protesting the volume I'm trying to create with my anger, "you basically told me to choose them! What the fuck?"

"We're not stupid. Your father wanted you to be happy, we weren't about to push against that by suggesting someone else, like Marco did. Best for us to fly under the radar and figure out a way to fix all of this for good."

"So, you see, we didn't really have a choice. Since you couldn't make the right decision on your own, we decided to help that along," Iris chimes in, as she returns to the bench seat.

"By kidnapping me," I spit.

"Let's call it an aggressive relocation tactic," Otto smirks.

Iris smiles, reaching out a hand with two small white pills in it.

"What are these?"

"They'll help with your pain," she says nonchalantly.

"But what are they? Can I see the bottle," I ask again, taking the pills from her and inspecting them for any kind of identifying markings or name brands.

"I don't have the bottle anymore, I just keep a little pill thingy in my purse. Trust me. Those are for pain, I keep them in a separate little spot so I remember what they are."

"I'll pass," I grimace, handing the pills back to her, "I don't exactly trust you when it comes to pharmaceuticals."

"Suit yourself," she huffs, popping the pills into her own mouth and dry swallowing them, "but that headache isn't going to go away with water."

"Jesus," I mutter, rolling my eyes in disgust.

"Back to the matter at hand," Otto continues, "Since you couldn't follow through on such an easy plan, we had to make some necessary adjustments and set up a plan to move you outside of the city and out of the way."

"You need to speed up story time, Otto," Iris interrupts.

"And you," she adds, "need to finish that water, maybe rinse your mouth out, and try to look as presentable as possible. You're about to meet your new pack," she states, pointing to a spot in the distance over the bow.

I glance to where she's pointing and I see another boat heading in our direction. I don't even know what body of water we're currently in, just that I can't see anything at all around us except open water. The fact that there's another boat rapidly approaching can only mean this is whoever we're scheduled to rendezvous with.

"So what? You're just going to hand me over and think you'll be able to continue on with life as you know it," I question, incredulous that they think they can get away with this, especially after telling me everything about their betrayal.

"Of course not. I mean, that was the original plan in getting rid of you but, after the debacle back at the Sylvan, Remi and Dmitri's untimely arrival, we definitely won't be able to go back to normal life," Otto replies, using his fingers to make air quotes when he says 'normal', "but we'll make our own new normal."

"Then why even go through with this? You know my father will never stop hunting for me. Neither will my true mates," I choke out, unable to even voice their names, the pain of losing Simon coursing through me all over again, "and when they find you, they'll kill you."

"No one is going to find us, our associates will make sure of that. All new identities, a fresh new start anywhere we want," Ben says over his shoulder, "and all we have to give them, is you. We're safe and you're silenced."

"You're all insane! You can't do this. You can't force me to mate with someone else!"

"We won't have to force you, Sloane," Ben says, shutting off the engine and turning from the wheel, "You're not actually mated yet and you're already a day past due for your heat suppressant. You're about to board a boat full of alphas. Your own body will make the choice for you eventually."

CHAPTER THREE

Hudson

I'm barely keeping my shit together, standing in the waiting room at the hospital, counting down the minutes until they wake up Simon and start testing him. Sloane's been gone just over 32 hours and I am losing my fucking mind.

I know I need to focus and do my part to help find her, but I seriously can't think past wanting to destroy everything. I have to resist the urge to physically attack anyone who comes near me, outside of my packmates. I want to burn everything to the ground until I find her.

Brooks and I have been working nonstop with Ricci and his people to try to figure out where Ben and Otto would have taken her. Without tech support, though, we haven't gotten very far. Ricci's girl is in the wind, which leads us to believe she was working with Ben and Otto the whole time.

I'm not ashamed to admit that I'm hoping Simon will wake up with no issues, ready to jump on this problem. I know he needs to recover and I know he's going to be in a lot of pain, but I also know how much he loves our girl. And love is a hell of a motivator.

I continue to pace the length of the room, one hand shoved in my pocket, the other tapping out an annoying rhythm on my thigh. I know it's annoying because Brooks keeps tossing me aggravated looks, between tugging on his hair and checking his phone, but he hasn't said anything.

He keeps all of his feelings and frustrations shut up inside, I have to move it out. Sitting still right now is not an option and Brooks knows it. So he lets me annoy the shit out of him with my pacing and my tapping, while systematically checking in with every single one of our soldiers to see if they've uncovered anything.

Once we're done here, we're going to visit Leone and Vincent. We've still got them detained and they won't be going anywhere anytime soon. We have his sister at a secondary location as a countermeasure in case he doesn't want to cooperate.

I was way fucking off with my assessment of Marco, but I'm hoping that everything with Leone still adds up. At the very least, he set us up to the fucking feds, so I'll be able to relieve a little frustration by beating some information out of him.

A nurse pops her head into the door, "Your packmate wanted me to let you know that they're starting and he'll be out with an update as soon as possible."

I growl involuntarily, not appreciating my current territory being invaded by an outsider.

"I apologize for my associate," Brooks attempts to smooth things over when the young nurse looks like she might start to cry, "he's under a lot of stress right now, as you can imagine. Thank you for letting us know, though."

She smiles at Brooks before closing the door quickly, avoiding more of my reaction, in spite of Brooks' attempt at normalizing my behavior.

"You need to get your shit under control," he says to me, his attention immediately going back to his phone.

"I rather like being unhinged, thank you," I snark, "I think it will help, in the end. When we find her. I need to be a little dissociated, you know. Maximum annihilation."

Brooks shakes his head, but doesn't say anything. He knows I'm right and I know he's here for it. He just can't let himself devolve into such a state, as much as he wishes he could.

After several more minutes of pacing and tapping and pacing, the doors open and Kaiser steps into the room, blessedly alone.

Brooks lurches to his feet and we both rush to him, when we see the tears sliding down his face.

Brooks reaches him first, wrapping him in a hug. I slide in behind him, wrapping my arms around him and gripping Brooks, sandwiching Kaiser between us. Anyone looking at us would probably laugh their asses off, given that Kai is about six inches taller than both of us, but neither of us give a shit right now. Comforting Kai is more important than anything right now.

"It's okay, it's okay," Kai gasps out, his voice hitching, "he's okay."

Brooks steps back, gripping the back of Kai's neck and pulling his forehead down to his, "He's okay?"

"Yeah," he chokes, "everything…he's okay, his toes, he can feel them. He's speaking, he remembers us. No memory loss."

I exhale deeply, pressing my face between Kai's shoulder blades and nuzzling his back. I grip Brooks arms, squeezing him with relief. He's okay. We're all okay. We're all going to be okay. We just have to find our little omega and everything will be okay.

After a few more moments of comforting each other, we pull back and regroup. Brooks and Kaiser sit down together, I resume my pacing. Even though Simon is okay, there's still a hell of a lot I need to walk out.

"Tell me everything," Brooks instructs.

"He's in a lot of pain, obviously. They turned down his pain medication so that they could evaluate him without interference. He remembers everything that happened, I asked him questions about the past, the present, what happened at the Sylvan. He remembered all of it."

"Thank god," I mutter, rubbing my hand up and down my face before cramming it back into my pocket.

"When I say he remembered all of it, he remembered who was there. Ben and Otto and Iris," Kaiser stresses her name, "Iris was in on it from the start."

Brooks takes a deep breath, then shakes his head, "We figured she was involved in some way, now we know. It doesn't change anything, but at least we've got the info. Finish telling us about Simon."

"Okay, um, they checked his reflexes, they poked his feet and his legs, and he could feel all of that, too," he chokes out, pausing to pull himself back together again.

Brooks clasps his shoulder tightly, giving him a slight shake before letting him go again.

"Now that we know he's going to be okay, we can turn our total focus on getting Sloane back. He remembers she's gone, obviously, but I don't want him to overexert himself trying to help. No one is to bring him anything other than a phone, got it." Brooks states, staring at me pointedly.

I turn and throw my hands up, "I won't bring him anything, swear."

Brooks narrows his eyes at me, probably trying to gauge my sincerity, which is 100%. *I* won't be bringing *him* anything. I can't stop the nurses or orderlies from giving him things that I leave here, though. Or giving him deliveries that are obviously addressed to him. Not that I would do that. But, just in case, you know.

"It's not going to be easy to keep him out of this," Kaiser tells him, "he's already asking for more information, updates on what we've found so far. I'm hoping that they keep his pain meds up and he's too loopy to protest."

I make a mental note to talk to the doctor about that. I'll just drop a few semi realistic anecdotes about how Simon has had difficulties in the past with pain medication. A history of vomiting and delusions should be enough to keep the dosage low. I'll make sure to appear real concerned just to sell it fully.

"I do not trust the look on your face right now," Brooks directs to me.

"I am 100% trustworthy. Besides, I'm going with you, remember? How can I get into trouble if I'm with you?"

"I don't know how, but I know it's going to happen. He needs to rest, Hudson. He can't jump back into things like nothing happened. He almost died," he snaps, the emotional overload of the past day and a half coming through in his voice.

He closes his eyes and pinches the bridge of his nose, "I'm sorry. I'm sorry, okay. We just, we need to focus and we can't be working against each other here."

"We all want the same thing, Brooks," Kaiser says gently, reaching over to squeeze the back of his neck, "now that we know Simon is going to be okay, we can focus everything we have on Sloane."

"I know, I'm just…trying to keep it together. We have to get her back," Brooks looks between the two of us, his eyes red rimmed and glassy. He's fighting the tears again. We all have been, on and off.

I take a moment and drop into the chair on Brooks' other side, looping my arm over his shoulder so I can encompass him, but squeeze Kaiser as well.

"We're all in, Brooks, you know this," I tell him, pressing my cheek to his, "you're not the only one lost without her."

Kaiser drops his arm over mine around Brooks, rubbing his hand up and down my back. At the same time, he nuzzles his head on Brooks' shoulder, drawing us all closer together.

"We're going to get her back, Brooks. We won't sleep, won't break, until she's back with all of us."

We spend the next few minutes immersed in our mixed pack scent, comforting one another. Kaiser is the first to move, standing up and pulling Brooks after him. I follow them up when Kaiser reminds us that we only have another few minutes to visit Simon before they move him again.

"They turned his pain mends back up before I came out here, so no guarantees he's coherent."

We follow Kaiser down the hallway until we reach the sealed doors of the ICU. He presses the intercom, letting them know that he's returning and has brought the two of us with him.

The actual unit is small, only eight rooms total. I can see Simon through the clear glass walls of his room, the curtains pulled back to give us a straight view of him. The bed is lifted slightly, putting him at an angle that looks almost like he's sitting up.

Even though Kaiser already told us he was okay, actually seeing him now - eyes open, no tube down his throat - it hits me. He's okay. I feel like I'm able to take a deep breath for the first time. The feeling only lasts a moment, though. Simon's okay, but where is our little omega?

Simon gives us a drowsy smile as we all troop through the door together.

"Thank God, Brooks, tell them," Simon mumbles, "my equipment delivered. I need…I need…laptop," he trails off, eyes half closed as the drugs work through his system.

"Just sleep, Simon. Let them take care of you, we've got this," Brooks tells him, moving to the side of the bed and gripping his hand.

"No. I…help," he pleads quietly, eyes closed now, "I have to. No one else is…I just need my laptop, iPad…" he trails off again, fighting the exhaustion so clearly on his face.

I take my post next to Brooks, wrapping my hand around Brooks and gripping Simon, too.

"Brooks is right. For once," I chuckle, "Just sleep, man. We got this, we'll keep you updated."

"My phone," he questions, barely audible now as sleep pulls at him.

"I've got it, baby. I'll make sure you have it when you wake up later," Kaiser tells him, leaning down to kiss his cheek and forehead.

"Mmm, ok," he mumbles, finally succumbing to the drugs and drifting off into oblivion.

"I'm going to stay with him until they get him moved to his new room. I'll make sure his phone is ready and charged, but once he's secured, I'll join you guys at the warehouse."

Brooks reaches across Simon's bed, grasping Kaiser's hand in acknowledgement. We take turns leaning down and rubbing our faces along Simon's, scent marking him to get rid of some of the hospital stink. Kai gets comfortable in the bedside chair and we bid him goodbye before heading out of the unit and down to the car.

I stalk through the parking structure, looking forward to the absolute ass kicking I'm going to deliver to Antonio Leone. I'm also looking forward to getting some answers from him. About the raid and about Sloane. He's an easy target for all the rage I have inside right now.

As I climb behind the wheel, Brooks closes his door, "We need to keep Leone alive as long as possible."

"I know."

"We need to get as much information from him as we can, Hudson. Not just about Sloane, but about everything."

"I know," I spit tersely.

"I just need to make sure you keep your head in the game. You can't lose control in there, Hudson. I know you've got a lot pent up and you want to unleash a lot of that on him, but you can't kill him yet."

"I know, okay, I know."

"Vincent on the other hand, Vincent is expendable," Brooks tells me, clapping me on the shoulder before buckling himself in.

I can feel the evilness of the smile creeping across my face. Antonio's third is definitely not necessary for the end game here. My chest loosens a little with the idea that I'll be able to unload some of this rage and not have to hold back.

CHAPTER FOUR

Simon

I think I'm moving.

I manage to force open one eye and see ceiling tiles, one after another. I'm laying down but I'm moving.

A dinging sound.

There's a metal ceiling. I roll my head to the side. Kaiser.

Moving again.

Stop. Counting. I'm sliding now, blinking, surrounded by people.

Laying down again, but not moving.

I feel a hand in mine. I squeeze. I know that hand. I've held it a thousand times.

Why can't I wake up?

I need to find something. I feel like I'm floating. Swimming. Sinking.

I'm so heavy. I'm stuck. I need to get out of here.

Focus.

Focus.

Kai.

I try again, forcing my mouth to move.

"Kai," I croak, barely audible. A rasp and vibration of sound, but I feel him squeeze my hand.

"Simon," he whispers, "I'm here, baby, you're safe, just sleep."

"I'm lost," I choke out, my throat so sore, "Kai. I can't…" I trail off, losing my train of thought again.

So heavy.

I feel scruff nuzzling my shoulder and face. That scent, so familiar.

"I know you," I whisper.

"You do. I'll take care of you, baby. Sleep."

"I can't," I mutter, this time forcing my eyes open. Just a slit at first, the lights in the room on low, so I pry them open further.

I let my head loll to the side so I can see Kai.

"I love you."

He smiles softly at me, "I love you, too."

"I love…someone. Someone else. I love…Sloane. Sloane," I groan, trying to force my brain back online, knowing they've pumped me full of drugs for the pain. My chest is currently a huge, raw, ache. My throat, swollen and thick feeling.

I can't wallow here though. Sloane.

"Sloane, Kai. Where is Sloane?"

He shifts next to the bed, nuzzling his head back into the crook of my neck. His breath puffs against my face a few times before he starts a low purr. So soothing.

I feel my eyes drifting shut, my body going lax, softening into the mattress.

"Kai," I breathe out, "I can't…don't let me."

"Sshh, baby," he whispers against my cheek, "you need to go back to sleep."

"Where is Sloane?"

He doesn't reply, just increases his purr, gripping my hand tight now.

"Where," I try to ask more forcefully, his silence is telling.

The panic starts to overcome the effects of the drugs coursing through my system. I manage to get my eyes open again. Kai's face is next to mine, resting on my shoulder, tears rolling down his cheeks.

"Kai, please," I rasp. The effects of the drugs rapidly dissipating now that full blown panic is rocketing through my system, "tell me they didn't take her, Kai. Tell me that someone got her. Kai. Tell me."

"I can't tell you that, Simon," he utters, his voice hoarse with emotion.

"Oh God," I mutter, horrified by the implications of his admission.

"We're working on it, Simon. You need to sleep and recover. That needs to be your main focus right now."

"How can you possibly think I would be able to do that, Kaiser. Knowing that Sloane is out there somewhere, that someone else has her? Are you fucking kidding me," I hiss, the pain in my chest suddenly piercing, for an entirely different reason.

My sweet Sloane, gone. Her last memory of me, lying on the ground and bleeding out. That I couldn't save her. I haven't told her how I feel, truly feel about her. I don't even want to imagine what she's going through right now.

Her mother. I remember now. Her mother was there. Ben and Otto.

I can find her. I know I can, but I need to start now, before the trail gets cold. I need my things.

"Kai. How long? How long has she been gone? I need my laptops, both of them. My iPad," I take a deep breath, my chest beginning to loosen now that I can focus on actually helping her. "I can find her, I know I can, but I need my things."

"Simon. You can't…the doctor said you need time to recover. You almost died," he chokes out, "we thought we lost you, too."

"Kaiser, I know. It was scary, I was scared, but I can't be sidelined on this. You and I both know I'm the best shot we've got to find her, but I have to start as soon as possible. The longer we wait, the further away she'll be," I end my mini rant on a coughing fit, the mucus in my throat from breathing tube choking me briefly before Kaiser holds a straw to my mouth.

"Brooks said no."

"I don't give a good goddamn," I rasp, between sips of water, "he might be my boss, but he's not in charge of me. I have to do this, Kaiser. I have to."

He looks at me for a moment, his eyes flicking over my bruised face and chest. His face tightens when his eyes cross over the bandages mummifying my upper body. He finally meets my eyes, smiling softly again.

"I love you, Simon Costa. I'll get you what you need, but you have to promise me that you won't overdo it. I can't lose you to get her back. I can't lose either of you," he whispers against my lips, kissing me gently before pulling out his phone.

"I have to keep Brooks in the loop," he says, dialing Brooks and putting it on speaker.

"Is Simon okay," Brooks' concerned voice comes through.

"I'm fine," I answer him, "a little sore, a little tired, but fine."

"Why are you awake - why is he awake, Kaiser?"

"Ready to get to work, buddy," Hudson asks, talking right over Brooks and his concerns.

"Just got done convincing Kai to get my things for me, but he wanted to check in with the boss first," I reply to Hudson, ignoring Brooks continued ranting about my being awake and wanting to work.

"Does anyone fucking listen anymore," Brooks shouts over everyone, clearly exasperated at this point.

"Sure we listen," Hudson snarked, "we listen and then we make our own assessment of the situation."

I can just imagine the half smirk on Hudson's face as he says that and it makes me want to laugh. I don't, of course, because pissing off Brooks more is not going to get me what I want.

"Brooks-" Kaiser starts, but I cut him off.

"I can't sleep, Brooks. You can't expect me to sleep through this. I know I need to recover, I totally get that, but there will be plenty of time for that once we get Sloane back."

"Simon, you need to understand..." he trails off, I hear as he clears his throat before starting again, "it was really close, Simon. We thought we had lost you, too. We need you, Simon. You are important to all of us."

"I know, Brooks. I love you guys, too. I promise I won't overdo it. I can't move out of this bed anyway, so it's not like I'm going to start running around trying to find her."

I hear Hudson snort and I know I've gotten through to him before Brooks responds, "Just don't be stupid, okay? Kaiser, stay with him. Keep him on a short leash."

"Yessir," Kai responds.

"I'll find something, Brooks. I'll find her."

"I know you will, Simon. I just don't want to lose you in exchange for getting her back, so just be a good boy," he chuckles.

"We'll send you whatever information we get out of Leone and Vincent," Hudson adds before they disconnect.

"Alright. Boss man is on board now, too. Please get my stuff," I tell Kaiser, pouting just a little in an effort to get him to move faster.

He laughs, "Calm down, killer. I'll get your stuff, I promise. Just maybe let me enjoy the fact that you're sitting up and talking to me instead of dead in that alleyway, okay?

I reach out and palm his cheek, ignoring the stretching pain across my chest as I rub my thumb across his bottom lip.

"Trust me when I say, I'm glad I'm not dead, too. I will not do anything to compromise my recovery, Kaiser. I don't want to leave you guys, but I also can't imagine trying to live without her. I have to do this."

He covers my hand with his, holding it against his face as he nuzzles against it, "I know, baby. I also know that we are much better off with you helping us, so I'm just going to sit here and make sure you don't do anything stupid."

"You can sit there after you get my stuff," I grin at him.

"I already asked Anton and Bea to go pick up your stuff," he smiles sheepishly, "I knew you would wake up wanting to help and, even though Brooks said no, I wanted to be prepared. Plus, I know they want to check on you. Just made sense."

"Bea been calling every hour on the hour," I ask, smiling at the love that floods me when I think of Bea Conti. My mother didn't do much with me, growing up. She got pregnant during a fling with one of Conti's lower ranking soldiers. He didn't believe her, didn't step up and she didn't pursue it.

Luckily she was a live-in housekeeper and Bea Conti had a heart of gold. Once I was old enough to walk, she started having my mom put in with the other guys during the day. She always said it was more efficient that way, mom could focus on her job without having to worry about me and the boys could learn how to play gently since I was so much smaller.

In the end, though, Bea and Anton basically adopted me. I love her like I should love my own mother, but she never gave me the chance. Bea gave me everything a mother should have, so she holds that spot in my heart.

"She probably would have showed up a lot sooner if I hadn't constantly reassured her that you were okay."

"So you're going to use her concern to get my stuff here, so you don't have to take your eyes off me. You're a sneaky shit, huh?"

"It's one of the reasons why you love me so much," he replies, flicking his tongue out to lick against my thumb.

"Okay, none of that, Romeo. I need to focus. When do you think they'll be here?"

"Should be soon. I messaged Anton about an hour ago, just before Brooks and Hudson left. In the meantime, I am going to grab the doctor on duty to give you a quick once over, since you're determined to stay awake now."

I smile as he rises from his chair and heads to the door to hunt down the doctor. Unfortunately, that means I'm alone and without a distraction now. My mind inevitably drifts back to the kidnapping. The shooting.

When they initially woke me and the surgeon was assessing my mental status along with the reflex assessment, he did tell me that I might have some amnesia or spots in my memory due to the trauma. I wish that was the case. I wish I couldn't remember.

When I initially arrived at the building, everything was totally normal. I was escorted to the basement to work with their tech girl. We were sharing information and discussing ways to approach the search. After a few hours, when I was getting ready to wrap it up and return to the warehouse for the night, she suddenly became agitated.

I remember that she said she had to make a call, then left the room. I started packing my things up, when someone I didn't recognize came into the room. He hit me so fast that I didn't even have time to register what he looked like.

By the time I came to, I had been moved to another room and tied to a chair. Ben, Otto, and Iris were in the room with me, discussing their plans to get Sloane. I was going in and out, I caught just snippets of conversation.

They were using me as bait to get Sloane to the building.

They were planning on handing Sloane over to someone as part of some kind of deal.

Eventually, Brooks called to check in with me. Otto held a gun to my head, made sure I answered appropriately so that Brooks knew I was in distress and they needed to come get me. We played right into their hands.

Brooks thought I was signaling him surreptitiously. He didn't know they were already ahead of us. They had access to the building's cameras and as soon as they saw the guys had entered the building, they untied me and began moving me down to the main room.

Their plan was to go find Sloane, wherever she was, but then she was approaching outside and all they had to do was force me through the door with the gun to my head. My girl looked so scared, I can see her face in my mind's eye, the horror in her eyes when she saw the gun against my temple.

When they forced her into the van and restrained her, I lost it.

"Good morning, Mr. Costa, I'm Dr. Seymur."

I turn my head to see who's entering my room, thankful to be pulled from my reverie before having to relive the gunshot. I can still hear Sloane's screams echoing in my head as they took her away

The doctor accompanying Kaiser is an older gentleman, graying hair and smile lines. He comes directly to the side of the bed, wasting no time listening to my heart and inspecting the bandages around my upper body. He walks through the room, checking the various other machines hooked to me and making notes in the tablet he carries.

"Well I would be lying if I told you it was good to see you awake, but at least you're not in distress. I wish you would let yourself recuperate a little. Since I can see that's not going to happen, keep your call button close and alert the staff to any kind of new symptom you might have."

"Thanks, doc," I said, reaching a hand out to shake.

He grasps mine, shaking a few times before warning me, "Don't overdo it, whatever it is you are planning on doing, because I will come in here and I will put you out."

I chuckle at first, but then note the seriousness on his face.

"It's my job to make sure you end up getting out of here and I will do what's necessary to make sure that happens," he tells me, finally releasing my hand. "Now, I'm sure mountain man over there is going to make sure you don't get crazy, but I figured I'd add my two cents."

"Yeah, of course. I swear, doc, I won't overdo it. I want to get out of here, too."

He nods at me, very serious, before turning and walking to the door. He pauses before leaving, "Make sure to call down your meal preferences at least an hour before chow time and they'll let you add in food for him, too."

"Thanks, so much."

As the doctor swings open the door, Anton and Bea are waiting on the other side. Anton has a case in each hand, along with a bag over his shoulder, leaving Bea to carry a huge bouquet of flowers.

Bea smiles warmly as she approaches, setting the vase of flowers on the side table before bending over and gingerly hugging me.

"Sweet boy, how are you," she asks, pulling back and cupping my cheeks.

"It hurts, but not too much. I'll survive," I say, returning her smile.

She pats my cheek before stepping aside and letting Anton take her place.

"Not sure where you're gonna be able to set all this up, but I brought everything Kai told me to," he says, reaching out and clasping my shoulder gently.

"Thanks, Anton," I place my hand over his and give it a squeeze.

"I can't tell you how thankful we are that you made it through, *figlio*. Anything you need, my boy, anything," Anton murmurs, "Just keep us in the loop and we'll do everything we can."

"Thank you Anton, Bea. We'll make sure to let you know if we need anything," Kaiser smiles, shaking Anton's hand and embracing Bea.

"Are you sure you don't need me to stay? There's nothing pressing at home, I can stay and help. Keep an eye on you and get you whatever you need," Bea smiles.

"I've got it, Bea. I promise. If anything changes, we'll let you know."

Bea leans over and kisses my cheek before taking Anton's elbow and following him out the door.

"Let's get all this set up, then," Kaiser huffs.

Kaiser wheels in two extra over the bed hospital tables before positioning them around me, creating two spots for my laptops and screens, and another where I can take notes. He plugs them all in, connecting them together and to power sources, before letting me take over to get them on the network.

"Should I hack the hospital network or ask nicely for access," I joke.

"Depends," he responds, "will they be able to track you if you hack it? Because you'll probably get a better signal if you hack their main network as opposed to the guest access they would give you."

"Good point, hacking it is."

"What's your approach? I mean, we don't know anything. Just who took her. Beyond that, it's been a guessing game."

"It's only a guessing game because you didn't have me," I smirk at him.

"Okay, wonder boy, walk me through it."

"First, I'll hack the cameras at the Sylvan building. I find which direction the van went in, then follow traffic cams to figure out where they went."

"That seems way too easy," Kai says doubtfully.

"It does and it probably won't end there, but it's the best place to start. I'm sure that they likely transferred vehicles and probably split up, but it gives me a starting place."

Kaiser nods while I turn my focus onto getting into the hospital network and getting access to their wifi for each of my laptops. Once that's set up, I work on hacking the security footage at the Sylvan.

It takes a couple hours of work, but I'm finally in. It takes me another half hour to sift through all of the different angles and recordings.

"Bingo," I mutter.

"You find something?"

"I've got the right feed, now it's just a matter of tracking the van through the city and see where they end up."

"I'll take it. First fucking lead we've had since she was taken."

Kaiser leans forward and watches as I stream through the various views of the different cameras on the outside of the building. We can clearly see Ben driving and Iris in the passenger seat. Otto remains in the back with Sloane.

They pull out of the alleyway next to the Sylvan building and travel east. Next step is to get into the city network so I can track it beyond the building cameras. Now that I know they were traveling east on Sylvan and have the time stamp, this will be much easier.

I hacked the city network years ago, leaving my own backdoor in their system so I can access it anytime I need to. Comes in handy with our line of work. It takes no time at all to get into the city cameras and access the feeds that I need.

I track the van through the city. They don't make any evasive maneuvers, no switching cars or multiple turns to try to hide what they're doing. They drive directly to the docks on the southeast side of the city.

Once they pass into the dockyard, the city cameras are of no more use. It takes me less than twenty minutes to get access to the dockyard security. Definitely set up by an amateur.

I flip through the various feeds, using the timestamp from when they arrived to find out where they end up amongst all the acres of equipment and boat slips. The dockyard is used by various crime families and legitimate corporations to move goods.

Boats range in size from barges to commercial fishing boats, down to a few small speed boats and just about everything in between. It's smart to keep smaller boats alongside the larger transporters. You never know when you'll need to slide around law enforcement.

"Okay, I got it," I tell Kai, pulling up the main security feed on the larger screen. He leans over to watch with me, gripping my hand.

The van comes to a stop next to a boat slip on the south side of the dockyard. There's a medium sized, nondescript boat docked that Iris immediately heads toward once the van stops. Ben climbs out and walks around to the sliding side door.

When he slides the side door open, Otto staggers out, holding a wad of fabric against his shoulder. I thought one of the guys got him with a shot, but I wasn't sure. Ben climbs into the van and drags Sloane out behind him. Even though the footage is grainy at best, I can see the utter devastation on her face. Ben has a gun pressed to the back of her head while he waits for Iris to come back and pat her down, but it doesn't matter. Sloane's not fighting back.

I watch as Iris pulls the handgun out of the back of her pants, the magazine from her pocket, keys and phone. She pulls off a bracelet before patting her down once more, forcing her to remove her shoes and shake them before she moves back to the door of the van.

Iris turns to Ben, now holding a rag in one hand. She motions with her head until Ben puts his gun away and reaches out to grip Sloane in a tight bear hug from behind. Iris steps up and forces the cloth over her face. She struggles, but it doesn't last.

Kai's fingers tighten on mine and we watch as Sloane slumps in Ben's arm. After another few seconds, he swings her up into his arms and they walk together toward the boat that Iris left running. Otto grabs a bag out of the back of the van and follows after them.

Ben carries her onboard, followed by Otto while Iris unties the moor lines before stepping up to the wheel. Iris begins to maneuver the boat out of the slip and into the waterway that runs through the dockyard. Eventually, the waterway leads to the river, then out to the bay.

"Fuck," Kai whispers, "fuck. They got her out on the water? How they hell are we going to find her now?"

"Don't stress yet," I reassure him, "I still have a few tricks. Boat type and size, I can get the gas tank volume, see how far they could make it before they needed to refuel. Where they could refuel, how long it would take-"

"Okay, I get it," he cuts me off, "I'm just scared, Simon. I'm scared we're not going to get her back."

"We are going to find her, Kaiser. It's only a matter of time before I track them down."

He drops his forehead down to rest on our clasped hands, taking a deep breath, "I believe you. I just hope we get her back before anything else happens to her."

CHAPTER FIVE

Sloane

My stomach twists as the other boat pulls alongside ours. Though boat is a loose term as it's nearly twice the size of ours. They pull up next to us, trying to maneuver into place so we can transfer over by the swim deck, but the water is too choppy. After trying for over ten minutes, they eventually just drop a rope ladder for us to use.

I don't want to go, but Ben makes it clear that I don't have a choice. He holds a pistol against the back of my head until I start climbing after Iris. He lets me know that he'll have the gun trained on me the entire time, even once I'm out of physical reach of him.

As I reach the top, a set of large hands grip me under my armpits and hauls me onto the deck. The man shifts me to the side, but keeps his hands on me until I'm steady on my feet. I look up at him and take a moment to catalog his features.

I need to remember every asshole I come into contact with, just in case I'm able to get away. I want to be able to point my men in the right direction for revenge.

This man is tall. Almost as tall as Kaiser. He's shirtless in spite of the weather, wearing long cargo pants and his hair is cropped short to his skull, dark in color. His eyes are a dark brown and his nose is crooked like it's been broken once or twice. He leers at me, making it a point to take a deep sniffing breath and I'm able to see that several of his top teeth have gold caps. How cliche.

I grimace at him, making sure he can see the disgust in my face, before wrenching away and moving back toward the railing. He smells like sweat and hot iron. It's taking everything in me not to gag.

"Follow me," the man says to Ben before turning and heading around the deck to the rear bridge.

I fall in line behind Ben and Iris, Otto taking up the rear. We follow him onto the bridge, then down a flight of stairs to the lower deck. Several people are gathered here, scattered around the room in various stages of fucking, while two men lean casually against the bar observing the scene.

The shock of coming upon such a scene has me frozen in the doorway, but Ben resolves that with a firm shove between my shoulder blades. I stumble into the man leading us, forcing me to catch myself by bracing my hands on his bare back.

His skin is hot and smooth. For one, treacherous and disgusting moment, I can almost convince myself to slide my hands along the rest of his body, but I yank myself back before letting my hormones dictate anything to me.

My stomach churns as he steps aside to lean casually against the wall, giving me a more clear view of the space we've been brought to.

A short, stocky man has a petite brunette bent over the arm of the couch, driving into her from behind. He's grunting and sweating as he grips both of her hips and pounds into her. I can't see her face, but based on the sounds she's making he's either very good at what he's doing or she's a very good actress.

Another man is sitting on the couch, a redhead kneeling between his feet and bobbing her mouth up and down his cock while he leans back, arms crossed behind his head. She's clearly done this before, as she doesn't stutter or gag, taking his considerable length to the back of her throat. His dick is big, like, almost as big as Kai's - though I'm not comparing - so I'm impressed by her ability to swallow it without a flinch.

On the next couch over, there's a man laying on his back. A very well endowed blonde is riding his face, rolling her hips and grinding her pussy down onto his mouth. A second blonde is riding his cock just as hard, squeezing her own tits and pinching her nipples while she writhes on top of him. Both moan encouragement to the man under them, even though they're doing all of the work.

I cross my arms and squeeze myself tight, trying to disassociate myself from everything taking place in front of me. I refuse to acknowledge the show being put on. Just as I refuse to acknowledge the scent of sex and alpha on the air and the way my body is reacting to it.

As my eyes continue to sweep from couch to couch, unable to look away, I finally notice a small table next to the bar and the two men seated at it.

Enzo Gallo and his second, Anthony. Before I can lunge at him, Ben has turned and is pressing the pistol into my ribs.

"Do not make a scene," he hisses, "do not move and keep your mouth shut."

He prods me once more with the pistol to get his point across, then turns back to the room to address the men at the bar. At least, I'm assuming that's who he's addressing, since everyone else is otherwise occupied.

"Thank you for having us, Egor. Enzo tells us that you're open to making a deal."

The man on the left remains casually slouched on the bar, resting on one elbow while holding a low ball in the other hand. He takes several sips while watching Ben which gives me a chance to scrutinize his features and commit them to memory.

I'm thankful for anything to focus on, other than the debauchery I'm in the middle of. It's hard to focus between the moaning, slapping flesh and sounds of wet sex, but I force my eyes to take him in.

He's tall, though he tries to hide it with his posture. He's trying to make us feel at ease by making himself smaller. He takes pride in his appearance. He's clean shaven and his hair is styled just so. His clothes are plain, but expensive. Clean but well tailored.

He has fair hair and pale skin, ice blue eyes and a broad nose. His shirt is unbuttoned, revealing a strong and well muscled torso with a smattering of hair. I don't see any evidence of tattoos or scars, but his nose is crooked just like the man who hauled me onboard.

He's not conventionally attractive, but I can't deny he has a certain air about him. He oozes strength and masculinity, there is zero question of who's in charge as long as he's in the room. This is the man that I need to be most careful of.

The second man is equally intimidating, though he's not trying to hide it. He has two long scars down his face, starting just under his right eye and disappearing into the neckline of his shirt. The scars are identical, just an inch or two apart from each other, probably made at the same time.

He has short cropped black hair and dark eyes, dead eyes. They flick over our group without a hint of feeling and a shiver runs down my spine. I don't want this man's attention on me for any reason.

Finally the man on the left answers Ben, his russian accent thick but easily understood, "With the right payment, I am willing to deal with you."

Ben grabs my arm and yanks me forward, pushing me out in front of him and almost knocking me into the redhead on her knees, "And is this acceptable payment?"

I growl at him and try to yank my arm away, but he just grips tighter. I know it's going to bruise, but I don't care. I'm not going to let them trade me like a piece of meat for a better life for them, especially if the women around this room are any indication of what I have to look forward to.

Ben slides his hand down my arm and bracelets my wrist, yanking my arm up behind my back until I squeal.

"Don't damage the merchandise," Egor commands, unfolding from the bar and stepping toward us.

Ben eases up, allowing my arm to fall into a more comfortable position, but doesn't release me.

"She's not exactly cooperative," Ben warns, "she needs to be reminded of her place."

"That's good," Egor responds, as he continues to stalk toward us, maneuvering between the writhing bodies, "we want one feisty. Stubborn. No one wants to breed a pathetic weakling. Strong women breed strong sons."

He steps up to us, gripping my chin and tilting my face toward the light, turning my face back and forth and inspecting my features. He slides his hand down to collar my throat and forces my head to the side, dropping his nose into the crook of my neck and taking a deep breath.

Ben knows me well enough, he pressed the pistol into my ribs the second Egor got close to us. If I was wholly suicidal, I would spit in Egor's face after driving my knee into his nuts. Since I want to make it out of this alive, I stand stoically while he runs his nose up and down my throat, his chest rumbling.

This close, his scent fills my nose. He smells like molasses and roasting nuts. Combined with the pheromones already saturating the space, I can't stop the involuntary shudder that runs through my body. My stomach drops at the same time, physically repulsed by the reaction my body is having.

"You smell like *plushka*, sweet omega. I can't wait to taste you," he breathes into my ear as he pulls away.

"That is never going to happen," I grit out between clenched teeth, fighting the urge to sniff deeply for more of his scent.

Egor lets out a booming laugh, "We'll see, sweet omega. We'll see."

I start to open my mouth and Ben yanks my arm up again. I grunt in pain, but decide to keep my mouth shut, so he lets me relax.

"Nikolaj, take my guests to the upper deck. We can finish negotiations over a late lunch."

The gold toothed man pushes himself off the wall, turns and exits the sitting room onto the deck. Ben pushes me ahead of him and I follow Nikolaj with Ben at my back and, I'm assuming, Iris and Otto behind them.

We cross the deck and take the promenade toward the bow, climbing a short flight of stairs to the upper deck. There is a sail shade over a portion of the deck, covering a long table and chairs, set with multiple place settings. There are two portable propane heaters directed toward the table, warming the area significantly.

"The weather from our homeland is much like this, we enjoy it whenever we can, but you should be more than comfortable," Nikolaj says, leading us to the table and pointing out the heaters.

He directs me to the first chair to the right of the head, pulling it out and encouraging me to sit. Ben takes the seat next to me, Otto and Iris across from us. That leaves three more place settings available.

Assuming Egor is going to be seated at the head of the table, I'm curious to see who else is set to join us. As I ponder who else might be dining with us, Nikolaj steps up next to me and begins to fill my water glass. He makes his way around the table, filling everyone's glass before stepping behind the head chair and crossing his arms casually.

"A guard dog who serves guests," I snark, "how novel. What other tricks can you perform?"

Ben fists his hand in my hair, snapping my head back painfully and pressing the pistol into the side of my neck.

"Shut. The fuck. Up. I'm not going to tell you again, Sloane," he threatens.

"And I'm not going to tell you again, *mudak*. Hands off," Egor's rumbling voice precedes him through the door toward the back of the deck, the alpha tone causing my nipples to tighten painfully.

The bark has a different effect on Ben, who releases me as quickly as he grabbed me.

"If you truly wish to negotiate, I suggest you keep your hands to yourself for the remainder."

"Just a reminder for her to be respectful, Egor. My apologies."

"As I said before, we happen to appreciate a strong woman. One who's not afraid to speak her mind. I won't hold anything she says against you," he smirks at me as he takes his place at the head of the table.

"I'm not worried about that," Ben replies.

"Good, because we don't manhandle our omegas. Better to keep them compliant and more…agreeable."

"Are we waiting for additional guests," Otto interjects, attempting to break the tension.

"Yes, of course," Egor responds to Otto but continues to observe me, his eyes flick down to my chest, his lips quirk to one side as he sees the obvious evidence of my reaction to his entrance, "Enzo and his second will be joining us momentarily."

I can't help the disdain that comes over my face, lip curling at the mention of that asshole joining us.

"You don't want Ben to manhandle me, you should ask what Enzo Gallo does to a girl on a first date," I sneer.

Egor's eyes narrow, just as I hear Enzo and Anthony making their way up the stairs. He glances to the right, watching as they meander across the deck and join us at the table. Thankfully Enzo sits next to Ben, so I don't have to see his face.

"I'd like to start off by saying thank you to Enzo, for arranging this meeting and thank you to Egor for accepting," Otto says, holding his glass up as if he's making a toast.

I scoff as Enzo raises his glass in response, "You are most welcome, though there's nothing I wouldn't do for my most lucrative business associates."

Iris titters and blushes at Enzo. I can only imagine the look he's giving her right now. I hope it's just a look and they haven't actually been together. That thought has me wanting to gag.

Egor scoffs, "We're here to discuss business, not coo over each other like a bunch of *deti* at a *devichnik*."

Enzo clears his throat, "Of course, Egor. I apologize, I was just trying to make them feel comfortable-"

"Shut the fuck up, Enzo."

For a man as full of himself as Enzo, his silence is telling, and another shudder wracks me. If Egor wasn't an absolute scumbug wanting to breed me against my will, I could maybe actually like him just for the simple fact that he can shut Enzo up so quickly.

Fuck no, I immediately yell in my head. *You do not, cannot, are not going to like this man. It's bad enough that he smells good, he has no redeeming qualities. He is the scum of the earth and we want nothing to do with him!*

While I've been mentally berating myself, the conversation has continued to flow around me. Basically, what they told me on the boat. New identities, new lives in exchange for me.

"We have everything set up onboard to provide new identities, along with all appropriate documents for you.

You can stay anchored next to us, we should be able to complete everything within the next 12 to 24 hours."

"Can we also get alternate transportation? I'm sure that this boat was seen on surveillance and it is registered to an identity that is easily traced back to me," Iris requests.

"Not a problem, you can stay onboard here, then. I'll have a new ship brought to the marina for you, we can sink this one before we head back. Anything else?"

Otto, Ben, and Iris exchange glances, seeming to agree without speaking. Each of them shake their heads.

"Then the agreement as stands, new identities for the three of you, set up with a complete back story, real estate holdings, etc. First, you'll assist with transporting the omega to the private airport, then you'll be taken back to the marina for your new boat and new life."

"Why me," I blurt, interrupting their discussion and turning to Egor with narrowed eyes, "you have enough money, clearly, why wouldn't you just go to a surrogate to get what you want? Then you can hand pick the characteristics, genetics, everything you want."

Egor chuckles, shaking his head slightly, "You have no idea who I am, do you, *plushka*? Where my money comes from? Going to a random surrogate is not exactly an option."

"I don't care. I just want to understand why I've been brought into this. I get that they think I was in the way of some business deal they were trying to make," I say, waving a hand towards Ben and Otto, "but why am I so valuable to you?"

"Your designation, for starters. Omegas are very special," Egor purrs, "Plus, you gravely insulted Enzo here, so he made it a point to bring you to my attention, in hopes that I would be interested."

I can't stop my lip curling again, hearing his name. I know he's sitting just feet from me, but it's easier to ignore him since I don't have to see him.

"When we saw your pictures, well, it was an easy decision," Egor chuckles, his smile chilling, his eyes burning into me, "Do you know how rare omega's are, *malyshka*? How difficult it is to find one? Especially in countries where women are a lower population?"

I swallow compulsively, my mouth suddenly dry, "Yes."

"And you are a smart girl, so you understand the cost of commodities when it comes to supply and demand," he continues in a low voice, completely devoid of emotion or intonation.

This time I nod, unable to speak with the horror and disgust of where this conversation is heading.

"I deal in flesh, *plushka*, but I specialize in omegas. Any woman can spread her legs to satisfy a man, as evidenced by the scene currently unfolding below deck, but how many women can go into heat? How many can breed? Take an alpha's knot, while begging for more?

Pussy so hot and tight that any alpha would lose his mind to be inside of it."

"You-you're disgusting," I choke out.

"Hmm, some would agree with you, not anyone at this table, though. It's not just where my money comes from, after all. The flesh trade, and especially the selling of omegas, finances everyone at this table."

"It doesn't finance me," I hiss, "I would never, never support or participate in something like this."

"*Plushka*, you most definitely will be participating," he replies lasciviously, "In no time, as a matter of fact, if the information I have been given is accurate. You see, my pack and I have been looking for our own omega for a long time. And now that we don't have to wait any longer, we're going to take full advantage of the situation."

"I will never be yours," I spit vehemently.

"Oh, you will, *malyshka*, you will. Pretty soon you'll be begging for me, for us. You might not know what happens when you go into heat fully, but I do. I've seen it time and again. You see, we always make sure to deliver product when they're most susceptible."

"You're sick. I don't want you or your pack, you can't force me. I will fight you."

"*Moy sladkiy*, no one is going to force you. That's the beauty of omegas. Once you're in heat and there's a viable alpha close, you'll be presenting until one of us mounts you."

"No," I whisper in disgust.

He reaches out, tucking a stray hair behind my ear, his fingers lingering and dancing down the side of my neck, "Yes, *plushka*, yes. I've seen it before. You'll forget everyone else exists except for the alpha in front of you, you won't know anything except the burning between your thighs and the need to be stuffed with cock, knotted and filled with cum."

His smile turns predatory when he feels the tremors coursing through my body, the glint of tears in my eyes.

"So beautiful," he murmurs, "I hope you save some of those tears for me."

He grips my throat again, pulling me close to him as he whispers in my ear, "I want to taste them after you beg me to fuck you, when you realize you can't control yourself, when my cock is all you crave and you're covered in my seed. I'll lick them off your cheeks, even as you ride my dick and beg for more."

CHAPTER SIX

Brooks

We've been working over Antonio and Vincent for the last few hours, but we're no closer to finding Sloane. We're deep inside one of our warehouses, a converted space we refer to as The Vault that was soundproofed and outfitted with plumbing. Makes clean up a breeze.

The two of them are immobilized and strung up next to each other, naked. Ankles strapped to spreader bars, wrists tied together and hung on a hook high enough that their toes barely touch the filthy floor.

At this point, I don't think we're going to get anything important out of them. It's become very apparent that they didn't have anything to do with Sloane disappearance or the call to the Feds accusing us of human trafficking. They don't know anything. It's kind of pathetic, actually.

He didn't even come up with the story he gave Sloane. Vincent heard the story from one of Enzo Gallo's soldiers and passed it along to Antonio as fact. Antonio took it upon himself to share it with Sloane. Gallo has definitely moved up on my shit list.

I almost feel bad. Almost.

Sloane is fucking missing though and I am going to do absolutely anything and everything I can to get her back. Even if that means beating and torturing these two men within an inch of their lives.

"I say call it," Hudson huffs out, "they clearly don't know shit. We need to focus our attention somewhere that might actually be helpful."

"Agreed," I grunt, landing one final punch to Antonio's left kidney. They might not be at fault, but they're a good outlet. Not to mention that he tried to get my girl. Feels like justice to me.

"I'll gladly put them out of their misery," Hudson mutters, digging around on the tool bench, looking for something specific.

"Just make it quick, just because we don't need him alive any more, doesn't mean that you have time to play with them."

He chuckles darkly, holding up a short, stainless steel jab saw, "You got it, boss."

He stalks up to Vincent, yanking his head back by his hair and angling him so he's facing Antonio, then starts sawing across his throat. Vincent grunts a few times, barely struggling. We've taken most of the fight out of him already.

I can tell the moment he hits the carotid, bright red blood arching across the space to splash on Antonio's face and chest. Hudson laughs maniacally, not stopping with the saw until his head is practically hanging off.

"Jesus, dude," I mutter, "is that really necessary?"

"I figure, since he won't be able to witness his own death, I should make Vinny's here as bad as possible for Antonio to have as his final vision."

Hudson walks up to Antonio, Vincent's blood dripping from his arm and hand. He grabs Antonio's chin, forcing his head back and drives the jab saw into the side of his neck. He twists once all the way around, then yanks it out.

Hudson jumps aside, as the blood sprays out onto Vincent before slowing to a drizzle and dripping onto the floor. The jab saw clatters to the floor as Hudson tosses it aside, walking toward the exit.

We step into the tiled anteroom together, stripping off the jeans we changed into when we got here. The jeans go into a bag and tossed back into The Vault, to be disposed of by the cleaning crew later. The anteroom was added for ease of cleaning, as well.

We start the shower heads installed on the opposite wall, stepping under before they're even warm and start scrubbing down. Top to bottom; hair, face, body. Scrub under the fingernails, in all the cracks and crevices on our hands. Every single trace of what we've been doing for the last few hours, gone.

Hudson pulls the hose off the wall, pointing it at the floor and walls, rinsing away the rest of the blood we dragged in. When the crew comes in to clean The Vault, they'll sanitize in here, as well, before taking everything to burn.

We have our hands in several funeral homes around the city. Very lucrative business. Comes in handy for destroying evidence on the fly.

We dry off together and exit naked. The clothes we arrived in, neatly folded on the table outside the anteroom, just as we left them. We quickly dress and I begin checking my phone as we make our way to the car.

"Simon found something," I tell Hudson, almost in disbelief.

"What," he shouts, entirely too close to my ear, then reaches for my phone, trying to grapple it out of my hand.

"Calm the fuck down," I growl before shoving him off, "let me finish reading. Fuck."

"Sorry," Hudson whines.

"Hey, it's okay," I tell him, reaching out to pull him close, my alpha instincts kicking him to comfort him, even though he's an alpha himself.

Since Sloane was taken, we've found ourselves acting out of character more frequently. The idea that she became such an integral part of our pack in such a short time, without even mating, to change our very natures with each other shows how true mates can affect each other.

As soon as we get her back, I'm mating her. I don't care where we are. I'm dragging her to the nearest private area and making her mine. Permanently.

"He followed the route the van took; they ended up at the dockyard. They took her on a boat. He's working on tracking down where they went from there."

"Fuck, a boat? Fuck, fuck. They could be anywhere, man," he groans, raking his fingers through his hair and grabbing fistfuls of the short strands before yanking them in frustration.

"Let's get back to the hospital, see where he's at tracking her down, okay? I'll call Ricci while we're en route and give him an update."

He nods once, reaching out and squeezing my shoulder before heading back in the direction of the car. Once we're on the road, I pull up Ricci's contact and call.

"Brooks," Ricci answers after one ring, his voice tense.

"Morris, we got something."

I relay all of the information I got from Simon quickly. I know Morris is hurting just as much as we are, albeit in a different sense. He's also struggling with the guilt associated with her kidnappers being two of his pack.

If Morris wasn't Sloane's father, I probably would have gutted him by now. How can you be so close to someone and have no clue how corrupt they are?

"I can be ready to move whenever you need me. Remi and Dmitri are on standby, Marco as well. Whatever you need from me to get her back, Brooks."

"I know Morris, we'll keep you in the loop. I don't know what kind of situation we'll be walking into, keep some of your top guys close, alright? We might need more than just the seven of us."

"Of course. I'll get Marco on it."

"Good. Stay sharp, okay. I'll call again soon."

"Thank you, Brooks, for everything."

With the betrayal of Ben and Otto, plus his tech girl seemingly involved as well, Morris is struggling with his empire. Not sure who to trust, who to include, he's relied on us to handle a lot of the heavy lifting when it comes to looking for Sloane. He's reached out to his other alliances, but is still unsure of who's reliable.

I disconnect and Hudson lets out a snarl that I know he's been holding back since he heard Morris' voice. Hudson is struggling to be around anyone other than pack right now, but especially Morris and Marco.

Once we heard the story from Morris, about how Ben and Otto were trying to get him involved in the flesh trade, especially in kidnapping omegas, Hudson lost his shit. I was pretty close, myself.

I don't know how Morris let it go and didn't look into it further when they brought up making an alliance with Egor Volkov. Russian pig. Scum of the earth. Aside from the run of the mill human trafficking he's involved in, he also kidnaps omegas.

He then sells those omegas to the highest bidder, waiting to deliver them until they're deep in heat and completely mindless. At that point, they'll present for anyone who smells good to them, who's compatible. It makes me sick.

The fact that Ben and Otto were obviously somehow involved with that cretin makes me murderous. I pray every minute that he is not who they ran to for rescue. That he's not the one that my *tesoro* is with right now.

Morris told me that she's now missed her heat suppressant shot. I haven't told any of the guys about it yet because I know they'll lose their shit. Especially Hudson. I'm barely keeping it together, the idea that my mate could go into heat at any time and we're not with her?

This knowledge, combined with the fact that she might have been taken to the most notorious human trafficker I know of, is eating away at me. The faster we find Sloane, the better off we'll all be. I can't maintain this veneer of civility.

Even beating Antonio Leone to within an inch of his life didn't release half of the tension I'm carrying.

My fingers tap tap tap on the center console while Hudson maneuvers us through afternoon traffic downtown. I drop a quick text in the group chat.

B: On our way now. Need anything?

Si is quick to answer, as I knew he would be. If he has his laptops set up, his messages will sync there and he can respond quickly.

Si: We're good, bossman. I could use a Monster or two, but the nurses keep telling me no.

Simon follows that with the cry laughing emoji. He might find that amusing, but I most certainly do not.

B: I have to agree with the nurses, asshat. Your heart literally stopped just a day ago, I don't think you need to crank it up right now.

B: And you better not be giving those nurses trouble.

Si: I'm not, I swear. You really think Kai would let me get away with that?

Si: Besides, I've been too busy to ask for anything actually. I'm so close to finding her Brooks, I can feel it.

B: I hope you're right, Si, it's killing me.

Si: I know, I feel it too. We're gonna get her back.

B: We'll be there in 5. You sure you don't need anything?

Si: Swear we're good, they've been feeding both of us.

I send a thumbs up emoji and drop my phone back into the cupholder.

"Everything good," Hudson asks.

"Yeah, Simon thinks he's close. No proof or evidence, just a feeling, but I fucking hope he's right."

"Me, too, brother, me too."

We ride the rest of the way in silence. Before getting out of the car, I reach into the back and grab Sloane's overnight bag, the one she left at the house. I want it to be available quickly if we need it. Since we've been splitting our time between the hospital and Ricci's downtown offices, I figured it would be smart to leave it in Simon's room. Just in case.

The silence stretches, no words exchanged as we park and climb into the elevator. Dead silence as we stalk the halls to Simon's room. We're all on edge, not knowing where Sloane is and if we'll get to her in time. Carrying her bag is a harsh reminder.

Walking into Simon's room, the tension ratchets to 100. Kai is sitting next to the hospital bed, hands clenched in fists on his thighs, his head down and shoulders tense. Simon's eyes are narrowed, while he taps furiously away on his keyboard.

I can see the muscles in his jaw bunching in time with the information flickering across the screen in front of him as it lights up his face. Whatever we just walked into is bad. I send a silent prayer up that it's something we can recover from.

"Well I don't like how this feels," Hudson grunts, barely restraining the growl in his voice.

Simon's eyes flick our way for a brief moment before going right back to the screens in front of him. Kai finally acknowledges our presence by tipping his head back and pinning us both with a grim look.

"I suggest one of you starts talking," I snap out.

They exchange a look, but still, neither of them speak.

"NOW," I snarl.

Simon hunches into himself slightly before recovering, nodding to Kaiser as if encouraging him to be the one to share whatever horrors they've uncovered.

Kai clears his throat, "It's just a suspicion right now, we don't have any evidence-"

"Circumstantial, yes, but very telling," Simon interrupts him, shooting daggers at the side of his head.

"One of you better get on with it before I lose my shit, and I can guarantee you do not want that to happen in here," Hudson hisses, baring his teeth at Simon and Kaiser in turn.

"Fine. Fuck it. Simon checked all of the security footage for public arenas that they could have reached by boat in the time they've been gone, calculating the need for refueling. They didn't show up on any of them."

"So, they could have docked somewhere private," I point out.

"Yeah, let me finish, okay," Kai says on a sigh, dragging his fingers through his hair, "While he was reviewing security footage for the public docks, he came across footage of Nikolaj Petruk onboard a small yacht heading out. He went back through the footage with facial recognition, just to be sure, but there's no evidence that the boat he was on docked anywhere, either."

Hudson rasps out a laugh, "So let me get this straight. Sloane is on a boat that can't currently be found and Nikolaj Petruk, second hand to the most notorious human trafficking piece of shit on the planet, the pig that was colluding with the two men currently holding our girl hostage, is also on a boat, in the same fucking area and also can't fucking currently be fucking found? FUCK," Hudson is yelling by the end of his rant.

I drop Sloane's bag and scrub my hands down my face, my greatest fear appearing to be coming true.

"We need to find her Simon," I rasp, "as soon as possible, we need to find her. Whatever you need, whatever I can get you, we need to find her."

"I know, Brooks, I know. I'm doing everything I can, okay? I know what we're facing, if they're really meeting up with Petruk."

"It's not just Petruk, I would bet everything I own that Volkov is on that boat, too."

"I didn't see him board…" Simon trails off, directing his focus back to the screens, "I can review the footage again."

"Don't bother, you won't see him. I'm surprised you saw Petruk. Volkov won't risk being seen, but if they are meeting up, then I can guarantee he'll be there for the pick up."

"Why," Hudson questions, confused by my insistence on this fact.

I take a deep breath, glancing between all three of them before dropping the bomb I've been holding onto since this all started.

"Sloane is just over two days past due on her heat suppressant shot."

Simon's fingers stop on his keyboard, Kai stares at me like I just lit his grandma on fire. Hudson scoffs, then laughter spills out his mouth. Not good laughter, the laughter of a man pushed way past his breaking point.

Hudson bends over, bracing his hands on his knees, braying laughter before turning abruptly and locking himself in the bathroom. The sounds of destruction follow soon after. Luckily there's not much in there he can damage except himself.

"I didn't think this could get worse, Brooks," Kai admits quietly.

"How much time do you think we have," Simon asks.

"Given the fact that she's been spending so much time with us, her body is already primed for a heat. Without the shot, it's just a matter of a few days. Assuming they're taking her to Volkov, she's going to be put on a boat full of alphas. I would say two, three more days tops before she's completely out of it. She's probably already in the early stages and doesn't realize it."

"Christ"

"Fuck"

Simon and Kaiser mutter at the same time. I can't agree more. The second I heard the name Petruk, my stomach dropped to the floor. We are in some serious deep shit and I'm not sure we're going to be able to climb our way out of it.

Our girl, our mate, is somewhere on the open water, on her way to being given or sold to Egor Volkov. And we know fuck all. I can feel my facade cracking, the more this information loops in my brain. It's like static filling my ears and I can't think of anything beyond the fact that we won't be able to get her back because we don't know where she is.

CHAPTER SEVEN

Hudson

I'm almost positive I've broken at least three of my fingers. Possibly cracked a knuckle or two. I'm thankful for my steel toe boots though, broken toes suck.

I brace my back on the door and slide down until my ass smacks the floor and I splay my legs out. I take a moment to survey my surroundings before shutting my eyes and shutting everything out.

The bathroom is no longer functional. Then again, I'm pretty sure I'm no longer functional.

I can hear them talking on the other side of the door, their muffled voices occasionally loud enough that I can hear as they plan how to find her. My little omega.

I thump my head back once, twice. Harder each time until my teeth clack together and I bite my tongue. The physical pain numbs all the other pain, at least for a moment.

Egor fucking Volkov. The thought of my baby in the vicinity of that russian fuckstick…too much for my brain to deal with. Hence, the now non-functioning bathroom.

We've got to get her back. I don't know if any of them truly understand where I'm at mentally without her here. I told Brooks that I was unhinged and I think that was probably an understatement.

I've never in my life felt this bond with anyone. Sure, I'm tight with the guys, we're family, we've been together our entire lives. Even their love can't touch what I feel for her. They took a piece of me when they took her from me and I'm pretty sure it was my humanity.

I will destroy everything in front of me, burn a path of destruction through this world until I get her back. I don't care what I have to do or who I have to take out to get to her. There is no punishment, no repercussion devastating enough to keep me from getting her back.

We've built a lot in this city, but I will throw it all away if that's what it takes to get my baby back. If it gets that bad though, I'm sure Simon would create a whole new life for all of us and we could just disappear. As long as we have Sloane back, I'll be a fucking pig farmer in Belarus for all I care.

I realize that the voices from the other room have stopped. No one is going to knock to check on me, they know me well enough to know I went in here to be alone in my devastation. I also realize I can't stay here any longer.

I drop my head forward and let the desolation creep close, embracing the pain one more time before pushing it into a little ball in my heart and hoisting myself to my feet. I brush off the debris as best I can, not wanting to track broken tiles and glass back into the room, I kick my boots against the jamb as I open the door.

Kai's next to Simon's bed, Simon propped up, silently tapping away at his keyboard. Brooks is across the room, staring out the window at the rapidly darkening sky. Once they hear the door click shut, all eyes are on me, assessing.

Brooks checks me from head to toe, noting the discoloration of my right hand. Simon must have noticed too, as I hear the ping of the nurse light coming on.

"I assured them I'd pay for any damages," Brooks tells me, "but I doubt they were expecting an entire remodel."

"Yeah, well, you know me, go hard or go home," I shrug, "where we at?"

There's a light tap on the door before a nurse slips in and heads directly to Simon. She reaches behind the bed and turns off the call light before looking him over.

"What can I help you with this evening, Mr. Costa?"

"Not me, him," he points at me before focusing back on his screens. I don't think I've ever seen him this obsessed before. I'm thankful for it.

The nurse glances at me, then at Brooks, before settling back on me, "You're not my patient."

I barely stop the snarl from escaping, but my lip curls up on its own at her tone. She doesn't miss the aggression and disdain emanating from me and immediately directs her attention back to Brooks.

"It's nothing against him or any of you, but he's not my patient. I can't treat him without him being evaluated by a doctor and having orders."

"Then find a doctor," Brooks dismisses her with the tone of his voice alone.

She scurries away, hopefully listening to Brooks and finding a doctor. I'll need the fingers taped at a minimum if I'm going to be effective going forward. I could do it myself, but I don't have any supplies here.

"What have we come up with? What's next?"

"Once your hand is checked out, we're taking a ride across the river. Volkov's boat left from a dock in Leone's territory. We're going to go ask some questions."

"Excellent," I reply, bringing my hands up to crack my knuckles and just barely stopping myself in time.

"I've got surveillance embedded in all of the surrounding public docking areas to alert me when and if any of them are caught on camera. I'm coordinating with Ricci to get a long range drone in the air," Simon adds.

"A drone? Are you shitting me," I chuckle.

"Not shitting you, the newer commercial models can go up to 8 miles. If I can calculate a trajectory based on where each left the docks, I can try to quarter the area and see if I can get eyes on them. Assuming they're together and stationary, that will make things easier…" he trails off, distracted by something on his screen as he begins typing furiously, completely focused elsewhere now.

Brooks steps up next to me, knocking his shoulder into mine. I nudge him back before turning and dropping my forehead to his for just a moment. I head over to the bed and push myself into Simon's space, rubbing my face against his aggressively. Because I love him and because I want to irritate him for funsies.

I catch a hint of Sloane, when I inhale down by his neck. I start sniffing around and find one of her t-shirts tucked under the blanket against his chest. Someone grabbed it from her overnight bag and slid it in next to him.

I smile sadly and drop into the chair next to Kai, gripping his hand with mine and bringing it to my mouth for a quick kiss. I love them all, the realization of how much didn't really hit me until this shitshow.

They've just always been there. Simon being shot, the idea that we might not all be together forever; I resolve myself to make sure they know how much I care.

"We're heading to the docks as soon as we're done here," I state, looking at Brooks, knowing that the best time to ask questions is at the same time the boat left to begin with, the same people should be around working.

He nods, opens his mouth to say something, when the door pops open again and an older guy in a long white coat comes through. The nurse from before trails after him, a tray of supplies in her hands.

"Mr. Costa, so glad to see that you're not overdoing it. I hear your friend here might need a little assistance though," he greets Simon, chuckling as he turns to me, "I'm Dr. Seymur. Let's take a look at that hand."

I try really, really hard not to be a dick, but it doesn't work. As soon as he takes a step toward the bed, the growl rumbles from deep in my chest. Kai slides his hand around the back of my neck, trying to ground me.

It actually does the opposite, reminding me of the fact that I have an injured pack member behind me and my protective instincts flip. The growl gets deeper, turning into a snarl when the doctor continues to approach.

"Hudson," Kai snaps, close to my ear, "we're all safe. He's here to help. You and I are between him and Simon. Let him look at your hand."

He continues to squeeze the back of my neck rhythmically. When that doesn't work, he presses himself close to my back and starts to purr. I try to let go of the tension, pushing myself back into him, but it's not until I feel Brooks take up on my other side that I can finally force myself to lift my hand and let the doctor take a look.

"Impressive alpha instincts," he murmurs as he turns my hand gently.

I grunt in response. I don't care what this dipshit thinks and I certainly don't want to engage in conversation with him.

"Can you feel this," he taps the tip of each finger.

"Yeah."

"Good, that means there's no nerve damage. We should take x-rays-"

"Fuck. No," I grind out between clenched teeth.

"Fine, fine," he sighs, "Just keep in mind that you were never seen and this never happened, because I'm not going to be responsible if there's permanent damage."

"No one's going to blame you, doc, just fix the fingers and you'll get your payment, this isn't our first rodeo" Brooks instructs, dropping his hand to my shoulder, adding his touch to Kai's to help keep me grounded.

I close my eyes and focus on Brooks and Kai, managing to make it through the entire taping process without lashing out. I stay focused until I hear the door shut, just to be on the safe side. No reason to fuck up a guy who's trying to help me just because I'm completely unstable.

Brooks gives my shoulder one final squeeze before stepping away and I open my eyes. Kai hugs me from behind, burying his face in the back of my neck and rubbing his scent all over me before pushing me up and out of the chair.

I flex my hand, checking the tape job and the movement. Satisfied that he actually did a decent job, I turn back to Kai and return the favor, rubbing my face against his obnoxiously until he pushes me away. I swoop down on Simon, purposefully blocking his screens with my head as I rub against him one more time before heading out with Brooks.

"You good to drive or you want to take shotgun," he glances at me out of the corner of my eye as we ride the elevator down to the parking garage.

"Nah, I'm good, gives me something to focus on."

He nods, then ushers me out of the elevator.

"You think anyone there will really out Volkov," I ask as we climb into the Macan.

"I think that depends on how convincing we can be, with fist or finance. I'll give them the whole fucking world if they can give me any information or, I'll point you in their direction. Hopefully one or the other will be enough."

I nod, hoping he's right. Hoping we can get to her in time.

Shit. I block that thought off before it can take root. Focus. Docks, intel, Volkov. I cannot have another meltdown right now.

We cross the river and follow the frontage road down to the docks. This side of the river, there's no guards or fences to protect anything, finances aren't as high here, so I make sure to park the Macan under a nice big pool of light, courtesy of one of the only working security lights in the place.

It's no wonder this is where Volkov docks his boat. No one would suspect that one of the richest criminals in the country would stoop so low as to use this place. Hopefully that means the people here are desperate for an influx of cash.

The only worrying thing about this situation is the fact that Leone never uttered a word about Volkov. So either he's incredible under torture or he had no idea that Russian piece of shit was shipping out on his territory. Sloppy, sloppy.

I slide my Glock out of the holster mounted under the steering wheel and slide it into the holster built into the inside of my leather jacket, next to the custom SOCOM alpha knife I've been carrying since that night. Brooks does the same, pulling his from the holster under his seat. I'm hoping we won't need them, but it's always better to err on the side of staying alive.

Since I decided to park under the lights, it's a bit of a walk to the main building, which I'm assuming houses the offices. We slip through the shadows side by side, taking in the surrounding area, hunting for anyone we can pump for information if those in the office turn out to be a bust.

It's late and I don't see anyone else out and about, but I do note a few houseboats with lights shining within. We can stop by and introduce ourselves later, if the need arises.

Pushing into the building, the smell of stale cigarettes and mold assails me. Glancing around the interior, I can see that no one cares about the upkeep here. Cobwebs are gathered in all the corners, the carpet is worn clear through in several places, and there's an overflowing ashtray on the desk.

There's no one in the tiny lobby area, but the smell of fresh cigarette smoke wafts down the back hallway. Someone is definitely here.

"Knock, knock," I yell loudly, stepping between Brooks and the hallway and sliding my hand into my jacket. At least if someone comes up behind us, I'll hear the door opening as a warning.

A few seconds later I hear footsteps coming toward us, not hurried or stomping, then I hear, "Eddie, that you?"

I ease the grip on my pistol, but don't release it completely. Unless whoever this is comes around the corner hates Eddie and wants to shoot him dead, I'm confident I'll be able to draw fast enough to defend us.

A short, grizzled, wrinkly raisin of a dude comes around the corner, a half smoked cigarette hanging out of the corner of his mouth. It's really weird because he looks like he hasn't seen the sun in years, he's so blindingly white, but he's so wrinkled he looks like leather left in the sun.

"You're not Eddie," he blurts, blinking owlishly at the two of us, the cigarette dangling for dear life, "Eddie send you?"

"Sorry man, but I don't know who the fuck Eddie is. I do have some questions you could help me with, though."

"Eh, I don't know, I'm not really the answer man around here, you need to come back in the morning, talk to Mickey," he scratches the side of his neck, pushing his wiry beard to one side, then ashes his cigarette in the already overflowing tray on the desk.

"If you're the one who's here at night, then we need to talk to you," Brooks steps up next to me, "and anyone else who's normally here this time of night."

"Alright then, shoot," he cackles, pulling out a second cigarette that he lights using the half burnt one he'd currently smoking. Mashing out the first cigarette I notice the yellowed skin around his first two fingers and thumb. I gag internally. Clearly a longtime smoker.

Brooks pulls his phone out, flipping to the picture of the yacht that Petruk was seen on, "We need all the information you have about this ship. Logs, manifest, captain, destination - anything."

Watching Raisin closely, I notice when his eye twitches. Most people might miss this in the sea of wrinkles he has on his face, but I saw it. I knew.

"I don't know nothin about nothin about that boat," Raisin says confidently, mashing out the second cigarette, "now if you'll excuse me."

Too bad he doesn't know who he's dealing with.

Faster than he can react, I grab his beard, wrapping it once around my hand before yanking him close. I slide the SOCOM out of my jacket and hold the point just under that twitchy eye.

"See, the problem with that answer," I tell him, "is that I don't believe it. Now, unless you want to lose this eye, I suggest you tell me what you know."

He sputters, at first, continuing to deny his knowledge. I put a little pressure on the tip, just enough to break the skin so he can feel the burn. A perfect red droplet runs down his face and he whimpers.

"I am not fucking with you, my man, I will pop these fuckers right out if you don't start talking."

"I don't wanna die, man!"

"Then tell me," I yell, spittle flecking his face as I lose my cool.

"I can't win man, either you kill me or he does," Raisin starts crying and I smell the acrid stench of urine laced with fear.

"Fuck's sake, man," I shove him away from me and step back quickly, almost stumbling over Brooks in my effort to get away from Mr. Pee Pants.

"We're not going to kill you, if you tell us everything. We'll give you enough money to disappear," Brooks tells him, pulling a thick wad of cash out of his coat pocket, "this is just a taste of what we can do for you."

Piss Raisin is shaking now, slumped against the wall, trying to pull his cigarettes out of his shirt pocket. His eyes dart between the two of us as he finally wrestles it free and taps a fresh cigarette out.

"You need to make a decision quick because I am twitchy as fuck right now. I will leave you bleeding out on this floor and find someone else willing to take this money and spill their guts. You get me?"

He nods, "Yeah, yeah, I get you, but listen. I-I need the money tonight. They're supposed to be back late tomorrow and I can't be here, man, I can't be here when they get back."

"Tomorrow? When," I bark.

"I-I-I," Pissy stutters around his fresh smoke, shaking so hard he burns part of his scraggly mustache trying to light it.

"I'll have the money delivered. Speak. Now. I'm losing patience," Brooks adds the last through gritted teeth.

"Okay, man, okay," he takes a deep drag of the cigarette before starting, "it was an unexpected visit. Petruk called yesterday morning saying they needed the boat ready to go as soon as possible, outfitted for two to three days. He showed up with a bunch of his guys, some women. They all loaded up and said they'd radio when they were on their way back."

"Two to three days? You just said they're coming back tomorrow, which is it," I bark again, enjoying the way he twitches and whines each time I dominate him.

"I know man, that's what he said originally. But I guess they're coming back early because he radioed a few hours ago and said they'd be back mid-day tomorrow. They needed the boathouse cleared to dock, moving precious cargo or something."

I take a step toward him, the overwhelming urge to shove my knife in his guts because I know that the precious cargo is probably my little omega and this fuck helps Egor fucking Volkov traffick women and omegas. Brooks grabs my shoulder, yanking me back before I can clear the counter and get close.

"How many guys, exactly, got on the boat," Brooks asks, pushing me behind him.

"Um-I-um, six or seven guys and um, four girls."

"You're sure," Brooks steps toward him, "seven guys max?"

"Yeah, for sure, man. I didn't count them, specifically, but yeah, that's about what I saw. The chicks, for sure, four of them, man. The two blondes," he shakes his head, then holds his hands in front of his chest, mimicking giant breasts.

"Christ," I mutter, trying to step past Brooks.

"I'll make sure your money is delivered tonight," he tells him, stepping in front of me and snapping a picture of his face, "I'll send this to my associate now so he knows who to deliver the money to, okay?"

He sounds so sincere, I almost believe him, until I look over his shoulder and see who he's sending the picture to. Pissy pants will be dead before morning. Probably floating out in the marina. A 'freak accident' causing him to drown, most likely.

Brooks likes accidents, especially when he can make sure someone else makes it happen. Even though I'm the best at what we do, he doesn't like us to get directly involved unless it's something deep.

I shove my knife back inside my jacket and follow Brooks to the door, fighting every urge to turn around and take care of him myself. Brooks pulls the door open and shoves me out it, in front of him, effectively blocking my way back inside.

"Sometimes I think you know me too well," I chuckle, making a beeline for the car with Brooks on my heels.

CHAPTER EIGHT

Sloane

After the absolute horror of being in close proximity to Egor Volkov, I am thrilled to be locked in one of the staterooms. Even if it is on the lower deck and even if it is close enough to the lounge that I can hear the 'party' currently taking place, I'd rather be here than in the same room as him or any of the other animals on this boat.

I can no longer deny the effect they have on my body. The lack of suppressant is becoming very obvious and I can admit that I am terrified of what will happen if I don't get out of here soon.

The room they've put me in is basic and bare, a bed with side tables, some cabinets along the wall, a small walk in closet. The closet is empty, save for extra pillows, blankets, and sheets for the bed. Same with the cabinets and side tables.

The drawers don't even come all the way out, so no chance of using them as weapons. The attached bathroom doesn't have a mirror, just a one piece marine toilet and sink, a shower head mounted on the wall, no curtain. Nothing in the cabinets here, either. No cleaning spray or chemicals.

The longer I'm in here, the more I think that others may have been held here. Most boats this size have fancier staterooms. There's nothing in here I can use to hurt myself or anyone else. How many other omegas have been in here? How many were in the same state of preheat as me?

My first heat was barely a blip; triggered by Brooks and Hudson, then shut down by Iris. The second was at the Academy and simply a reflex of biology. I've never been around this many viable alphas and I only know what to expect based on what I was taught.

I remember the first time, feeling hot and twitchy at the hotel. I can look back and realize that I was wanting for a nesting space, which explained the agitation. I can feel those same urges now, though not as strong, I can recognize what they are.

My symptoms are inconsistent, but increasing in strength. I'm hot and sweaty, then cold and crampy. Egor's scent was teasing me at lunch, his pheromones and overall dominance in that space, making my pussy clench and release a lot of slick. Not heat levels, but more than usual.

And I know he could smell me. They could all smell me, but no one made a move. He said he wanted me mindless and I'm afraid that's exactly what's going to happen, sooner rather than later.

At least I have the comfort of knowing that he's the biggest alpha here, so no one else will touch me in fear of his wrath. I just have to fight through it, as long as I can while praying that I find a way out of this. Or that someone rescues me. Either or at this point, I don't really care as long as I get out of here.

Based on how I'm feeling now, I figure by this time tomorrow, I'm going to be in quite a bit of pain. According to the education we received at the Academy, the basic stages were pre-heat, which is where I am now. Hot flashes, urge to nest, mild increase in pheromone production. Check, check, and check.

Beginning heat will be signaled by an ongoing fever, mild cramping, increase in slick, and low grade sexual need. The overwhelming need to nest will also present. This quickly morphs into a full heat which will include rolling waves of severe need, marked by intense cramping that can become debilitating if not relieved.

With some assistance, such as knotted dildos and masturbation, an omega can make it through heat on their own. It's not necessarily satisfying, but it gets the job done enough that the omega can function.

Being in a full heat, with compatible alphas available, it would be nearly impossible for an omega to deny being mounted. They would likely beg for it, just like Volkov claimed. That's why it was drilled into us in the Academy to track our heat cycle and ensure we had multiple plans in place to handle it. It's too easy for an alpha to take advantage of an omega in need.

The entire basis for Volkov's criminal empire. The entire reason why I'm here right now. Just thinking about the things this man has done, that Ben and Otto and Enzo have helped him do, makes me sick to my stomach. My heart hurts thinking of all the omegas before me and the horrors they've been dealt.

No longer able to resist the urge, I grab the blankets and sheets off the bed, tossing them into the closet along with the pillows. I pull the other blankets and pillows off the shelves and add them to my pile.

The first thing I do is tuck a pillowcase around the overhead light. I need to be able to see, but the light is too harsh. With the pillowcase in place, it's much more soft.

I start with a sheet, then layer two blankets. The pillows create the base, nestled together with just enough room for me in the middle. I fill it with sheets and two more blankets over the top.

I climb in, but the scent isn't right. It's too clean, missing the comforting alpha pheromones I need to settle. My own scent is agitating more than anything. Being alone like this, so far from home in a makeshift nest, I can't help but think about the nest back home that the boys put together for me.

I never got to see it. And even if I do, it won't be the same. Not without Simon. I hold the blanket to my face to muffle my sobs. It's doubtful anyone would be able to hear me, unless they were in the main room, but I'm not taking any chances.

I don't want someone to walk by and hear me crying, thinking they need to check on me. The longer I can be left alone the better. Not just because I do not want to see or deal with anyone right now, but because the less pheromones I'm exposed to, the slower my heat will come on.

At least, that's what I tell myself. It's not true, my heat is going to progress no matter what, but at least I can suffer alone.

As I cry myself into utter exhaustion, I make a vow to myself and to all the omegas who were brought here before me. Once I get out of this, I will not stop until Egor Volkov and all of his pack are dealt with. Permanently. I may not have involved myself in the business much up to this point, but I have my father and my mates at my back. I will make him and anyone associated with him pay with their lives.

CHAPTER NINE

Kaiser

My eyes burn from lack of sleep, but I still can't take them off of Simon. The grittiness of each blink just accentuates the fact that he's alive; that I'm really seeing him and not a ghost.

The absolute roller coaster of pain from the last three days has done a number on me. My heart hurts, the constant tug of war between being so thankful Simon is alive and the pain of Sloane still being gone, almost too much to deal with.

I'm so sleep deprived that it takes me a few seconds to realize Simon is looking at me, calling my name.

I snap to attention, "Yeah? What," I ask, talking over him.

"Your phone," he's telling me, "your phone."

I blink a few times, then register the buzzing sound as my phone vibrates on the table next to me.

"Shit," I mutter, snatching it up quick and answering it. I see it's Brooks so I immediately put it on speaker phone.

"Sorry, boss, sorry. Zoned out for a minute."

"Have you slept at all, Kai?"

"Have you," I counter, not hiding the frustration in my voice.

"More than you," he fires back, "I catch a few every couple hours. We're not going to be any use getting her back if we're not taking care of ourselves. Get some shut eye."

"Yeah, okay," I mutter, not trying to hide the sarcasm. Multiple nurses have offered to wheel in an extra bed or even just switch out the chair with a recliner, but I refused.

I need to stay awake, I need to see Simon. See him okay and sitting in front of me. Every time I close my eyes, I see him in that alleyway and I can't get through that. If I fall asleep with that image, I know I'm just going to repeat it in my nightmares.

"I'm assuming you got some information," Simon interjects before I get myself in real trouble.

"Yeah. Okay, here's what we got. Petruk boarded the yacht with seven men and four women. He doesn't have a destination, but reported they would be back tomorrow midday. He wanted the boathouse at the marina cleared for them because they were bringing back precious cargo that needed to be unloaded in private."

"Fuckin hell, I hope you took care of whoever told you that shit once you were done questioning him. He knows what kind of 'precious cargo' they're transporting."

"Brooks wouldn't let me deal with Raisin Pissy Pants, but he called in Mac. Guy'll be floating in the marina by dawn," Hudson answers.

"Raisin Pissy Pants," I ask, bewildered. No matter how long I've known Hudson, the shit he comes up with sometimes still has the ability to throw me off.

"Ha, dude pissed himself when I got a little loud. And he was sooo wrinkly, man," he laughs, "guess maybe you had to be there. But then you would've had to smell him and that, I wouldn't wish on anyone."

"You're lucky I love you, you weird ass sonofabitch," is all I can reply. Apparently his coping mechanism is being weirder than normal.

"Anyway," Brooks stresses, "we need to decide how we want to handle this. Are we waiting for them at the dock or are we sending out the drone? Simon, can you run a few scenarios, odds of success, things like that? Give us an idea of our next move?"

"On it. You guys coming back here or heading to the warehouse?"

"We're stopping at the warehouse, gonna grab some fresh clothes for all of us, then we'll be up there. Hopefully Simon will have some ideas by then, we can discuss how to get our girl back."

"Right," I swallow hard, ignoring the stabbing pain in my heart and sending up a short, quick prayer that we find Sloane before anything serious happens.

"We'll see you soon, have those reports ready."

"Yeah, I got it. See you soon."

"See you soon," I echo, disconnecting the call.

"You need to sleep, baby. It's going to be a few hours before they make it back here, do you want me to call the nurse? See if the doctor will give you something?"

"I don't want-I can't be out like that. I know, okay, I know I need to sleep," my eyes well up, throat thick as I see it again in my mind's eye, "but every time - every time I see you, laying there."

Hot tears roll freely down my cheeks, soaking into my beard. I reach out and grip his hand hard, laying my head gently on his shoulder. I shudder, inhaling his subtle scent, barely discernible beneath the hospital disinfectant and the lingering scent of Sloane.

"I've never been that scared in my life," I whisper, "when I saw you laying there, all the blood. Then the surgery, not knowing if you would be you when you woke up, if you'd be able to walk."

He nuzzles his head against the top of my head, "I'm here, baby, I'm alive. I'm still me and I still love you. Let them bring in a bed for you, we can line them up together and drop the rails. You won't be able to sleep right next to me, but you'll be able to reach out and touch me. Know that I'm right here."

"I still don't know if I can, it's not that I don't want to-"

"Just try, okay," he pushes the nurse call button and smiles indulgently, "be a good boy."

I chuckle, "Don't get sassy with me, you won't be laid up forever. I'll be able to put you back in your place eventually."

"And you know I love it when you do," he kisses me gently on the forehead, "but for now, just let me be in charge."

"Fat chance," I mutter before stretching up and plucking a light kiss from him.

"Sorry to interrupt, gentleman, but I need to get to that call light," a voice I recognize as the nurse from earlier comes quietly from the foot of the bed.

"Ah yeah, sorry," I slide back and stand up so she can reach the light.

"What can I do for you guys?"

"Can you bring in another bed for him," Simon smiles at her, "line it up right here so he can have his own space, but we can still be close?"

She huffs out a breath, looking back and forth between the two of us a few times before finally answering, "It's not something we're supposed to do, he shouldn't be so close to you, just in case he flails or something in his sleep. But, he also looks like he's dead on his feet, so I'm going to let it fly. Also because I know you'll go above my head and create an issue if I don't."

"Thank you, truly," I paste on the most sincere smile and point it in her direction.

"Yeah, yeah, save it for day shift, they eat that sweet shit right up. Give me a few, we have some unused rooms right now so I'll be able to wheel one right over."

In less than ten minutes I'm set up with my very own bed. With the beds pushed together and the side rails down, the beds sit almost flush. It's not the most comfortable bed I've enjoyed and the pillows are almost as thin as the blanket, but I'm going to make the best of it. Especially since I grabbed another one of Sloane's t-shirts to keep close.

"Talk to me," I ask Simon quietly.

"About?"

"Anything? I just want to hear your voice while I try to sleep, I think it might help."

"Okay," he chuckles softly, reaching across the bed and squeezing my hand, "I'm working through the probability of our success on rescuing Sloane based on two different scenarios, waiting until they dock tomorrow midday and finding where they are and confronting them on the water."

I stretch out onto my back as his voice turns into a soft, soothing buzz, draping her t-shirt across my chest so I can smell Sloane with each inhale. I sink quickly, the sleep deprivation taking a larger toll than I realized. I can feel my body sinking into the bed as Simon's buzzing fades into the distance.

The bed shifts suddenly, Sloane's giggles and Simon's overdramatic "sshhhhh" bringing me out of my fog.

Glancing to the side, I see the two of them trying to quietly climb into bed with me. Sloane is in the same red bra and pantie set she was wearing the night I taught Simon to eat her pussy, Simon's wearing his regular black boxer briefs.

"We were trying to surprise you," Sloane whispers, crawling across the bed on her hands and knees.

"I was going to show Sloane how you like me to suck your dick," Simon adds, tugging the blanket down slowly.

"Be my guest," I tell them both, pushing the blanket down to reveal my nakedness, cock already at half mast with the idea of the two of them touching me at the same time.

"Come here, beautiful," Simon pulls her against him so they're both kneeling between my legs, Sloane's back to his chest, "he usually likes me to start sucking him off when he's still semi soft, likes the feeling of getting hard in my mouth, but I think we should give him a little show first.

Sloane moans as Simon slides his hands up her body, cupping and massaging her breasts for a moment before popping the front clasp and pulling the bra off. He pinches and twists her nipples until she cries out, rocking her hips back into his lap.

"Look how hard he is, Sloane. See what your sexy body does to him?"

"Not just her," I tell him, "the two of you together."

"Then let's work together," he whispers in her ear, pushing her down until she takes me in her hot little mouth. Her lips stretch tight as she takes as much of me as possible. Simon spits in his hand, gripping my cock and stroking in time to Sloane's sucking.

"Shit," I mutter, watching her swallow my dick while Simon strokes me.

I groan when I feel Simon wrap Sloane's hand around my balls, teaching her how to squeeze and roll them, just how I like. I drop my head back on the pillow. Watching them together right now is too much, I don't want to blow my load in her mouth, I want to feel her pussy.

"Get on top of me, cara, ride my cock," I grunt, reaching down to tug her away from my cock.

Simon keeps his hand fisted around my dick while Sloane yanks her panties to the side and climbs on top of me. I brace my hands on her hips and guide her down, Simon positioning my cock at her opening. I let out a long breath as she sinks down onto me.

Her pussy is so hot and tight and wet as she slowly takes me. Her slick coats my cock, dripping from her pussy. The sexy little whimpers as she takes me deeper make me impossibly hard.

Simon presses close to Sloane's back, meeting my eyes over her shoulder as he reaches both arms around her body. He slides one hand down to circle her clit, lifting the other to twist and pluck her nipple.

She's fully seated now, my cock deep inside of her. I can feel her pussy twitch and throb around me as Simon rubs her little clit, faster and faster. He alternates between her nipples, twisting and tugging on them in turn. Her slick slides down my balls, pooling underneath us.

I groan and push myself up, determined to be involved in this sexy show.

Sloane cries out as my cock shifts inside of her as I sit up, penetrating her deeper than before. I smile wickedly, pushing her back against Simon to support her while I suck a breast into my mouth.

Simon tucks both of her arms behind her back, holding her still while I suck and bite across both of her breasts.

"Please," she sounds so sexy when she begs, "I need you to move, please."

I slide my arms under her legs, her knees over my elbows, before gripping one ass cheek in each hand. Between Simon and I supporting her, I use my grip to slide her back and forth on my dick while still laving her nipples.

Her cries become muffled. I flick my eyes up to see Simon tongue fucking her mouth while I rock her on my cock. Watching them together gives me an idea. I want to feel her cum on me, but we're nowhere near done with her yet.

I lean back, knowing Simon will support her upper body, and I shift my grip from her ass to her hips. I angle her pelvis so my cock rubs the front of her pussy wall each time I stroke into her. I start to rock her harder down onto me, pushing my hips up at the same time.

Simon breaks the kiss as Sloane starts panting and mewling. I watch a bead of sweat roll down between her breasts as she starts to beg again.

"Please, please," she cries, "I'm so close, please."

She stiffens, her toes curling as she lets out a hoarse scream. Her pussy squeezes me so good, her slick squirting out around my cock as she cums. I want to push my knot into her and fill her with my cum. The urge is almost overwhelming, but I want to see her and Simon together more.

Once her body relaxes, pussy pulsing around me, I slide her off my cock and back against Simon. I kiss her gently, brushing sweaty strands of hair off her face.

"We're not done with you, cara," I tell her, licking across her bottom lip before sealing my lips to hers. Our tongues swirl against one another as I reach between us and pull her panties off.

"Lay on your back," I tell Simon, pulling Sloane against me so he has room to maneuver and taking a moment to slide my tongue against hers a few more times until Simon is ready. At some point he removed his boxers and his cock is hard as a rock, laying against his stomach, balls tight to his body.

I lift Sloane up and spin her around so we're both facing Simon. I take her hand in mine, reaching forward and stroking both our hands up and down his cock. His breathing increases as we continue to stroke him lightly up and down.

"Do you want to fuck him, cara," I whisper in her ear, "Do you want to ride his cock until he fills you with his cum?"

"Yes," she pants

"So do I. We're both going to fuck him, together."

Her breath hitches, "Oh," she squeaks.

"Do you like the idea of that, beautiful," Simon rasps.

She nods, crawling forward until she's straddling his hips. I reach down and grip his cock, holding it for her, like he did for me. She slides down his cock and they both groan.

"How does she feel, Simon? You like pussy on your cock, baby?"

"Fuck," he mutters, "she's so hot and tight."

"You have to ride him a bit, cara. Once I'm fucking his ass, he's going to cum quick and I want to make sure you get to enjoy yourself again."

Sloane leans forward, bracing her hands on his shoulders as she starts rolling her hips against his, grinding her clit into his pelvis. Simon slides his hands up her thighs and around until he's gripping her ass, moving her faster against him.

Her breathing increases, sexy little moans and mewls falling from her mouth. I slide my hand between her thighs from behind, coating my hand with her slick. Once it's nice and wet, I slip two fingers between Simon's cheeks, dragging them up until I can press them into his tight asshole.

He groans and his back arches, pushing his cock deeper into Sloane. She gasps and I start to scissor my fingers inside of him, prepping his asshole to take my cock, making sure her slick is deep inside of him.

Using my clean hand, I gather more of Sloane's slick and stroke it up and down my cock. When I'm slippery with it, I shuffle closer, gripping my cock and pressing it to his tight hole.

"Push out, baby, you know the drill," I tell him, easing my cock into him slowly.

"Oh fuck, jesus," he mutters, "I'm not going to last, fuck, that feels too good. Oh, shit, shit."

His rant ends on a groan as I push my cock deep.

"Ride him, cara," I whisper to Sloane as I start fucking in and out of Simon's ass. She leans back against me, wrapping her arms back around my neck and using her grip on me as leverage to fuck him.

I can watch over her shoulder as her breasts bounce, her nipples red with the abuse we gave them, the bite marks stark against her white flesh. The marks are just that, marks. They'll fade quickly, but I'll enjoy them while they're there.

We fuck Simon together, her pussy squeezing his cock while I fuck his asshole, rubbing across his prostate with each stroke. I can tell he's close by the noises he's making *and the fact that his ass is twitching and clenching on my cock.*

Using my clean hand, I reach around Sloane and start to play with her clit. I rub tight little circles with two fingers, increasing my pressure as her hips start to stutter against him.

"Cum for him, baby. Let your little pussy squeeze his cock, show him what it feels like, coat his cock with your slick, cara, give it to me," I continue to whisper filthy things in her ear until she stiffens against me.

"Oh god," she breathes out.

At the same time, Simon cums with a shout, his ass tightening around me convulsively. I fuck him right through it, using the twitch of his tight hole and the throbbing of his prostate to chase my own orgasm.

My jeans are too tight, squeezing my dick painfully. My balls are heavy and full, aching for release.

"Fuck," I groan, "how long-"

"Ssshhh," Simon cuts me off.

I glance up at him and he points across the room, "The nurse brought in recliners, Brooks and Hudson are sleeping. You've been out about three hours. Not nearly long enough," he adds sternly.

I groan again, "Are you sure they're asleep?"

"Yeah, they've been out for awhile, Hudson finally stopped snoring about ten minutes ago."

"Thank god," I grunt, reaching under the covers and popping open my fly. We might be as close as can be, but they don't need to hear me jack it in a hospital bed.

"What are you doing," Simon asks, curious as he watches me lick my hand before spitting quietly into the palm.

"Unless you're gonna talk dirty to help me along, just be quiet and let me get through this quick," I grunt, taking my cock in hand. I'm so hard I know I'm not going to last long, whether Simon decides to help or not.

"Oh, okay," he says, smirking slightly before, "I miss feeling your cum in my ass. The way is leaks out all day after a good fucking. I love feeling you inside of me. I want to feel you inside of me while I'm inside of Sloane. I want you to fuck me into Sloane. All of us on our knees together, fucking like animals."

My hand flies up and down my shaft. The imagery he's giving me is so close to what I just experienced in my dreams, I'm cumming in my hand by the time he's done telling me what he wants.

I muffle my groan, cupping as much of my cum as I can, knowing I need to try to sleep more and I would prefer not to sleep in my own cum stain. Simon hits me in the chest with a box of tissues.

"Clean yourself up and get back to sleep."

"Yessir. Finding your inner dom while laid up in the hospital, huh? You know I'm gonna fuck that right out of you as soon as you're better?"

"Oh, I'm counting on it," he chuckles, "now let's all get some sleep, okay?"

Simon shuts off his extra monitor and closes down his laptops while I clean myself as best I can. I toss the tissues over the edge of the bed, hoping I wake up early enough to clean them before a janitor or nurse shows up.

"I love you, Kaiser," Simon whispers in the dark, sliding his hand across the space and gripping my hand.

"I love you, too, baby," I squeeze his hand.

"I love you both, you dirty dogs," Hudson whisper shouts from across the room.

CHAPTER TEN

Sloane

The cramps wake me up. Low and twisting, they're manageable right now, but I know they'll get worse. I feel like I'm burning up and I desperately need to go to the bathroom, but I don't want to move out of the false safety of my little cocoon.

I shift in my nest, trying to relieve the pressure on my bladder and realize that I've leaked a small puddle overnight. There's no way I can leave this room soaked through like I am. How the hell do they expect me to walk off this boat basically dripping everywhere?

Egor said they were going to transport me to an airfield. How does he think that's going to work when my scent is going to be calling to every alpha around? Even if they manage to find me new clothes, it's not like I'm going to stop leaking.

I roll onto my knees before pushing back the blankets so I can stand. I contemplate stripping off my pants and wrapping myself in a sheet so I would be more comfortable, but ultimately decide I don't want to risk having less layers between me and the world.

I step out of my nest and listen briefly at the door before pushing the door open. No one is currently in the room, but someone had been while I was asleep. It had to have been Iris, as there's no discernible scent. If it had been an alpha, I would know, and I don't think Egor has any betas onboard.

There are several towels folded at the foot of the bed, along with a change of clothes and shoes. There's also a note, confirming it was Iris, letting me know that I needed to shower and change. I should be ready to disembark by 1 o'clock and it would be helpful if I folded one of the towels to keep under me once we leave.

Disembark? Like this is some kind of cruise and I should be excited to be here? That woman is going to regret the day she involved herself in all of this. I don't know who's going to have more fun torturing her; my father or Hudson.

I do need to shower though. And change. I can appreciate the towels and still hate her guts.

I move into the small bathroom and realize that there's no lock on the door. Shit. I need to shower. I'm sticky and uncomfortable and I know it's only going to escalate once I leave the room and have to smell all the pheromones lurking out there.

I just want five minutes to try to center myself and fight some of this off. To just get clean and maybe feel normal for a second or two. As I keep looking around the space, a thought hits me and I go back into the stateroom.

The shoes Iris brought me are athletic shoes, each with laces. I take the shoes back into the bathroom and start pulling the laces out quickly.

I tie one end of the first lace onto the doorknob, then tie the other end to the drawer pull. That won't work on its own, because the drawer would just slide open when they pulled on the door. So, I take the second lace, tie one end onto the drawer pull and the other end around the base of the sink spout.

It's not foolproof. I imagine an alpha would be able to wrench it open pretty quick. Right now though, it looks like they only have Iris checking on me and she definitely won't be able to break that. By the time she goes to get someone, I'll have had time to get dressed.

Still not 100% sold on my plan, I strip and jump under the spray before it's even warm. I do my best to keep my hair out of the water, quickly washing myself as best I can with the crap tiny soap bar she left.

I'm washed and out in under five minutes. I dry off and redress in less than two, folding a hand towel and securing it between my legs with my underwear. It's not much, but it's my only option.

I take the shoes and laces back into the room, then sit in the corner furthest from the door and start relacing the sneakers. I'm halfway through the second shoe when there's a tap on the door just as Iris pushes it open and comes in.

She glances around the space before spotting me in the corner. She starts walking toward me and I immediately stiffen, my lip curling. A low growl starts in the back of my throat, warning her out of my space.

Iris is stupid, though, so she just keeps coming. As soon as she's within striking distance, my leg lashes out, driving my heel into her gut.

"Ooof," she heaves out, dropping back so fast she doesn't have time to stop herself. She lands heavily on her ass and winces.

I pull myself up into a squat, back to the wall with a shoe in each hand. Not sure how much damage I can do with a trainer, but we'll figure it out if she comes any closer. I don't want anyone in my space right now, least of all this traitorous bitch.

I continue to warn her off with growls and snarls. She's watching me warily now, perhaps finally figuring out how much I loathe her and how much danger she might be in, being alone with me.

Still on her ass, she scoots backward, pushing with her hands and feet. Once she's back near the door, ten feet away or so, she finally speaks.

"I just came to check on you. I didn't realize you were so far along already, I thought we would have time to get you off the ship and to the airfield."

"Fuck. You. Iris. I don't need or want your help."

"And I understand that-"

I cut her off, "About time. You understanding."

I hiss out a breath, a low cramp wavering my attention briefly. Luckily the towel seems to be working to absorb some of the slick. I know it won't last, though.

"I'm your only option right now, okay? Unless you want one of Egor's men in here helping you," she questions, a salacious smile on her face, "are you ready, then, to accept your fate?"

I let out a snarl, launching to my feet and halfway across the room. I'm on her before she can pull the door open and escape. I grab fistfuls of her hair and toss her back down on the floor. Straddling her, I use my knees to pin her arms down and wrap my hands around her throat.

"You are a worthless piece of shit and I want you to die," I scream in her face, squeezing as hard as I can while she struggles beneath me, "I'm never accepting another pack, never!"

Her face is turning purple, her eyes watering as she tries to buck me off. I'm younger though, and stronger. Not to mention my protective instincts were triggered the second she opened that door and tried to invade my space.

Just as she weakens and her eyes start to roll up, the door slams into us, knocking me loose. Before I can recover, I'm wrapped in a bear hug from behind and lifted off the floor, my feet dangling as I'm held against a hot, hard body.

I snarl and kick, trying to break free of whoever is holding me, my instincts screaming at me to get away and protect myself. The arms only tighten, then a warning growl sounds next to my ear, the sound vibrating through me before settling between my legs. The growl turns into a purr and I can't stop my body from relaxing.

My feet touch the ground, but my legs won't hold me up and I find myself on my knees. The same body surrounding me, pressed tight to my back. I recognize him, his scent. Egor has come for me.

Egor's purring changes back to a low growl and he rolls his hips into my ass. I can't stop the shudder that runs through me, my nipples hard as diamonds and the towel mostly useless as I feel the slick gathering between my thighs.

"Sweet, *plushka*," he whispers, "you smell good enough to eat. The spice of your slick mixed with your rage. So savage, so perfect."

He punctuates each sentence with a roll of his hips, rocking his hard cock against my ass. His arms are a steel cage around me, I couldn't get away if I tried. The problem is, I'm not trying. My brain is screaming at me to get away from him, but my body is not getting the memo.

"I don't think you're ready for us yet, *moy sladkiy*. But let's see, shall we," he nuzzles his face into the crook of my neck, one arm banding tight around my middle while the other hand slides up to cup my breast.

He squeezes my breast roughly, then pinches and tugs on my nipple. At the same time, I feel his teeth graze my neck.

Oh fuck no.

I throw my head sideways as hard as I can, my chin catching his nose, at the same time twisting my body away from his. I drive my elbow back into his side and it feels like striking granite, but I don't stop.

I scream as I fight him, the threat of his mating bite enough to bring me back to my senses. He finally lets me go and I scramble across the room as fast as I can. I squat in the corner again, pressing myself as far back as I can get.

Egor is still on his knees inside the doorway, his cock straining against the zipper of his slacks. Iris is nowhere to be seen. Nikolaj and the man with the dead eyes are standing together in the hallway, blocking the door but watching. Nikolaj is casually stroking himself through his pants, the head of his cock peeking out of the top of the waistband.

The man with the dead eyes, not so dead anymore. I shudder at the heat I see in them, the way his eyes stroke over my body, focusing on my chest and my pussy as if I'm bare before him. I watch as he takes deep, sniffing breaths and a low growl rumbles out of him.

"Don't worry, *plushka*, I won't let Aleks have you yet. You need to be broken down and ridden a few times, really and truly mindless before you're ready to take the pain Aleks likes to deliver."

Nikolaj snickers and my eyes dance between the three of them, a snarl building in my throat.

"Since Iris is likely out of commission now, thanks to your little tantrum, we'll have to come up with a different escort for you. In the meantime, don't leave this room."

I maintain my defensive posture, not moving or speaking, not even blinking until Egor heaves himself off the floor and all of the men exit. Even with the door shut, it takes several long moments before I'm able to drop onto my knees and attempt to relax.

Staying focused is becoming harder, especially now that the room is churning with alpha pheromones. My body is coated in a thin sheen of sweat and the towel in my pants is soaked through. My cramps are continuous and much more painful. After becoming so aroused, even if it was against my will, my body is begging for release.

I pray that we're close to docking, that my father or my men are close to finding me. Even if I can escape at this point, it won't do me any good. I'd be jumped by the first weak alpha I ran into.

Even with laws in place to protect omegas in heat, not all alphas are strong enough to resist or care to, as evidenced by the assholes currently holding me captive. I know that a time will come when I won't be able to fight them anymore. My body will take over and I'll be at the mercy of my heat.

I'm so scared and I don't know what to do. If no one rescues me in time, I'm going to be forcibly bred by Egor and his pack. If I manage to escape, with no one around to help me, how likely am I to make it to a safe space or hospital before I can't function anymore?

I stay tucked in the corner and draw my legs up to my chest. I wrap my arm around my knees and hug them tight, keeping my eyes trained on the door. Escape or give in? Rescue or run? I keep rolling my options around and around as I wait for the door to open and lead me to my fate.

CHAPTER ELEVEN

Brooks

"Check, check, go for Brooks," I hold the PTT button clipped to my cuff and whisper into the microphone tucked into my collar.

"Check, Brooks," Simon responds from his hospital bed across the room. He's verifying everyone's equipment, ensuring that everyone is able to communicate as we prepare to rescue Sloane.

Simon will be our eyes in the sky. Pulling their security feed and watching our backs while we're on the ground. Infiltrating in broad daylight is going to be much more difficult than going in at night, but we don't have a choice. Hopefully the addition of Simon keeping an eye out will give us an advantage.

Remi, Dmitri, Morris, Marco, Hudson, Kaiser and I are all working together to get stripped down and geared up. If the hospital staff have anything to say, no they don't. They watched us all march in here together, closing the curtains to prepare for war and we haven't been bothered once.

Morris insisted on coming, so of course Marco insisted as well. I wasn't looking forward to dealing with their dead weight, but I was pleasantly surprised. This isn't some run of the mill operation that I would send any soldier on, this is Sloane we're talking about. I only want top tier people on this.

They might be a few decades older than the rest of us, but you would never guess it. Sure they're both a little gray around the temples, maybe a few more smile lines, but their bodies are just as hard, just as young looking as ours. And I'm thankful for it.

Assuming the guy from the docks was correct, we're seven on seven for Egor's men. If Ben, Otto, and Iris are still onboard, we'll be a little outnumbered, but not by much. The four women were purely entertainment and will likely duck and cover once the fighting starts.

"Okay, let's review one more time before moving out," I announce, moving back toward Simon's bed and the largest monitor set up.

"Morris and Marco will enter on the southside of the docks, coming across the footbridge here and setting up on the southeast side of the building. Remi and Dmitri, you'll park behind the warehouse on Dunlap after dropping those two off and make your way into the marina on foot through the industrial park here. Hudson, Kai, and I will enter the marina in the berth of a fishing boat which will dock on the northeast corner of the boathouse."

I glance around, making sure everyone is paying attention, taking in the hard looks on each face.

"Simon will be able to tell us when he sees them approach. He'll keep us updated on movements around the dockyard, if we're going to expect company, whatever is going on. Once the docking doors on the boathouse close, we move in. Whoever gets eyes on Sloane first grabs her and gets her the hell out and onto the fishing boat."

I slap Hudson on the shoulder, knowing he's practically foaming at the mouth now that we're this close.

"Any questions?"

A chorus of 'no' and head shakes follow.

"Alright, load up."

Kai, Hudson and I crowd around Simon, getting as close to him as we can without putting too much pressure on his wounds. We take turns nuzzling him, covering him with our scents.

"Bring her back, yeah? Just bring her back in one piece, okay," he looks at each of us in turn.

"You're gonna be right there with us," Kai whispers to him, "you'll be with us each step. We're gonna get her."

"You really think I'd come back without her, dude," Hudson adds, leaning down and butting his forehead against Simon's like some kind of psychotic billy goat.

I reach down and squeeze Simon's hand, "We're gonna get through this, get her back, and then you can focus on recovering, okay?"

"Deal," he answers, squeezing me back.

The others wait quietly by the door while we say our goodbyes to Simon and we all head to the elevators together now that we're done. If the staff thinks it's weird that we're all dressed in black tactical gear from head to toe in the middle of the day, they don't mention it.

On the other hand, they know who we are and probably don't want to rock the boat.

I talked to Dr. Seymur this morning, giving him a head's up that we would be bringing in an omega, likely in the early stages of heat. Like most urban hospitals, they have an entire wing dedicated to omega care, including some isolation rooms specifically designed for an omega in heat.

We'll be able to ride it out with her or she can be sedated. Whichever she chooses. Either way, she'll be in this building and we'll be able to take turns standing guard if she opts for the sedation. We'll be able to watch over her and Simon.

The elevator reaches the parking garage and we separate into our two groups. After exchanging some hand shakes and fist bumps, Remi, Dmitri, Morris and Marco head to their Q8. Kai, Hudson and I climb into our Macan.

Tension is at an all time high as we head toward the marina. Kaiser used one of our contacts to rent a fishing boat and captain to transport us across to the marina on Leone's side of the river. Once there, the captain will anchor the boat and leave on foot.

As the three of us head down the gangway to our rented vessel, Simon's voice crackles in my ear, "Marco and Morris are crossing the footbridge now, Remi and Dmitri are parking at the warehouse, Brooks and the boys are boarding the boat."

"Check," I respond.

"Check," echoes through the earpiece as everyone else checks in.

The captain nods to each of us, ushering us into the berth under the cockpit. As the boat gets underway, I go through a double check of all my weapons. Two pistols, one on each hip. Two magazines for each. Kbar on my left thigh.

Hudson and Kaiser are outfitted the same, although Hudson added brass knuckles to his kit. Now that we've got solid information on where Sloane is and who has her, he's ready to bathe in their blood.

"Remi and Dmitri in position, Morris and Marco in position, Brooks and the guys entering the main waterway of the marina. Eta for docking, 4 minutes."

Another round of checks flow through the earpieces.

I shift restlessly from foot to foot, almost bouncing as adrenaline starts to flow. We're so close to getting her back, we can't fuck up now. Everything has to move without a hitch.

The boat hits against the bumpers on the side of the dock. We hear the captain greeting someone from the marina and throwing them a line to tie off. His footsteps cross the deck as he exits the boat.

Now we wait, but we don't have to wait long. Not ten minutes later, Simon informs us that a boat matching the description we were given has entered the main waterway.

Captaining the ship is Aleksandr Petrov, Egor's other pack member and lieutenant.

"Fuck," I mutter, "how did we miss that information?"

"Mr. Raisin obviously wasn't very forthcoming with his information," Hudson replies.

"Or he didn't see him board. He didn't see Volkov either, did he," Kai asks, glancing between us.

"Now that you mention it, no, he only mentioned Petruk and six or seven other guys. If he had seen Volkov or Petrov I think he would have said that specifically," Brooks answers, rubbing his chin, deep in thought.

"What are you thinking," Hudson asks quietly, "I know that look. You think we're missing something."

"How would Volkov and Petrov get on that boat without anyone seeing them? And if they're on the boat, how many others are on the boat without being accounted for?"

"Shit. You really think they could have smuggled more people onboard? What? Once they were out on the water?"

I tap my PTT button, "Simon, do you have a visual of anyone else on deck aside from Petrov?"

"Negative. Petrov is alone on deck."

"Okay, listen up everyone. We didn't have any indication that Petrov would be onboard. He wasn't seen boarding at the marina, which means that they may have had additional people brought on once they were on the water. Stay sharp, we may be facing more than we anticipated."

"They could have fifty men on that boat and I'd still be going in," Morris hisses through the comm, "I'm getting my daughter back and putting an end to this betrayal."

"Reign it, Morris," Hudson hisses back, "stay cool and keep your head in the game otherwise someone will end up hurt."

"Who would have thought Hudson would be the voice of reason," Kai chuckles between the three of us, not engaging his comms.

Hudson jabs him in the ribs with an elbow, "I might have gone off the deep end when they took her, but I'm not so deep that I can't recognize other crazy."

"I disagree," Kaiser murmurs, reaching out to flick the back of Hudson's earlobe.

"Now, now children, they're going to be docking any minute," I interrupt them before they can get into a full out slap fight, "so let's be ready to fuck them up and not each other, yeah?"

"Whatever," Hudson mutters, narrowing his eyes at Kai "I'll get you back later you big, dumb, shit."

"Bring it on, princess, I'll be waiting," Kai responds with kissy noises.

"Doors are closing, dock is clear in all directions, move," Simon's order comes through.

We move together as a unit, out of the berth and onto the deck. We each palm a pistol and form a triangle, covering all sides as we make our way to the boathouse. I can't see the other men approaching, but I know they are.

Each team is entering at a different point then converging on the boat. Our goal is to get Sloane out with as little noise as possible. Between me and Morris, we have a lot of the police force in our pocket, but that doesn't mean we need them showing up because of a firefight.

"Everyone is go," Simon intones, meaning we're all at our points of entry, "countdown in 3, 2, 1."

As soon as Simon hits one, we push through the doors all around the boathouse. Morris and Marco entering from the south side, Remi and Dmitri from the main double doors and the three of us sliding in from the back, next to the waterway.

Two women are standing on the swim platform at the back of the boat, smoking. Both wearing next to nothing in spite of the weather; one is a tall redhead, the other brunette. All of us immediately train weapons on them.

"Permission to come aboard," Hudson snickers, dropping off the gangway and onto the dock behind them, bringing his pistol back up and pressing it to the neck of the brunette, "tell me where she is and you don't have to die."

"Hudson," I warn.

"Tell me," he snarls, jamming the pistol up behind her ear.

Before any of us can react, the redhead spins around and sweeps Hudson's legs. As he hits the deck, she grabs the brunette and attempts to jump over him to get back into the cabin.

Hudson grabs her ankle and yanks her hard enough that they both fall, the redhead's face smacking the deck. She rolls onto her back and kicks at Hudson's face, blood streaming from her obviously broken nose.

So much for thinking they were just entertainment.

While Hudson wrestles the redhead, the brunette regains her feet and scrambles across the deck to one of the built-in bench seats. Wrenching the top open, she pulls out a pistol just as Kai and I drop onto the deck next her.

Kai grabs her wrist with one hand, directing the pistol away from us before landing a hard punch to her temple. She immediately crumples, unconscious.

Hudson has the redhead pinned to the deck, both hands wrapped neatly around her throat. He leans down so they're nose to nose, whispering, "You know what they do and you defend them, so you can die with them."

He adjust his stance so his knees are pinning her wrists, then grips her chin with one hand and a fistful of hair at the crown, "I wish I had time to make this hurt," he tells her before violently twisting her chin up at the same time yanking her head to the side.

Hudson pushes himself off the redhead before moving to the brunette, still unconscious at Kai's feet. He rolls her onto her stomach before pressing a knee into her back and pulling her head up by her hair. He drags his kbar across her throat, blood spraying the benches as her life gurgles away.

Kai and I have nothing against killing women, especially ones involved in Sloane's kidnapping, but we know Hudson needs the catharsis. Hopefully he'll be able to put himself back together once he purges all of his murderous intentions and we have Sloane back.

He drops her lifeless body back to the deck, stomping through the pool of blood and tracking it across the deck as we approach the rear cabin doors. I press myself to the door, listening intently for any indication of movement on the other side.

I assume anyone in there would have heard the scuffle on deck and come out to investigate, but you can never be too sure.

I slowly pull the door open, making sure to stay behind the door while Kai and Hudson are on the other side but clear of the opening. Nothing happens. Hudson glances in quickly, then again more slowly, signaling that we're clear.

We enter into a bar area. It's empty now, but the lingering scents of sex and alpha hang heavy in the air. Thankfully, there's no hint of Sloane's scent here. Pushing further into the room with Kai and Hudson at my back, I take a deep breath, opening my mouth slightly to get a full sensory scent on the room.

I snarl, a growl pumping out of me.

"Gallo. Both of them, Enzo and Antonio. Ben and Otto. Five other alphas. The women are all betas."

Hudson pushes his PTT, his voice echoes in my ear, replaying my information to the rest of the team. Adding that two of the women are dead and the other two should be killed on sight, and these are just the scents detected in the bar, could be others onboard.

We move through the bar and into the hallway beyond. This hall stretches the length of the ship and ends in a stairway to the other levels. Now that we're beyond the stench in the bar, I taste a hint of Sloane on the air.

Hudson and Kai scent her, too, purring growls erupting from them almost simultaneously.

"Fuck she's close," Hudson rasps, pushing in front of me and taking short, sharp sniffs as he follows her scent down the hall.

Kai's close at his back, his face a mask of determination as they trace her scent.

"Stop," I hiss, "we need to clear these rooms."

"No, we need to find Sloane. Priority numero uno," Hudson responds, creeping further away.

"Listen to me, dumbshit. We need to get her off this boat, which means we need to come back down this hallway and we're going to be fucked if anyone hiding in these rooms decides to come out."

"I don't give a single fuck. I will stand in front of her and take a bullet if it means getting her now."

"Let's not joke about getting shot, okay," Kaiser chimes in, pressing in close to Hudson as they both come to a stop halfway down the hall, "she's definitely in here."

"There has to be some kind of ventilation, or something, blocking her scent," Hudson adds, "it should be much stronger given how deep she should be by now."

"Yeah, this isn't their first rodeo, remember," I reply, giving in and crowding in behind them, "it's probably where they keep any omega they get their hands on. Prevents anyone from getting too crazy."

Hudson leans forward and presses his ear to the door. Kai presses his nose to the crack around the frame.

"I don't hear anything."

"There are three alpha scents, but they're old and faded. I don't recognize them."

"Alright then," I click my PTT button, "we've found where they're holding Sloane. Continue to clear the ship, we're going in. We'll check in when we're secure."

Hudson wastes no time pushing into the room. We pile in behind him and shut the door quickly, not wanting to alert anyone outside of our presence, but also in an attempt to keep her scent contained. And it's strong.

Her pheromones hit me like a punch to the gut. My breath whooshes out and I double over, practically dropping to my knees as my cock is suddenly hard and throbbing. I glance to my left and see Kai struggling as well, one hand gripping his massive erection through his tac pants, rhythmically squeezing and stroking as if he can't control himself.

Hudson is across the room, pulling Sloane up out of the corner and into his arms. He fists her hair and sucks at her mouth, pressing her against the wall and dry humping her while she mewls and tries to rub her whole body against him.

"Mine," he rumbles against her mouth, hands dropping to her legging and tearing at the fabric, "Mine," he snarls again when she tries to help him, whimpering in need.

Kai and I approach together, needing to be close to her, to scent her and feel her body.

Hudson whirls, blocking her from our view and snarls, snapping his teeth. His eyes are so completely dilated I can barely see the blue, his face is flushed and his chest heaving.

"Fuck," Kai murmurs, "what do we do?"

"Just stay back and let him ride it out, we'll be right here. He won't hurt her."

"Not on purpose, you mean."

"Judging by how she looks and smells, she'd enjoy it anyway."

"I've heard some horror stories about alphas in rut, that's all I'm saying."

"Me, too, but I know Hudson. I know his heart and he won't hurt her."

Kai groans, cupping his balls and squeezing as we watch Hudson manhandle Sloane. He pushes her onto her hands and knees in front of him, but facing us, just a foot or less away. He grips either side of her legging and pulls, tearing the fabric in half completely.

"Please," Sloane cries out, "please, I need you."

He growls in response before shredding her panties and the towel she apparently had shoved down her pants, throwing the fabric away from them. From this vantage, all I can see is her lower back and the curve of her ass, but her skin is flushed and covered in a sheen of sweat.

Hudson presses between her shoulders with one hand until her upper body is flat to the floor, while tearing at his pants with the other. His cock springs free, angry red and already weeping cum for her. She pushes her ass up higher, presenting her slick soaked cunt for him to take.

I can't resist anymore and drop to my knees, pulling my own cock free. I just hope that the guys are handling everything else because there's no way we're going to be able to leave this room right now. I pull the comm out of my ear and focus on the scene unfolding before me.

Sloane lets out a keening wail as Hudson drives his cock into her and my fist tightens reflexively on my own dick. Kai has his cock in one hand, his other shoved down his pants and gripping his balls tight. If she looked up, she'd be able to stroke her tongue across both of us, we've managed to shuffle so close.

We stroke ourselves, listening to Sloane's cries and the sounds of slapping flesh. Our cocks are practically touching as we get as close to Sloane as possible without angering Hudson. An alpha in rut is almost as dangerous as an omega in heat.

Hudson throws his head back and howls, loud and long, as he ruts on Sloane. His hips slamming against her ass so hard and fast, they're almost a blur. He leans forward, clamping his hands on her shoulders and holding her down as his hips snap faster, growls and grunts now pouring from his mouth.

"Fuck, fuck," Kai chants under his breath, eyes glued to Hudson absolutely dominating our little omega.

The scent of Sloane thickens in the air as Hudson wrings orgasm after orgasm out of her. The pounding of his cock into her heat sensitive little pussy is enough to set her off time and again. She's a shaking, sweaty mess by the time he pulls her up against him.

He wraps one arm around her middle, pinning her arms to her sides, his other hand fisting in her hair and yanking her head back. He forces her down onto his knot at the same time he clamps his teeth into the side of her neck. His groan is muffled against her flesh, his teeth staying embedded even as his body shudders with release.

I watch as Sloane's tight little pussy swallows Hudson's knot. Her slick seeps around his cock, dripping from his balls as she screams her way through another orgasm. I remember the feeling of that tight pussy squeezing my knot, as I blew my load in her over and over again.

My balls tighten painfully, my cum shooting across her thighs and her pussy, landing where she and Hudson are joined. Kai grunts next to me and I watch as his cum lands across mine, marking her with all of us.

Sloane is limp against Hudson, so spent and used that she can barely moan, even as two beads of blood chase each other down her neck. Hudson's tongue snakes out, catching the blood before it can be absorbed into her shirt. He licks and sucks at the wound, making sure it will scar, cementing the mating between them.

I shift back on my heels, taking a breath and trying to clear the fog. Sloane's pheromones are in full effect now. She's saturated the room with her scent and her need. My cock is still rock hard, in spite of the fact that I just came all over her. I glance over and see Kai is in the same predicament.

I don't know how we're going to make it off this boat. I'm mesmerized as I watch Kai yank his shirt off before crawling forward and sandwiching Sloane's body between them.

CHAPTER TWELVE

Hudson

My brain comes back online, just as I feel my shirt being tugged over my head. I give Sloane's mating mark one final lick before blinking my eyes open and seeing Kaiser tongue fucking Sloane a few inches from my face.

I can't help myself. I lick a path across Sloane's cheek and onto Kai's before wiggling my tongue against her mouth, wanting to be let in on the fun. Kai breaks the kiss to pull Sloane's shirt over her head and I moan at the feeling of her slick, hot flesh against mine.

Kai's hands dance across my chest as he searches for the clasp to Sloane's bra. He finally tugs it free and his hands slip away. His abs are hard, pressing against my forearm where I'm still holding Sloane to me. I let go of her hair and run my hand up his back, reveling in the feeling of his hot, hard body in contrast to Sloane's softness.

Why have I never done this before, I think to myself as my free hand glides over his shoulders. I lose all train of thought when I feel Kai's hand brush against my balls. He's rubbing Sloan's pussy, circling her clit then running his fingers up and down her lips. Her lips that are stretched tight around my cock.

His fingers drift over my cock where Sloane and I are joined together, the sensitive spot just under my knot. When I don't protest, he slides his hand down further, cupping and squeezing my balls before stroking back up to Sloane's stretched pussy.

"Fuck," I groan in his ear, "if you keep that up I'm going to stay knotted in this pussy all day."

Sloane whimpers in protest as Kai breaks the kiss, "please, more, I need you," she moans and starts rocking in my lap.

"You have to share, asshole," Kai mutters back, nipping my bottom lip before he slaps my balls.

My knot shrinks so fast from the stinging pain that I whimper, even as Sloane's pussy gushes out the mix of our cum. Coated with the scent of us together, my dick starts throbbing, easily recovering from the slap, in the face of satisfying my omega.

Kai pulls her from my arms and turns, laying her out on her back like a feast. He pulls the remains of her leggings off and pushes her thighs obscenely wide. Sloane's pussy is swollen and pink, oozing more slick and cum as her hips shift and she begs for more.

"I need you inside of me, please, Kai, please, please. It hurts, make it stop," she moans, lifting her hips in offering to him.

"Don't worry, *tesoro*, we're going to take care of you," Brooks whispers, shuffling around so he can scoop her up in his arms, "but not here."

He straightens and turns toward us, his bulging hard-on at eye level. How he wrestled that back into his pants and zipped them is a mystery to me.

"Put your dicks away and get it together, we can't stay on this boat and ride it out, we need to get back to the hospital."

He walks over to the bed and lays Sloane down in the middle of it. Grabbing two corners, he brings the blanket across Sloane, then rolls her back and forth until she's tucked in like a sexy little burrito.

I slap Kai on the back of the shoulder, breaking him out of his own stupor, "Let's listen to Brooks just this once. The least we can do is make it to the car, right?"

"Easy for you to say, you've already had her. I just got a front row seat and a teasing invitation," he groans, squeezing himself hard.

"We just need some fresh air. Fresh air will definitely help. Let's get moving," I push myself to my feet, wincing as I zip my pants over my straining cock. Seriously, I don't know how Brooks did it so easily.

"Yeah, fresh air, okay," he mocks, taking several deep breaths before standing next to me and wincing as he drags his pants up over his balls. He holds his hard on against his stomach with one hand, trying to zip his pants with the other, but it's not working for him. Hell, I struggled and I'm not half as girthy as he is.

"You need some help with that," I chuckle.

"You gonna hold my dick for me, asshole?"

"I mean, I was gonna offer to zip you, but I guess I can hold it, if that's what you need," I shrug, then wink at him, not really sure what's come over me. I suspect it has something to do with the crazy mix of pheromones in the room right now and the mating high I'm still rocking, but I don't look too deeply at it right now.

"Jesus," he mutters, shaking his head, "I'll hold it, you just help me zip."

I step close, probably closer than necessary, but he smells really fucking good right now. He has one hand on the head of his dick, still holding it and uses the other to tug the sides of the waistband together.

"For safety purposes," I whisper, sliding a finger into his pants between his dick and the zipper, keeping it in place as I tug the zipper up.

He hisses when my knuckle brushes against the underside of his cock head, trailing across the tip before I pull it away, "You can handle the button, I'm sure."

"Now that you two are done flirting can we please get the fuck out of here," Brooks voice booms through the tiny space, making Sloane whimper in her cozy blanket wrapper.

We both turn quickly, the hint of alpha in his voice enough to motivate us. If he's stressed enough to use it, we need to get moving.

I hurriedly toss my shirt back on, hitting the PTT in the cuff, "Report Simon?"

"I disconnected your comms when I realized you were compromised so no one would accidentally get an earful.

They cleared the ship. Volkov and Petruk were not onboard, only Petrov, who they secured and will be delivered to the Vault. Otto, Ben and Iris were transported away by Remi and Dmitri, everyone else was neutralized. Morris and Marco went back to the hospital to wait on you guys, the Macan was delivered outside. Clean up crew is en route now that you've come to your senses."

"What do you mean they weren't onboard," Brooks snarls, "where the fuck are they?"

"No idea," Simon replies, "but I'm sure we'll be able to beat the information out of one of them."

"Keep me posted as soon as you learn something new."

"Aye, aye captain," Simon snarks.

We exit the back of the boat, the same way we came in. I climb the ladder to the gangway first, reaching down to take Sloane from Brooks and waiting as they climb up after. We walk around the entirety of the ship and exit out the southside of the building to the waiting Macan.

Kaiser pops open the back door for me and my precious little roll up. At some point during our short walk, she managed to fall asleep so I do my best to keep the jostling to a minimum as I squeeze us into the backseat.

In a shocking turn of events, Kai slides into the backseat with me, lifting her legs onto his lap and leaving Brooks to drive.

"Do you even know how to turn it on," I blurt as Brooks gets behind the wheel.

"Shut all the way the fuck up," he grinds out, clearly not digging my jokes. Or maybe it's his blue balls, either way I'm not that easily dissuaded. I got my baby back and all's right with the world.

"I'm just saying, it's been a long time since you've been behind the wheel, my man, and I'm not sure I want to take my life into my hands, freshly mated and all."

"Don't remind me," he snarls over his shoulder, starting the car and yanking it into drive so hard I'm sort of worried he might snap the damn gearshift right off.

"Oh, I get it, somebodies just jealous cause I got there first," I snap back.

"Hudson, do not make me dom you. Shut up and let me focus."

I sit back with a huff, snuggling Sloane's upper body close to my chest. I pull her up and nuzzle my face into the blanket against her neck, nudging it aside enough that I can lick along the mating mark some more.

My hormone driven brain really did a number with that. It's high up on her neck, just under her jawline, moreso towards the front of her throat than the side. There's no way she would ever be able to cover this. Not that she should want to, but it's very obvious she belongs to someone.

My dick throbs with the primal claiming instinct. I focus on the mating mark, searching inside until I find her nestled there, a new warmth in my soul. I knew we were true mates, knew from the first time I scented that ripe pussy that she belonged to us. Having the bond just confirms it.

The path between us fresh and new, so tight and full. Even in her sleep I can feel her reaching for me, her love washing me clean. Pure instinct has me returning the motion, pushing everything I feel for her into the bridge connecting us.

Her eyelids flutter, briefly opening and connecting with mine. She gives me a sweet smile and mumbled, "love you" before drifting back out again. I nuzzle my cheek to hers, coating her in my scent before a troubling thought crosses my mind.

"Is it normal for her to be sleeping like this," I ask, concerned with how out of it she seems, "I mean, not like I've done this before, but it just seems weird."

"Yeah, not what I was expecting," Kai agrees.

"I mean, everything I've read about it, supposed to be like a three day long orgy or something. Raw dicks and sore puss all around, yeah? One round shouldn't have put her out like this."

"It didn't," Brooks mutters from the front seat, "I sedated her."

"What," Kai and I snarl at the same time.

"It wasn't safe for us to stay in that room. We needed to get her off the ship and you two weren't getting the memo. Seymur gave me a shot, in case she was too far gone, so I decided to use it."

"That's fucked up, dude. It was supposed to be her choice," Kaiser grits out between clenched teeth, pulling her legs against him protectively.

"Her mom drugged her. Against her wishes, during her first heat. You think that's not going to bring up some serious issues when she wakes up," I add.

"What were you thinking," Simon hisses through the earpiece, no longer needing the PTT to hear us, since we're in the Macan and it's wired.

"I was prioritizing the mission, getting her out safe. That was the goal, right," he barks, Kai flinches but I throw it off, my protective instincts overriding the power in his bark.

"She was safe enough in that room, no one would have gotten past us," I bark right back, hugging her against me, "you should have given her the choice."

"Enough, both of you," Simon shouts into my ear, into all of our ears, "she needs to be checked out by a professional and placed in an isolation room. Just focus and get back here in one piece."

The remainder of the ride is spent in tense silence, Kai and I cuddling Sloane's limp form while Brooks seethes in the front seat.

Brooks pulls into the hospital drive, taking the first turn toward the parking garage.

"Drop us off at the ER entrance," I snap, "Kai and I will make sure she's looked over and taken care of."

"I don't really think that's necessary, Seymur can check her over once we get upstairs. Don't you think Simon should see her before she's isolated?"

"She needs to be checked, Brooks, by a specialist. Seymur isn't good enough," Simon answers via the comm units, "I know she's safe, I can wait a few days to see her."

Brooks snarls, but turns around and drops us at the entrance to the ER.

"Let me know once you have a room," he grunts out, staring straight ahead, not acknowledging either of us.

"Yeah, okay," Kai responds, squeezing my shoulder before we turn together and head inside to get Sloane situated.

CHAPTER THIRTEEN

Sloane

The cramps wake me up again. Low and twisting, my whole body aches, my mouth is dry, and my head feels like it's filled with cotton. I try to blink, but my eyelids are so heavy. I'm so hot. I moan in frustration, realizing that my heat is still riding me and I'm sandwiched between two hard bodies, an equally hard cock nestled between my ass cheeks.

"Ssshh, little omega, you're okay, we've got you," Hudson rumbles against the back of my neck, his body hot against mine. One of his hands slides up my leg, across my abdomen and cups my breast. My very naked breast.

"She needs water, Kai," Hudson says and the body against my front shifts forward, then turns, breaking contact with my body. I whimper at the sudden absence and chill, Hudson tugging me more firmly back against his nakedness to warm me up.

I feel a straw tapping against my bottom lip and I open just enough to suck down some icy cold water. I moan as the chill fills my mouth and cools my parched throat.

"Open your eyes for me, *cara*, let me see them," Kai whispers, pressing gentle kisses to each closed lid. I manage to pry one lid open, squinting up at him through blurry vision. I can just make out the shape of his face and the hazy outline of his naked torso.

"What happened to me," I rasp out, my throat still feeling dry and scratchy in spite of the water, "we were on the boat, I remember…I remember…Hudson and, um, and you and Brooks…watching."

I can feel the flush spread across my face and down my chest. In spite of the fact that I'm already unbearably hot, I feel even hotter remembering how Hudson dominated me. I bring my hand up clumsily to feel his bite, only to come into contact with a gauze wrap.

Hudson grabs my hand, bringing it to my shoulder so he can lean over and kiss my fingers, "The doctors insisted on cleaning and bandaging it, baby, but it's there, I promise."

And a wave of reassurance washes over me, tempered with love and patience. Just a trace of worry.

"Oh, Hudson," I whisper, trying to turn toward him so I can take him in my arms, but he holds me tight to keep me from moving.

"Easy baby, we have the rest of our lives to explore that. Right now we need to talk quick because Dr. Mason said we won't have much time between the sedative wearing off and your heat kicking back in, full throttle."

"So we need to talk about what you want, before this gets too out of hand," Kaiser adds, setting the water on the side table and climbing back into bed with us, "In spite of the fact that we're naked already, we will support whatever you decide."

"Yeah," Hudson murmurs against my neck, "we just got naked because Mason thought that would make you come out of it quicker. Of course, I wasn't about to argue about having this hot little body pressed against me."

"Nothing is better than a Sloane sandwich," Kaiser agrees, pressing to my front, his hard dick hot against my thigh, and slides his arm around Hudson's back, squeezing me tight between them.

"Come out of what? What aren't you guys telling me," my question ends on a moan when Hudson bites at the gauze, directly over his mating mark.

"Hudson, keep it together, man," Kai chides, the motion of his arm making me think he's rubbing Hudson's back, although he seems to be rubbing a little low.

"Where's Brooks? What happened on the boat, Kai," I try again.

"Your heat is going to come back with a vengeance any minute now, Sloane, so we need to know if you want us to help you through it or if you want to be sedated again," Kai replies, completely ignoring my questions.

"Oh," I squeak, flashing back to the mind numbing pleasure of Hudson rutting me on the boat, pinning me to the floor and fucking me hard and fast, slamming me onto his knot and marking me as his forever.

"Ooooh," I moan, slick sliding down my thigh as my body tightens in anticipation.

"You have to use your words, *cara*, what do you want us to do?"

"Please, I want you, Kai. I don't want to be sedated. Where's Brooks? Can he come back, too?"

"Brooks is with Simon, baby, he's in a time out," Hudson murmurs.

"SIMON," I shriek, "he's with Simon? Simon's alive? Where? What? Can I see him?"

I catch Kai by surprise, pushing him onto his back while I try to scramble over him, "OH MY GOD," I scream again, "where is he, take me to him!"

Kai grabs me around the waist, pulling me back against him before I can make it off the bed, "You can't leave the isolation room, *cara*, not until your heat is over. We're in the hospital, he's just a few floors below us. I promise, he's alive and he's doing well. I will take you to him just as soon as it's safe."

He squeezes me so tight I struggle to breathe for a moment, not realizing that I've been unconsciously rubbing my body back against his. I can feel his precum sticky on my ass from where I was rocking into him and I moan at the hedonistic feeling.

"Don't worry, baby, we'll take care of you," Hudson whispers.

I glance over my shoulder and see Hudson has his chin propped on Kaiser's side. From my angle it looks like he's pressed right up against Kai's back. That…can't be right though…can it?

"There something going on here I need to know about?"

"Dr. Mason thinks it is a secondary manifestation of our mating bond, your feelings influencing mine into recognizing something that I've been denying."

"Yeah," I cock an eyebrow at him, my brain still too foggy to fully comprehend his weird medical speak, but not so foggy that I'm immune to the feeling of Kaiser's hard cock rubbing on my ass. I wiggle back against him until his cock slips snuggly between my ass cheeks, then rock my hips slowly.

"He thinks he wants my dick," Kai moans in my ear, "just like you," he adds before sucking my lobe into his mouth and nibbling it.

"We talked it out before you woke up," Hudson adds, "so we'll see where it goes."

I continue to rock my ass back against Kai, moaning when he cups my breast and tugs on my hardened nipple. I feel Hudson's hand slide from Kai's hip onto mine before delving his fingers between my thighs and teasing my clit.

"You are so wet, little omega, making a mess all over Kaiser's dick like a good slut. You want that knot, don't you."

"Please," I pant, "please, fuck me."

"Oh, don't worry, *cara*, I'm going to fuck you until you scream for me. Then I'm going to do exactly what Hudson did," he tells me, licking along the shell of my ear, "give you my knot and mate you."

"Please, yes," I whimper, my pussy throbbing as my heat ramps back up, slick pooling beneath me.

"Such a good little omega, show Kai what you want," Hudson encourages, sliding his arm under Kai's and pulling it away from me so I can push myself up onto my hands and knees.

I feel the bed shifting as Hudson pulls Kai around behind me. I glance over my shoulder and see them kneeling side by side, Hudson has one hand on his cock and the other wrapped around Kai's.

Kai glances down as his dick, then at Hudson, "You really think you can handle that?"

"Ssshhhhh," Hudson admonishes, "that's not why we're here right now, just think of it as a bonus feature. Instead focus on that."

Kai's gaze switches back to my ass and soaking pussy on display just for him. I part my knees further, then drop down onto elbows, tilting my hips and giving him a full view of my wet, weeping pussy.

"Look at that. Pink, wet heaven, just for you. She's so hot and swollen, so tight," Hudson murmurs to Kai as I feel two fingers slip inside of me, "she needs to be ridden hard, like a dirty little slut."

I whimper when Hudson pulls his fingers away, "Please, oh god, please, I need-"

"I know what you need *cara*," Kai rumbles from behind me, the bed shifting and I feel his hands drop to my ass cheeks, squeezing and kneading them before sliding one hand up my back.

He grips the back of my neck, his fingers curling around Hudson's bite and eliciting a full body shudder. He uses his other hand to position his cock against my slick soaked entrance before he pushes just the head inside. I moan, pushing myself back onto him until he's seated fully inside of me, stretching me so good.

"Such a good girl, *cara*, you take my cock so well," he tells me, making me whimper and preen at the praise, as he starts to rock in and out of me, "You look so sexy split on my dick, your little pink cunt swallowing me up."

Kai grips my hips tight, holding me in place as he curls his upper body over mine, his hips angled so his cock drives down inside of me. I can feel my orgasm building almost immediately, my pussy throbbing around his dick and slick coating my thighs.

"Harder," I moan, needing him wild like Hudson, making me cum so hard this wildness I feel in my chest has some release. The orgasm is building inside of me, but just out of reach, like a tease I can sense but can't grasp.

"You'll take what I give you, like a good little slut," he groans, driving into me again and again, the same smooth strokes, equally paced and dragging along my inner pussy walls.

I clench, trying to keep him inside me, or maybe it's to push him out? I don't know anymore, I'm mindless with need, clawing at the bed sheets and bucking against him. The tension is almost too much.

"Fuck," Hudson moans, "I can't even describe how you're making her feel, but don't stop, it's delicious."

"Please," I cry out, "I can't take it, please!"

"Almost there, baby, almost there," he grunts, snapping his hips against my ass a little harder now, a little faster.

I'm on the verge of sobbing. My legs are shaking and my body is on fire, I can feel sweat trickling down my body and my pussy is soaked.

Kai slides one hand from my hip, around to where we're joined. He uses two fingers and starts circling my clit.

Faster and faster with his fingers, harder with his cock until I scream.

I collapse forward on the bed as waves of pleasure pulse through me. My pussy spasms around his dick, slick pumps out of me with each contraction. Little sparks of electricity seem to trace over my body, even my lips are tingling with the pleasure he's torn from my body.

I'm keening as he continues to fuck me through every twitch and tremble, hard thrusts pushing the head of his cock back and forth across my g-spot. I'd heard of it, of course, but had no idea the pleasure it could bring, the pleasure he continues to wring out of me.

"Come here, *cara*," he whispers, wrapping his arms around my waist and pulling me up against him, "I'm not done with you yet."

He crosses one arm around my hips, holding me tight to him as he grinds up into me. The other crosses up between my breasts and wraps around my throat. His thumb presses up under my chin, turning my head away and giving him access to my throat.

My head rests against his upper chest, our size difference so much more apparent like this. I'm like a tiny doll compared to him, a tiny little fuckdoll. God, I love it when they use me like this.

I feel Hudson in front of me. Reaching out and tearing the gauze off my mating mark, he leans into me, licking and sucking the mark until I'm moaning and whimpering between them.

"I want to watch your face when you cum this time," he murmurs against my throat, "You're going to cum for me, with Kai's dick deep inside. He's going to knot you and fill this sweet pussy while marking you forever."

Hudson leans back after one final lick, then slides his hand down between my thighs. He strokes my clit before reaching down further and cupping Kai's balls. Kai's groan vibrates through me while Hudson strokes and fondles both of us.

"Oh, fuck," Kaiser groans, his body tight and hard behind me, "make her cum already, I can't deal with you."

Hudson snickers, his hand stopping whatever he was doing to Kai, returning to my clit. Using two fingers, he rolls my clit while Kai starts thrusting up into me again.

"Oh," I gasp out, "yes, right there, please. Oh, harder, please!"

"Is this what you want, baby," Hudson murmurs, twisting his fingers around my clit and pinching it between his knuckles. He squeezes in time with Kaiser's thrusts, stroking and squeezing my hard little clit until Kai and I are both soaked with slick.

Kai presses his cheek to the side of my head, growling as his thrusts become harder, more wild. He lets out a snarl before pushing me down one last time, driving his knot into me as my orgasm crests. I scream again, the pleasure fracturing me.

I can feel his cock pulsing inside of me, his hot cum filling me, just before I feel his thumb under my jaw, forcing my head to the side. His teeth sink into my neck, right underneath Hudson's mark and I let out one more sobbing, hoarse yell.

I feel Hudson's hot cum splash across my abdomen, his pleasure flooding me, overwhelming me, as I feel Kai for the first time. He's like sunshine in my soul, so warm and bright. His love, like a hot blanket, wrapping me tight.

Kai eases his teeth from my neck, licking and sucking at the stinging mark. His nose nuzzles against Hudson's mark as he tends to his own, the three of us bound together now through me. I close my eyes and wallow in the feeling, my need easing momentarily while Kai is still locked inside of me.

Hudson cups the side of my face, stroking his thumb across my cheekbone. I open my eyes, watching him as his eyes trace across my features, something akin to awe on his face.

"You're so beautiful," he whispers hoarsely, touching his forehead to mine before bringing his other hand to his chest, "I can feel you both now and you're so beautiful, that you can give this to me - to us. For once in my life, I think, I don't know what to say, how to explain. I can feel you and it's beautiful, but so much more."

I press my lips to his gently, lovingly, before cupping his face in both of my hands and feathering soft kisses all over his face. I go back to his mouth, licking softly along his lower lip until he opens for me. I explore his mouth slowly, our tongues sliding together and sharing the warm glow from the bridge now embedded inside of us.

I feel Kai's lips travel up my neck and across my cheek, pausing to flick his tongue against the edge of my lips before doing the same to Hudson. I feel him leaning over my shoulder, obviously giving Hudson attention and I can't help but open my eyes, wanting to see.

I watch as Kai trails kisses across Hudson's cheek before licking at his ear. He bites the lobe gently before sucking it into his mouth. Hudson moans into my mouth and I break the kiss, turning to kiss and lick the underside of Kai's jaw, so close to my face.

I can hear the sounds of them kissing now, even with my face buried in Kai's neck. It's so heady, so exhilarating being trapped between them as they enjoy each other.

"Explain this to me," I murmur, giving Kai's throat one more kiss before directing my attention back to the two of them.

They break the kiss, Hudson sucking Kai's lower lip into his mouth before letting it go and kissing me again. He tries pushing his tongue into my mouth, but I laugh and turn away.

"No. I'm lucid for a minute, maybe two and I want to know what the heck is going on between you two," I cock an eyebrow at Hudson, "not that I'm complaining. It's incredibly hot, but how? Why? What does Simon think? God, Simon…"

"I promise, *cara*," Kai says, kissing my shoulder, "he's okay. He had to have surgery and he's going to have quite the scar, but he's healing up."

"And he's cool with all this," Hudson chuckles, "he's actually painfully jealous because he can't join us."

"Yeah, I don't know about that," Kai mutters, sucking gently at his mark.

"I'm just-I didn't think, it wasn't…obviously something changed. The mating?"

"That's the theory," Kai says, nuzzling both of the marks, "he could feel how you felt, while we were watching you, and it opened up something inside of him. I still think it's fucking weird, but I'm not complaining."

"Of course you're not, I'm hot as fuck and I know how to slang this dick," Hudson replies, gripping his half hard cock.

"Jesus," he mutters, trailing his mouth down my neck and across my shoulder, his unbound hair tickling across me, "I don't bottom, so you can slang that dick somewhere else."

"Everyone wants a piece of this, we'll see," Hudson snarks, grabbing my hand and bringing it to wrap around his cock, "she loves it."

"I do," I moan, feeling him so hot and now hard in my hand, seems to bring my body back online.

"Shit," Kai hisses, his knot easing as my pussy contracts, our pent up fluids soaking the bed underneath.

I can feel my body flush, heat spreading up from my pussy and across my chest, my cheeks, even my ears feel like they're on fire. I whine as Kai's softening cock slips out of me and the sudden emptiness I feel.

"We got you baby," Kai croons in my ear, lifting me in his arms and holding me while he adjusts positions. Leaning back against the wall of pillows at one end of the bed, he situates me on his lap facing Hudson.

Kai hooks his arms up under my legs, his elbows under my knees and spreads me obscenely. He brings his knees up on the outside of my legs so he can rest his elbows on his thighs. My upper back is resting against his chest, but the rest of me is essentially hovering, supported by Kai's arms.

Hudson kneels between our legs, bracing his knees against the inside of Kai's thighs and pushes into me with one hard thrust.

"Yes," I throw my head back against Kai's chest, "please, fuck me, please, I need you!"

"Such a dirty girl, my little omega. Don't worry baby, I'm going to fuck you as much and as long as you need."

Hudson grips one of my ass cheeks in each hand and yanks me toward him, using the position to fuck me on and off his cock without moving his body. He rocks me easily back and forth, with Kai supporting me, driving me onto his cock until I'm mewling and panting, begging for more.

I can feel the slick trickling down my ass crack and dropping on Kai and the bed. Kai's cock is hard again, rubbing on my ass each time Hudson rocks me onto his dick.

"Hudson please, I need it," I whimper, still feeling empty even with his cock pistoning into me, "please Hudson, please."

"I got you baby, I got you, sshh," Hudson pants out, switching his grip from my ass to my waist, holding me still and snapping his hips so his cock drives deep and hard.

He starts railing me, one hand on my waist and the other I can feel under me, stroking Kai's cock in time with his thrusts. Kai's moans mingle with mine, his chest vibrating with his growls of pleasure, pushing me closer to the edge.

"You close, Kai," Hudson grunts, "you gonna cum for me? I want you to cum all over this pretty pussy. You're gonna coat this hot little cunt in your cum and I'm going to fuck it into her. You ready?"

"Fuck," Kai spits out, "fuck yes."

Hudson pulls out of me, causing me to cry out in frustration, but he brings Kai's cock to my pussy. He's stroking Kai, his knuckles slipping up and down my wet pussy while he jacks him off.

Kai's whole body tightens under me, he grunts out a breath and I feel his cum splashing across my pussy, mixing with my slick before Hudson shoves his dick back inside of me.

"That's both of us, baby, all our cum, just for you, just for you," he groans, pushing the rest of the way into me, his knot squeezing into my swollen, abused pussy and setting off a chain reaction of pleasure between us.

My body stiffens, toes curling as my orgasm rolls through me. My pussy milk Hudson's cock, pumping me so full and keeping my orgasm going. Kai's relaxed beneath me, letting his knees down and bringing my legs into a more comfortable position as I ride this out.

Hudson collapses forward, catching himself on his arms stretched on either side of Kai's hips. Kai eases my legs down, reaching around me to pull Hudson against both of us, taking his weight onto us. Hudson brings his arms around Kai's back and I revel in the feeling of being snuggled between the two of them hugging each other.

After a few minutes, Hudson eases back and hooks his arms behind me, one under my ass and the other across my back.

"I know Kai's a big guy, but I don't think it's fair to crush him. Plus, someone needs to fetch water and since he's not currently engaged, he volunteers," Hudson chuckles, pulling me tight against him before shuffling around and sitting down next to Kai with me astride his lap.

I moan lightly, not happy about being moved, my back now cold and bare. I reach an arm out to find Kai, but he's already moving off the bed. I let out a long, high pitched whine. I want my mates.

It's bad enough that I'm not in my own nest, back at the warehouse, the nest I never even got to see or enjoy. I've been kidnapped and terrorized and now I'm dealing with my first full blown heat.

"*Cara*, I'm here, I'm not leaving you. I'm just getting water. We have to stay hydrated or we're going to be in real trouble," he attempts to soothe me, his voice coming from across the room.

"We're doing the best we can, baby, considering we had no options, no time to plan, and we're stuck in the hospital," Hudson murmurs, stroking his hands up and down my back.

"I don't want excuses, I want him back in this bed. Now," I snarl, reaching the limit of my patience. I'm hot and needy and I want him in this bed.

"I'm here, I'm here," he placates, the bed shifting as he crawls back toward us, several water bottles in hand.

He cracks one open and holds it up to my mouth, tipping it slowly for me. Hudson grabs one for himself and Kai finishes the one he opened for me once I'm done. He tosses the empty bottle off the edge of the bed and snuggles up next to us, laying on his side and draping his arm across my back.

Hudson loops one arm around me and the other under Kai's neck, holding us all together. I yawn so hard, my jaw pops, creating a chain reaction that rolls through all of us, Hudson making sure his yawn is over exaggerated and loud.

"Naps all around then," he murmurs before kissing my temple and rolling slightly to kiss Kai on the forehead, "we won't leave you, baby."

Kai finds the blanket, kicked over to the other side of the bed and surprisingly still dry. He drapes it over the three of us, laying back down and tucking his arm around us again.

I drift off slowly, the warmth of their love soothing me from the inside out. The scents of us combined the room, comforting the feral part of me, the wildness eased for the moment.

CHAPTER FOURTEEN

Sloane

I've lost all track of time in this room. The low lighting and lack of windows, no interruptions from the outside, and the constant burning need deep in my pussy combines to leave me a horny, confused mess.

During the short reprieves I get while knotted by one of them, I've managed to sort of figure out how things work. I've also come to really love the set up of the room and hope that my nest at home is similar, though more personal.

The room is a basic square, with the bed taking up the majority of the space. The bed is large, a custom made pack size with high head and foot boards at either end. There are supports that run from end to end, creating a wood formed canopy that's currently draped with various fabrics to create curtains around the space.

The whole surface is covered in pillows and blankets of various sizes. There are multiple layers of waterproofing, but it's still incredibly comfortable.

There's a few chairs around the room and an attached bathroom. We've made use of every space and surface in here, I think. The only way they've managed to get cleaned up is by taking turns fucking me in the shower. I don't want either of them far away from me.

There's a small vestibule just outside the door where food and water is delivered for us several times per day. No one is allowed in the room except for pack members, while I'm still in heat. So the food is delivered and one of them brings it in. It's mostly just protein shakes and other liquids. Things that are easy to consume in between sessions.

I'm currently sprawled across Kai's chest, his cock knotted deep while Hudson tries to get me to drink some bone broth. I'm so tired, though. Weak from not being able to prepare, not mentally or physically ready to endure an ongoing heat like this.

We had extensive nutrition classes designed to help us prepare for a drawn out heat. How to calorie load in the weeks leading up to our heat so that we could be deprived during that time and not suffer too much. How to eat the right combination of foods to ensure optimal health for a pregnancy, if we decided to breed during our heat.

I didn't have a chance to do either of those things. I made the choice to go through this, knowing that I wasn't fully prepared, but it's a lot more draining than I ever could have imagined. I'm absolutely exhausted, my body driving me to take them one after another with limited rest in between.

"You have to drink, *cara*. I know you're tired, but you have to keep your strength up if you want to continue," Kai encourages, cupping my cheek to support my head, allowing Hudson to pour the hot liquid directly into my mouth.

"Should we call the doctor," Hudson whispers to Kai, "I don't like how exhausted she feels."

"I know," he murmurs.

Kai turns my face toward his, sliding his thumb under my jaw to keep my head from lolling the other way, "Can you look at me, baby?"

I grunt, slitting my eyes just enough that I can see his face, not wanting to go through the effort of opening them all the way. I need to preserve my strength, even if it's just the little bit I save from not opening my eyes.

"If you don't drink the rest of this bone broth, I'm going to call the doctor," Kai warns, voice like steel but I can feel his unease and worry swirling inside of me. It's cocooned in caring and love, but it's strong.

I huff out a breath, irritated but understanding. The fact that I can feel their worry thumping through me is probably the biggest motivator. I open my mouth and make a concerted effort to swallow all of the broth.

I smile sleepily at both of them before snuggling back down against Kai's chest and closing my eyes, hoping for a few more minutes of peace and maybe a hint of sleep.

"Maybe we should call Dr. Mason," Hudson starts again, "she wasn't ready for this, we should have sedated her from the beginning."

"I didn't realize it would be like this. It's only been two days. If it lasts beyond tomorrow, I don't think she'll make it."

"Can she be sedated now? I know that's not what she wanted, but I can't watch her waste away like this, it's killing me," Hudson whines and I can feel his sincerity echo inside of me.

"Don't talk about me like I'm not here," I mumble, voice muffled by Kai's chest, but I refuse to move anymore than I need to, "I'm fine."

"You're not fine, *cara*, you're exhausted and drained. I think you've lost five pounds already. Do you want to be sedated? Now you know what it's like, we can be better prepared for next time."

"No," I brace my arms on Kai's chest, pushing myself into a seated position, straddling his lap as his knot deflates and he slips out of me.

"No sedation," I emphasize, looking each of them in the face and pushing my conviction through the bond.

"We have to do what's best for you, Sloane," Hudson counters, "even if that means something you don't want."

"What about what's best for the baby?"

I can feel shock reverberate through them, incredulity then denial.

"Neither of you thought about that, huh? No heat suppressant, no birth control. The fact that you've both been railing me for two days straight, never occurred to you that you'd get me pregnant?"

I can feel as their shock turns to surprise, joy. Then Kai sits up abruptly, pulling me against his chest and ravaging my mouth. His tongue thrusts against mine as his hands drop to my ass, dragging my pussy up his now hard cock.

"Fuck no, my turn," Hudson growls, wedging his arms between us and snatching me off Kai's lap, "mine!"

Feral dominance runs through the bond. Self satisfaction, pride, and overwhelming desire. Hot, all consuming passion. I can't tell who it's coming from, mingled together and overlapping.

Hudson tosses me down onto my stomach before wedging a pillow under my hips.

"Just relax and take it, baby," he mutters before driving his cock into me.

He has one hand on my hip, the other braced next to me as he fucks me hard and fast. I hear Kai spit and I turn my head enough to see him kneeling next to me, eyes focused on Hudson's cock pumping into my slick soaked, used pussy while he strokes himself.

"Fuck," Hudson groans, "I'm gonna pump you so full, if there isn't a baby in there now, there will be."

I moan and whimper, my body limp and exhausted, but throbbing with desire. He shifts back, gripping each of my hips and pinning me down while he pounds his dick into me.

He drives into me with a shout, my pussy clamping down on his knot. He groans, dropping his forehead down to rest on my lower back as his cock throbs inside of me, spurt after spurt of cum filling me.

"Open wide," Kai mutters.

My eyes snap open when I realize he's not talking to me.

I can hear the wet, sucking sounds as Hudson takes Kai's cock into his mouth. Kai groans, the bed shifting as his hips pump back and forth, fucking Hudson's mouth.

I whimper, "I wanna watch."

"Not this time, *cara*, I'm too close. The scent of your freshly fucked little pussy just does it for me," Kai groans, "fuck yeah, Hudson, you like that, don't you. Take this cock, fuck, take it."

Kai grunts once, then again and I can imagine how he looks. Face scrunched, head thrown back, one hand fisted at his side while the other is fisted in Hudson's short hair. His cock pulsing as he cums in his mouth.

My whole body shudders at the imagined visual.

"Good boy," Kai chuckles, stretching out beside me and draping an arm across my back before nuzzling into my neck and licking at his mark. Something they've both become obsessed with over the last few days.

Hudson hooks his arm under my hips and holds me to him as he rolls us onto our sides. Kaiser pushes against us, squeezing me between them, their arms wrapped around each other. As much as I love this time with them, I can't help but wonder how different this will be in the future and how all of us will fit together then, especially once Brooks and Simon are mated with us.

I guess Hudson's newly awakened bi instincts will probably go a long way into making everyone feel connected. At least when it comes to Kai and Simon. Not sure what side of the line Brooks is falling on here, but that might change when we're mated, just like it did with Hudson.

Speaking of.

"Is Brooks going to join us? I know you said he was in a time out, whatever that means, but I was just wondering, how it would be with all of us, I know Simon can't...I just thought-" I cut myself off with a huge yawn, exhaustion coming back quick now that I'm relaxed again.

"Maybe you should just take a nap, baby, while you have time. We can talk about Brooks later," Hudson whispers in my ear before dragging his mouth down to his mark and dropping a featherlight kiss on it.

"What happened? Something went down between the boat and the hospital, while I was passed out, what aren't you telling me?"

"We just don't want you stressed, *cara*, you need to get through this heat and then we can discuss everything," Kai says, brushing gentle kisses across my cheeks as my eyes flutter shut.

"I'm stressed right now, not having my whole pack, not being in my own nest, being kidnapped and harassed," I snap, "now you're both lying by omission and I'm tired and cranky and if you don't tell me what's going on I swear I won't talk to either of you once we make it through this!"

"You have to talk to me, you're having my baby," Hudson growls against the back of my neck.

"I don't have to do anything I don't want to do. Besides. It could be Kai's, you don't know," I sniff haughtily, pretending that I'm not laying here naked stuffed full of cock.

"Yeah, could be my bun in that sexy little oven," Kai chuckles, "so she can ignore you all she wants."

"Don't act like you're above me here, bro, you don't want to talk about it, either."

Frustrated with their back and forth and the fact that they're still not telling me anything, I take all of the anger and irritation that I'm feeling and push it out through the bond. I'm tired and I want answers, so I push that through, too.

The last thing I drag out is the sadness. That Brooks and Simon aren't here. That they're playing with me instead of being honest. That they're making jokes instead of explaining things to me.

I push all that out to them before closing my eyes and closing myself off. I don't even know for sure what I'm doing, just that I want to block them out. They don't get to share my feelings if they can't be respectful of them. It's not fair for them to decide what I should and shouldn't know, to exclude me when it comes to something that directly involves me.

"Don't be like that, *cara*," Kai whispers, hurt lacing his tone, "we're just trying to do what's best."

"We're trying to protect you, baby," Hudson adds, "take care of you."

"You just went through something traumatic and we're just trying to enjoy this time with you before we have to go back into discussing traumatizing things."

I refuse to answer them, keeping my blocks firmly in place while they try to cajole me into letting them back in and taking a nap. As soon as I feel Hudson's knot release, I struggle out from between them, fighting them the whole way.

Kai tries to hold me between them and I snap my teeth, inches from his face. Growling low in my throat, I leave long scratches down Hudson's forearm when he tries to hold me in place.

I finally break away, scrambling across the bed until I'm in the complete opposite corner from them. Like I did when I was in the closet on that boat, I make a Sloane size pillow pit and cover it with layers and layers of blankets. Crawling inside of it, alone, I make sure to stick my arm out and give them the finger for a solid thirty seconds before digging down into my pile and forgetting they exist.

I'm staying right here until they either agree to tell me what's going on, why Brooks isn't here and what happened on the boat or until my heat is complete. At which point I'll leave this room and find Brooks myself. I'm so hurt and angry that I can't feel anything else. Certainly no urges to let either of them fuck me.

I remember them telling us at the Academy that certain things, strong emotions or serious illness, a fracture in the pack, could interfere with a heat cycle. If the omega was under a great deal of stress, she may skip her heat or have a dysfunctional one. I think I'm dysfunctional, then.

I feel the bed shifting and it feels like one of them is moving towards my side. I let out a warning growl and the movement stops; the bed shifts again but in the opposite direction this time. Satisfied that they're going to leave me alone, I let my body relax and drift off to sleep.

Some time later, I'm awakened by voices.

Brooks and Kai are arguing, but I can't make out all the words, buried under the blankets as I am. I don't want to move and let them know I'm awake, but I want to hear what they're arguing about. Since no one wants to be honest with me, this might be the only way I find out what's going on.

I listen for a few more minutes, sound still muffled, when I feel the bed shift, like someone sitting down and then a door shutting. Frustrated at not knowing what's going on, I decide to make a move. Shifting forward slightly, I push one of the pillows out of the formed ring around me, giving me an opening I can see out of.

Hudson is sitting in one of the chairs across the room, a blanket tossed across his lap, Brooks is sitting on the edge of the bed and I can't see Kai, but the light in the bathroom is on. Brooks leans down, peaking into the opening and smiling slightly at me.

"Hello, *piccoletta*, how are you feeling?"

"Yeah, I'd like to know, too," Hudson mumbles.

I extend my arm and give him the finger again, "I'm not talking to him," I tell Brooks.

"I see. Do you want to talk to me?"

"I just want someone to tell me what's going on. Why you weren't here," I tell him, voice cracking, "What happened on the boat? No one wants to upset me, but I am already upset, thank you, so if you could just be honest with me, I would appreciate that."

"I can do that. Do you want to stay in there or do I get to see you?"

"I haven't decided yet. Start talking and I'll let you know."

Brooks takes a deep breath, tugging his fingers through his hair briefly before angling his head so we can maintain eye contact without him having to lean over completely.

"I needed to get you off that boat. We had already lost a lot of time, Hudson rutting you and us watching, obviously. I am not complaining, about anything that happened, we couldn't have fought it if we tried, but by the time I snapped out of it, I was worried about how long we had been there."

I nod as best I can, buried as I am and smile up at him, letting him know I'm listening and I understand.

"When I put you on the bed and wrapped you up, you were so out of it. Your scent was so strong you were even pulling me in again. I wanted nothing more than to strip bare and fuck you for hours. But, at the end of the day,

I'm the one responsible for everyone's safety. So I made a decision and I injected you with a sedative that Simon's doctor gave me before we left to rescue you."

I swallow hard. That's not what I was expecting. So many thoughts rush through my head, I have a hard time compartmentalizing all of them. Mainly it brings to the forefront the issues I have with Iris. Getting appropriately drugged at the Academy by a doctor was one thing, being stabbed with something against my will is a whole different ballpark.

Being sedated against my will isn't exactly amazing anyway, but the feelings of inadequacy and abandonment that stem from Iris' treatment of me suddenly resurfacing definitely doesn't help. The fact that Brooks' did it for a good reason, and the fact that I understand why he did it still doesn't make it better.

In my panic and anxiety, I let my blocks slip. Kai slams out of the bathroom, nothing but a towel in his hand at the same moment Hudson pushes up from the chair, his blanket dropping to the floor. Both of them rush over to the bed, wary but obviously concerned.

Brooks has a look of utter confusion on his face when Kai turns to him, growling, "I told you this needed to wait. She's not in the head space to deal with this right now."

"Not your call," Brooks retorts, "she's a grown woman and can make her own decisions. I'm tired of you guys locking me out. I'm the one in charge here! Or did you two forget it?"

Brooks' yelling, though not directed at me, causes me to flinch and whine which isn't missed by Hudson, now crawling across the bed toward me. He reaches into the open space where the pillow used to be and hauls me out, up into his arms, making sure not to destroy my pseudo nest.

He sits down and cradles me to his chest, tucking my head up under his chin and purring. The soothing vibrations rock through me, combined with the warm touch of his naked skin against mine and I feel myself relaxing bit by bit.

"You're my brother, and I love you," Kai tells Brooks, "but if that hadn't worked to calm her down I would have fucked you up."

"Bring it on," Brooks steps back, opening his arms in a 'come get some' type gesture, "If that's what you need to forgive me, I'll take the beating. You better believe I'll give as good as I get, though."

Kai growls, stepping into Brooks for a moment before hesitating. He feels my fear spike through the bond, not wanting the two of them to fight, but especially not wanting them to fight over me. He glances over his shoulder at me and I reach a hand out, wanting him close to me, comforting me, instead of fighting with Brooks.

"Now she knows, you can go," Kai tells him, climbing onto the bed and shuffling across to us. Hudson stretches his legs out, letting Kai sit between them, facing us. Kai drapes his legs over Hudsons and scoots close enough that their junk is touching under me and I'm cradled between them.

Brooks gives us one last sad, longing look before turning toward the door.

"Wait, Brooks," I call to him, keeping my head tucked against Hudson but making eye contact across the room, "you didn't even let me say anything."

"I think their response was a good enough indication that you're pretty upset, *tesoro*. I'll let them calm you down and we can talk soon," he smiles sadly before turning away again.

"Stop turning away from me, Brooks Conti," I hiss, "and don't you dare try to tell me how I feel. I'm so sick of you big idiots trying to do what's best for me without actually consulting me. I have a brain, you know!"

Hudson chuckles, nuzzling his cheek against the top of my head, "Oh, she's mad and it's so cute. She's like, shit what was that movie we watched when we were kids. The animated one with the llama? She's like the villain who got turned into the tiny evil kitty. What the fuck was it called?"

"Emperor's New Groove," Kai answers, bewildered.

"YES! She's like, tiny fluffy Yzma."

I turn my head and bite his nipple until he yelps, grabbing my hair and yanking until I let go.

"Next time I'll bite it right off. Don't test me right now, I'm barely over being angry with you!"

"Yes, ma'am," he nuzzles me again, pushing his face down into my neck so he can kiss his mark.

Brooks continues to watch us, a combination of pain and longing so obvious on his face. I'm not mad at him. I know he didn't want to do it, he had to. I get it. It's not him I'm mad at, it's all the feelings that his confession brought up. All the insecurity and pain, especially at having been so close to Iris during my confinement.

"I am upset, yes, that's pretty clear, given their behavior. It's not at you, Brooks," I tell him, reaching a hand out between Kai and Hudson, gesturing him closer, "it's at the situation and the feelings it brings up. Iris put me through a lot, as a kid and more recently with all this bullshit. It's a lot to process and your confession only brought it to the surface."

He takes a few steps closer to the bed and I smile encouragingly. He pulls his shirt over his head then strips off the rest of his clothes before crawling onto the bed with the rest of us. Once he's close enough, Hudson and Kai let me go so I can slide onto Brooks' lap.

He sits cross legged and I straddle his lap, looping my arms behind his neck and pulling him down for a kiss. His hard cock is trapped between us and I tilt my hips just enough that I can rub my wet pussy along the underside of his base.

He moans into my mouth, one hand dropping to my ass and dragging me harder against him.

"Fuck, I missed you, *tesoro*," he confesses while peppering my face with kisses, "I felt like my heart had been ripped out. I was so scared, so scared we wouldn't get you back."

"Sshh," I press my lips to his lightly, "I'm here now, we're together. I'm in one piece and everything is going to be okay."

He squeezes me tight against him, his arm like a steel band wrapped behind my back, locking me to him. His other hand still gripped onto my ass cheek, grinding my pussy against him.

"Are you sore," he whispers against my shoulder, trailing kisses across every body part he can reach.

"Not much," I moan as he sucks the sensitive spot just under my ear, "they took care of me while I was out of it. I wouldn't care, even if I was, I want you."

"And you can have me," he murmurs, switching his attention to the other side of my neck and licking a slow path up across both of the mating marks there.

I shudder from the brief contact. The pleasure of his slow and gentle exploration of my other men's marks causes slick to flow out of me, soaking his coak and dripping down off his balls.

Moaning from behind has me craning my neck to try to see over my shoulder. Brooks chuckles, then murmurs into my ear, "You want to watch them, *piccoletta*? My naughty little voyeur."

Brooks bites on Hudson's mark and I cry out. The marks are so fresh and new, every little caress is like a shot straight to my pussy. I know the sensation will dull over time, but right now it's like a fire in my bloodstream every time he touches one of them.

Brooks grips each ass cheek and starts rocking me harder against him.

"Kai has his mouth wrapped around Hudson's cock," he whispers, making sure my clit is rubbing with each stroke, his thick cock nestled perfectly between my pussy lips, "he's taking him so deep, baby, swallowing him down. He's going to make Hudson cum in his mouth, then I think he's going to fuck his ass."

Hudson groans and I can hear the wet, slurping noises as Kai quickens his pace.

"Please, let me watch," I pant, grinding myself down onto Brooks cock as his hands knead my ass.

"Anything for you, *tesoro*," he tells me, kissing my forehead before using the grip on my cheeks to lift me up and help turn me around.

Brooks stretches his legs out in front of him, almost touching Hudson's leg while Kai kneels between them. Brooks pulls me down onto my knees, facing away from him and straddling his lap. He presses his cock against my slick soaked opening, then grips each hip and pulls me down onto him.

"Oooooh," I let out a long moan, reveling in the feel of him deep inside of me, before dropping forward to brace my arms on his thighs and ride him while I watched Kai and Hudson.

"Oh no, baby, you can watch, but you're still going to know it's me fucking you," he loops his arm around my waist and pulls me flush against him, "ride like this baby, I want to have access."

I twine my arms back around his neck and arch my back, driving my pussy back down onto his cock. He slides one hand up to tease and tweak my nipples, the other dropping to my clit and roughly circling.

Using my knees, I lift up and drop down on his dick, watching as Hudson grips Kai's hair and drags him off his cock.

"Open your fucking mouth," Hudson tells him. When Kai does, sticking his tongue out for good measure, Hudson spits into it before sealing their mouths together.

"I want to fuck you," Hudson snarls, breaking their kiss to leave bites across Kai's neck and shoulders.

"Not gonna happen," Kai pants out as Hudson pulls him upright by the hair before leaning down to bite at each of his nipples.

"So fuck yourself on me, I don't really care how you do it, I just want my dick in your ass," Hudson tells him, wrapping his hand around Kai's cock and stroking him hard and fast.

Kai pushes Hudson back, pinning his arms to his sides and stretching himself out on top of him. He savages his mouth, biting at his lips while sliding his hips against him, their cocks rubbing together.

I grind myself down harder and faster on Brooks, chasing an orgasm as he expertly strokes and circles my clit. I didn't realize watching them would be so hot, my pussy is soaked. Brooks continues to lick and nibble on their mating marks, only driving my arousal higher.

Kai slides down Hudson's body, taking his cock into his mouth again. He wraps his fist tight around the base of his dick, stroking him hard, in time with his mouth. I'm mesmerized by the sight of his mouth working up and down, his spit sliding over his fist and making a mess of the two of them.

Brooks pinches my clit before grinding me down hard on his cock, his knot popping inside of me. I howl as my pussy convulses around him, my back arching so hard I find myself staring at the ceiling, but only for a moment.

Brooks yanks my head to the side, teeth sinking into the crook of my neck and back on my shoulder as he marks me. I cry out, my pussy squeezing and milking his cock as I feel his cum pumping inside of me.

I refocus on Hudson and Kai when I hear Hudson grunt, "Fuck"

Kai pushes himself up to his knees, taking his cock in hand. I watch as he spits a mouthful of Hudson's cum onto his own cock and uses it to stroke himself roughly.

"Cum on me," Hudson moans, "I want to feel your hot cum on my cock and balls, give it to me."

Kai groans low, reaching down to squeeze his knot with his other hand as his cum splatters across Hudson. Squeezing his shaft, he shakes every drop out onto Hudson's stomach and hips, Kai's sticky cum dripping down Hudson's dick.

Once he's spent, he drops down across Hudson, their legs tangling together as they kiss and nuzzle each other. I let out a soft moan as Brooks tends to his own mark, now linked with us forever. I savor the contentment I feel flowing between the four of us before snuggling back into Brooks and allowing my eyes to drift closed again.

CHAPTER FIFTEEN

Simon

The nurse helps me hobble back into my room, just as my phone pings an alert. They finally took the catheter out yesterday, but still make me call for assistance when I need to piss. Apparently I'm a fall risk so I can't walk around alone.

I guess it's a smart move, considering I have to use the bathroom in the hallway instead of the one in my room. It's been cleaned out and the shower is functioning, but the toilet was cracked to shit after Hudson stomped it and they can't do construction until I'm discharged.

Apparently, pissing in the shower drain isn't sanitary, or so the nurse informed us when she caught Hudson doing it. So now we all have to walk around the corner when the need hits.

The nurse helps me swing my legs back into the bed before raising it up again as I grab my phone.

H: Sloane's heat ended early, too much stress according to Doc Mason

H: We'll be up once she showers, don't want to incite the rabble

H: I told Kai not to wash his beard though, you can snuggle all in there and live vicariously

My dick perks right up at the visual of Sloane in the shower before my mind drifts to images of what Kai would have been doing to have her scent so imbedded in his facial hair.

H: Sorry you couldn't join in, man, I promise you'll get some just as soon as Seymur clears it

H: In the meantime, I will gladly suck your dick if you need it

H: Don't mean to brag, but I think I'm pretty good at it

H: And I need the practice if I'm going to catch up with you two

B: Please shut the fuck up

K: He doesn't need the temptation when he can't participate

K: Don't be a dick

I stare at my phone, not even sure how to respond to all of that. Hudson's normal crazy with this new addition of sudden onset bisexuality is just a bit much for me.

He is hot as fuck, I can't argue with that, but it's just weird. We grew up together and he was straight as an arrow. All of the sudden he wants the dick, too? I'm still working to process it fully, though I am definitely intrigued.

I told Kai it wouldn't bother me if they fooled around or fucked while they were locked up with Sloane. We've known each other all our lives. As long as he keeps it within the pack, it's okay with me.

Besides, I've done enough research to know how crazy it can get with an omega in heat, especially as an alpha. I'm okay with them hooking up, I'm just not sure I'm ready to get involved.

"Is there any way I can take a shower," I ask the nurse before she can leave, one hand on the door. Up to this point, I've been getting sponge baths every time they do a dressing change, but haven't been able to actually shower or wash my hair.

"I'll have to see if someone is available to help you. We can't have you in the shower alone, but it's against policy for a female employee to watch while you bathe," she replies, turning toward me, "unless one of your friends wants to help?"

I groan inwardly, "I was actually hoping to shower before they got back. Our omega, she was in heat…they're on their way back up now…" I trail off.

"Right, okay yeah, Seymur said something about that. You want to shower before they get here, put on a fresh face for your girl. I get it. Let me see what options we have."

I take a deep breath and stare at my phone for another few minutes, finally settling on:

Si: ETA?

There's too much to unpack in those texts and I'd rather just focus on trying to get myself clean before Sloane shows up.

K: She's in the shower now, maybe 10-15 min

Si: Thanks, see you soon

Just as I hit send, the nurse pops back into the room, holding the door for another nurse carrying a plastic shower chair behind her. Dr. Seymur enters behind them.

"How are you feeling today, Simon?"

"Good Dr. Seymur, thank you, what's up?"

"I heard you wanted to take a shower. I'm going to remove your bandages and just do a quick wound check while the ladies get the chair setup. You'll be able to shower on your own, but you'll have to call to have them assist you out. I don't want you walking on a slippery shower floor on your own, got it?"

"Yessir, I appreciate the help."

"Alright let's take a look."

Dr. Seymur helps me sit up and then unwinds the gauze bandages. The incision starts just between my pecs and travels down to just above my belly button. It's roughly 10 inches long and ugly as fuck.

Doc keeps telling me that it'll heal up and won't be too noticeable, especially once my chest hair comes back in. I don't care about some ambiguous future date when it won't be noticeable, I care about now. About Sloane seeing me after so long being gone and me being damaged. Broken.

"Everything looks good. We'll pull the staples tomorrow before you're discharged. I think that'll go a long way into making you feel better."

"Thanks, doc."

He nods, shakes my hand, and heads to the door, "Make sure you use that call button, Simon. No playing around with your health."

I check my phone, five minutes has passed since Kai texted me back. Should give me enough time for a quick wash and dry. I pull a clean pair of sweatpants out of the bag next to the bed and toss them on the pillow so they're ready for me to put on when I get done.

"Ready to shower," my nurse asks, stepping to the side of the bed to escort me across the room, "It's important that you stay facing away from the shower spray. It's okay for your incision to get wet, but you don't want to soak it, okay?"

"Got it."

"Stay in the chair the entire time. You can cover yourself with one of these," she sets a handful of towels on the shelf, far enough away that they'll stay dry but I can still reach them, "when you ring for us, but do not get up for any reason, okay?"

"Aye, aye captain," I mock salute, as she helps me sit in the chair. She shows me how to operate the shower head, adjusting the temperature and giving me a bottle of all in one cleanser.

"Sorry we don't have anything fancy for you, but I'm sure she'll just be happy to see you."

"I wasn't expecting much, so thanks for this. I just want to be clean for her," I say, smiling awkwardly at her as she backs out the door.

"Do not get out of that chair," she tells me one more time before the door clicks shut and I'm alone.

I lift my hips and shuffle out of the dirty sweats I currently have on, then adjust the temperature quickly. Once it's nice and warm, I take a minute to direct the stream across as much of my body as I can reach. Across my shoulders, down my back, my arms and lap and legs.

I feel like it's been ages since I felt water on my body. Since I felt clean. I can't bend over, so I'm not going to be able to give myself a deep clean, but I'll be able to wash what's important.

I squirt some of the generic soap into my hand before scrubbing all the important areas - pits, junk and ass, though the ass is a little difficult since I'm not supposed to stand. I get myself rinsed off, before wetting my hair.

It's a little awkward, since I can't tilt too far back without my chest hurting, so the water dribbles down my face and into my ears. Nevertheless, I am going to get myself clean if it's the last thing I do.

I lather up the soap in my hands before scrubbing my fingers through my hair. For the first time in a long time, I contemplate cutting it. The strain from having to hold my arms up for so long to wash the length is frustrating.

I take a break, letting my arms rest across my lap, tilting my head back as far as is comfortable to keep the soap off my face. I hear muffled voices on the other side of the door. Shit.

A few seconds later, there's a tap on the door and Sloane's sweet voice, "Simon? Hudson says the toilet is broke so you're definitely not using it, but I wanted to make sure. Is it okay if I come in?"

I freeze. I don't want her to see me like this, naked and helpless. I haven't had a chance to discuss my worries and fears with her, to try to sort out my own issues before this shit storm descended on us. Now I'm sitting here, soaking wet and limp dicked, soapy hair and an ugly ass scar.

"Simon, are you okay," she asks louder, tapping at the door again, "please, I need to see you, Simon."

"Answer her, dick, you're freaking her out! She thought you were dead," Hudson yells through the door.

"Yeah, uh, yeah, sorry, I'm just, uh, just trying to wash my hair," I finish lamely.

"Oh," I hear, then her murmuring to the other guys before the door opens and she slides in. She's wrapped in two hospital gowns, her hair still wet, looking freshly scrubbed and so painfully beautiful.

Meanwhile, I'm sitting in a shower chair, one hand covering my junk and the other holding the shower head to keep my chest from getting wet.

"Oh, Simon," she whispers, tears trickling down her cheeks as she crosses the room, dropping to her knees in front of me, "I thought, when he shot you, I saw all the blood."

She chokes up and starts sobbing. Scooting forward, she rests her forehead on my knees and wraps her arms gingerly around my waist.

"Hey, hey," I whisper, slipping my fingers into her hair and massaging her scalp, "I'm here, beautiful, I'm alive. I'm okay, Sloane, it's okay. Shit."

I hiss, pulling my hand out of her hair to wipe my face. When I sat up to comfort her, I forgot about the soap in my hair and now it's in my eyes, all over my face.

"Shit, ow, fuck," I mutter, clamping my eyes shut and trying to wipe my face, then rinse my hand at the same time without getting Sloane soaked, too.

"Let me help," she takes my hand and pulls it away from my face, then I feel a wet washcloth wiping across my eyes and down my face. She takes the shower head from my hand, rinsing the cloth I assume, and brings it back to my face for a second wipe down.

"I'm sorry," I whisper.

"For what," she whispers back, trailing her fingers across my face after handing back the showerhead.

"For being such a clumsy ass?"

"I love you, Simon, clumsy or not," she rests her forehead to mine and I feel her breath ghosting across my lips, "when I thought you were dead, I didn't know how I was going to live without you. You complete me, just like the rest of them do."

She kisses me softly, trailing kisses across my cheeks and forehead.

"Let me help you," she whispers again, sliding her hands up into my hair and pushing it back from my face.

"Okay," I sigh, knowing I can't possibly be any more pathetic at this point, handing her back the shower head and cupping my junk with every ounce of awkwardness I possess.

I keep my eyes shut as I feel her step behind me, her fingers sifting through my hair. Her short nails scrape against my scalp and I can't help the moan that escapes. After going days with barely any physical contact except from medical staff, it feels like pure heaven to have her hands on me.

She scrubs gently at my scalp before running her fingers through the length, scrubbing the ends and then rinsing all the soap out.

"I'm assuming you didn't get any conditioner, either, huh," she asks.

"Yeah, not a chance," I chuckle, "we're not exactly at the Hilton, beautiful."

"Yeah, I noticed," she mutters, wrapping a towel around my hair and gently rubbing the strands as dry as she can.

I pull one of her hands around and drop a kiss on the inside of her wrist.

"I love you, too, Sloane. So much. When they had you in that van, your face, the look on your face when you saw me…" I trail off, choking up before I can finish.

She leans down, resting her cheek against mine, her other arm wrapping around the front of my shoulders while I continue to kiss her wrist.

"You got me out, Simon. You might not have been able to be there, but the guys told me everything that you did. I wouldn't be here without you."

We stay that way for a few more minutes, taking comfort from one another, even though I am painfully embarrassed and pathetically naked. One hand still cupping my junk as if I can hide it from her.

"Okay," she pulls back, "let's get you dried off and dressed. Brooks said you had some information you wanted to talk to us about."

"Yeah, um, just hand me a towel and get Kai to help me back out to the bed. I left my sweats out there."

"I can help you, Simon," she chides, approaching with another towel and attempting to dry me off.

"Please, Sloane," I snap a little, "Kai can help me."

O-okay," she murmurs, turning quickly, but not before I see the look of hurt on her face.

"Sloane, I didn't-"

The door closes behind her before I can finish. It's another minute before Kai comes in, his face stony with disapproval.

"Did you really have to be a dick to her? She thought you were dead the entire time she was gone," he admonishes, stepping up with a towel and drying me off my front, before helping my stand and drying my back.

"I didn't mean to hurt her, I didn't-don't want her to see me like this, like a broken, pathetic thing. I don't…you know, it was bad enough before. Now. Now, what do I have to offer, huh. Even less than because now I have this ugly fucking scar, I couldn't save her from being taken. I'm fucking worthless to her, man," my voice cracks and the first tears slip free.

"Goddamnit, Simon," Kai grumbles, hugging me to him as gently as he can while I try to control my sobs so I don't injure myself, "you are so far from worthless it's not even funny. We wouldn't have found her without you. She loves you just as much as the rest of us. I can feel that, man, she can't hide that. Her love for you is just as bright as the rest of us."

"Well then I wish I could feel it, too," I hiccup, "because feeling like this is worse than being shot."

"You trust me, right? She loves you, with everything she is. As soon as you're better, we'll make it permanent and then you can feel it, too," Kai promises, still holding me gently and dropping a kiss to the top of my head.

"I didn't mean to hurt her," I whisper again, wanting him to know that I really didn't mean it.

"I know, I know. Let's just get you out there and dressed. You guys will work it out, you need to talk to her. Tell her how you're feeling if you can't wait to feel it for yourself."

"Yeah," I nod, leaning on him as he walks me out of the bathroom and across the room to the bed.

Sloane is sitting with Hudson in one of the recliners that the nurses brought for them to sleep in the other night. He's got her tucked into a little ball, her head up under his chin and his arms wrapped tight around her. Brooks drapes a blanket across them both before dropping into the other recliner.

Leaning against the edge of the bed, Kai helps tug the sweats up for me, reaching over to press the call button for the nurse. Once she rebandages me, I'll throw on a t-shirt or something. For now I sit back on the bed gingerly, letting Kai lift my legs for me.

Just as he gets my second leg onto the bed, Dr. Seymur pops into the room.

"They're doing shift change out there, so I figured I'd be helpful and come wrap you up," he says, waving a roll of gauze.

"Sure, doc."

Kai steps around, giving him room to work while I sit as still as I can with my arms up. Seymur starts at the top, wrapping and wrapping all around my torso until the incision tape is covered in two layers of overlapping gauze.

I look up and see Sloan watching me from across the room, her eyes trained on the scar running the length of my chest as Seymur covers it. She doesn't appear shocked or disgusted, so I guess that's a plus.

"You didn't get it too wet, so we'll definitely be able to remove the staples tomorrow before you leave."

"Remove the staples," Sloane pipes up, "are you sure that's okay?"

"Yes, of course, Sloane, right? I'm Dr. Seymur," he introduces himself, turning so he can look at her, "I've been taking care of Simon here since he got transferred to my floor. The general timeline for suture removal from surgery like this is 6-10 days. His incision is healing well, nice and pink, no puss or evidence of infection. He'll be perfectly fine having them removed."

"If you're sure," she whispers, concern etched on her face.

"I am sure. And having them removed will help him in the long run, make it easier for him to move around without pinching and pulling. He'll heal much faster with them out."

"Thank you, Dr. Seymur," she murmurs, still looking concerned but apparently content enough to listen to him.

"Of course," he nods at her before turning off the call light and heading out the door, "I'll be signing the discharge paperwork tonight, so you'll be able to leave after first rounds in the morning."

"Thanks, doc," Hudson calls, the rest of the guys echoing the sentiment.

"Now that we're alone, you want to tell me what crawled up your ass in there," Hudson asks quietly, in deference to Sloane being in his lap, but the look he shoots my way is full of murder.

"Not really, no," I answer calmly, "that's something that I will discuss with Sloane when we have time alone."

"You hurt her, dick," he hisses.

"Yeah, I know and I'll discuss it with her when we're alone. Just because we're all in this together, some things are still personal, private between the two of us. Not everyone is as free and easy as you, Hudson."

"You better make it right, that's all I'm saying," he narrows his eyes at me, "if you don't I'll piss in the ventilation ducts in the basement every fucking morning."

"You're disgusting," I mutter, cracking a small smile as Sloane giggles at Hudson's threat.

"Now that Hudson got his hissy fit out of the way, what did you want to share with us, Simon," Brooks asks, tucking his hand under the blanket so he can rub Sloane's leg.

"Right, okay, hand me my laptop, babe," I hold my hand out, taking the laptop from Kai as he sits on the bed next to me, "Dmitri sent over some information I wanted to share with everyone. Let me just pull it up. He sent an email, so it's kind of oddly worded."

I situate the laptop on the hospital table, tapping in the password before pulling up my email.

"I'll just read it to you, that way you get the full context," I look around quickly, making sure they're all on board.

"Okay then. He says, 'we've gathered information from our colleagues that we thought should be shared with you in the interest of safety. All three were involved in stealing rare artifacts, making regular trades with their counterparts who they did meet with on the boat. Unfortunately, the others had alternate transportation scheduled and were not able to attend the reunion. Our colleagues are convinced that they will want their artifact back along with their missing piece. No known timeline, just a strong assurance, so it's important that you stay alert and the artifact is protected at all times. Please let us know when Sloane is feeling better, we would really like to see her. Make sure to ask her about Iris' new purple necklace, lol' and that's that."

I glance around the room, gauging everyone's reaction. Sloane's eyes are wide and she's chewing her lower lip, but otherwise doesn't seem too worried. Brooks looks like he's ready to murder everyone in his path and Hudson is squeezing Sloane so hard, I'm surprised she can breathe.

"Tell us about Iris necklace, *cara*."

"I have no idea what he's talking about. I don't think she was wearing a necklace. I think I would've noticed one, especially if it was purple," she scrunches her face up, thinking hard.

"Okay, but he's writing in code, right? So what other kind of purple necklace might she have had," Brooks asks.

"Oh, that" Sloane giggles, "yeah, I forgot about that."

"Well," Hudson jostles her a little, "don't leave us in suspense."

"I tried to kill her. She pissed me off, right when my heat was starting so I pinned her down and I choked her. Almost had her, too, but then Egor came in and stopped me."

"Egor? You call that fuckstick by his first name," Hudson growls.

"Matter of survival, remember," she snaps back, "didn't think it would be in my best interest to piss off the human trafficker."

"Easy, you two," Brooks interjects before Hudson can respond, "you know she didn't mean anything by it, don't be an ass. Sloane, we need to know what happened on that boat. We know you weren't raped, Dr. Mason did an extensive exam-"

"What," Sloane screeches, in what I can only assume is intense anger.

Kai winces and presses his hand briefly to his chest, "She's pissed," he murmurs to me.

"WHILE I WAS UNCONSCIOUS? YOU HAD SOMEONE TOUCHING MY BODY WHILE I WAS UNCONSCIOUS?"

Hudson's gripping her tight around the middle and upper body as she struggles to get away from him and go after Brooks. She's putting up a decent fight, too. I'm actually impressed, given that I've worked out with Hudson and I know how strong he is.

"Listen, Sloane, we didn't know what happened to you. We didn't have any information, nothing to go on and we couldn't exactly ask you. Dr. Mason wanted to examine you anyway, before assigning you a room, so WE," Brooks stresses the 'we, "decided to ask her to do an internal exam and make sure that you hadn't been violated."

Sloane stops struggling.

"You were in on it," she asks over her shoulder, narrowing her eyes at Hudson.

"We agreed on it, yes. We didn't want you to wake up with us, naked and in heat, if you'd been raped. We would have kept you sedated and dealt with the consequences."

"Huh," she sits back in Hudson's lap, seeming to relax right before slamming her elbow back into his stomach.

"Oof, fuck," he wheezes, trapping her against him, "you're a violent little thing. I love it."

He nuzzles into her neck from behind, while she crosses her arms and ignores him.

"Maybe later you can choke me, too," he mutters against her shoulder, purring.

"Pervert," she snaps, but I can see her face softening.

"It wasn't an easy choice, Sloane," Kai finally deciding to add his two cents, "but we wanted to make sure you were okay. If you're that mad, then you need to be mad at all of us."

She sighs, "I'm not really mad, just a knee jerk reaction, you know. I appreciate you looking out for me, even if the idea of it makes me uncomfortable."

"Now that we've got that all straight," I smile at her, "you want to tell us everything?"

"Honestly, there's not much. They kept me locked up in a state room most of the time. The whole idea was that they were going to trade me to Egor and his pack in exchange for them to have a new life set up somewhere. Egor planned on keeping me and breeding me."

Kai tenses up beside me, a growl rumbling from his chest. Hudson growls low, yanking Sloane down against him and tightening the blanket around her again. Brooks snarls so loud, I flinch back from him for just a moment.

"Fuck," Hudson spits, "I'll fucking kill him!"

"Hudson, I need to breathe," Sloane squeaks and he immediately loosens his grips.

"Sorry, baby."

"It's okay, I know you're upset. Nothing happened, though. I didn't go fully into heat until he was already off the boat anyway. His plan was to have me taken to an airstrip and then flown south to his estate on the coast. With the travel time, I would have been completely out of my mind once I was there. But you got to me in time and I'm okay."

"They didn't do anything to you," Brooks asks.

"Nothing serious, mostly just threats and insinuations about what they would eventually do to me. Like I said, I was locked up most of the time."

"If that's the case, then why would they be so keen to get her back? She's obviously gone through her heat, so they wouldn't be able to use that to get her to comply. She's very likely pregnant already by one of you," I wonder aloud.

"Not to mention that they literally kidnap omegas for a living. If they want to breed so bad, they know how to get them," Hudson adds, "I know our girl is special, but if she was just meant to be payment, well, they didn't have to put up anything anyway, since Ricci has them now."

"He did like that I was, um, feisty. He mentioned, several times, that he liked that I had fight, that I would breed strong sons."

"Yeah you will," Hudson mutters, biting her neck before sliding his hands under the blanket.

"Hey! Hands to yourself, mister, we're having a serious conversation here. Need to be prepared if they really are going to come after me," she laughs, pushing at his hands and trying to get him back on track.

"Okay, let's set up a meeting with Ricci and the rest. They want to see her anyway and we can talk face to face, get more information," Brooks looks to me, "you want to go to the compound or have them come to the warehouse?"

"Wherever you think is best, I'll make do."

"No, I want you to be comfortable. If you think you can hack it at the compound for a few hours, we'll go there once you're discharged and then head home. If you'd rather go right home, then we can have Ricci come to us. You are what's important in this equation, Simon."

"Let's just go to the warehouse," Sloane smiles at me, "Simon should be home where he's most comfortable. Dad and Marco and the others can make the drive for once."

"Yeah, I think I'd just like to go home," I agree, smiling back.

"Great, now that that's all settled, I'm going back to sleep," Sloane announces, pushing up from Hudson's lap.

"You can sleep right here, with me, baby," Hudson reaches for her, trying to pull her back.

"Hell no, recliners are for losers. I'm sleeping with Simon and Kai. A hospital bed is still a bed and better than this," she says, waving her arms at Hudson and Brooks.

Hudson makes a grab for her again, but she just laughs and skips across the room to climb up next to Kaiser. He lifts her over his body, bringing her down between the two of us, but still on his bed. She smiles up at me, her eyes sparkling with happiness and love.

I smile back at her, "You heard the lady, it's bedtime. I'm sure we can all use the extra sleep."

I close my laptop and push the hospital table to the side before pushing the button to recline the head of the bed. Once I'm semi reclined and I have my pillows tucked around me to keep me from rolling my sleep, I click the overhead lights off. Hudson gets up to pull the curtains over the windows that look out onto the ward.

I reach my hand out to Sloane, smiling into the dark when her fingers curl around mine.

"Goodnight," I say to the room, my heart warm and full as they all echo it back.

CHAPTER SIXTEEN

Sloane

"I am not leaving this room, Simon Costa. Whatever this thing is with your attitude and being hot and cold with wanting me around, get over it because I'm not going anywhere!"

He continues to study the surface of the hospital bed table. Apparently, the ugly faux wood grain is more interesting than anything I have to say. He puffs out a sigh, drumming his fingers on his thigh like he's the one who's frustrated and not me.

"Simon, you need to talk to her because this is getting childish," Kai calls from across the room.

He and Brooks are working on gathering all of the supplies and clothes that have ended up here over the past several days. Hudson already took the laptop and monitors down to the car, now we're just waiting for the doctor to come in and remove the staples.

Simon keeps telling me to go down to the car with Hudson, to ride back to the warehouse and wait for him there. I can't imagine leaving his side. For the past week I've thought he was dead and now it's like a miracle having him back, in front of me, breathing. I'm keeping my eyes on him as long as I can.

"I'm not squeamish, you should know this by now. Whatever you think you're trying to save me from seeing, let it go, please," I plead, sliding my fingers through his and squeezing his hand.

He doesn't squeeze back, though. His hand stays rigid in mine, like he's fighting the urge to pull away from me or something.

"Simon, you're hurting her, which means you're pissing me off. If you don't talk to her, I'll have Hudson do it. I'm sure you'd love that," Brooks tells him pointedly.

"Fine, it's fine, okay, you can stay," Simon blurts out right as Dr. Seymur comes into the room, a small tray in hand.

"Good morning folks, how is everyone this morning? You ready to go home?"

"Absolutely, doc," Simon replies, "let's get this over with so I can sleep in my own bed."

Dr. Seymur chuckles, "Yes, I'm sure you're looking forward to that. Just remember, nothing too vigorous okay? Generally we recommend that you wait until about four weeks to resume sexual activities, but if you're careful and he or she does all the work, it's safe after about 10. Just make sure not to do anything that will aggravate your wound, if it hurts stop immediately."

I can feel the heat suffuse my face. I will never get used to how casually everyone discusses my sex life.

"Don't worry, doc, I'll keep them in line," Kai tells him, "but we gotta get him outta here first, so what needs to be done?"

I send my gratitude through the bond and he smiles back at me. Having true mates who can feel your emotions is quite convenient at times. Although I'm sure the fire engine red blush streaking across my face would have signaled anyone anyway.

"Yes, of course. The paperwork has all been signed, his prescriptions were sent to the pharmacy downstairs. We just need to get these staples out and he's free to go."

"Let me help you," I murmur, sliding my hands under Simon's t-shirt and tugging it gently over his head. I lay the shirt on the side table and take his hand again. This time, he actually wraps his fingers around mine.

I don't know what his deal is, but I'm going to get to the bottom of it eventually. Just not here, preferably when we're alone and he's actually ready to talk to me instead of one of the others pushing him to it.

Seymur removes the gauze wrap, then reclines the bed so Simon is almost completely on his back. There's a strip of surgical tape down the center of his chest, covering the incision and the staples holding it together. His chest is littered with healing bruises, a patchwork of yellows and greens where they performed CPR, used a defibrillator to bring him back.

Kai had told me exactly what happened, but seeing it up close and personal is staggering. The fact that he pushed through all of this, refusing to rest in order to get me back makes my heart swell.

"If you could feel her now, Simon," Kai tells him quietly, "she's glowing for you, man."

"True mates," Dr. Seymur asks Kai, as he slowly peels the tape off the wound.

"Yeah, just waiting for Simon to recover enough that I can bring him into the fold."

"My wife and I are true mates, one in a million chance. Met her on a field rotation during Doctors Without Borders. She was a nurse from Greece, assigned to the same tiny village in Cameroon. Been together 32 years now. This might pinch a little, but if it really hurts, let me know," he tells Simon as he positions the staple remover at the top of the incision.

Simon nods and Dr. Seymur pops the first staple out. Two small beads of blood well where the prongs were embedded, but no reaction from Simon. I kiss his knuckles gently, still holding his hand while Dr. Seymur works down his chest.

"Has your link evolved over the years," Brooks asks, tone laced with the same curiosity I can feel curling through the bond.

"It has, actually, quite a bit. It's probably been a decade or so since any major changes, but in the beginning we could only share feelings, sense how each other was feeling and send feelings across. Eventually we were able to send single words, impressions of where we were or what we were doing. Now, as long as we're within a certain proximity, we can actually communicate pretty effectively just using the bond. And I always know where she is, could find her even if I was blind."

"Amazing," I whisper, "I've read about it, of course, learned about it in the Academy, but I've never actually met someone who's experienced it."

"This is going to sting," Dr. Seymur tells Simon before wiping down his chest with an alcohol pad. Simon hisses between his teeth, his hand tightening in mine.

"I've heard it can be even more intense when it's a group. My wife and I, just the two of us. If the link is supported between more people it's supposed to be stronger and more easily developed. Science hasn't found the end to what can be accomplished between true mate bonds," Seymur adds, moving the head of the bed back into a sitting position and helping Simon swing his legs off the side of the bed.

Simon reaches for his shirt, holding it against his chest like a shield, head bowed "Can we get this covered up. Just get my shirt on, please."

"Of course, I'm sorry, here," I reach for the shirt and when I pull it away, he flinches. From me.

"Simon," I whisper, hurt coloring my words.

"I'm sorry, just please, please," he whispers, and I see a tear drop on his clenched fists.

Kai shuffles me aside gently, Brooks pulling me into his arms, "I'll finish up here. We'll meet you down at the car. Brooks will take care of you, Sloane."

Kai kisses me gently on the forehead before blocking my view of Simon and Brooks tugs me toward the door. I watch over my shoulder as Kai kneels down in front of Simon, holding him gently while Simon's head rests on his shoulder and he cries.

The door shuts behind us, blocking them from view and my heart twists in my chest.

"It's okay, *tesoro*, it's not you. He has some shit he needs to deal with and, until he does, he's going to struggle."

He loops one arm around my shoulders, tucking me under his arm and leading me toward the elevators. His phone starts ringing just before we step in, so he pauses to pull it out. Smirking, he shows me the screen before answering it.

"She's fine," he tells Hudson, "just a little misunderstanding. We're headed down to you now."

We step into the elevator as he responds, "Yeah, it's just Simon and his new found baggage."

I can hear Hudson speaking on the other end, but can't make out his words.

"I told him if he didn't discuss it with her, then I would let you talk to her about it."

"No, you can't tell her now. No. You need to give him time to talk to her. I don't know, like a week?"

They keep going back and forth while the elevator descends. I rest my head against Brooks' chest, listening to his heart thumping under my ear and soothing myself with the love I feel through the mating link.

I wish I knew what Simon's issues were. I can't fix them if I don't know the problem. I wish he was healed enough that Kai could mate him already, bring him into the link so that he could just feel everything.

It's just about impossible to suffer miscommunication when you can literally feel everyone in the group.

The elevator slides open and Hudson is waiting on the other side. He drags me against him, pinning my arms to my sides as he nuzzles his cheek against mine. He drags his tongue down the side of my neck before planting a kiss on each of my mating marks.

"You okay, little omega?"

"I'm sure Brooks told you I was," resting my chin against his chest I smile up at him, "just as I'm sure you can tell that I'm okay."

"Not totally okay. Simon's being a real dick and I don't like it."

"Not on purpose. At least, I don't think it's on purpose. None of you idiots will tell me anything, but from what I've overheard he's having some personal issues he needs to work through. So, even though it hurts, I'll put up with it until he can talk to me about it."

"Or until I'm fed up with him and tell you myself," Hudson mutters, pulling me toward the car and helping me into the front seat.

"Ooh, shotgun, must be my lucky day."

"Nah," he laughs, reaching across to buckle me in, "I just wanna hold your hand for the drive."

"More like you don't want me holding her hand. Or anything else, while you're driving," Brooks snarks, climbing into the seat behind me.

"Can you blame me? It's distracting!"

"Does Kai have the keys already or are we waiting for them to come down?"

"Nah, Kai has the keys. We can head over to the warehouse and they can meet us there once they make it down here.

"Sounds good, let's go."

"You know, at some point we're going to need to move my things to the warehouse. I need my clothes, makeup, pictures. You know, stuff."

"We stocked your bathroom with all of your favorites and we did move some of your clothes there in anticipation of you moving in," Brooks replies, "but yes, we will have to make time to move the rest of your stuff."

"We have to make time to get you some new clothes, too. Won't be able to squeeze into those sexy little outfits for much longer," Hudson winks as he throws the car in reverse and heads out of the parking garage.

"We don't even know for sure if I'm pregnant," I smile at him, squeezing his hand.

"Baby, we stuffed you like a cream filled donut. There is no way that you made it through that without eating for a bun in the oven."

I burst out laughing.

"I think you have your euphemisms mixed up, there," I tell him.

"Whatever, you're knocked up. I don't need a fancy test to tell me that. I do need a fancy test to tell me if it's mine though, probably. Maybe he'll just come out handsome as his pops and we'll know he belongs to me."

"Does it really matter, though," I ask, brushing off the niggling worry that he might actually want me to take a paternity test.

"Of course not," he hurriedly adds, "that little guy belongs to all of us. Don't worry, baby, I'm gonna love him no matter who he comes out looking like. I just want to be able to tell everyone that my cum is king."

"Jesus christ," Brooks mutters from the back.

"What? Kai got her just as many times as I did, you were in there once. Just want to prove that my swimmers are supreme."

"For crying out loud," I laugh, "can we at least wait until we're sure I'm pregnant before you start shouting from the rooftops how virile you are?"

"I am so virile, baby," he pulls my hand to his mouth, nibbling my fingers, "I am going to show you just how virile I am as soon as we get home. Gotta christen every room we can, starting with my bedroom."

"Not so fast, beefcake. Morris, Marco and the rest are coming over to discuss the situation with Volkov. You don't have time to christen anything," Brooks cuts in, "you'll be too busy whipping up something for a late lunch."

"Fuck man, come on. We can order in!"

"Hudson, I'm moving in. We can christen whatever we want whenever we want after we deal with my father. I'm not going anywhere, beefcake."

"Okay, no, that's not it. You gotta pick something else, baby, that's not gonna fly."

I cackle at the serious look on his face. Like I would really walk around calling him beefcake. I roll my eyes as he pulls into the parking garage under the warehouse.

"I'll help you cook, hot stuff," I smile, "then you can pick whatever spot in the house you want to fuck me, once everyone is gone."

I feel my cheeks heat even though I fight it. With everything we've done together, you'd think I could talk dirty to my mate, but apparently my body hasn't gotten the memo yet.

"Deal, except no on the hot stuff. Keep working on it, baby, you'll find something."

We climb out of the car together, Brooks going around to open the rear and unload all the junk they brought back from the hospital.

"You," Brooks says, shoving two bags at Hudson, "can go put this stuff back in the basement. Then meet us upstairs."

"That's bullshit! Why do I have to go to the basement?"

"You know exactly why, now go to it," he hands him the monitor and points to the elevator.

I smile and push up on my tiptoes so I can give him a little kiss on the nose.

"You're cruel," he tells Brooks, waiting as we grab the rest of the bags and follow him to the elevator.

"And you're unbearable," Brooks retorts.

Hudson gets off the elevator at the next floor up, leaning in to give me a smacking kiss and promising he'll see me soon. Brooks and I stay on, up to the main floor.

It hasn't been that long since I've been here, but it feels like coming home. I can scent all of the men as soon as we exit, their unique pheromones mixing in such a way that it immediately calms me. The scents are a little stale, but embedded everywhere. Brooks loops his arm around my shoulders, pulling me close and kissing me on the forehead.

"I love you, Sloane Ricci, soon to be Conti. Welcome home."

"You know you still need to ask me, right? Properly. With a ring. And it better be romantic."

"Everything you want, *piccoletta*, always," he smiles down at me before tugging me close and leading me down the hallway toward their private wings. I remember heading this way when Simon took me to his room to shower, but I'm not 100% sure how the set up goes back here.

Last time I was here my tour got cut short. I know the common areas, the middle level with the gym and indoor pool, the movie room and the wine cellar in the basement. I know the kitchen and dining room, the sitting area from the first time I came here. I never got to see their suites or my rooms. My nest.

"Hey, what's going on in that head of yours. This is a happy day for us, *tesoro*."

"I know, I was just thinking about the last time I was here, that I never got the full tour or the chance to see my rooms and nest. And now, if I am pregnant, I'm not going to get to use it for a long time."

Brooks drops his bag on the floor and tugs me into his arms. He cuddles me close, rubbing his cheek against the top of my head. He starts purring quietly, flooding me with love.

"You're here and you're safe. We're all together. We have the rest of our lives to use that nest, Sloane. Besides, Simon will be healed by the time you're cycling again, so we'll all be able to christen it together, the way it was meant to be all along."

"You're right, I know," I tell him, voice muffled as I nuzzle my face into his chest, "but I'm still allowed to be sad about it."

"I don't want you to ever be sad, *piccoletta*, especially if there's something I can do to fix it."

"You can't stop me from being sad," I laugh, pulling away and reaching down to hand him back his bag and get him moving again.

"I'm sure I can try. And I will. I don't like it. No one else is going to like it either, so be prepared for all that."

"What about when I'm going through crazy pregnancy hormone spikes and there's no good reason for me to be sad? You can't fix something that's just wonky biology."

"We'll deal with it when and if that happens," he smiles, pushing open a door and ushering me in.

The room is obviously Brooks, his scent the strongest, though old. I guess no one has been spending much time here, so that makes sense.

The room is overly masculine, but streamlined and modern at the same time. The sitting area consists of two low slung couches with a chrome and glass topped coffee table. There's a small bar area in the corner along with a basic kitchenette.

The bed dominates the other room. A towering four poster, California king. The posts are thick, dark wood that match the dresser and wardrobe. There's a small office area tucked in the corner between two doors, which I assume lead to the closet and bathroom.

"Well," he asks, "what do you think?"

"It's very you," I smile, "dark and broody, but sturdy and reliable."

"I do not brood."

"I'm very sure you do," I walk toward him slowly, still smiling.

He opens his arms when I get close, letting me slide my arms around his waist before holding me close. I press up against him, kissing his chin and jaw until he tilts his head down and catches my lips with his.

I moan softly when his tongue slips past my lips and explores my mouth slowly. He slides one hand into my hair, rubbing the back of my scalp while keeping me tucked in close with the arm still around my waist.

"I knew it, you fucker," Hudson yells from the doorway, scaring the shit out of me.

"Hudson! Don't sneak around like that," I yell back.

"I didn't mean to scare you, little omega," he stalks into the room, spinning me away from Brooks, "forgive me?"

He starts kissing all over my face and neck, muttering "sorry" after each peck. I can't help but laugh.

"Fine, fine, you're forgiven. Don't do it again, though!"

"I won't, promise. I don't like feeling you scared, little omega," he presses his face into my neck, licking at his mating mark.

"Don't start," I admonish, "we don't have time, Brooks said so."

I moan when he bites down, sucking on the mark.

"We really don't, Simon and Kai are back, plus we still need to figure out lunch. Ricci is going to be here in less than an hour."

Hudson hums against my neck, gripping my ass cheeks and walking me backwards toward Brooks bed. One of his hands creeps between my thighs from behind, cupping my pussy through my leggings. I moan again when he presses against my clit.

"Alright, nope," Brooks slides in behind Hudson, pushing one arm between us, pinning Hudson's arm to his side. He breaks his grip, then twists him away from me, popping him in the back of the knee and taking him to the ground, face down.

Brooks stands up, slapping Hudson hard on the ass before tugging me around him and trying to make it out the door. Before we take two steps, Hudson's arm shoots out and wraps around Brooks ankle, yanking hard so Brooks drops to his knees.

"Shit," Brooks manages to choke out as he falls.

Luckily, he let go of me and didn't take me down with him. I back toward the door, giving them room to wrestle around, but keeping an eye on them at the same time.

Hudson uses the grip on his leg to pull him down further, climbing on top of him and then sitting on his back. He leans forward, wrapping one of his arm around Brooks' throat and giving him a noogie.

"Take that, bitch," Hudson grunts as he digs his knuckles into Brooks' skull.

Brooks grunts, rocking his hips until he has enough momentum to roll Hudson off him and onto his side.

"You forget, I know your weakness," Brooks taunts, kneeling on one wrist, while reaching across his body to pin the other. With his free hand, he starts tickling Hudson's sides.

"Fuck, no, stop, uncle, uncle," Hudson pants, twitching and bucking, trying his best to get away, but not able to coordinate his limbs like he wants.

I can't help but laugh at their antics. I love the relationship they have with each other and I'm so happy to be a part of it. Watching them act like this, still being able to enjoy such simple things and act so ridiculous makes me realize how great they will be with children.

Being a mother this young was definitely not on my agenda, but at least if I am pregnant, I'll be going through it with them. The fact that we're true mates pretty much guarantees that I am pregnant right now, since we're perfectly matched on every level.

I smile softly, imagining what a baby of ours would look like. Would he be tall like Kai? Funny like Hudson? Smart like Simon? Bossy like Brooks? Does it matter? As long as he's happy, he can be any or all of those things.

I blink myself out of my reverie, realizing that Brooks and Hudson are still on the floor, both staring at me.

"What are you thinking about, *piccoletta*," Brooks asks softly.

"So intense, little omega, so beautiful. What's on your mind?"

I smile at them both, turning and stepping into the hall. I glance over my shoulder at them, "I like Sebastian if it's a boy, Ophelia for a girl."

I feel their shock, then surprise through the bond. Then the same warm and intense love they must have felt from me. The feeling is quickly overshadowed by intense desire, dominance, and self satisfaction. Hudson clearly likes the idea that he knocked me up.

"Don't even think about it," Brooks yells before I hear a thump and more sounds of them struggling.

I laugh, finding my way back to the kitchen and checking the food situation. Nothing fresh which isn't a surprise. There's a lot of frozen meat, which doesn't help since I have less than an hour now to throw something together.

I check the pantry, finding some dried pasta and jarred sauces, but not much else suitable for feeding a group.

Judging by the shelves in here, they like to snack a lot. Chips, Pop Tarts, cookies, instant noodles, and various other highly processed junk.

I step back out into the kitchen, just in time to see Kai come around the corner behind Simon.

"I'm perfectly capable of walking around by myself, you don't have to babysit me."

"I just want to make sure you get yourself situated okay, that's all."

"I know, and I love you for it, but I need to be able to do things on my own."

Simon pauses halfway across the room once he finally sees me standing there. He smiles awkwardly, standing frozen on the other side of the island.

I clear my throat and give him back a brief smile before turning to Kai, "Can I use your phone? There's not much food here, so I'm going to call and have some stuff delivered."

"Of course, *cara*," he tells me, walking around the island to hand me the phone before scooping me into his arms and holding me bridal style before whispering, "don't be sad, baby. Everything will be okay."

I nod against his chest, sniffling up any tears, refusing to let them fall. I know Simon isn't hurting me on purpose, but it does still hurt. Kai holds me until I've got myself together and I plant a light kiss on his cheek once he drops me back to my feet.

Simon made his way to the sitting room and got himself into a chair while Kai was comforting me. He's currently trying to pull his legs up onto the ottoman without bending over.

"Please go help him before he hurts himself," I murmur, sending my love straight down the link to him.

He kisses me on the forehead before crossing the room to help Simon.

I use his phone to dial Marcino's Deli and Grocer. They deliver groceries to the compound every week and Eli Marcino happens to love me. I went to school with his son and defended him aggressively when he started getting bullied for being gay.

"Hi Monica, it's Sloane Ricci, is Eli there?"

"Oh, hi Sloane! I heard you were back home! How's life as an omega?"

"I would love to tell you all about it, Monica, but I'm in a pinch and I need some stuff delivered as soon as humanly possible."

"Of course, of course, I'm so sorry! Let me get him."

I give Eli a rundown of everything I need. Not just stuff for lunch today, but enough to make a quick dinner later and a few days worth of basic fixins'. Hudson and Brooks come in while I'm talking, giving me kisses before moving into the sitting area with Simon and Kai.

"The warehouse on Easton and Bay. Have Benny call this number when he gets close, I'm not sure where he should deliver. Thanks again, Eli! You're a lifesaver."

"Anything for you, *figlia*. He'll be there in ten."

I walk across the room and hand Kai his phone before plopping down on the couch next to him, "You'll get a call in about 10 minutes from Benny. He's the delivery guy, just let him know where to park and he'll bring everything in."

"Sounds like a plan," he replies, draping an arm around me and tucking me against his side, "hopefully they'll get here before your pops. We'll look like a bunch of assholes, inviting them here with nothing to offer."

"Papa won't care," I smile, "he knows you guys have been taking care of me, that Simon was in the hospital. Knowing him, he's probably bringing a bunch of crap with him."

"Hopefully some of those salads the chef made for lunch the other day. That cold pasta with the peas and the white sauce? Amazing," Hudson says, "Think it's too late to actually ask for some of that?"

"Yes" I laugh, "they're definitely on their way by now. Next time we go over I'll make sure that Isa makes some for you, okay?"

"We do need to schedule some time for you to get over there and pack up your stuff. Do you think you'll need a moving truck? Or will we be able to move everything?"

"Honestly, I'm not sure how much I would even bring over here. Since I don't know what my suite looks like," I stare pointedly at Brooks, "I don't know what I can fit."

"Don't worry, *tesoro*, we'll make sure you get the full tour this time including your room and the nest. I'm sure you'll have plenty of room to bring over everything you need."

"I have a lot of clothes. And shoes. Jewelry, purses - a lot of purses. Bathing suits and pajamas and -"

"Trust me, little omega," Hudson interrupts, "it will all fit. I've seen your current closet and your new rooms. Whatever you want to bring will fit in there. Guaranteed."

I narrow my eyes at him.

"Don't be so impatient," Kai says, shaking me gently before dragging me up onto his lap, "you'll see it soon enough and you'll love it."

"Fine," I huff, just as I see Kai's phone light up on the arm of the couch.

"It's Benny," I say, just as he answers.

"Yeah, not a problem, head north on Easton, there's a pull around, I'll meet you there….there's a freight elevator if we need it….how much," Kai asks, jerking around to eyeball me.

I shrug, "We needed food."

"Okay, I'll bring another guy down with me. Thanks," he hangs up the phone, "what the hell did you order, *cara*?"

"Enough," a retort, bracing my fists on my hips, "we all need to eat and Simon needs a lot of protein to help heal and I like fresh fruit for breakfast."

"I love it when you're sassy, little omega," Hudson whispers against my neck, sneaking up behind me and wrapping his arms around my waist, "makes me wanna fuck it right out of you."

"Is there anything I do that turns you off," I ask.

"Nope, not a thing."

"Alright, Hudson go with Kai to help with the food. Her family is going to be here soon and we don't need your pheromones floating around choking everyone," Brooks directs.

"Ugh, you suck," Hudson complains before following Kai out toward the elevator.

"Brooks, would you mind, giving us a few minutes," Simon asks quietly, the first words he's uttered since we all sat down together.

"Of course, I'll go follow them down, wait for your dad down there," Brooks smiles at me, brushing a kiss across my cheek before heading toward the elevator with the others.

I turn back toward Simon, hoping he's going to share his feelings with me, giving him an awkward half smile before taking Kai's seat on the couch. I tuck my feet up under me and lean against the arm of the couch, giving my full attention to Simon.

He clears his throat, looking anywhere but directly at me. His hands, the ottoman, the window across the room.

"Ah, okay, this is…really hard for me," he clears his throat again, "hard to admit that I might not be good enough or that I might not fit in…"

He trails off and I want to refute what he has to say. I want to argue with him, tell him that he fits perfectly with me, with us. He's more than good enough for me and I love him so much. But I bite my tongue. I know he needs to get this out, so I watch him and wait.

"I know, um, that I'm not an alpha, I don't have all the extras, so to speak. Just, ah, plain old Simon, you know," he chuckles in a self deprecating way, glancing at me out of the corner of his eye, still staring out the window.

"And now, you know, I couldn't even save you from being taken and all I have to show for it is this hideous new scar. I can't even stand to look at it, so I'm sure that it's even worse for you."

"Simon-" I try to interject.

"Just let me, let me get it out, okay? I'm just going to, ah, you know, I'm not good enough for you and I get that. I know that. And having you just, you're so nice to me, all the time. Even now that I fucked up so bad with letting you get taken. And I think that you're trying to convince yourself to, um, love me. Like you have to take me in too, because of them, because of Kai. And I just want you to know that, you don't have to-"

"I'm going to stop you right there," I seethe, biting my tongue no longer working, "you do not get to tell me how I feel. Or assume to know how I feel. I don't even know where to begin with all of the garbage that just came out of your mouth."

I shake my head, angry and frustrated and hurt.

"You think so little of me, Simon? That I'm so shallow I could only ever want an alpha? That everything I've said to you up to this point is a lie, that I would lie about my feelings for you?"

"That's not what I was trying-"

"Stop. Just stop. I don't know what your problem is, but based on the crap you just spouted, I'm going to assume you have some serious self image issues you need to work on," I'm on my feet now, on the verge of shouting, "none of which has anything to do with me!"

I stalk closer to him, wanting him to see my anger and hurt, since he can't feel it like the others.

Tears stream down my face that I barely notice as I continue, "Don't you dare try to tell me how I feel. You don't know and if you keep this shit up, you never will. I love you, Simon Costa. I love you just as much as I love Hudson and Brooks and Kai, but I'm not going to let you keep hurting me like this. It's not fair to me and it's not fair to them because they have to feel it."

"Sloane," he pleads quietly, lifting a hand as if he might reach for me.

"Until you figure your feelings out, leave me alone," I turn away from him, the first sob escaping from my tight chest. I stumble around the coffee table and out into the hallway, tracing my steps back to Brooks' suite, since I know it's the closest one.

Remembering the layout, I cross the room in the dark. I climb into his monstrous bed, burrowing under the covers on the far side. I know it's only a matter of time until one or all of the others come for me, but I'm going to stay right here for as long as I can and just let the anger and tears flow.

CHAPTER SEVENTEEN

Simon

I struggle to push myself up from the chair, wishing I had picked one of the hardback ones instead. Just as I finally push upright with a grunt, Brooks comes stalking back through the kitchen.

"What the fuck did you do, Simon," he growls at me, baring his teeth.

I'm so focused on getting to Sloane that his threat barely registers.

"I'm going to fix it," I mutter, "I just have to find her."

"What did you do," he asks again, calmer now but no less angry.

"I tried to talk to her, okay? Tell her how I was feeling, my fears and struggles, but it got away from me. I-I-I told her that she didn't have to be with me, that I knew she didn't really want me."

"You've gotta be fucking kidding me," Brooks pinches the bridge of his nose, "Good luck fixing that, is all I have to say. She's…I can't even describe how she's feeling right now. And right before her dad is supposed to be here? Could you have fucked the situation anymore?"

"I know I fucked it up, okay, but I didn't mean it. I just have to find her-"

"No," he cuts me off, "no you're going to leave her alone right now. Morris and Marco are going to be here any minute and we need to discuss Volkov. We don't have time to deal with your shit on top of that right now."

"I'm sorry Brooks, I, it just, it got away from me."

"You said that already, doesn't make it better. Go back and sit down, I'll find Sloane. Hudson and Kai are on their way up with the groceries. I don't know what her plan was for feeding everyone, but I'm sure they can figure something out. That is assuming they don't strangle you first."

"Please tell her I'm sorry," I whisper, horrified at myself, stumbling back into the sitting room.

I gingerly settle back into one of the high back chairs next to the fireplace. Not the most comfortable thing to sit in, but easier for me to get in and out of on my own. I thump my head back against the headrest, hating myself even more, if that were possible.

I don't know what's wrong with me, why I can't just get past these feelings. I want to listen to what the others have to say, to believe that Sloane really does love me and wants to be with me, but something in my head just keeps telling me I'm not good enough.

I'm not man enough because I'm not an alpha. I don't have a knot, I don't purr. I had to have Kai explain to me how to eat her pussy for fuck's sake. Not to mention the fact that I haven't topped in a long ass time, so I would probably shoot my load as soon as I got my dick in.

Fuck. I need to redirect. I can't just sit here and wait or my stupid insecurities will take over completely and I won't be able to function.

I push myself back up, even though Brooks basically ordered me to sit and relax. It's much easier this time, the hardback and seat giving me a more stable base to push up from. I was actually listening when she ordered and I know that she's having premade salads and pasta delivered in addition to the groceries.

I go into the kitchen and preheat the oven so we can keep the pasta warm until everyone is ready to eat. I pull down plates and cups from the hutch, setting them up on the island so we can form a self-serve kind of food line once we're ready.

I'm just laying out the silverware on the table when I hear Kai and Hudson come off the elevator. Instead of just carrying bags like I thought, Hudson is actually pushing one of the small garage carts piled high with containers and bags. Kai has three or four bags in each hand.

"I guess we won't have to worry about food for awhile," I quip as Hudson pushes the cart around the island toward the oven.

"Yeah," Kai agrees, barely looking at me, "she knows we like to eat."

Hudson doesn't reply at all. Doesn't even acknowledge that I spoke to him.

"I started the oven, so we could keep things warm until everyone is here. And got the table set, plates out. Should

I go down and get wine? Or is it too early? I would need someone to tell me what to get, you know I can't pick out wine to save my life. Or maybe we should just stick to water and whatever."

I finally manage to stop myself from rambling. Hudson still won't look at me, moving to the refrigerator to put away the other containers. Kai half smiles at me, shaking his head and emptying the bags he's carrying into the pantry.

"Please," my voice cracks, "I didn't mean to. I tried to fix it, Brooks wouldn't let me. I don't know what's wrong with me, but I can't lose you, too. Either of you."

Kai steps out of the pantry, taking in my reddening eyes and pathetic attempt to keep the tears at bay. Hudson finally looks at me, though his face is decidedly blank.

"You really hurt her, asshole. Like, really fucking bad. I can't even describe the combination of pain and sadness and anger that she had, but I can tell you that I really didn't like it. I can also tell you that, if it wasn't you who made her feel that way, I would kill the fucker who did," Hudson fumes.

"I love you so much Simon, you know that. You trust that. Why can't you trust it from her? Or when I tell you it's real? Because I can guarantee you that she loves you just as much as she loves the rest of us. You're destroying something so beautiful and you're going to end up miserable for it," Kai says softly.

"If you keep it up, she won't forgive you. WE won't forgive you. Get your shit together and talk to her. Really, actually talk to her. Fix this, man," Hudson pleads.

As we stare at each other across the expanse of the kitchen, the distant sound of a door closing lets us know that at least Brooks is on his way back. Hopefully he convinced Sloane to come with him and hopefully she doesn't totally fucking hate me.

I suck it up and turn toward the opposite entryway, waiting to see who's going to come through the door. At the same time, the interior alert goes off, letting us know that someone has entered the vestibule downstairs. Brooks steps into the sitting room from the opposite side, Sloane tucked up under his arm, hair disheveled and face blotchy and red.

She's drowning in one of Brooks' old hoodies. The sleeves rolled and bunched up at her wrists, the hem hanging almost to her knees. She's so painfully adorable that it only strikes that much harder when she won't meet my eye.

"Assuming that's Morris and guests, I'll go show them up," Kai says, stepping past me to draw Sloane into his arms for a brief moment. He murmurs something in her ear, kissing her tenderly before heading out the opposite door to the elevator.

"Did you get the pasta in the oven to warm," Sloane rasps, heading toward Hudson who's now pulling out all the salads he put in the refrigerator to begin with.

"I did, little omega," he pulls her against him, rubbing his chin against the top of her head, "everything is taken care of, just go snuggle up on the couch or wait for your pops to show, okay? We got this."

"Okay," she sniffles a little, "Love you."

"And I love you, baby," he spins her around and lays a smacking kiss right on her mouth, before continuing to make overly obnoxious noises as he plants kisses across her cheeks, forehead and face until she's giggling and pushing him away.

She turns toward the door to head out to the elevator and Hudson smacks her ass so hard she jumps and hisses at him.

"Just trying to keep you on your toes, baby," he winks at her.

"How is she," I ask Brooks quietly when he comes to stand next to me.

"How does she look," he retorts, "because that's about as good as she feels."

"Fuck," I mutter.

"You're going to fix this and you're going to do it tonight. I don't care what it takes, open up every dark door you've got, but we can't be divided like this, especially now."

"I-I can do that. I will do that."

"Good," he says, stepping away and heading toward the door. No doubt wanting to greet Morris and the rest as they come off the elevator.

"I just want you to know that I'm throwing you under the bus," Hudson tells me when we hear raised voices coming off the elevator, "besides, he'll be less likely to hit you with your heart and all. Maybe take off your shirt so he can really see the scar."

"Fuck you, dude," I retort, recoiling slightly when Morris stalks into the room, the air practically crackling with his anger and dominance.

"I finally get to see *mia piccola stella,* days she's been home, *voi tienila lontana da me, il suo cuore è spezzato, spiega qualcuno, ADESSO,*" he yells, stopping just shy of the kitchen area so he can look all of us in the face.

"Papa, *fermati! Per favore, lascialo,*" Sloane pleads, tugging on his arm.

"No, *mia figlia,* I know they saved you, but not to turn around and make you sad again. You're home, safe. You should be happy, but look at you. *La tua tristezza gioca con il mio cuore.*"

"Papa, *è maleducato parlare quando non riescono a capire.*"

"I don't care what they understand. If they can't take care of you, they don't deserve you!"

Hudson snarls at Morris, sliding around the island so he can advance on him.

"STOP," Brooks barks, tugging Sloane to him and keeping her squeezed against him, "this isn't helping the situation. If anything, it's making it worse."

Marco steps up to Morris; Remi and Dmitri lingering in the doorway, observing but not looking like they're going to intervene. Kai pushes between them, coming to stand just behind Brooks.

Marco wraps an arm around Morris, "Forgive him, he's not thinking clearly."

"Not thinking clearly, my ass, look at her Marco," he gestures at Sloane, "tell me that's the face of a happy mate."

"Papa-"

"It wasn't one of her mates," I interrupt, "it was me. I'm struggling and I took it out on her. It's my fault. If you want to be angry at someone, be angry at me."

"You're suddenly not one of her mates? I was under the impression that she would be connected to all of you," Morris cocks an eyebrow at me, still glowering.

"I-ah, that is, I'm not an alpha. I can't mate with her. I'm not, um, mated with her, sir," I stammer out, not used to having the full attention of an angry alpha fixed on me.

"Doesn't mean you're not her mate, or that you can get away with shit like this," he points at Sloane for emphasis, "you hurt my baby like that again, Costa, and it won't matter that you just had your chest cracked open, because I'll crack open your skull, yeah?"

"That's enough," Brooks steps forward, "I understand you're upset, but this is our pack, our issue to deal with. If he deserves an ass kicking, one of us will deliver it."

"I didn't know you could speak italian, little omega," Hudson says, pulling a pan of lasagna out of the oven, "you gonna teach me all the dirty words?"

"I'll make you flash cards," Sloane smiles at him, thankful I'm sure, for breaking the tension in the room.

"Let's eat," Brooks adds, directing Sloane toward the kitchen to grab a plate, "I think Sloane ordered half the menu from Marcino's so we should have a lot of options."

I step around the island and start to pull salads out of the fridge while Hudson pulls the rest of the pans out of the oven. Kai steps up behind me, grabbing the salad bowl out of my hands.

"You aren't supposed to be lifting anything, go sit at the table."

"No, I'm not supposed to lift anything over five pounds. That salad is definitely not five pounds."

"Doesn't matter, you're supposed to be relaxing. The better you take care of yourself, the faster you'll recover."

"I can't just sit around doing nothing, Kai, that's not who I am."

"You could have died, Simon. I thought you had," Sloane says quietly from behind us, "please just sit down and stop overexerting yourself. You help enough with your other skills, you don't have to do this, too. Please."

It's the soft plea in her voice that has me stepping back and following Kai's orders to go sit at the table. I don't want to make things worse by pushing my luck right now.

"I'll bring you a plate," she tells me, gently trailing her fingers down my arm as I walk by. It brings me hope that I haven't completely ruined everything. I know I can't keep pushing her away, but I also don't know how to make myself stop.

Everyone else forms a line around the island, helping themselves to the various dishes set out before joining me at the table. Sloane sets a plate down for me before setting her plate down and taking the seat to my right.

"Thank you," I murmur, briefly reaching out to squeeze her hand.

"Can I get anyone a drink? We have water, soda. I can run down to the cellar and get a bottle of wine," Brooks asks.

"Water is fine, we need to keep our heads about us for this discussion," Morris responds.

"Can we get through lunch first, papa, before we have to bring all this up again?"

"Of course, *stellina*," he smiles indulgently at her.

We all focus on eating, the silence occasionally broken with small talk. Remi and Dmitri volunteer to help

Hudson clean up and load the dishwasher while the rest of us move into the sitting area. Sloane helps me back into the comfortable chair, handing me my laptop and iPad before sitting between Brooks and Kai.

Morris and Marco take the opposite couch. I'm a little surprised that they sit together at one end, as opposed to taking each side as I would have thought. I remember Sloane telling us her theory that Marco secretly wanted to be with her father, maybe there's something to that after all.

"Well let's get this show on the road, shall we," Morris starts, "Have you gotten any information out of Petrov?"

"We haven't had a chance to talk to him yet," Brooks replies.

"Who's Petrov," Sloane asks.

"Aleksandr Petrov, one of Volkov's lieutenants," Morris answers, "We secured him onboard the ship and had him transferred to a warehouse to be interrogated. I assumed someone would have taken care of him by now."'

"We had more important things to deal with, Morris, but I can assure you that he's next on the list."

"Aleks," Sloane whispers, shuddering, "he was the one with the dead eyes, Egor said he would hurt me."

The chorus of growls that sound around the room, from Morris and Marco to Hudson and Dmitri in the kitchen, Brooks and Kai. If I was a lesser man, I would probably piss myself at the amount of aggression suddenly pouring into the room.

"Did he touch you, *piccoletta*?"

"No, ah," she clears her throat, "Egor just threatened me, that Aleks was particularly rough while, um, during…sex. That he would hurt me when he got his turn."

"Do you want to tell us what happened, Sloane," Marco asks gently.

"I honestly don't think that it will shed any light on what's happening or what their plan will be. I was locked in a state room most of the time and I only overheard the one conversation they had when we first got onboard."

"I don't think that's why Marco is asking, *cara*," Kai murmurs, "he wants to know if talking will help you process it."

"Oh," Sloane looks at Marco, her eyes glossing over, "thank you, but no. I'm not really ready for that. I mean, if it would help, obviously, but right now, no, that's just not something I want to do. Thank you."

"Okay," he sits back, draping an arm around Morris, "just know that we're all here for you and ready to listen when you're ready to talk."

She nods slightly before burrowing under Kai's arm and pressing her face into his chest, inhaling his scent.

"Let's discuss what Dmitri got out of the others," Brooks cuts in before anyone else can ask Sloane something.

"They were separated during the questioning process. Dmitri worked Otto, then Ben. Let Ben hear everything that happened to Otto, figured it would soften him up a bit," Morris starts.

"And it worked," Dmitri adds from across the room, "before I could even start on him, he was spilling his guts."

"I had Dmitri include everything in the email."

"So now we just have to figure out why they want Sloane so bad and when they're going to make a move. They've got to know we won't keep Petrov alive, so if they want him back, they're going to make a move soon."

"They won't know where he's being held, so that's good for us. We'll be able to keep him under wraps and get all the information we need out of him," Hudson moves around the couch to sit on the other side of Brooks.

"What about Iris," Sloane asks quietly, her voice slightly muffled against Kai's chest, "What did you do with her?"

"We haven't done anything with her, yet. She's going through withdrawals pretty hard, so we're letting her suffer through that before we try to question her," Marco replies quietly.

"And you're going to kill her, right? Once you're done with her," Sloane turns toward her father.

"Yes, *mia figlia*, she'll be disposed of."

Sloane nods, "Good."

Brooks leans over and kisses Sloane on the temple, rubbing her back and murmuring something in her ear. She smiles up at him and I would give anything to have her smile at me like that right now.

"Do we wait for Volkov to make a move or do we go to him," Dmitri asks, standing behind Morris and Marco, arms crossed while Remi takes the chair next to me, "I think that's the most important thing in this equation."

"I say we wait him out," Hudson chimes in, "He's gotta make a move soon if he wants Petrov back, he knows we won't keep him alive. We know this city, we each have cops in our pocket, work crews and packs all around the city. Let him come to us."

"How would he approach? You think he's going to reach out and try to set up a meet or just sneak back into the city," I ask, opening my laptop so I can take notes, since it seems we might start talking about an actual plan soon.

"I don't see him as the sneaking type. Especially if he wants Sloane and Petrov. No, he's either going to reach out or have another pack come to us with an offer, I think," Morris muses, rubbing his chin.

"I want him dead," Sloane says quietly but firmly, "him and Nikolaj and Aleks. I want all of them to suffer."

"That's the plan, *stellina*," Morris assures her.

"We need to put our people on alert. Let them know to keep their ears and eyes open, report anything suspicious, anything having to do with Volkov," Brooks tells me and I quickly pull up my email. I have an encrypted program that I use to send emails to the other packs under us, ensuring that I can be blunt and to the point, and not be concerned that the emails might be used later as evidence.

I put together a quick email, pulling pictures of Volkov and Petruk to attach. I put all our top packs on alert, letting them know to report anything they hear or see that involves them. I also tell them to keep an ear out for anything about kidnapping omegas or other human trafficking.

"Sent," I let Brooks know.

"Hudson and I will go to the Vault tomorrow," Kai looks to Morris, "We'll get everything we can out of Petrov."

"You want some help," Dmitri asks, dead serious.

"Realistically, I probably won't be doing much," Kai responds, "except cleaning up after him. He's got a lot of angst to work out."

Hudson chuckles maniacally, "You are more than welcome to join us, actually. Let me show you how it's done."

"As long as you promise to let me get some in, too," Dmitri replies.

"You got it," Hudson nods, "You can meet us here in the morning, say 10?"

"I'll be here."

"Alright then, I look forward to seeing you work," Hudson smirks.

"So we're on the same page," Marco questions, "we'll wait. See what we get out of Petrov and see what intel we can get from the packs around us."

"In the meantime," Morris cuts in, "you won't let Sloane out of your sight or I'll be bringing her back to the compound."

"You can't take me home like a wayward child, papa."

"I can and I will, *mia figlia*, if they don't keep you safe."

"She's not your responsibility anymore, Morris," Brooks holds up his hand when it looks like Morris is going to argue, "she will always be your daughter, and I respect that, but she's our mate, soon to be wife-"

"Mother of my child," Hudson adds, cheekily.

"And we'll be responsible for her," Brooks finishes, slapping Hudson on the back of head.

"*La mia dolce bambina,*" Morris breathes, "Why didn't you tell me? I'm going to be a *nonno!*"

"Because we don't know for sure," Sloane tries to calm Morris down, "it's too soon to know anything. I haven't had any tests, nothing is confirmed, papa. Don't get ahead of yourself, okay? I promise, you'll be the first person we call once we know for sure."

Morris laughs, clapping Marco on the back, "I'm going to have a grandson!"

Sloane huffs and flops back against Kai, rolling her eyes.

Marco smiles and shakes his head, obviously willing to humor Morris, "Let's leave them to it, then. We can go home and start planning a nursery."

Marco winks at Sloane before standing up and pulling Morris along with him. Everyone else in the room stands except me. The stink eye from Sloane keeps me firmly planted. Everyone exchanges hugs or hand shakes, Dmitri confirming he'll be here at 10 before Brooks walks them to the elevator to escort them out.

Sloane stretches her arms above her head, arching her back and yawning. Hudson slides up behind her and squeezes her in his arms, nuzzling into her neck.

"You tired, little omega?"

"So tired," she yawns again, "I have two days to make up for."

"It was a fun two days, though, you have to admit," Hudson murmurs into her neck, still kissing and nuzzling there.

"Early pregnancy symptoms include fatigue," I add, smiling. The idea of having a baby is daunting to say the least, but amazing at the same time.

"Not you, too," she pouts.

"Statistically speaking, the likelihood of you being pregnant is significant. An omega going through heat without birth control, with compatible mates to service her has a 79% chance of conceiving. Change that to true mates and it changes to 92% chance."

"See? See! Even science is on my side," Hudson exclaims.

"Our side. You don't know it's yours, bro," Kai flicks him in the forehead.

"I had her first, I'm sure that Si can find some statistic that proves it's most likely mine."

Kai lets out an aggrieved sigh, face palms Hudson and pushes him back at the same time he yanks Sloane into his arms. Hudson stumbles back and lands on the couch.

"You're just jealous," Hudson mutters, tucking his arms behind his head and getting comfortable while we wait for Brooks to come back.

"You guys need to get over it," Sloane says, pushing away from Kai and coming to sit next to me, "it doesn't matter who contributed the DNA, you're all going to be fathers."

"You know, I'll love him either way, baby, I just want everyone to know that my swimmer's got the gold medal."

"Get over yourself," she narrows her eyes at him.

"Not a chance, little omega."

"Are we ready for the tour, then," Brooks asks, strolling back into the room, "I figured we can start with all of our suites, then end with hers and the nest so she can catch a nap."

"A nap sounds delightful," Sloane smiles at him, standing up then offering me a hand.

CHAPTER EIGHTEEN

Sloane

The moment has finally come for me to see the space that they created for me in the warehouse. I'd be lying if I said I wasn't nervous. They took me through the rest of the main living floor, taking the time to show me each of their suites.

There was originally office space in the corner of this floor. A larger office for Brooks to use and a small space that Kai and Hudson shared when they needed it. The office's had their own entrances and were also connected through a bathroom.

The smaller office was made smaller, more insular for nesting purposes and also to expand the bathroom. The bathroom was very basic, utilitarian to begin with and now has a spa-like feeling, with the addition of a large, jetted tub.

Or, so I've been told. Hudson has been trying to psych me up by dropping little hints about what I have to look forward to in my new space.

"Ready, *tesoro*," Brooks asks, giving my hand a squeeze. I can feel his anticipation and nervousness, too. Hudson's excited and Kai is a mixture of excitement and nervousness, like me.

"Yeah," I blow out a breath, "let's go."

Hudson holds one hand over my eyes, sliding his arm around my waist to help walk me forward into the room. I hear the door open and he shuffles me forward slowly until we must be towards the middle of the space.

"Ready, little omega," Hudson whispers.

I nod against his hand and he pulls it away. I open my eyes slowly, spinning to take in the entire space.

I'm stunned.

It's so beautiful, I don't even have words. The entire space is painted a light lilac color with deeper purple accents.

There's a small sitting area with a plush white loveseat, purple pillows and a throw blanket. There's a small ottoman and side table along with a few candles. The bed is in the back corner and looks like it's big enough to fit all of us, if I wanted it to.

There's a large, deep purple upholstered headboard that stretches up almost to the ceiling. The bedding is a combination of white and different shades of purple, with additional throw pillows and decorative pillows gathered around.

There are small nightstands on either side decorated with delicate paper lamps that give off a warm glow. There's also a small glass water jug with a cup as a lid and a few small candles.

Hudson shows me to the opposite end of the bed where there's a second door leading to the walk in closet. Definitely big enough to fit all of my things from home, just like they promised.

"What do you think," Simon asks, shyly.

"I love it," I sigh, "It's beautiful."

"And we're not even halfway there yet," Kai winks, tugging my hand toward the other door in the wall, what I'm assuming is the bathroom.

Kai pulls the door open with a flourish, bowing and sweeping his arm toward the room. I smile and chuckle a little, rubbing his back as I step through into the bathroom.

It's even more stunning than the bedroom.

The same purples were used in here, but also some muted greens and blues. It does have a very spa-like feeling, especially with the huge jetted tub that they added. I think it could easily fit the five of us. The same can be said of the shower right next to it.

A clear glass enclosed space, I can see that there are three shower heads mounted on the wall, two of which are removable. There's a small wooden bench inside and a matching shelf that has various body products, along with shampoo and conditioner.

There are candles scattered around the space, on the counter and around the tub. The lights are on a dimmer, which Simon demonstrates. The lights can even be operated from the bathtub or the shower. There are speakers mounted in the ceiling, so I can play music while I'm relaxing, as well.

"This is amazing, truly," I smile at all of them, "even better than what I have at home."

"We wanted to make sure it had everything that you liked. And that it was big enough for all of us to join you, if and when you want us here," Brooks takes my hand, pulling me across the space toward the closed door on the opposite side.

"If there's anything in there you want changed, just let us know," Hudson tells me as we reach the door to the nest, "we have time to renovate before we get to use it anyway."

I roll my eyes and he winks, rubbing his hand in circles on my lower belly. I swat him away before encouraging Brooks to open the door.

"Remember, we all worked together on this to make it perfect, just for you. Only our scents will be in this space," Kai says, coming up behind me and resting his hands on my shoulders. I lean back into him briefly, absorbing his warmth and the feelings of love and possession traveling down the bond.

"I'm sure it will be perfect," I tell them all, "because you made it for me, for us, to use."

Brooks pushes open the door and steps back, allowing me to enter the space ahead of him. I flip the switch on the wall, illuminating the space with soft, diffuse lighting. There's a chair rail all around the room and the lighting is mounted beneath, giving just enough light to see and enjoy the space.

The majority of the space is a raised platform bed, taking up over half of the room. There are curtains mounted on the ceiling, hanging down to drape around the space, easily rearranged to cover as much or as little of the bed as I want.

There are two low chairs next to the bed, along with some larger cushions, giving different options for sitting around the space. The overall feel is deep and utter contentment. I can easily imagine losing myself for days in here with my mates.

I turn back to them, all huddled around the door, watching.

"I love it," I whisper, "it's so perfect."

Hudson presses his hand to his chest, rubbing over his heart as he takes in the feeling of sheer happiness and love that I'm sending to them. I wish Simon was healed enough to be brought into the fold so he could experience it, too.

Of course, if he could experience everything I was feeling, we wouldn't be in this awkward predicament.

"Baby," Hudson whispers, reaching for me, obviously taking note of my sudden change in mood, "what's wrong?"

"I'm just tired, really tired. I do think I need a nap."

"Okay then," he turns with me in his arms, "let's get you tucked in."

He maneuvers me through the bathroom and across to the giant bed in the corner. He folds back the corner, then reaches for my pants.

"Hey, hands off, sir," I tell him, pushing his hands away.

"I'm just helping you get comfortable, baby," he leers at me, reaching for my pants again.

"I can handle that myself, thank you very much," I laugh, pushing him away again.

"Alright, alright," Brooks steps up to Hudson, wrapping an arm around Hudson's neck and dragging him backwards, "she's perfectly capable of getting herself into bed."

"Just let me help," Hudson gurgles as Brooks makes it to the door, manhandling him through it.

"Sleep well, *tesoro*, we'll see you in a few hours. If you're not up for dinner, I'll come get you."

Kai steps up to me, laughing as Brooks drags Hudson away, "Do you want company, *cara*?"

"Actually," I stretch up on my tiptoes to plant a kiss on the side of his neck, "I was hoping Simon might stay with me. I'm sure he could use some sleep, too. Good for his recovery."

Kai smiles down at me, hugging me against his body and teasing my lips with gentle kisses, "I think that's a great idea."

I lean around Kai to smile at Simon, "What do you say, Simon? Want to take a nap with me?"

"Ah, um…I think, yeah, I guess that could probably be good. Uh, just, we have to put a pillow between us, just in case, I have to make sure to stay on my back," he stutters so cutely, a blush spreading across his cheeks.

"I think we can handle that," Kai says, pushing me toward the bed, "Sloane should get in first, so you're closest to the edge. Then we can get you both tucked in."

I shuck off my jeans and t-shirt, leaving me in a pair of comfy undies and a tank top. I slide under the corner that Hudson already folded back, tossing some pillows to the foot of the bed and gathering some others to tuck around Simon for safety.

Kai pushes Simon toward the bed, stepping up behind him to undo his jeans and push them down. Kai kneels down and tugs the pant legs off as Simon uses his shoulder to balance and lift each leg.

"I'm going to leave my shirt on," Simon says quietly, throat clicking as he swallows.

"That's completely fine, however you're comfortable," Kai tells him, helping him into the bed.

Once he's settled, Kai and I tuck pillows on either side of him, up under his arms so he can't roll. It will also keep me from accidentally rolling into him, as well.

"Okay, sleep well, you two. Like Brooks said, we'll come get you if you're not up for dinner," Kai says, leaning down and giving Simon a kiss.

I brace my hands on my knees and lean over Simon so Kai can give me a kiss, as well. He humms against my lips before grasping my neck lightly and tilting my head so he can kiss his mating mark.

"I love you," he tells me, kissing me one last time before grasping Simon's hand, "and I love you."

"I love you, too," we echo.

I reach over Simon, tugging the pull cord on the small paper lamp, shutting off the light on that side. I leave the lamp behind me on, giving just enough light that I can see around the room, but not bright enough to disturb my sleep.

I snuggle down under the covers, loving the feeling of the fresh, crisp sheets against my exposed skin. I take a deep breath, appreciating the scents of pack overlaying the general cleanliness of the room.

I reach out tentatively, finding Simon's hand under the covers and curling my fingers around his.

"Is this okay," I whisper.

"Of course, of course it's okay," he whispers back.

I take a deep breath, wanting him to open up to me, but not sure how to push that along without making him feel defensive. I don't want to have to force him to talk to me, but maybe given the opportunity he'll want to.

Maybe this time he can be honest and not hurt me so much.

I turn toward him so I'm on my side and hugging the pillow between us. I tuck our entwined hands against my stomach and slide the other up and down his arm, slowly.

"You know, when I found out you were alive, I practically threw Kai out of the bed trying to get out of that room and get to you," I laugh, "I wanted to see you with my own eyes, see you and touch you so I knew it was true."

He squeezes my hand tight in response, but doesn't say anything.

"They wouldn't let me out of the room, of course, but it didn't change the fact that I needed to see you. The last memories I had," I stop for a moment, choking up a little, "I really thought you were dead and I didn't know how I was going to go on without you. I love you, so much, Simon. I just want you to know that."

We lay together in silence. I continue to stroke his arm while I listen to the sounds of his steady breathing, just appreciating that he's here with me, even if the silence feels strained.

"Before you were taken, I had a conversation with Hudson and Kai, about my issues. My…feelings," he starts quietly.

There's a brief pause before he starts again, "I don't know how to talk about how I'm feeling. I didn't do a good job talking to them about it, either. I don't want to hurt you Sloane, that's not my goal, I want you to know that."

"I know," I tell him, tucking his arm more firmly against me, "I don't like it and I'm not going to let you keep doing it, but I do know you're not doing it on purpose."

"The easiest thing I can say to explain is that I don't feel like I'm good enough for you, for this situation."

I lay quietly next to him, continuing with soothing strokes on his arm. I'm determined to let him talk it all out this time. I will bite my tongue for as long as it takes.

"We talked, before, ah, about how, um sexually inexperienced I am, with women. Right. And I remember, you assured me, you were, uh, okay with that and with me still wanting Kaiser."

"That hasn't changed, Simon. I don't care that you haven't been with a woman before me. I've never been with a man before the four of you. We'll learn together," I lean forward and place a tentative kiss on his arm, just under his t-shirt sleeve.

"I don't feel, like, I don't, I'm not an alpha. I can't do all the things they can for you. I can't purr to comfort you and I can't knot you, I can't get you pregnant, I can't help you during your heat. I can't even give you an orgasm without Kai standing by to help me. I'm just a pathetic beta who doesn't add anything to this dynamic."

"Simon. That's not true, I mean, Jesus, Simon. Is that how you've been feeling?"

I desperately want to see his face, look at him, but worry that he'll shut down if we're eye to eye. He seems to be able to confess things to me, here in the semi-darkness, and I don't want that to stop.

"I can't help it because it's true. What benefit am I to you, Sloane? What's the point of me being here?"

"Simon. Listen to me. I don't need another alpha, I need you. You who remembers what my favorite foods are, my favorite designers, my favorite color. You're so smart and kind and make me feel wanted. I don't need you to purr or growl or anything else that isn't you. Just because you can't knot me, doesn't mean you can't help me through my heat. I want you there, inside me just like the others, when the time comes again. You're my mate, too, Simon. Mine."

"I hear what you're saying Sloane, it's just so hard for me to believe it. I don't know what's wrong with my brain that the words just don't want to penetrate. Trust me, it would be so much easier if I could just push everything aside and believe you."

"Soon enough, Simon, you won't have to try to believe it, because you'll be able to feel it. You'll know deep in your soul that I love you and you belong, because you'll be able to feel me."

"And I can't wait for that day, I just hope I don't fuck all this up again between now and then."

"Just keep your intrusive thoughts to yourself and we should be fine. Just remind yourself that I love you and your brain is lying."

"I wish it were that easy," he sighs, squeezing my hand.

"I know something that might help, and it is easy," I whisper, leaning close to kiss his arm again.

I let my lips trail across his upper arm, flicking my tongue out to lick gently before pulling away, "You game?"

"I, uh, don't know…what are you suggesting?"

"Well, one of the things you're so hung up on is our sexual compatibility and having an orgasm really helps me sleep. Since you're not cleared for actual sex yet, let me show you what I like," I murmur, tucking his hand down between my thighs, "then you can show me what you like."

Being in the dark makes me bolder than normal. And being with Simon, who never takes the upper hand, means that I need to step out of my comfort zone and try to bridge this gap a little.

"I-I-I, uh, I, sure, ah yeah, okay," he stutters and I can picture the red staining his face as his hand clenches in mine.

"Just relax," I whisper, shifting around so I'm up on my knees, "I'll show you exactly what I like."

I cup my hand under his and spread my knees apart before sliding them both under the waistband of my panties. Putting pressure against his first two fingers, manipulating them like they're mine, I press them against my clit.

Letting out a low moan, I direct him, "Here, just like this," moving his two fingers with mine to rub and circle my hard clit.

"That feels good," I whisper breathlessly, "just keep going like that, get me warmed up."

I rock my hips gently against our hands, changing the pressure with each stroke across my clit. I can feel my pussy releasing slick as he pushes me higher.

"Now, just like this," I push his hand further between my thighs, curling his fingers with mine and pushing them inside my weeping hole, "and your thumb, your thumb on my clit."

I whimper when he starts moving his fingers inside of me without prompting. I pull my hand away as he curls his fingers and strokes them in and out, rubbing across my clit with his thumb at the same time.

"Yes, Simon, yes" I moan, rocking my hips against his hand, "just like that, please, just like, don't stop, don't."

"You feel so good, so hot and wet," he murmurs, his voice husky with lust and need, "I want to feel you on my dick, Sloane."

"Oh yes, soon, please," I pant, "please harder, Simon. On my clit, harder. I'm so close."

He slides his fingers all the way inside, curling them to keep pressure on my g-spot, but not moving them. He presses down hard with his thumb, rubbing in rough circles while I whimper and moan, fucking against his hand as much as I can.

"You are so sexy, the noises you make, fuck, my dick is so hard," he moans, still circling and circling my clit.

"Simon, I'm going to cum, I'm going to, please, don't stop, don't stop, don't stop. Oh, oh yes," I cry out, back arching as my pussy squeezes his fingers. He keeps circling his thumb, pushing my orgasm higher and higher until it almost hurts.

I grab his forearm, squeezing, "It's too much, please," and he stops, fingers still buried inside of me, but he stops circling my clit.

I let the orgasm settle through me, my breathing slowly returning to normal, before I let go of his arm. He pulls his hand out of my panties and I watch as he shoves his fingers into his mouth, licking and sucking my slick off them.

"You taste so good, Sloane. Like candy, like cinnamon candy. I want to eat you out everyday."

"As soon as you're better, I promise you're first in line," I tell him, snuggling back down next to him and stretching my arm out until it's braced over the pillow separating us and resting on his upper thigh.

"Fuck," he mutters as I trail my hand up his thigh to his hard cock, stroking him through the thin layer of cotton.

"Tell me what you like," I whisper, squeezing his balls gently before tugging the elastic down enough that his cockhead pops out the top.

"Pull my boxers down, beautiful, and take me in your hand."

I adjust a little so I can reach both hands over, tugging his boxers down while he rocks his hips so his cock springs out. I make sure his balls are clear of the elastic before laying back down and wrapping one hand loosely around his hard dick.

"Get some slick on your hand, lube me up good."

I slide my hand down my panties, rubbing against my pussy until my hand is soaked with slick, before bringing it back up to his shaft. Wrapping my hand around the head, I stroke down once and up again, making sure that he's coated.

"That's it, Sloane, I want you to squeeze it, tight. Just under the head," he groans, as I grip him tight, "right fucking there, yeah. Stroke me, baby, just the head, just like that."

I squeeze him tight, ringing my fingers around his cock and stroke hard and fast over his head. My slick lubing my strokes so my hand flies up and down, his breath panting out the faster and harder I go. His hands are fisted in the pillows on either side.

"Fuck, baby, just like that, yes, yes, harder," he grunts, flexing his hips and pushing his cock through my hand faster, fucking my fist.

"I want to taste you again," I tell him, stroking harder and faster, watching precum ooze from the slit in his dick and wanting it in my mouth.

"You can taste me, beautiful, I'll cum right in that pretty mouth, fuck yeah I will," he grunts, "tighter, baby, harder."

I squeeze his dick so hard, I'm scared I'm hurting him, but his groans of pleasure only spur me on. I flick my wrist as fast as I can, jacking his dick while he pants.

"I'm gonna cum, baby, open wide, put that mouth on my cock, swallow it, swallow it all," he grunts, just as my mouth seals around his cock. The taste of us combines on my tongue and I whimper at the heady taste.

He grips my wrist, slowing my strokes as his cum pumps onto my tongue and I swallow every drop. He stops me altogether, wrapping his hand around mine to squeeze his dick one last time, stroking up to make sure I get every bit of his cum in my mouth.

"Fuck, Sloane, that was…" he trails off, pulling my hand off his cock and bringing it up to his mouth, cleaning every trace of slick off my hand.

"I know," I whisper, "I felt it too. You didn't hurt yourself? Pull anything?"

"No," he chuckles, "I'm good. More than good. Maybe we can actually sleep now? On a positive note, with a little happiness onboard."

I smile against his arm, tucking it right back against me once he's done cleaning my hand.

"I think that sounds like a great plan."

CHAPTER NINETEEN

Kaiser

I'm so fucking happy this morning, I whistle all the way down to the parking garage. Well. Mostly because I'm happy. Partly because it pisses Hudson off and he's a cranky ass this morning. I think it's because Sloane decided to sleep in her own room last night with me and Simon instead of christening his bed with him.

To be fair though, we didn't christen anything, either. I didn't think it would be fair to Simon since he can't participate. Although I would love to know what the two of them got up to during nap time. Neither would spill the beans, but I could smell her arousal in the room. It didn't make it easy to fall asleep.

Waking up between my two favorite people, though? Simon's hand tucked into mine with Sloane half draped across my chest; nowhere else I'd rather be.

"Dmitri here yet," I ask when the elevator opens into the garage level.

"I haven't heard from him, but he still technically has about 15 minutes before we leave. Maybe he's not punctual like the rest of us."

"Punctual my ass. The only time you're ever on time is when one of us is ushering you along. Do you even know how to tell time?"

"I know how to tell you to fuck off, does that count?"

"Jeeee-ZUS that was lame. You get enough sleep last night? You're a little off your game."

"You're a prick, you know that," he snaps, turning and flicking my earlobe as hard as he can.

"Ow, you asshole," I reach out and slap the back of his neck with my knuckles.

"Shit," he wraps one hand around the back of his neck, but reaches out with the other to yank on my beard.

"Damnit," I hook my ankle behind his and topple him onto his back, following him down to the ground so I can pin him.

I straddle his waist, kneeling over him. I trap his wrists under each knee so he can't fight back, then I settle my weight back, directly over his hips.

"I win. And I'm not letting you up until I make you suffer," I smile, leaning back and crossing my arms.

"Bring it on, you can't break me."

"I think we both know that's not true. I know every single tickle spot you have, but that's not what I have in mind right now. I think you're cranky because you're feeling left out," I smile down at him, shifting back far enough to give me access to his dick but still keep his wrists pinned. It's great being so much taller than everyone else.

I slowly unzip the front of his jeans, pushing the flaps apart so his rapidly hardening cock is framed between the open zipper. I reach down and cup his balls, completely ignoring his dick in favor of rolling and tugging his sack until he moans and tries to buck up against me.

"Poor Hudson, feeling neglected? Let me help you out," I mutter, wrapping my fingers around his dick and squeezing. I stroke him lightly a few times until he growls in frustration.

"Jack it like you mean it or let me go so I can take care of it myself."

"You think you can boss me around, you have definitely lost your mind. But I have no problem reminding you who's in charge," I tell him, giving his dick one last stroke before releasing it and moving to my pants.

Hudson groans in frustration when I pull my hard dick out and start stroking it. I spit in my hand, stroking it around the head and getting it nice and wet. I start stroking my cock with one hand, reaching down and massaging my balls with the other.

Being in bed with Sloane and Simon and not being able to touch either one left me with an aching hard-on this morning. I was able to ignore it until Hudson started with his bratty behavior. Now he can watch while I take care of it.

"One day, I'm going to bend you over and really show you. You're gonna take my cock like a good little boy," I groan, precum leaking out to drip on Hudson's dick. I grip my dick and wipe the head up the underside of Hudson's, smearing my pre cum all over him in the process.

"Fuck, please," he grunts when I rub my dick up and down against his, wrapping my fist around both of them.

"Suck my cock like a good boy and I'll let you cum," I tell him, releasing his arms so he can push himself up into a sitting position. I rise up on my knees so my dick is closer to his mouth and he swallows me down.

I hiss out a breath when I feel my cock tapping the back of his throat. He gags a little before wrapping his fist around my base. Hudson starts to jack me and suck at the same time, working his fist in time with his mouth until I'm panting and ready to cum.

"I'm gonna cum in your mouth and you're going to swallow all of it," I groan, grabbing a fistful of his short hair and pushing his mouth down hard on my dick, his gagging turning me on even more.

"Take it, take this cock like a good boy, choke on it," I snarl as my cum shoots into his mouth. I grunt with each spasm, as he gulps it down. Sucking and licking my cock, making sure he gets every bit.

"Such a good boy," I tell him, pushing him back to the floor and wrapping my hand around his throat. I pin him down to the ground with that hand, then spit in the other and wrap it around his cock.

I press my thumb to the underside of his cock head, stroking it hard and fast while I squeeze his throat just a little. Not enough to cut off his air flow, but enough to remind him that I could if I wanted to.

"Open your mouth," I order, and he does.

I spit in his open mouth, "Swallow it."

And he does, "Such a good, good boy. Are you going to cum for me now, like a good boy? Are you going to cum all over yourself? Pull your shirt up, I want to watch you cum all over. Make a mess on yourself."

I stroke him hard, squeezing his cock with each upstroke until he's panting. I know he's close, I can feel him throbbing in my hand. Just a few more strokes and he'll be shooting his load. And just like I told him to, he pulls up his shirt.

"Cum for me, like a good little boy, Hudson. Cum all over yourself."

"Fuck, fuck," Hudson grunts, his cum shooting across his abs and chest, sticky white ropes decorating his skin alongside all of his tattoos. I stroke him through it, making sure that every drop is painted on his own skin.

Keeping him pinned with the one hand, I take the other off his dick and start rubbing his cum into his skin.

"You're going to wear yourself, under your shirt, so you remember that you're my good little boy. And as a reward, I'll make sure you get some alone time with Sloane, okay?"

He groans, "You're still a prick, but jesus you make me feel good, you dirty fuck."

"Yeah, you love it," I push myself up, giving him a hand and yanking him to his feet before walking to the sink in the corner. It's currently a greasy mess, since Hudson's been using it to store his motorcycle parts, but it's better than walking around with cum on my hand all day.

"Fuck yeah, I do. I can't wait for Simon to get better so every single one of us can get naked together."

"Pervert," I laugh, knowing that I'm looking forward to the same damn thing.

"Alright, 5 more minutes then we leave without him," Hudson announces, heading toward the Macan.

"I'm sure he'll show, he seemed pretty into it yesterday. Maybe he just doesn't want to get stuck hanging around here with everyone, just wants to head right into the action."

"Either way, get in. I'm going to pull out onto the street and park so he can just get in and we can go."

"You just can't wait to get your hands on Petrov, huh?"

"You know it."

I slide into the passenger seat, clicking the buckle while Hudson pulls out onto the street. He loops around the building and into the pull around in front of the guest entrance. He puts it in park, just as a figure comes around the corner on a GSX-R.

The crotch rocket pulls in behind us, the rider pulling off his helmet and revealing Dmitri. He swings off the bike and approaches Hudson's side.

"Any way we can park it in the lobby or down in your garage? Not that I don't trust the area, I'd just feel better if it wasn't out on the street," he asks, pushing his hair back from his face.

"Sure," I call across Hudson before he can answer, unbuckling and pushing out of the car to open the lobby doors for him.

"Thanks, man, I've put a lot of work into it and just want to make sure it's safe," he says, pushing it up the curb and into the lobby.

"No worries, Hudson is the same way," I tell him, letting the lobby doors swing shut and lock behind us, "no one will be able to get in there except for us and Simon and Brooks who have received an alert that we went in. You're covered."

"Alright then, what's the plan," he asks as we both climb back into the car and Hudson heads toward the Vault.

"Absolute fuckery," Hudson responds, "however we can accomplish it. We'll try to get him to talk, obviously, but I have a feeling that he's not going to be in a sharing kind of mood."

"Okay, so we take turns or what? Normally I do this with my brother and we have a pretty good partnership, I just don't want to step on your toes, especially in front of this asshat."

"Hey, I'm good with whatever, feel free to step in whenever you want. I mostly just want to beat the fuck out of him, Kai is the question man today."

"Gotcha. Kai, you okay if I ask some questions, too? I got some information a few days ago from Cartouchi, Morris' club manager and I want to see if it pans out."

"Something to do with Sloane," Hudson growls.

"No, with Iris or rather who Iris was meeting with at Finesse when this whole shit show started. She's still coming off whatever drug cocktail she's been using so she's no help. I just need to know if the intel is accurate."

"You gonna share with the class," I ask, definitely not appreciating the shady ass vague descriptors he's using.

"I can, as long as I have your word that you won't interfere. This is Morris' issue to deal with and he doesn't want anyone stepping in."

"We're on the same side, dipshit, we won't step on his toes unless he asks us to help," Hudson mutters.

"I'm just saying. Morris is struggling right now. He's trying to keep up his image and having the Conti pack step in to clean up a mess for him will just dive bomb his efforts."

"We're not going to do anything," I retort, "We want Morris to regain his status. It doesn't exactly help us to be in an alliance with someone who can't keep his people in line."

"Low blow, dude," he tells me, "the only reason I'm not going to kick your ass is because it's true. But don't kick him when he's down, man. His daughter was kidnapped, he was betrayed by his closest pack members and he doesn't know where it ends."

"Let's just be honest with each other, okay? Just get it all out in the open so we can move forward and work together to make Petrov pay," Hudson adds, turning onto the parking ramp that leads to the garage below the Vault.

"Iris was trying to get one of Morris' low level soldiers to give her his daughter," Dmitri blurts, "At least, that's the information that Cartouchi was able to get after investigating why she was at the club."

"An omega," I ask quietly.

"Yeah," he sighs, running his fingers through his hair a few times, "I guess the guy bet more than he could afford during a card game, couldn't pay the pot. Iris was trying to convince the guy to trade his daughter in exchange for the debt. The game was backed by Enzo, who we know now, was backed by Volkov."

"Enzo Gallo is out of commission, permanently. One of you guys took him out on that boat, so what's the issue," I ask as we pile out of the Macan and head toward the elevator.

"According to Cartouchi's source, the deal was already made. Morris is concerned that Volkov is going to come for the girl, even though the deal was technically with Gallo. They won't let an omega slip away, especially one who was basically handed over on a silver platter."

"I'm all for making sure that some young girl doesn't end up in Volkov's hands, but why doesn't Morris want help?"

"He wants to handle it on his own. It was arranged by Iris with his soldier, so it's his problem. He wants to try to repair some of the damage by making a showing against trafficking, especially trafficking omegas. He wants to save her, but also make a point."

"Okay," I respond, stepping off the elevator outside the Vault, "I get it, I'm for it. I usually let Hudson warm them up a little before I start questioning them, make sure they're in an open state of mind, but you can ask whatever you need to when you're ready. Just know that we will step in if Morris can't handle the situation."

"We'll handle it," he replies, determination threading through his voice, "we're not going to let anyone else be taken."

"Alright, you know we're going to report everything to Brooks, so we'll be back up if you guys need anything," Hudson adds, stripping his jacket off and tossing it on the table before bending down to unlace his boots.

I step up next to him and start disrobing, letting Dmitri know, "We don't take anything into the Vault with us. Everything stays out here, we have jeans or sweats you can change into. Those will stay in the Vault for clean up once we're done."

He nods once before stepping up next to me and pulling his jacket off, quickly followed by his sweater and undershirt. Once we're all naked, Hudson tosses me a pair of jeans, grabbing a pair for himself.

"What size are you, Dmitri? You look like you'd fit Brooks, maybe."

"34 waist."

"Yeah, alright," Hudson says, tossing a pair to Dmitri, "let's go."

Once he's got the jeans pulled up, Hudson pulls open the door to the vestibule. Closing it behind Dmitri, he crosses to the main food to the Vault, gripping the handle.

"He's been in here a few days, you know, might be a little ripe," Hudson warns, "we've been keeping him alive with a central line that one of our little EMT friends has been changing out, and she hoses him down when she comes by, but it's just basic care."

"Fuck," Dmitri mutters, the smell hitting us like a wall when Hudson pulls the door open. Stale body odor, piss and shit, anger, rage, and hate all mix together to form a severely off putting stench.

We move into the room, circling Petrov where he hangs from the ceiling. A spreader bar is attached at his ankles keeping his legs locked apart, with just the balls of his feet touching the floor. There's a second spreader bar with a neck stockade immobilizing his upper body.

A steel ring circles his neck, a bar spread to each side and resting on the tops of his shoulders. His arms are bent at the elbow, his wrists locked at the ends of the bar.

Chains attach to the bar on either side of his head, keep him lifted just enough that he can't get traction to move his body.

Dried blood coats his chest and arms. He's obviously spent quite a bit of time struggling against the bar, trying to get himself loose. He won't be able to, but it looks like he's put up a good fight. He doesn't move, doesn't acknowledge our presence, just continues to hang there without even a muscle twitch, eyes closed and seemingly relaxed in spite of the situation.

"No wonder you like to hurt women, Lexi," Hudson mocks, staring down at his dick, "I'd be mad as hell if that's all I had to work with, too."

Hudson chuckles when he doesn't get a response, "Maybe you didn't get the joke. You have to hurt them because they can't feel that," he reaches out and slaps his dick as hard as he can, "when you put it in."

Aleksandr grunts quietly, barely reacting to something that would have very likely brought me down. Dick slaps are no joke, especially when it's coming from Hudson. He might think slapping is for bitches, but he delivers them like a pro.

"Where are my manners, though. So sorry, let's get you cleaned up," he walks to the hose laying on the floor a few feet away.

Hudson aims the hose at his face, unleashing a stream of water. I can only imagine how cold it is with no water heater in the building, and winter coming to a head outside. Probably feels like tiny needles drilling into his face.

He moves the hose down to his body once Petrov starts sputtering and choking. No matter how stoic you think you are, the threat of drowning is no joke. Hudson moves toward him, the pressure of the hose increasing with each step closer, until the sprayer nozzle is practically touching his dick.

This guy is seriously fucked up. I'm not ashamed to say I'd be begging for mercy if my dick was taking a beating like that. The pain from the ice cold alone would be enough to get me to cave, let alone the hammering the water pressure is delivering.

"Now that we have a clean canvas to work with, let's get started," Hudson sneers, tossing the hose to the side and moving to his workbench. I lean back against the wall, keeping the room and Petrov in my line of sight while waiting for Hudson to do his worst.

"You sure the normal approach is going to work, here," I ask him quietly as he searches through his tools, Dmitri at his side taking in the selection.

"It's just a matter of finding his weakness. Clearly he doesn't care about his cock like most men would."

"Or maybe he inflicts pain because he likes it, too and he wants to share it," Dmitri adds.

"If he liked it, he'd have a boner right now. Nah, there's something else, something…I'll figure it out. I always do," Hudson adds, finally deciding on a handful of heavy duty, metal BBQ skewers that he had sharpened like knives.

"I can tell, you're the strong silent type, right? I respect that, I do. So, we're just gonna get started, do a little tenderizing so to speak. When you're ready to talk, just let me know."

Hudson pulls one of the skewers free from the pack, sticking his finger through the loop on the end and spinning it around while he slowly circles Petrov. He keeps spinning and spinning the skewer, eyeballing Petrov's body from top to bottom. Suddenly he stops and, almost quicker than I can track, spins the skewer off his finger and slams it into Petrov's left biceps from behind.

Petrov grunts again, hissing out a breath before gathering himself and blanking out. He's going to be tough to crack, but I trust Hudson to be able to do it. I just don't want to be stuck here all day waiting for it.

A few more trips around, a few more skewers, still nothing.

"How you feeling, Lexi? Need to get anything off your chest," Hudson asks, petting his chest as he circles around again.

Once he's behind Petrov, he cocks an eyebrow at me, tilting his head at Petrov, asking silently if I saw the twitch. It was barely noticeable, but I saw it. When Hudson was petting his chest, Petrov's forearm twitched, likely from him fighting against making a fist. His eyebrows drew together for just a fraction of a second, too.

I half nod, turning my head to the side at the last minute. Yes, I saw it, but I don't know what it means. Obviously something with his chest being touched, but is it his chest in general or the fact that it's a man touching him? A little bit of homophobia? Or just that it was a more gentle touch and the part of the body doesn't matter at all?

"I'd like to get this show on the road, you know. I have questions, my colleague here has questions. It would go a lot faster if you would be a little more cooperative," Hudson murmurs, leaning close to his back and making sure his breath coasts over the back of Petrov's neck.

This time there's an obvious shudder. Still not 100% on the trigger, but it's either gentle touch or the fact that Hudson has a dick and he's so close to him. Hudson being Hudson, he pushes up against Petrov so his chest is plastered to his back.

Petrov grimaces, his whole face tightening as Hudson stays pressed against him, even going so far as to bring his arms around and give him a hug. Petrov's a little homophobe bitch.

"Oh, Lexi, I almost forgot. Hope you don't mind a little cum between friends. You see, I had a little session this morning and my dom decided to rub cum into my chest and make me wear it because I'm a good little boy," Hudson chuckles against the back of his neck, making sure to slide his chest against his back a few more times.

"*Otstan' mudak,*" Petrov hisses, trying to swing his body away from Hudson. He doesn't go anywhere though, Hudson's got a good grip on him.

"Is that anyway to treat a friend. I just want to cuddle with you, Lexi," Hudson whispers right into his ear, sliding his hands up his chest and across his pecs.

"*Ostanovis' ublyudok*," Petrov roars, his feet scraping across the floor as he tries to get purchase to swing away from Hudson.

"We all know you can speak English, asshole," Dmitri pipes up, leaning back against the workbench, using a slim filet knife to clean his nails, "so just agree to answer a few questions and I'll put Hudson here back on his leash."

"*Ne proiskhodit,*" he seethes, teeth clenched.

"Hmm, I don't speak Russian, but assuming you're not cooperating. Hudson, why don't you give him a hand?"

"I'd love to," Hudson snarls against Petrov's neck, reaching around and slapping his hand down between Petrov's legs, cupping his cock and balls all in one go.

"*Ostanavlivat'sya, net,*" he yells.

"STOP," he yells, this time in English, right as Hudson starts laughing.

"Oh, naughty boy, Lexi," Hudson drops his hand to reveal that Petrov now has a raging hard-on, "you're not a homophobe at all, are you? You loooooove the cock, that's your issue."

"Fuck you," he screams, his Russian accent thick as spittle flies from his mouth, "I'm not a fag!"

"Yeah, I think that tells a different story," Dmitri gestures with the filet knife.

Poor Petrov isn't a grower, either. I mean, he's not even average size. I seriously think my thumb might be a bit bigger. That's a rough life.

"Nothing wrong with taking the dick, my friend," Hudson tells him, coming around to face him.

"I don't want dick, I don't take dick, I'm not a fag," he yells again, this time ending his sentance by trying to spit at Hudson. Unfortunately, he's fairly dehydrated in spite of the central line keeping him going, so he doesn't produce anything worth spitting.

"Listen, I'll make you a deal, okay," Dmitri chimes in while Hudson continues to tease Petrov by running his hands across his chest and arms, then down his abs, coming within inches of his cock, "same as before. Answer our questions and I'll get lover boy here under control."

"Let me add, I'm not a rapist, but I'm sure I could find one easily enough. Most guys just want a warm hole, won't even care it's an asshole and not a pussy," Hudson whispers, leaning close to his face to add, "I'll do whatever it takes to get the information we want."

Petrov's eyes bounce around the room, landing on each of us before whipping around in the dark.

"Okay," Hudson starts toward the door, "let me just grab my phone."

"Stop," Petrov croaks, "stop, *pozhaluysta*."

Hudson swings back to stare him down, waiting for him to say the words.

"Whatever you want to know, just promise you'll kill me at the end. I can't go back to Egor after this."

"Of course we're gonna kill you, fuckstick, you really think we'd let you out of this,'" Hudson laughs before slapping him on the cheek.

"What do you want to know," Petrov asks, defeat in his voice and every line of his body.

CHAPTER TWENTY

Dmitri

I call Marco on the way back to the compound, letting him know to gather Morris and Remi in his office. I didn't call Morris directly because I knew he would want me to relay everything immediately and I'd rather wait until we're all together.

Marco is more levelheaded. He'll be able to get them together and I'll only have to go over everything once, then we can come up with a plan. We're going to have to work together with Brooks and the others, no way around it. Kai assured me that Brooks would be fine letting Morris handle the girl, though.

As I turn down the private drive to the compound, I reach into my jacket for the gate pass. I've traveled this enough times on my Gixxer that I know exactly when to hit the button so the gates swing open perfectly for me to zip through. Nothing sucks like having to wait on a gate to swing wide enough when I'm on my bike.

Winter might be here, but sometimes I just need to feel the wind rushing over me. It's like therapy. Any time there's a hint of sunshine and the roads are clear of snow, I take it out.

I cruise right up to the main house, parking in the family garage adjacent to the circular drive. Ever since we figured out that Ben and Otto were traitors, Remi and I have been staying at the main house with Marco and Morris, just in case. We don't know who else Ben and Otto had on payroll, but we're working on vetting everyone on the property now.

I enter through the back, stopping just long enough to hang my jacket and put my helmet up in the closet. Isa's a stickler for having everything in its place. Moving past the kitchen, I make a quick pit stop and grab a bottle of water out of the game room next to Morris' office.

I push into the office and see Morris leaning on his desk, Marco beside him and Remi is seated on the couch across the room.

"What did you find out," Morris wastes no time.

"Let him get in the door, *cucciolo*," Marco admonishes, "he'll tell us everything he can."

"You want a beer," Remi asks from the couch.

"Nah, I'm on for something a little stronger once we're done here."

I plant myself in one of the chairs in front of Morris' desk, "You want the good news or the bad news?"

"Is any of it actually good," Morris counters.

"Eh, better than the bad, anyway."

"Just start from the top and go through it all," Marco interjects before Morris can ask something else.

"Okay, the girl's name is Mariella, she turned 22 last month. Her father agreed to the bargain with Iris. According to Petrov, they're supposed to collect the girl from the Hawthorne in three days."

"What, her dad's just gonna drop her off at a hotel with no explanation and expect her to stay there? That doesn't sound like a grand plan," Remi points out.

"According to Petrov, this is something they worked out with Gallo. There's a room there that has a separate ventilation system, he makes sure they're checked into that room. Once the omega is alone, he releases a gas to drug them, then moves them out through a hidden entrance. The parent or significant other, whoever - continues to stay in the room like normal."

"They do this enough that they have a room set up specifically for it," Remi asks, disgusted.

"It's not the only hotel like it, I guess. Petrov says they have contacts around the country set up like this. Parents sell their kids, partners trade for money or release from a deal. Sometimes an unlucky omega is traveling alone and just gets nabbed."

"That's fucked up," Remi interrupts again.

"Shut up and let me finish, fuck."

Remi gives me the finger then motions me to continue with my story. I swear to christ, he's 8 years younger than me instead of 8 minutes. Maybe he was deprived of oxygen during the birth.

"Anyway. In this instance, Nikolaj or Aleksandr meet Gallo at the hotel for the pick up and the rest is history. Petrov is convinced that Nikolaj at a minimum will still show to get the girl. They'll contact the father and let him know that the deal is still in place."

"Even with Gallo dead? He still thinks they'll go through with it?"

"Petrov said that omegas take precedence over any other deal because the amount of money they get. If the father believes the deal is still in place, he'll take her to the hotel.

Gallo would have already had a reservation in their name for that room. It would just be a matter of Nikolaj or Egor gaining access to the room."

"And since they're already familiar with the hotel set-up from working with Gallo in the past, it likely won't be too hard for them to get in and out with her," Remi muses.

"So we'll need to keep an eye on Mariella and her dear old dad, get to the hotel ahead of him and make sure she's safe before she ends up drugged," Marco sums up.

"Basically, yeah, except-"

"Except, what," Morris spits, "There is no exception. I told you we would rescue this girl and we will."

"Yes, except," I stress, holding up my hand to keep him from interrupting me, "that I was in that room with Hudson and Kaiser. They heard everything I did and they will tell Brooks that Nikolaj for sure and possibly Egor are going to be in town in three days time. You know they want a piece of him."

"So, we work with them," Marco starts.

"No. I said we would handle this and we will, it's our responsibility to make sure this girl is safe. Sloane is my daughter, I will get justice for her, too."

"I told them you wanted to handle the girl on your own and they agreed. But we will have to work with them, it's the only way we can ensure the girl is safe and Egor is neutralized. It just makes sense, Morry," I tell him, using his nickname and pleading with my eyes that he just be cooperative for once.

"We work together, they get Egor and we get the girl. It's a win-win, *cucciolo*," Marco tells him, agreeing with me for once.

Morris pushes up from the desk, pacing back and forth across the room. He scrapes his hands through his hair a few times, obviously struggling with having to share the spotlight. Especially with his daughter's mates.

I guess it must be hard, not being top dog anymore. I wouldn't know, spending my whole life serving. It's a hell of a lot less stressful down here, though, I can say that.

"Alright, fine," Morris finally relents, "call Brooks and set something up for tomorrow. We need to get a plan in place and move on this if we only have three days."

"On it boss," Remi says, standing up and pulling his cellphone out of his pocket before stepping out of the room.

Marco nudges my foot with his, bringing my attention up to him while Morris pulls his phone out of his pocket and continues to pace on the other side of the room.

"You staying in tonight," he asks quietly.

"Haven't decided yet. Thinking I might go blow off some steam at Blur. Depends on when we're set to meet Brooks."

"You just spent most of the day beating someone, that wasn't enough for you?"

"First of all old man, educate yourself. You want to look down on my lifestyle, how I choose to spend my personal time, but you won't even try it. Second, it's not a beating when it's between two consenting adults, it's an experience. Third, we didn't get a chance to beat him."

"Okay, but I don't want to try it because I don't get my kicks hitting women."

"It's not always women. But be honest, you never spanked a lady, *orso*? Pulled her hair, choked her a little?"

"Not the same thing," he looks at me with narrowed eyes.

"It's exactly the same thing, actually, just a little deeper and darker. And it's safer to do it at a club since there are rules and shit. Blur is one of the best out there. They have staff to cater to every need you might have."

"Spanking a woman in the heat of the moment, that's one thing. Talking about it before hand? Planning it out? Just doesn't tickle my pickle, you know."

"You should step out of your comfort zone once in a while, might learn something about yourself."

He chuckles softly, "It's true, I do want something more in my old age, *regazzo*. Different pussy daily is getting old, but I don't think BDSM is it."

"Or, maybe it's just the pussy part of the equation you need to change," I reply quietly, cocking an eyebrow at him.

It's no secret that Marco has the hots for Morris. Anyone with eyes can see that. Well, maybe not anyone, but I spend a fair amount of time around them and I've always suspected. It's only become more clear with Ben and Otto out of the picture.

Marco is always watching him. Even when they're out and Marco is picking up a chick to bang, he's still watching Morris. Probably trying to make him jealous or see if he'll join in, but it never seems to work.

"You might be right, but we don't always get what we want, unfortunately," he muses, pushing himself up from the desk, "I'm going to head over to the gym, I'll be back in time for dinner."

He heads through the door, clapping Morris on the shoulder as he walks by. Remi passes him on his way back in.

"They'll be here tomorrow by 11:30. Sloane wanted Isa to make brunch and they want to pack up some of her things to take back to the warehouse."

"Sounds like a plan, then. Can you have some boxes brought in, I doubt they'll bring their own," he replies to Remi before turning toward me, "Did I hear you're going out tonight?"

"Ah, I haven't decided yet, but I was thinking about it, yeah."

"Blur?"

"That was one of the options, just don't know if I have the energy for it tonight since I won't be able to sleep in tomorrow," I chuckle.

"If you're looking for some pussy, Morris, you need to come out with me," Remi tells him, slinging his arm around Morris' shoulders, "especially since he only runs pussy about 50% of the time. Plus, you don't want to get involved in his scene, trust me."

"*Ragazzino*," he grips the back of Remi's neck, "I don't think you could find good pussy with a flashlight and magnifying glass. I like experience, adventure, you know. Not these young things you take out."

He gestures at me before pushing Remi away playfully, "I can't believe you're related to this one, let alone twins. I wasn't looking for pussy anyways. I know where to get it if I need it. I was just checking in with my people."

"If I do decide to go out, I'll let you know. For now, I'm heading over to the gym, probably take a few laps in the pool, maybe hit the sauna. See you at dinner."

CHAPTER TWENTY-ONE

Sloane

I hate being late. My father has always been a stickler about punctuality and we are definitely running late. Plus, I know Isa would have put a lot of effort into the food since it's my first meal there in so long.

"Don't you dare touch me," I threaten Hudson with my eyelash curler when he tries to sneak up behind me.

"I just wanted a hug, little omega," he pouts, completely over exaggerating his bottom lip.

"Screw your hugs, hot lips," I turn back to the mirror to finish my makeup, "your hugs are what got us into this mess."

"Ew, hot lips? What are you, reading the worst endearment lists on Buzzfeed?"

"I just speak from the heart, now get out of here and make sure everyone else is ready!"

"But baby," he croons, trying to slip up behind me again, "I need a little hug, just to tide me over. We're not going to be able to do anything at the compound and I might just die from touch hunger."

"Hudson Briggs Alfera," I snap, turning back to him one more time so I can jam my finger into his chest, "get out of this bathroom and get everyone together or you won't be getting hugs for the next week!"

"Ouch," he pouts again, rubbing his chest as if I actually injured him, "you're so mean. Why you gotta use my government name like that, baby?"

"Hudson," Kai yells from out in my bedroom, "don't make me come in there and drag you out. You're stressing her out and you know it."

"If she just let me hug her, she wouldn't be stressed any more," Hudson replies, licking his bottom lip and waggling his eyebrows at me."

"OUT," I yell, pointing at the bathroom door and stomping my foot for emphasis.

"Okay, okay," he holds up his hands in defeat, backing out the door at the same time Kai comes in and wraps him in a headlock.

"Someone needs a spanking," Kai mutters, dragging Hudson backwards and finally leaving me in peace to finish getting ready.

"Can someone please let them know we're running late," I yell after him. I still haven't gotten my cell phone replaced and I really need to remedy that. Relying on everyone else for communication is a pain in the ass, plus I haven't spoken to Max or Emma in forever. I need and want to nurture my friendships.

I quickly finish curling my lashes, then slap on a coat of mascara. I'm skipping the foundation and powder today, definitely do not have time for that. I swipe a quick coat of lip gloss on, then deodorant and I'm hoofing it out the door.

The guys are all gathered in the kitchen, clearly waiting on me.

"Let's hustle, please," I plead, passing right by them without pause as I move to the elevator.

"Relax, *tesoro*," Brooks hooks an arm around my shoulders as we step into the elevator, "I'm sure your father will understand."

"I hate being late," I groan, "it's so disrespectful and selfish."

"Since this is an anomaly and not a constant, I'm sure your father will understand. It's a fluke. We just have to make sure it doesn't become a habit," Simon adds.

"You gonna sit up front and hold my hand, baby," Hudson smiles at me.

"You can hold Simon's hand," I reply, tucking myself against Brooks, "he needs to sit up front so he doesn't get jostled, being stuck in the back with us."

"Oooh, okay," he turns to Simon, "you're gonna let me get handsy with you, Si?"

"I suppose I can take one for the team," Simon rolls his eyes, barely stifling a laugh when we step out into the garage.

I slide into the back of the Q5, trying to be patient waiting for everyone else to climb in with me.

"Hudson," I snap, when he gets in and starts minutely adjusting everything, even though he's the last one who drove it.

"What," he cries, "I'm just trying to make sure everything is set properly. Safety first."

I lean forward between the seats, reaching out to twist his earlobe and yank him toward me.

"If you don't get moving now, I'm going to fuck every single one of them in front of you and not let you touch, understand," I hiss.

"Yes, ma'am," he squeaks and I let go of his ear, sitting back to nestle myself between Brooks and Kai.

"Is it wrong that that gave me a boner," Hudson whispers loudly to Simon.

Brooks leans forward and slaps him on the side of the head, "Move, Hudson, now."

"Fine," he mutters, spinning the wheel and taking us out of the parking garage, "you guys are so lame."

"Wanting to be on time and respecting my father's time are not lame," I admonish, "besides, you don't want to piss Isa off or she won't make that pasta salad that you like."

Hudson lets out a sad whine, "I love that pasta salad."

"I love you, poopsie," I smile at him in the rearview.

"My god woman, where are you getting these?"

I give him a kissy face in the mirror, then rest my head on Brooks's shoulder while squeezing Kai's hand in mine.

Simon flips on the radio and we enjoy the music while Hudson drives us out of town.

As we turn onto the private road, Hudson catches my eye in the rearview, "Think we can talk papa Morris into giving us a gate pass?"

"Would you give him a warehouse code," I counter.

Brooks replies, "I don't see that being a problem. I mean, we are a family now, especially if you're pregnant."

"Then I think he would be open to it. It makes sense for us to be able to access each other's homes, anyway. Never know when a quick response from someone on the outside might be needed," I muse, "Give me your phone."

Brooks hands his to me and I quickly call my father, "Please have the gates opened so we don't have to stop at each one. I feel bad enough as it is! Waiting will make us twice as late."

"You know it's me, papa, and you know I'm in a car with all of them, have Remi pull the security feed and let us in," she laughs.

"I love you, too, papa."

I hand Brooks back his phone, letting them all know that the gates will be opened and Hudson can head directly to the main house.

Papa and Marco are waiting on the porch as Hudson brings the Q5 around the circular drive. Kai slides out and helps me before opening the front and helping Simon. Hudson and Brooks come around the car, just as papa reaches the bottom of the stairs and squeezes me in a tight hug.

"How are you feeling, *stellina?*"

"Much better, papa, thank you," I push up on my toes and leave a kiss on his cheek before stepping around and hugging Marco as well.

"I know we haven't gotten a chance to talk about everything," Marco says quietly, "but I want you to know that I'm so glad you're safe and happy now. I love you, Sloane."

"I love you, too, Marco. I know a lot has happened and maybe someday we can hash it all out, but let's not drag it out right now, okay," I smile up at him before stepping aside and letting all the men shake hands.

"Isa prepared all of your favorites, but I'm sure that's not a surprise," papa tells me, slipping my hand onto his arm before leading me up the stairs and into the house.

"I'm so sorry we're late, I didn't realize the time when I started getting ready."

Papa chuckles softly, "*Stellina,* I remember what it's like, the beginning of a relationship, such passion. There's nothing to apologize for."

"Papa, please don't," I groan, blushing furiously.

"Okay, okay, sorry," he laughs, "let's eat and then we can talk business."

Papa directs us all into the dining room, platters and bowls lining the sideboard along with several carafes of juice and coffee on the table.

"It looks wonderful," I smile, "where's Isa?"

"Getting the biscuits out of the oven," she sasses from behind me, coming through the door with a large bowl draped with a towel in her hands, "you know I had to keep them warm for you."

"Thank you," I smile so big that I feel like my cheeks are splitting, "I'm going to miss this so much."

"You plan a day, every week you come back," she kisses me on each cheek, "I cook for you whenever you want."

"You can cook for the wedding," Hudson chimes in, "I don't think we could find anyone better."

"Absolutely not," I admonish, "she will be attending the wedding, not working at it! Besides. Brooks still hasn't asked, so there is no wedding."

"My girl, living in sin," Isa tsks, "good thing you have three other options if he doesn't ask."

She pats Brooks on the back as she exits the dining room.

"If that's the case, then allow me," Hudson pushes past Kai and drops down to his knees in front of me.

Before he can say anything else, Brooks is there, pushing him face down on the floor and straddling his back.

"I'm waiting for the right time, asshole," he says, rubbing Hudson's face into the tile so hard it makes a squeaking noise, "do not interfere."

"Speed it up," Hudson mumbles, "or she's fair game."

I roll my eyes at their ridiculous display, before stepping to the sideboard and grabbing a plate. Isa made so much food, I can't let it go to waste. I start with a slice of quiche, then some bacon, a load of broasted potatoes, a separate bowl for fruit, a biscuit. I pause for a moment, looking down at my plate and the rest of the dishes still waiting for me.

"I think this will take two trips," I laugh at myself, sitting down with my first plate and bowl of fruit, "but I'm definitely trying everything."

"Isa is pretty amazing," Marco adds, sitting across from me and pouring some orange juice for each of us.

Brooks finally pushes off Hudson, dragging him off the floor and joining Simon and Kai at the sideboard behind papa.

"Yes, thank you" I reply to Marco when he holds up the coffeepot.

"Caffeine isn't good for the baby," Hudson calls from behind me.

"According to the March of Dimes, minor caffeine consumption during pregnancy isn't a significant risk as long as it's limited to one cup. And we don't even know if I'm pregnant."

"Don't you think it's better to err on the side of caution," Kai asks, "just assume that you are and stay safe?"

"If any of you try to take my coffee away from me, I will punch you in the nuts," I state as succinctly as possible, adding cream and sugar before sipping it.

"Why are you researching caffeine consumption in pregnancy if you're not sure you're pregnant," Simon adds.

"Listen to me, all of you," I turn in my chair to face them, "if I am pregnant, I will be following the advice of a DOCTOR, not any of you. You can read and research whatever you want, but the DOCTOR will have the final say, so I suggest you get that through your thick skulls now so I don't have to actually nut punch anyone."

"You know it turns me on when you're violent," Hudson smiles lasciviously, licking his bottom lip.

I grab the biscuit off my plate and hurl it at his face.

"Do not push me right now, I am tired and cranky and I just want to enjoy my breakfast!"

Hudson stands there with a semi stunned look on his face, a half filled plate in one hand and biscuit crumbs on his face and shirt. I can feel his genuine shock that I actually retaliated, even if it was in the form of a baked good.

"I suggest you keep your comments to yourself for a little while, until she gets some food in her, anyway," Kai leans in to tell him, clasping his shoulder and giving him a light shake.

"He'd be better off keeping his mouth shut for the next five months until she delivers," Marco chuckles.

"At least I know *mia figlia* will stand up to you when she needs to. Makes a father proud," papa smiles at me before joining Marco on the opposite side of the table.

"I always knew she'd be a handful," Remi's voice comes from the doorway, "clearly the pregnancy hormones make it worse."

I glance over my shoulder and see him entering with Dmitri, "If you think I won't take you down, too, you're delusional."

Remi holds his hands up in a defensive gesture, smiling at me before making his way to the sideboard.

"Sorry we're late," Dmitri adds, slapping Remi on the neck as he passes him, "we decided to double check a few new security measures we heard you were, ah, running behind. Remi had to reset one of the new internal camera systems and it took a minute for the reboot."

"Thank you for checking on that," Papa smiles at them, "now get something to eat and join us."

I'm stunned. Papa has always, always been a stickler for time management. Is he getting soft in his old age? So weird.

Kai sits to my left, with Simon next to him at the end and Brooks sits to my right with Hudson on his other side. Remi and Dmitri get their plates before joining on papas side, splitting off to bracket them on either side. Dmitri next to Marco and Remi next to Papa.

It's odd to me how comfortable they are with each other, given that they've always had an employer/employee type relationship. They seem to have grown close in such a short time. I'm not sure what to make of it.

"The twins are staying at the house with you now," Brooks asks, pausing from his plate to take a few mouthfuls of juice.

"Yeah," Marco replies, "we feel better having them close."

"They're the only ones we're 100% sure of, that we can trust with everything. If anything happens, having them here will make a big difference," papa adds.

"And it's nice having others around, with Sloane moving out," Marco smiles at me.

"Which reminds me, we've kept Dr. Branson on payroll just in case, but we moved her to a penthouse in the city. Remind me to give you her information," papa tells me, finishing his coffee.

"Whose Dr. Branson," Simon asks.

"She took care of me when I was still living here. Gave me my shots every week, general check ups, stuff like that. She was really sweet."

"I hired her at the recommendation of the Academy. She retired from there; took care of generations of omegas," papa adds.

"What are her other qualifications," Brooks questions, "it would be helpful to have her available for Sloane during the pregnancy."

I roll my eyes so hard, I swear I see my brain.

"Can we stop planning for a pregnancy that we don't even know exists yet?"

"Okay, then let's assume for a minute that you aren't actually pregnant-"

"Ridiculous," Hudson interrupts, coughing the word out like a child.

I lean around Brooks, grabbing the biscuit off his plate and taking aim at Hudson. When I pull my arm back to sling it at him, Kai snatches the biscuit from me and hands it back to Brooks behind my back.

"Now children," Kai admonishes, "can we eat the food instead of playing with it?"

I turn in my chair so fast, Kai doesn't have time to react as I scoop up my juice glass and upend it into his lap.

"I think I've had enough this morning," I tell them all, pushing away from the table, "I'll be back when I'm ready to deal with all of you."

I snarl when Brooks reaches out for my hand.

"Do not. I will be back when I am ready," I snap between clenched teeth, throwing my napkin down on my chair and swinging the dining room door shut behind me.

I feel like I'm probably overreacting, but I can't stop myself. I stomp down the hallway, past papa's office and into the kitchen. I know Isa will be in there monitoring the feed for the dining room, making sure the dishes don't need refilling. I'm still hungry, but I am not going back in there right now.

"Oh my sweet child, get in here," Isa slides around the island to pull me into her arms, "you need me to go handle them?"

Her diminutive size means nothing when it comes to defending me. I have no doubt that she would march all five feet, two inches of her into the dining room and give my men a piece of her mind. She knows I can hold my own, which is likely the only reason she didn't already show up in there.

"Thank you, Isa, but no. It's my fault, I'm just feeling so sensitive this morning," I mutter, tears welling in spite of the fact that I'm angry and irritated, not sad.

"You come, sit down over here and I'll get you a plate going. Did you at least get to finish your coffee?"

"No, ma'am. And can I please have some biscuits, too. With your strawberry jam?"

"You know you get whatever you want in my kitchen," she rubs my back gently before placing a coffee cup in front of me, prepared just how I like it.

"There's just so much happening, Isa, I feel like I can't keep up. I'm happy, then sad and cranky. It's too much."

"You know exactly what's wrong with you, child, you just don't want to admit it."

"I'm too young to be a mother, Isa," I whisper, "I'm not ready. We've barely had a chance to get to know each other."

"Now you listen to me, Sloane," she snaps as she sets a plate full of biscuits down in front of me, "you have the biggest heart of anyone I've known. You might not have had the best childhood here with that witch of a woman, but you know love. You show love. Those men out there, they worship the ground you walk on. You think that, between the five of you, you won't be able to give that baby a loving home?"

"I'm so scared, Isa," I choke out, tears slipping down my cheeks, "I'm trying to be strong, to hide it, but sometimes I can't keep it inside anymore."

"You need to get it together, girl, because they're going to hunt you down whether you want them to or not, you keep it up," she gestures toward the monitors where I can see Brooks and Hudson standing next to the table, Kai sitting with his hand on Simon's shoulder.

I can't hear what's going on, but I can clearly see they're arguing with papa, surely trying to leave and find me. Hopefully he'll be able to keep them at bay while I try to pull myself together.

Isa goes to the fridge and pulls out two more carafes of juice. Pushing them into the hands of one of the other staff members, she directs the girl to inform everyone in the dining room that I'm fine and don't need anyone to come looking for me. Her eyes go wide for a moment, no doubt worried about delivering that kind of news to my angry alphas, but Isa assures her that papa will back her up.

I close my eyes and reflect back on the Academy teachings, taking deep breaths and repeating some of the calming mantras in my head. Isa steps to my side and slowly strokes up and down my back, helping to center me. Once I feel like I've managed to compartmentalize my feelings, I open my eyes and refocus on the screen.

Hudson still looks supremely agitated, but at least they're all sitting again. Crisis momentarily averted.

"I just wish I had had time to plan this, buy things, get a nursery together. Now we have, what, five months to try to buy everything we need AND get a nursery built. I don't even know where we would put one in the warehouse. It's just very overwhelming."

"Child, if you learned one thing growing up how you did, you should know money does a whole lot in this world. You could go out right now, buy everything you needed and get that whole warehouse renovated in time to welcome that little guy."

"I know, it's just…it was easier to deal with when it was a vague notion of the future, but this morning…when I went to the bathroom this morning, I could smell a change, ah, in my urine. I'm sure I'm pregnant. And I haven't told any of them," I finish miserably.

"They gonna know soon enough, it's just a matter of time until your whole scent changes, you know that."

"I know, I know," I mutter, stuffing a biscuit in my mouth after slathering it with strawberry jam, "but as soon as I tell them it all becomes real. You see how they are. I won't be able to leave the warehouse, they'll have me laying around all day with my feet up, not able to do anything on my own."

"Doesn't sound so bad to me," Isa cackles.

"Don't make me throw a biscuit at you, too!"

"You'll be fine, child, you know how to stand up for yourself. You let them moon and fuss over you, on your terms. When you've had enough, you let them know. It will all be fine, they were made just for you."

I smile at Isa, resting my head on her shoulder as she comes to stand next to me, reveling in the feeling of warmth and love I have for this woman. I pray she lives long enough that my baby will have memories of her, as well.

"I think maybe I should go up and take a nap. I didn't get much sleep last night and I'm sure that's not helping the situation. If anyone comes looking for me, you didn't see me, okay?"

"Anyone except your Pa, you know I gotta answer to the boss."

"Papa is fine, he won't bother me," I laugh as I give Isa one final hug and use the back stairway to head up to the second floor. It's a longer way around, but this way I'll avoid running into any of them.

Once I reach my rooms, I kick off my sneakers by the door and head across to the bed. I toss my sweater on the side table and crawl into the bed wearing just my leggings and tank top. I snuggle down under the covers, wishing I had my phone so I could set an alarm, but knowing Isa will tell papa where I am eventually.

I close my eyes, pressing one hand to my lower abdomen, cupping our new little life. For the thousandth time I wonder who he'll come out looking like. I don't care, at all, they're all going to be amazing fathers, I just want to know what he looks like.

Will he have a dimple, like me? Dark hair? What color will his eyes be? These are the thoughts that clutter my mind as I drift off to sleep.

CHAPTER TWENTY-TWO

Brooks

After eating, we all pile into the den, Remi offering to make drinks since Sloane is still MIA. I know she's sleeping now, probably in her room, I can feel it in the bond, but I'm not any less worried.

When we were apart, I could feel her distress through the bond. So many emotions, mostly sadness and fear. I wanted to find her, but Morris talked me down. He strongly believes she's pregnant, that she's experiencing the side effects of a massive hormone spike.

Normal gestation for an omega is just about 5 months, with the majority of changes happening in the early stages. She's likely going to be out of sorts for the next several weeks. Mood swings, sleeping more than usual, increased appetite.

"She's probably aware she's pregnant," Morris says as he drops down onto the couch next to me, "and that's why she freaked out a little. She's asleep now, right?"

I nod, "That's what it feels like, she's at peace."

"Then she'll wake up hungry and, as long as no one pisses her off again," he eyeballs Hudson hard, "she should be much better off."

"Unfortunately, there's nothing we can do about his personality, we've tried," Kai laughs.

"And for some reason, Sloane actually likes it," Simon chuckles along, "most of the time, anyway."

"You guys are so mean," Hudson sniffs, dropping into one of the chairs in front of the bar, "I'm totally telling Sloane when she wakes up. She won't put up with this kind of abuse against her baby daddy."

"God save me if my grandson comes out like you," Morris laughs, "I have enough gray hairs, thank you."

"Hey, you want him to be handsome, don't you? Not looking like a yeti," Hudson snarks, jerking a thumb toward Kaiser, "or a meathead" as he points at me.

"I just want him to be healthy and happy. And if you keep Sloane happy, he'll come out happy, so get your shit together - all of you - and figure it out."

"Trust me, we plan on it," I reply, "but let's talk about why we're really here."

"Volkov," Morris sighs.

"Volkov," I agree, "and the girl."

"Which I will handle," Morris jumps in, "it's my responsibility to fix what Iris did. I understand that you will be involved, after what Volkov did, I know you need your revenge, but the girl is my responsibility."

"I'm not arguing with you on that, Morris," I assure him, "whatever you want to do to ensure the girl's safety is fine by me, but we need to come up with a plan together so we're not stepping on each other's toes out there."

"If I may," Dmitri chimes in.

Morri waves a hand in his direction, encouraging him to speak as Remi walks around handing out drinks to everyone except Simon. He's not allowed to drink with his medication regimen.

"Simon can get into the hotel's system, figure out which room Gallo booked them into. He can also find floor plans for the hotel. We get into the room before they arrive, take out the father and secure the girl. Then we wait in the room for either or both of them to show up. Simple. Easy. Our best bet for getting them."

"Except there's no guarantee Volkov will enter that room," Kai replies, "we could go through all the effort and only end up with one of them."

"One is better than none," Remi adds.

"And if we have Nikolaj, he'll be able to lead us to Volkov or we use him to set up a trap for Volkov," Marco points out, "we'll still be able to end it even if we only get Nikolaj."

"And another girl will be saved," Morris adds quietly, "another omega; we have to take that into consideration."

"We are," I reply, "we will rescue the girl, no matter what. I just want to make sure that we put every effort into getting Volkov, as well. Sloane won't be safe until we can neutralize both of them. If we can work it out, to ensure both of them are there while rescuing the girl at the same time, that would be ideal."

"Is there any way we can communicate to Volkov that Sloane would be there, too," Kai asks, flicking his eyes in my direction briefly, but not willing to hold the contact, "lure him in with a kind of two for one deal?"

I can't stop the growl from rolling out of my mouth, the idea of Sloane in danger activating every protective instinct I have. We've just barely gotten her back, there's no way I'm putting her anywhere any kind of danger ever again.

"She doesn't actually have to be there," Simon adds quickly, "we just have to create some kind of scenario where he would think she's there."

"I don't know how we would do that, since we have no connection between us and them. No one we can pretend to secretly send information through," I point out, "we would have to make it seem like he's coming across the information by chance."

"Fuck, I have an idea," Hudson mutters, "but you probably won't like it and I'm not 100% sure it will work."

"Well don't just leave us in suspense, asshat," Remi calls from behind the bar, "what's the idea."

"We still have Alexis Leone being held at one of our other warehouses. No one knows we have her. We could use her to get to Volkov."

"How," I ask.

"We give her all the information, send her to Volkov. Make sure she knows what will happen if she double crosses us. She tells Volkov that she's seeking asylum because of what we did to her brother, in exchange she can provide information about Sloane. Alexis tells Volkov that Sloane is staying at the Hawthorne because we had a falling out and she didn't want to go back home to her father."

"There's a lot of variables in that equation that I'm not sure I'm happy with," Simon replies, "there's no way for us to guarantee that she doesn't double cross us. Not that she knows anything significant, but she could just as easily tell them it's a trap. Then we won't have any other way to get to them easily."

"I think our best bet is to stick with the plan as Dmitri outlined it. It's simple and to the point. We'll at least get our hands on one of them and save the girl," Marco adds, after listening to Hudson and Simon.

"I don't like the idea of releasing Alexis or of putting Sloane in danger again," I tell Hudson, "I appreciate your input, but I think we should move forward with the intent to save the girl and get whoever we can without involving anyone else."

Hudson nods, "I get it, it was probably a long shot anyway."

"So basically we have today and tomorrow to get everything in place," Remi questions.

"I'd say we need to be in place by late tomorrow night. I don't know when they're supposed to check into the hotel, but we need to be there before them so we can secure the girl," Kai replies.

"Her name is Mariella, can we stop calling her the girl, please," Dmitri says.

"I'll need her full name anyway, so I can find her or her father's reservation in the Hawthorne system," Simon says, opening up his laptop.

"Should be easy for you, huh," Hudson nudges him with his foot, "I bet they have shit security."

"We shall see," Simon replies, tapping away at his keyboard.

"Okay, while Simon works on figuring out the room and getting floor plans, let's expand on the plan," Marco gestures at Dmitri and Remi to move in closer.

"We'll have to check the floor plans before we can really nail everything down, but we can come up with something general," I glance around to see everyone paying attention except Simon, his attention currently absorbed by whatever he's doing on the screen.

"We'll have Simon watching over everything, just like when we went in after Sloane. I'm sure the hotel has security that he can infiltrate. If I remember the layout correctly, Remi can hang out in the bar, he should be able to see the entrance from there."

"Why do I have to hang out in the bar? I want in on the action."

Morris reaches across the table and slaps Remi on the ear, "You take orders, you don't give them."

"You're the least conspicuous," Hudson tells him, "Mid thirties, no tattoos, basic haircut. Put you in a suit and no one will look twice at you."

"Fuck you, Alfera," Remi snaps.

"Remi, shut up," Marco intones, "you're just mad because it's true."

"Goddaamn you guys. My own people, not on my side!"

"We need someone on the front and you're the least recognizable, especially if we put you in a suit like Hudson suggests. They know all of us, but Kai's about 8 inches taller than all of us and Hudson's covered in tattoos. Marco and Morris are packmates to the men who came to him for protection. They will stand out, you won't."

Remi makes a face, but then begrudgingly nods.

"Okay, Kai, Hudson and I will watch the outside doors, hopefully catch them before they even make it in. That leaves Dmitri, Morris, and Marco to infiltrate the room, however you want to do that, I'll leave it to you."

"If Simon's going to play eye in the sky, he'll be able to let us know if anyone gets past the four of you. I say we all go in together," Dmitri suggests, "the two of you can secure Mariella while I take care of her father."

"We'll have to see the layout of the room and where the hidden entrance is. If we're seen in the room before they make it in, we'll spook them. We have to make sure there's space for us to remain out of sight so they get all the way in," Marco says.

"Agreed," Morris nods at Marco, "but I do think it's important for all of us to be in there when the time comes. I'm sure Dmitri can take care of the father, but he needs back up, just in case. Then one of us needs to secure Mariella."

"Don't you think it would be better to have another woman there for Mariella," Sloane yawns from the doorway.

"Baby, did you get enough sleep? How are you feeling," Hudson murmurs, walking up and scooping her into his arms, "Do you want something to drink? Water, juice?"

He carries her across the room and drops gently onto the couch with her still clasped in his arms. She snuggles into his chest, letting out a contented sigh, and I can feel the love and happiness running through the bond to all of us.

"Juice would be nice, pineapple, please."

Hudson nods at Remi who jumps up to scoot behind the bar and get the juice.

"What do you mean, another woman should be there, *stellina*?"

"I mean," Sloane yawns again, "this girl doesn't know anything about anything, right? So she's checking into a hotel, probably told she's having a night out or mini vacation or something else equally fun, then finds a bunch of strange men in her room who also happen to be attacking her father. Not a great scenario."

"She makes a good point," I side eye Morris, irritated at myself that we didn't think about this.

"I don't have any women on payroll that I would trust to bring along. House staff have been vetted, but they're not exactly field ops. I don't think Dr. Branson would like to be an accessory to kidnapping, regardless of how much I pay her."

"I have some money movers that are female, but I'm not gonna lie, my soldiers are men. I don't like putting women in the line of fire, regardless of their capabilities."

"I'll go," Sloane says after gulping down a mouthful of juice, "I'll be safe with dad and Marco and Dmitri. She'll trust me and I know how to take care of myself."

"Abso-fucking-lutely fucking not," Kai snaps, turning on the couch to face her, "Have you lost your mind."

Sloane straightens in Hudson's lap, her head whipping to the side, "I don't know who the hell you think you're talking to right now Kaiser Pietro Moretti, but you better redirect that shit right now!"

Kai sits back, stunned to his core, I can feel his absolute shock pumping through the bond.

"Damn, baby," Hudson tucks Sloane tighter against him, "he's just worried about you. It's okay."

Sloane huffs out a breath and snuggles back down into Hudson's lap, tucking her head under his chin and going back to drinking her juice. But no matter the show she's putting on, her irritation is crackling through the bond like a live wire.

"I don't agree with you being there either, especially given the fact that we know Volkov wants you back. He's going to want retaliation for Petrov and what better way to do that, than by taking you back," I question her calmly.

"I'll be with three well trained men, one of which is my father. The three of you will be watching doors, Simon watching the cameras and Remi inside in the bar. You really think either of them will be able to slip through all that and get to me?"

"It's about keeping you safe, little omega. Out in public like that, even with us watching, there's a million things that could go wrong. We learned that lesson the hard way and we don't want to go through that again."

Sloane looks across the coffee table at Morris, "Papa?"

"I love you, my girl, so much. I couldn't stand it if you were taken again. While I agree that your suggestion makes sense, having a woman there, it can't be you. I can't risk it."

"Okay, okay" she rolls her eyes, "I'm out voted, I get it."

Hudson leans in and, cupping his hand around her ear, starts whispering something dirty and depraved, based on the redness in her cheeks and the sudden desire wrapping through the bond. No doubt we'll be able to smell her shortly if he doesn't reign it in.

She leans back against Hudson, relaxing and sipping her juice.

"Good girl," he murmurs against her cheek, running his fingers through her hair and adjusting her so she's tucked back up against him again.

"Now that Sloane's brought up the point though, how do we handle Marielle if she's uncooperative," Dmitri asks.

"Not the direction I'd like to go, but she is an omega and all three of us are alphas. One of us just has to dominate her until she submits, then hustle her out of there. Sloane waits at the warehouse for us, we take Mariella there to explain everything," Marco glances around the group gauging our responses.

"That's a good a plan as any," I agree, "Sloane will be at the warehouse with Simon, the warehouse is closer to the Hawthorne than the compound. My question is, what's your plan after you rescue her?"

"Yeah," Hudson adds, "doesn't seem like the best idea to kidnap a chick, off her dad, then let her go like nothing happened. I mean, what's your guarantee that she won't squeal?"

"Obviously we're going to explain everything to her," Morris retorts, "I figure she'll be pretty grateful that we saved her from a life of sexual slavery. I'll give her enough money to support herself for the rest of her life.

And we'll be there for her if she needs anything. I'm sure that's enough to keep her from reporting anyone."

"I think that would work," Sloane pipes up.

"Okay, then, assuming that Petruk hasn't shown at the time we get the girl out, Dmitri can join us downstairs while you guys bring Mariella here."

"That sounds good to me. I don't want to sit around the warehouse waiting on you assholes to take him down"

"Okay, I'm in," Simon's sudden announcement throws me for a second. He's always so quiet when he's distracted, plus I can't feel him through the bond.

"Show us what you got, hotshot," Hudson tells him.

"I'm fully integrated into their security. I'll get an alert as soon as they check in and I have all the cameras on that floor tagged. The floorplan shows five entry points on the ground floor. The main lobby entrance, the loading dock and an employee entrance, plus two alternate entries for guests which can only be opened by a keycard."

"You can lock those, right? Keep the cards from working," I ask.

"Of course," he smiles at me, laughing a little, "I'll freeze those two doors, leaving just the lobby which Remi will be covering and the loading dock and employee entrance. The loading dock has a large roller door for big deliveries, but also a smaller door next to the dock. Two of you should stay there while the other watches the employee entrance."

"I'll take the employee entrance, probably won't be as many people, easy for me to cover it on my own," Kai volunteers, "then Dmitri can join me there once they secure the girl."

I nod in agreement.

"Now, onto the suite. The hidden entrance is through an empty closet next to the room, labeled as a janitor's closet, but it's not actually in use. There's a removable panel in the closet which reveals the back panel of the wardrobe in the bedroom of the suite, which is also removable. So, not an easy entrance or extraction, but given that she'll be conscious and able to move on her own, should be a piece of cake."

"We won't be able to stay in the closet while they get in the room. There's no way we can all make it through such a small space and still have the element of surprise," Marco muses.

"What's the bathroom look like in comparison to the room," Dmitri asks Simon.

"Exactly what I was thinking," he replies, "There are actually two bathrooms, one attached to the bedroom and another just off the main sitting area. I figure two of you in the main bathroom, the other in the bedroom, that way you can cut off their exit."

"I like that idea," Morris looks at Dmitri and Marco for confirmation. They both nod back.

"The empty closet you'll enter through is in an alcove with the vending and ice machine. Next to the ice machine is an employee only entrance that leads to the freight elevator and down to the laundry room below the hotel. I'm assuming that's how he moved them out. Tossed them into a laundry bin and pushed it down like it's nothing important."

"The freight elevator has an entrance on each floor," I ask.

"Yes and it doesn't look like they're monitored. No cameras in the freight elevators or in the alcoves."

"Okay, so once we secure the girl, we take the freight down to the first floor and exit from there, less witnesses," Dmitri adds and the others agree.

"My suggestion, we get two rooms at the Hawthorne, under fake names, of course. Sloane and I stay at the warehouse, the seven of you check in and stay tomorrow night. They're supposed to be there day after tomorrow, but we don't know when they're going to show. We need to be in place in advance."

"Everyone in agreement on that," I ask, making eye contact around the room, to make sure we're all on the same page, "Good. I'll have Simon make the arrangements and I'll contact you with room information tomorrow morning."

"Can we go home now," Sloane yawns again, "I love you papa and I did want to pack some stuff today, but I am so tired and I just want to go home."

"Of course, *mia figlia*, you need to take care of yourself right now, just in case, okay?"

I stand, reaching down to shake Morris' hand, "Thank you for having us. As Isa suggested, I would like to make this a regular thing, maybe Sundays?"

"I think I'd like that," Morris grips my hand, then pulls me against him for a quick hug, clapping me once on the back, "I'll make Isa aware."

I walk over and scoop Sloane up, letting Hudson get up and say his goodbyes, bringing Sloane back to her father. I don't put her down, though, she can get all of her hugs while I'm still holding her. I've been missing her all day, especially after the tangle of feelings she was having when she left us.

As we follow Hudson down the hall to the front door, Sloane slings both arms around my neck and buries her face in my neck. Her warm breath puffs against my neck and I relish the contentment I feel coming from her.

"Will you nap with me when we get home," she murmurs, her lips brushing my neck with each word.

"I think I'd like that, *tesoro*, I think I'd like that a lot."

CHAPTER TWENTY-THREE

Sloane

I do not want to get out of this bed. I know I should, I know it's late based on the light coming through the edges of the curtains, but I just can't make myself care. Kaiser is pressed against my back, tucking my tiny frame back into his bulk, both of our arms tossed over Brooks who's face down on the mattress, but pressed to my front.

I'm trying really hard to rotate my time with each of them, since I stayed with Hudson the night before and I'll be with Simon tonight, I figured Brooks and Kai could share me last night. Brooks spent most of yesterday in and out with me napping. I loved having him so close.

I emailed Dr. Branson a million and one questions yesterday, letting her know I was pregnant and setting up a day and time for her to examine me. I'm going to tell the guys today, but I wanted to have a plan in place because I have a feeling they'll be just as overwhelmed as I was at first.

She did let me know that I should expect to be much more tired than usual and much more hungry than usual. I have to remember to put in another order with Marcino's, Branson said I needed to double my protein. And I've been craving sweets more than usual. And chips. I'll have to make a list before I call.

Now that I'm awake and my brain is online, the rest of my body is following suit. The scent of Brooks and Kai swirling around me is going straight to my pussy. I was so tired yesterday, I was already asleep when both of them crawled into bed with me. Now I'm taking advantage of the situation.

I wiggle around until I'm on my back, Kai groaning lightly as I jostle him. I slide one hand down Brooks' back, squeezing his ass while I slide the other down to grip Kai's semi hard cock. He groans when my hand makes contact, hardening quickly as I gently stroke it.

"*Cara,*" Kair groans, shifting back a little so I can stroke him fully.

"I want you," I moan, "touch me, please."

"With pleasure," Brooks whispers before slicking his tongue over my hardened nipple. He sucks and bites at the sensitive peak, pressing his other hand between my legs to stroke my clit in time with his tongue.

I spread my legs wide, throwing one leg over Kai's hip so I can spread as much as possible, giving Brooks room to work my pussy. I continue to squeeze and stroke Kai's cock while he moans his encouragement.

It feels so good, but I need more.

"Fuck me, please, I need it."

"Such a dirty mouth on you," Brooks mutters, pulling his fingers from my pussy and shoving them into my mouth, "we'll give you everything you need."

Brooks nods at Kai who grips my hips and flips me onto my side. He hooks his elbow under my knee and spreads me wide open. I feel his cock sliding along my pussy lips, from behind, his cock bumping my clit as he rocks his hips.

Brooks pulls his fingers out of my mouth and reaches down to grips Kai's cock, helping him get into position to push inside of me. I let out a soft cry as his cock stretches my pussy, slick leaking out to ease his entry. He rocks slowly at first, preparing my tight pussy to take his girth.

"Please," I whisper, the pressure of his cock against my g-spot almost too much to handle, "faster, please."

"I'm not going to tear you up, baby, be patient. Distract her."

I feel Brooks fingers return to my clit, circling and circling, driving me higher while Kai works me open. He leans forward to suck and bite my nipples, just as Kai's hips pick up speed.

"Ooh, yes," I moan as his hips snap against my ass, his cock sliding easily in and out of me now, slick soaking us both. The combination of Kai riding my g-spot and Brooks stroking my clit has me shaking and whimpering, begging for more.

Brooks pinches my clit, just this side of painful and I explode. My head kicks back against Kai's chest and I wheeze out a scream, surprised by the sudden climax. Kai groans, his chest vibrating against my back as his thrusts pick up speed.

"Fuck, baby, I love it when you cum on my cock, oh yeah, fuck, I'm gonna fill you up," Kai grunts, pushing me onto my front and following me over. He hooks his arm under my hips, holding me up and against him while the other is braced on the bed, supporting our weight.

I brace my elbows to keep my face out of the mattress while Kai pounds into me. He feels so good inside of me, I can feel myself building to another orgasm. The sounds my wet pussy makes are obscene as Kai rails me.

I cock my head to the side, trying to find Brooks. He's kneeling next to me, cock in hand, watching as Kai fucks me.

"Don't worry baby, I'm gonna fill you up next," he groans, watching Kai pound into me.

"He's gonna fuck this sloppy pussy just as soon as I'm done with it, fuck my cum deep inside you before he adds his. You want that, dirty girl, you want our cum inside of this filthy cunt," Kai pounds hard, his words zinging across my clit as his intense thrusts push me over the edge at the same moment I feel his cock throb with release.

I turn my face to muffle my scream in the comforter. Not that it matters, Hudson can feel everything going on right now, but maybe I can save Simon the torture.

My scream fades into whimpers as Kai slips his softening cock out of me. I can feel his cum mixed with my slick dropping onto the bed below me as Brooks shifts around and lines his cock up.

I squeal as Brooks lands a hard slap to my right ass cheek before thrusting into me, hard.

"Such a dirty girl," he groans, pulling out and slapping my ass again before slamming back into me, "with a dirty cunt."

He grips both my ass cheeks, fingertips digging in to the point I'm sure they'll leave marks. I love it. I love every dirty word and mark, I love how they use me behind closed doors, but worship me like a princess in front of others. It's our dirty little secret.

Brooks alternates between fucking my weeping cunt and pulling out to smack my ass. I feel Kai's fingers slip against my soaking pussy, finding my clit and squeezing it rhythmically while Brooks abuses my ass cheeks.

"You look so sexy with a red ass, *tesoro*, showing everyone what a naughty girl you are. Loves getting her little pussy fucked, but how will she feel when she starts taking cock here," and I cry out as Brooks pushes a finger into my ass.

"Do you like that, *tesoro*? Stretching both of your slutty little holes to take us. Who do you want in here first," he questions, sliding his finger in and out in counter to his cock pumping in and out of my pussy.

I can't answer, the feelinga are so overwhelming. The initial burn of his finger pressing into me has faded into an almost too full feeling. His cock rubbing inside of me with the added pressure of his finger is waking new nerve endings and feelings deep inside of me. I can't process the new sensations fast enough.

I moan in response, starting to rock my hips in time with his finger entering me.

"Such a dirty little slut, you want to be stuffed full, don't you," Brooks groans, picking up speed to match my hips driving back against him, "you just can't get enough."

I arch my back and let out a guttural cry as he pushes a second finger into my ass, scissoring them to open me further.

"Soon, baby, soon you'll be taking one of us right here," Brooks pushes his fingers deep, driving his cock in and out as Kai changes to rough circles against my clit, "but until then, I'm going to cum in this hot little pussy while you cum all over my cock. Cum for me baby, cum for me."

Between Brooks cock and fingers, Kai circling my clit, and Brooks filthy mouth, I feel myself hurtling toward an epic orgasm. My thighs are twitching and I can barely catch my breath as pussy clenches around Brooks cock. Kai pulls his hand away just as my upper body collapses to the mattress and I turn my face to the side, sobbing through the hardest orgasm I think I've ever had.

"That's it, my little fuckdoll, that's it," Brooks groans deep, driving into me one last time and I can feel his hot cum filling me.

After a few moments, Brooks leans down and kisses my lower back, slipping out of me, "I'll be right back, *tesoro*."

Kai pulls me against his side, curling around me as Brooks makes his way to the bathroom, likely to wash his hands.

I let out a contented sigh, feeling more relaxed than I have in awhile. As Brooks climbs back into the bed with us, a yawn sneaks out. I guess I'm more relaxed than I realized.

"What time 's it," I mumble, closing my eyes and wiggling back into Kai until I'm cozy as can be.

"Way past time for you to be awake," Kai tells me, tugging the ends of my hair gently, "you need to eat something."

"Kai's right," Brooks taps my nose, "you didn't eat dinner last night. You're going to waste away if you keep sleeping like this."

I yawn loudly, stretching my arms up and almost slapping Kai in the face.

"Mmmm, I suppose I could eat, but you're going to need to move," I tilt my head back until the top of my head is resting against Kai's chest and I can see his chin. He looks down, planting a light kiss on my forehead.

"Your wish is my command, *cara*," he rolls onto his back, taking me with him as I squeal and laugh. He rolls right off the edge of the bed onto his feet, the whole time holding me against him. He keeps me tucked against him, feet dangling as he makes his way to the bathroom.

"You wanna grab her some clothes while I get her cleaned up," he calls to Brooks as he steps into the bathroom and heads directly to the shower enclosure.

"I have to pee," I squeak out, as Kai tests the water temperature. He turns to carry me out of the stall, "put me down! I do not need you to carry me to the toilet!"

"Are you sure," he chuckles, sliding me down his body until my feet hit the tiles.

"Stay," I point at him, scurrying out of the shower and over to the toilet. Luckily he has the water running, and the glass is kind of frosted because I really need to go and don't need to fight with performance anxiety right now.

I sit on the toilet, trying to relax, counting in my head and focusing on anything other than the fact that Kai is less than 5 feet away from me. I take a couple of deep breaths, forcing myself to relax, relax, relax as I chant in my head. Finally, my bladder gets the memo.

Before I can reach for the toilet paper, Kai is stepping out of the shower and starting toward me, sniffing the air. Shit. I'd gotten used to the change in smell so it didn't even register that Kai would notice it.

"Based on your complete lack of reaction right now, I'm going to go ahead and assume you've known about this for a while," Kai accuses, his hurt and sadness squeezing the bond between us.

"I-I…yes, I noticed it yesterday," I grimace guiltily, "I swear I was going to tell all of you. This morning, actually. I was planning on telling everyone over breakfast."

"This is why you were so upset yesterday, flying off the handle?"

I nod, face flaming as I sit here on the toilet with him standing over me. Embarrassment seeping from my very pores.

"Sorry, *cara*," he says softly, "go ahead and clean yourself up, come shower with me."

He turns and walks back into the shower, giving me the opportunity to catch my breath and wipe. I follow him into the shower, sliding up behind him and wrapping my arms around his waist. I press my breasts against his ass and nestle my face against his lower back, breathing his scent deep into my lungs.

I can still feel the hurt lingering in the bond.

"I promise you, I was going to tell you all this morning. I even made an appointment with Dr. Branson for later today, so we could all go together. I just needed to wrap my head around it before sharing it. It's a lot for me, you know. It's not like we've known each other that long, we went through a completely traumatic experience between Simon and the kidnapping. I was hoping we would be able to spend time getting to know each other, but instead we're going to be parents."

"Are you-do you regret it," he chokes out.

"Oh, Kai, no," I murmur against his back, focusing on the life growing inside of me and everything I feel. For the baby, my mates, the future we have to look forward to.

Kai's breath hitches and he tugs me around in front of him, lifting me up so I can wrap my arms around his neck and my legs around his waist. He burrows his face into my neck and we hold each other tight, reveling in the incandescent feelings of joy and excitement. The warm water beats down on us from every angle, but we're lost in each other.

He slides his hand up the back of my neck, tugging my head back so he can seal his lips to mine. He slides his tongue against my lower lip and I open for him, meeting his tongue with mine and savoring the taste of him.

I tangle my fingers in his hair, holding him to me just as desperately as he holds me. His tongue sweeps through my mouth, dominating me, making me whimper and writhe against him as his scent intensifies around me. He growls against my lips, making my pussy contract and smear slick across his belly.

I can feel his hardened cock under me, sliding between my ass cheeks. He reaches down between us, pulling his cock up so it's trapped between us and I can rub my pussy on it instead of his stomach. He grips a cheek in each hand and rocks me up and down against him.

"I want to be soft and sweet to you, *cara*, but the smell of that slick sets me off every time," he grunts, adjusting my hips and dragging me down against him so his cock notches at my opening, "and I can't help but fuck you."

He slams me down onto his cock, knowing I'm wet enough to take him, still filled with cum and slick from our earlier antics. I throw my head back, letting out a hoarse scream as his cock splits me open.

"Touch yourself, Sloane because I'm not going to last," he snarls, dragging me up and down on his cock like I'm just a toy to be used for his pleasure. I reach between us, using three fingers to rub my clit roughly, already close just because of how he's manhandling me, using me.

I keep one arm locked around his neck, frantically stroking myself with the other as he fucks into me. I press hard on my clit, rubbing up and down quickly until I shatter, my pussy squeezing his dick as I cry out my pleasure.

"Fuck yeah, that's it, that's it," he slams me down once more, popping his knot inside of me and I clench around him. I scream as the pressure of his knot and his hot cum makes me orgasm again and again around him.

He growls softly into my neck, burying his face against me. His growls subside as he starts to lick and suck at his mating mark.

I hold him against me, stroking my fingers through his hair and murmuring how much I love him. Not caring about the passage of time or how the others might feel, I revel in this moment of joy and tranquility.

Until I hear Hudson let himself into the bathroom.

"You know I love you guys, right, but I'm starting to feel left out," he whines.

"You can't be inside her all the time, bro. Sharing is caring," his lips tickling against my throat with each word out of his mouth.

"Fuck, you knotted her, too," he complains as he joins us in the shower, wrapping an arm around each of us and squeezing tight, pressing against our sides.

I smile at him, wrapping one arm around his neck and pulling him close for a kiss, but keeping Kai tucked against my neck. Kai adjusts his grip on me, sliding one arm under my ass for support so he can tuck the other around Hudson.

"Sharing *is* caring," I murmur against Hudson's lips, "and I don't want you to feel left out. So, I'll share something with you that I've only shared with Kai, okay? Will that make you feel better?"

"Yes," he moans, as I feel Kai's fist against my thigh, wrapping around Hudson's cock and pumping.

"Or maybe Kai's making you feel better already," I whisper against his mouth, licking lightly against his lips before nipping at his jaw and neck.

"Tell me," he whimpers as I make my way down his neck, biting hard then licking away the sting.

I can feel his hips starting to shift, pumping his cock in and out of Kai's fist. His fingers tighten reflexively, squeezing into my side as Kai teases him.

"Please," he moans.

I'm not sure if he's begging me or Kai, but it's so sexy seeing him like this. Kai's fist speeds up, stroking roughly, focusing on the head of his cock.

I kiss him gently a few times, murmuring against his mouth, "I'm pregnant."

His eyes snap open, meeting him. His pupils are blown.

"Serious," he pants out, "for sure?"

"I smelled it this morning," Kai tells him, lifting his face from my neck to press his mouth against Hudson's.

"Oh fuck," his voice is muffled by Kai's mouth, but I can feel his hips kick against me, Kai's strokes speeding up as Hudson fucks against him.

Kai bites Hudson's bottom lip, tugging it before telling him, "She's going to start showing, everyone will know that you filled her pussy up so good. Such a good boy, pumping her full of your cum, now she's pregnant, you rutted that tight little pussy and she took your seed."

"Fuck," Hudson barks, his hot cum splashing against my thigh. Kai keeps pumping him, making sure every drop smears across my leg.

I press my mouth to his, plucking kisses as he pants against me.

"I love you so much, little omega, so much."

We stand like that, wrapped around each other, taking turns sharing kisses between the three of us. Kai's softened dick slips out of me, the sound of our mixed cum splashing on the tiles bringing us out of our little cloud of contentment.

"Let's get you cleaned up, little omega," Hudson steadies me as Kai sets me back on my feet, my hips aching from being spread so wide for so long, "you go over there."

Hudson pushes Kai toward the opposite shower head, grabbing the soap and dropping to his knees before me.

He lathers one leg and then the other, gently scrubbing and rinsing each foot. He makes his way up my legs, sliding his fingers against my pussy and back further between my ass cheeks.

He grabs one of the removable shower heads, directing it between my legs to rinse me, but letting it linger against my clit.

"No," I moan, "we don't have time for this."

He smiles wickedly before spinning me around and rinsing my ass, slipping his fingers into the crack to spread my cheeks apart. He kisses the back of my shoulder before putting the shower head back and soaping my back and sides. He slides his hands up my front, kneading my breasts and tugging on my nipples before rinsing me again.

"You're a tease," I complain, "and you're not helping."

"You don't even understand, little omega," he presses against my back, his newly hardened cock slipping against my ass, "I'm going to fuck you every single chance I can. The fact that you're pregnant right now, my cock is going to be like this all the time, wanting to be inside of that juicy cunt."

"Not now, sweetcheeks, there are two other men waiting on us right now who need to be let in on the secret."

"I do have a nice ass, but that one's not gonna fly, baby. Should I make you a list to try?"

"I think I'm doing just fine on my own, snookums."

"Oh, hell no," he laughs, grabbing the shampoo and working it through my hair, keeping his cock pressed tight to my ass.

"I'll finish up here," Kai tells Hudson, tugging him away from me, "I don't trust you to keep that thing under control."

"You shouldn't," Hudson laughs, but doesn't protest as he walks out to dry off, "I'm gonna stick it in her every chance I get."

Kai rinses the shampoo out before switching to the conditioner. Gently stroking it through my hair before rinsing it, too. He reaches around me to turn the water off, planting a gentle kiss on my shoulder before swinging me around and wrapping me in a towel that Hudson tosses to him.

"Did Brooks leave clothes out for her," he asks as he starts rubbing me dry, finishing by wrapping the towel around my hair and pushing me toward the door.

"Yeah, they're on the bed," he pushes open the door, "I'll get Brooks to start on breakfast. Or brunch, whatever."

He whistles his way out into the hall as Kai helps me on with the clothes Brooks laid out, a pair of jeans for Kai set out, as well. The sight makes my heart swell. My men, taking care of each other and not just me.

"We're all in this together, Sloane, we all love each other, even if it's not all the same kind of love, it's still love."

He tugs his jeans on before gripping my hand and tugging me out into the hallway. The smell of coffee gets stronger, the closer we get to the kitchen and my mouth practically waters. Everything smells stronger, sharper now.

Hudson smiles at me from behind the espresso machine, steaming milk for some kind of drink.

"I'm making you a latte, little omega," he winks, "less caffeine than a whole cup, with the same coffee taste you love. Just in case."

"A man after my whole heart," I smile back as I blow him kisses.

"Not the whole thing, *tesoro*," Brooks interjects, eyebrow raised, "he has to share you."

"I promise I'll save some for all of you," I reply, making my way around the kitchen, planting kisses on Brooks and Simon before accepting my latte from Hudson.

"Take Simon and sit down, food is almost ready," Brooks says, flipping the waffle maker open and sliding out four fluffy little squares.

"Smells delicious," I tell him, taking Simon's hand and walking toward the table. Hudson pulls out chairs for both of us.

Kai approaches with a platter of scrambled eggs in one hand and bacon in the other. Brooks is just behind him with a tray of waffles and various syrups. They set both in the middle of the table before joining us.

Simon and I are on one side, Brooks at the head of the table to my right. Kai is at the other end next to Simon and Hudson is across from me. I realize that Hudson and Kai orchestrated this, so that the two men who didn't yet know our surprise would be closest to me.

"You've been all over the place this morning," Brooks takes my hand gently, "everything okay?"

"Of course," I smile at him, "just a lot on my mind. I feel better now."

"Anything we can do to help," Simon asks from my other side.

"I do need a ride later and I was hoping that you all would come with me," I tangle my fingers with Simon's, reaching across the corner of the table to grip Brooks' hand as well, "I have an appointment with Dr. Branson."

Brooks hand tightens briefly, "And what are we seeing Dr. Branson for, *tesoro*?"

I tug Simon closer to me, resting my head against his shoulder, wanting to include him as much as possible. I want Simon to feel as much a part of this as all of the rest of them. He's so vulnerable right now, and until he's mated with Kai and brought into the loop, I'm going to give him every extra bit of love and affection I can muster.

"You're practically glowing, beautiful," Simon murmurs, kissing my forehead, "Do you have something exciting to share with us?"

"You," I smile up at him, "are you going to be a father. All of you are going to be fathers."

I beam at each of them in turn, reveling in the warmth and joy that flows through the bond, looping back and forth between the four of us. Mourning briefly because Simon can't enjoy it with us, but comforting myself with the knowledge that we won't have to wait much longer until he is.

Simon tugs me more firmly against him, wrapping his arms so tight I'm worried he's hurting himself.

"I don't even have words, Sloane," he chokes a little, "thank you, so much for allowing me to be a part of all of this."

"You're just as important as any of us," I whisper to him, cupping his cheeks and kissing him gently, "I love you so much, Simon Costa."

"I love you, too, beautiful girl."

Brooks clears his throat, "If I may?"

Simon kisses me once more before letting me go and nudging me to turn towards Brooks.

Brooks towers over me, standing next to my chair, but quickly squats down once I'm facing him. He squeezes me against him, burying his face in my neck and licks his mating mark.

"I can't even express how happy I am right now, *tesoro*. You are going to be an amazing mother. Thank you for choosing us."

"I'll always choose you, every single one of you."

"Group hug," Hudson yells, pushing halfway out of his chair until Kai grabs his arm and yanks him back down.

"No," Kai intones, letting go of Hudson's arms, but narrowing his eyes and pointing aggressively at him.

I laugh at the two of them, at the joy in this moment, the love between us and the life we're looking forward to.

Brooks reaches across the table for the waffles, piling several on my plate before going for the bacon and eggs.

"You need a lot of protein, you're eating for two now and you need to make sure you're staying hydrated," he starts pouring juice for me, "do you really think caffeine is good for you?"

"See this is why I made an appointment with Dr. Branson," I laugh again, "She can tell you that I'm allowed to drink coffee and eat whatever I want and make decisions without all of your input."

"And she'll be able to tell us what you need to eat and how much and she'll back us up if you're not taking care of yourself so well," Hudson tacks on.

"I'm going to start a spreadsheet. We can track your calorie intake, your macros and protein consumption. We can make sure that you're sleeping enough-"

"Woah," I cut him off, "everyone needs to calm down. Write your questions down and give them to Dr. Branson later. I just want to eat and go back to sleep. The only reason I'm out here right now is to deliver the happy news."

I hold up my fork when Hudson opens his mouth again, "Yes, it's perfectly normal for me to be sleeping this much. It will probably continue for the next 2-3 weeks. After that, my libido will significantly increase through the remainder of my pregnancy, so be prepared for that, too."

I grab the fresh strawberry syrup and flood my waffles while simultaneously hooking a strip of bacon on my fork and shoving it into my mouth. I crunch on the bacon while aggressively eyeballing all of the men around the table.

"Any other questions," I ask, stabbing into the waffles.

"Ah, I think we'll save them for the doctor," Simon mutters, watching as I continue to shovel food into my mouth.

"What time is your appointment," Kai asks.

"It's at 4. I figured we could go to see her and then the three of you can go to the Hawthorne while Simon and I come back here?"

"Who's gonna drive?"

"I can drive," I snap indignantly, "just because I don't do it that often."

"Okay, killer, okay," Hudson soothes me, sliding more bacon onto my plate, "you can drive whatever you want."

I smile at him briefly before diving back into my plate. The waffles are perfect, so crispy on the outside, but warm and fluffy inside. The bacon is nice and salty. I haven't tried the eggs yet, but I'm sure they're just as good.

We breeze through the rest of breakfast in quiet, happy companionship. The warmth pulsing through the bond is soothing as I finish off the last waffle.

"Everything was perfect, thank you so much," I sigh, sipping the rest of my juice, "I'm so full."

"And now you're ready for a nap, right," Brooks chuckles.

"Funny you should ask because I am, but I don't want to move."

"That's okay, *tesoro*, I'll carry you," Brooks smiles down at me, before scooping me into his arms and swinging back toward my room.

"Take your time, we'll clean up," Hudson winks as Brooks carries me past.

CHAPTER TWENTY-FOUR

Hudson

"When will she start showing? When can we hear the heartbeat? When will we know what she's having? Can you tell now? Is. It a boy? I think it's a boy."

"Hudson, schmoopsy, calm down," Sloane tugs on my hand, trying to reign me in, but we both know that won't work.

"Two big thumbs way down on that, little omega, do better," I kiss her on the nose before turning back to Dr. Branson, "Is it really okay for her to drink coffee?"

Sloane's growl is absolutely adorable, I don't know who she thinks she's scaring, but I'm here for it.

"Hudson, shut the fuck up," Brooks snaps, slapping me on the back of my head.

"Sloane said we could ask Dr. Branson questions!"

"And you can, Hudson," Dr. Branson cuts in, "just try to give me the chance to answer one before you ask another."

Sloane snuggles a little closer to me on the couch, rubbing my back and helping me to calm down a little. The fact that we're meeting in Dr. Branson's new living room is a little weird for me, shouldn't we be at an office or something?

"Next time, we'll have an office to meet in, but this was a little bit of a surprise, so I wasn't able to secure a space for us, yet," Dr. Branson says.

I look at her with wide eyes.

"You said it outloud, dipshit," Kai mutters from behind me.

"Oh, sorry," I grin sheepishly at Dr. Branson.

"Now, with your questions. She won't start showing for probably another 6 weeks or so. It's different for everyone, but anywhere from 4-8 weeks is when we would expect to start seeing a little baby bump. We'll hear the heartbeat at the next visit. We could probably hear it now, but I don't have the equipment here to do that. And no, we can't tell what it is yet. We'll do an ultrasound around 10 weeks and we'll be able to see what she's carrying."

"And the coffee? Cause we've all been talking about it and Sloane insists it's okay, but we all think it would be best to just hear it right from you, right guys?"

I glance around, waiting for them to agree, but realize they're all probably more scared of getting nut punched than getting a straight answer. I cup my hand over my crotch just in case.

"There aren't any definitive studies indicating that caffeine has a negative effect on a pregnancy. However. In general, even outside of pregnancy, high doses of caffeine lead to increased heart rate, high blood pressure, dehydration and headaches. My recommendation would be, if you can't completely stop drinking caffeine, limit it to 8 ounces or less per day.."

I smile at Sloane, hugging her to my side while also effectively pinning her arms down for safety, "Don't worry, baby, we'll start you on decaf. All the flavor, none of the danger."

She's so cute when she pouts.

"You know you'll step on that if you stick it out any further," I joke, kissing her bottom lip, then sucking it into my mouth for just a moment.

"Are there any other questions? I do have some pamphlets for you to take home; nutrition, exercise, stages of pregnancy, things like that. Eventually we'll talk about what kind of labor you want to have, where you want to deliver, and who you want to be there. It's something you can start thinking about now, but it's not an urgent decision."

"What does the appointment schedule look like," Brooks asks, "how often will we be bringing her in?"

"Generally the schedule is once a month for the first three months, then every two weeks, then once a week at the end,.."

"Whoa," I start before she cuts me off.

"BUT given the nature of your, ah, situation, we can meet as often as you like. I don't know if all of you will come to every visit, but the important ones will be in four weeks when we do the first ultrasound, then at the ten week visit when we figure out the gender. We'll listen to the heartbeat at every visit, so that's not necessarily special."

"Is there anything we should be on the lookout for, any kind of problems or complications she might experience," Simon asks quietly.

"It's highly unlikely she'll have any kind of complications. Given that you are a true mate pairing, your genetic material is super compatible. Her pregnancy should be easy and uncomplicated. Keep in mind that she's going to be more fatigued over the next several weeks and her libido will increase exponentially as her pregnancy progresses. Hormone fluctuations will likely result in some bouts of crankiness and general irritation, but that's probably the worst of it."

I drag Sloane onto my lap, nuzzling into her neck, scent marking her as much as possible. My dick has been hard since she told me she was pregnant and I'm not sure how I'm going to make it five months like this. I want to fuck her silly.

"Sorry, he's…really excited," Sloane tells Dr. Branson.

"No worries," she laughs, "you think he's the first alpha I've had to deal with? Most of them react that way. Something about seeing the manifestation of their virility as their partner grows through pregnancy. Or some just have a breeding kink."

I chuckle against her neck as Sloane chokes on her own spit.

"Breeding kink," she rasps out, finally clearing her throat.

"Some men like the idea of impregnating their partner, it turns them on to think of getting them pregnant, orgasming inside of them without using a condom or other birth control."

"Well now we have a name for it, perv," Kai flicks me on the back of the ear.

"Can we please be civil here people," I hiss over my shoulder at him.

"Nope," Kai responds, flicking my other ear.

"Baby, he's picking on me," I snuggle my face between Sloane's breasts.

"Oh my gosh, we really need to go now. I swear, I can't take you guys anywhere," Sloane admonishes, trying to push up from my lap. I'm not ready to let her go yet.

"When do we bring her back, doc," I ask, voice muffled in Sloane's cleavage, but I'm sure she hears me well enough.

"As I said before, we can wait four weeks as recommended, or you can come back in two. I don't think we need to meet any sooner than that. Plus it will give me time to secure an office space."

"Same time on the 27th," Brooks asks, looking at the calendar on his phone "you can email us with the new location."

"I will put it on my calendar, that sounds great. As soon as I have something set, I will email Simon. He's already reached out to me, so I have his contact information."

"He did," Sloane asks, her chest rumbling against my face as she speaks.

"Yes, he had some questions about a spreadsheet he's working on."

I chuckle a little, pulling back to check out Simon on Sloane's other side. Sure enough, his face is as red as hell.

"I just wanted to make sure that we're keeping track of everything properly. She needs to stick to a balanced diet, start a prenatal vitamin, she needs at least 96 ounces of water everyday."

This time when Sloane tries to move, I let her because she's just turning toward Simon. I don't mind her readjusting, she just doesn't need to get up yet. I keep my arms tucked around her waist as she leans over to hug Simon.

"I appreciate you wanting to take care of me," she whispers before kissing him.

"You appreciate him, but I get the growls? That hardly seems fair," I mutter against the back of her neck, nudging her braid aside so I can press kisses on her nape.

"You're trying to take my coffee from me. That I can't forgive right now," she sniffs before trying to lift herself up again. Luckily I'm so much stronger than her.

Unfortunately, I am not stronger than Kai. So when he forcibly pulls her up, I have no choice but to let her go.

"Thanks for seeing us, doc," I shake Dr. Branson's hand as we all shuffle out of her apartment and down the elevator to the parking garage.

Kai has Sloane tucked against his side, Brooks is pressed in on the other, so I squeeze in behind her. I wrap an arm around Kai and Brooks, squishing us all together as I drop my chin onto her shoulder.

"Not sure I can handle being away from you all night, little omega."

"You'll survive. You have Brooks and Kai to keep you company, plus you can facetime us whenever you want. Unless I'm asleep, anyway."

"I don't like it," I lick across my mating mark before tracing my tongue down her neck and across the others, "you'll be on the other side of town. Way too far away."

"In a completely secure building, with Simon, with some of your soldiers - hand picked, by you soldiers - stationed in the lobby. Not to mention that I do know how to use a gun and so does Simon. We'll be fine."

"I'm not worried about your safety, little omega, I'm worried about my dick. How am I going to make it 24 hours without unloading inside of you?"

"For fuck's sake," Brooks mutters, "are you serious right now?"

"You can cum in Kai's mouth and pretend," she giggles.

"It's good, but it's not the same," I whine.

"Wow," Simon blurts, "this is…are we really going to talk about this?"

"Don't worry Si, as soon as you're better, I'll cum in your mouth, too. I'm sure you're great at sucking dick, it's just not the same as Sloane's sweet cunt."

"Please stop," Sloane begs, just as the elevator doors slide open, "this is not a conversation for public consumption."

"I'm just trying to be honest," I follow them out of the elevator and over to the two cars. Kai drove over with Simon and Sloane in the Macan, Brooks and I took the Q5.

"Oh my god, are we going to get a minivan," I gasp, "Simon, start researching minivans. We need room for at least 4 carseats."

"Whoa, I am not a minivan mom. Not happening," Sloane snaps, "And 4 carseats? Are you out of your mind?"

"We need something big enough for all of us, what's better than a minivan? And I plan on keeping you pregnant, so we need all the carseats."

"Hudson, get in the car," Brooks orders.

"Okay, fine, sheesh. Guy just tries to help," I mutter, pulling Sloane against me before fucking her mouth with my tongue. I want her to imagine what my cock could be doing to her right now, instead she's going home with Simon while I'll be stuck in a hotel room with these two.

I let her go when her moans turn into sweet little whimpers and her hips start rocking.

"I love you, baby, I'll see you tomorrow."

"I love you, too, baby cakes."

"That's a front runner, still bad, but the best one so far."

She laughs before pushing me away and hugging Brooks, tugging him down to ravage her mouth almost as good as I did. Kai picks her up, of course. Which is totally unfair, but she seems to like it so I let it slide.

"Keep us posted, okay," Simon says as I hug him gently.

I tug on his braid a little, since I can't pick on him like I want to, "Will do."

Once we say our goodbyes, I climb into the driver's seat and watch as Sloane and Simon pull off into the opposite direction while we head to the hotel.

Simon checked us in under fake names, but we can't make fake faces, so we'll sneak in through the employee entrance and head up to the room without actually checking in. Once we're there, Simon will doctor the records to make it seem like we were checked in at the desk and given keys.

We have no idea who's in on the operation or even if Petruk and Volkov showed early to case the place, since Gallow is dead. We don't want to risk being seen in any of the heavily populated areas of the hotel.

Simon gave us magnetic cards keyed to open any door in the entire hotel, interior and exterior. We're meeting Morris and the others at the loading dock and giving them cards, as well. We'll go in through the employee entrance, they'll enter through the side guest door.

Our room is the floor below where the girl will be staying, their room is a floor above. We'll be closer to the ground floor to cover those doors while they'll be able to take the stairs down to the fake janitor's closet to get into the room.

We park in the staff parking garage, Brooks pulls the duffle we packed and we hoof it down to the loading dock where Morris and crew are already waiting.

"Sorry we're late, we had an appointment with Dr. Branson that ran over," Brooks tells Morris, shaking his hand before shaking the rest.

"So she finally came to terms with the pregnancy," Morris chuckles, "there's no other reason she would have been that out of sorts. I've never seen her so agitated."

"She did, yes, she told us this morning. I'm sure she'll want to tell you herself, so please pretend it's a surprise," Kai adds.

"Of course, of course. Big surprise for all of us," Morris winks at Brooks.

I pull the extra cards out of my back pocket and hand them to Morris, "Simon says no magnets, keep them away from your cell phone and treat them like gold because they will open every door in this place."

"Fancy," Remi mutters, turning the card over in his hands.

"Alright, everyone ready? Any questions?"

"We're good," Morris assures Brooks, "we'll be ready to move as soon as Simon reports they've checked in."

"Excellent, stay in contact. We'll be ready to go as soon as you are," Brooks replies, shaking hands again as we separate to enter the building.

Just as I swipe the card at the employee entrance, my phone dings to let me know that the Macan made it home. We cross into the main hallway and then the stairwell. The room Simon secured for us is directly next to the stairwell entrance, so it will be easier for us to slip in and out.

As I push out the door onto our floor, my phone pings again with a text tone. Sloane or Simon checking in that they made it back safe. We hustle into our room quickly and I pull my phone out once the room door shuts behind us.

I check the group chat.

Si: We made it in one piece, I'll work on updating the check in now.

S: I already miss you all so much

Sloan follows her text with several kissy face emojis.

H: We're in the room now

H: Not gonna lie, smells kinda weird

H: How much do they charge for these rooms, they're not even that big

S: I imagine they just seem small because the three of you are crammed in it together.

Si: Both rooms are updated with the correct check-in information. I'll let you all know when the girl and her father check in.

H: I love you two

H: Stay out of trouble

H: Or send pics

S: Just because I did that one time…

B: One time? Just one? You sure about that?

K: Wait, it happened more than once? Where the hell was I?

H: Hahahah, suckers.

H: She let me watch her ride Brooks on FT

H: SO fucking hot

K: Damn cara, when do I get to watch?

S: Oh my gosh, you guys. Stop.

Si: Sorry, I'm not exactly up for putting on a show quite yet. Think you'll have to wait for another time.

K: I'd rather be there when that finally happens anyway

B: Enough. I don't need to be stuck in a room with these two assholes wanting to fuck.

H: Lame

H: Maybe he's just jealous that we don't want to fuck him

H: I'm not opposed tho you know, if you ever change your mind

B: I'm going to put you in a sleeper hold and tie you to the bed if you don't shut up

H: Kinky

"Is it weird that we're all in this room together, but texting each other like we're not? I feel like this could be a twilight zone episode," I glance between the two of them, each on their own bed.

My phone pings,

B: Hudson is having an existential crisis. We need to talk him down. We'll talk soon, love you both

"So rude," I tell Brooks before climbing into the bed next to Kai, "can I be the big spoon?"

"No."

I collapse back on the pillows and huff out a breath.

"What are we supposed to do now?"

"Wait. Sleep. Whatever the fuck you want as long as it stays in this room," Brooks tells me, focused on his phone like it holds the secrets to eternal youth.

"What about whoever the fuck I want?"

"I don't bottom. So unless you're talking Brooks into something, you won't be fucking anyone," Kai says, pushing me across the bed so he can lay down next to me.

"Yeah, I'll pass. I love you guys, but I just don't feel a calling for the dick."

"No worries, you can watch and critique my performance," I tell him as I slide off the bed and whip my shirt off.

"That's not happening. If you whip your dick out while we're all in this room together, I will have no choice but to shoot it off."

"Damn, dude. Taking it a bit far, don't you think. Besides, this here is the baby maker 3000, you can't shoot it off."

Kai groans, "Not this again."

"We all know I have superior swimmers, the thickest of baby batter. I counted it out. I actually had her three more times that you did. And Brooks only had her once. It's totally mine."

"And none of us care," Brooks slaps me on the arm, "we just want him to be happy and healthy."

"I had a thought earlier," I gulp, sinking back down on the edge of the bed, "what if it's not a he. What if I make girl babies? What the hell are we going to do then?"

"Pray that she's an alpha," Kai asks.

"Hire armed guards 24/7 once she hits puberty," Brooks adds.

"One thing's for sure," Kai claps me on the shoulder, "she'd be the most spoiled princess on the planet."

"That's no lie," I smile, "Can you imagine? A mini Sloane? With my sparkling personality? That might be even better than a mini me."

"If she actually births a miniature version of you, we'd have to throw the whole kid out and start over, no lie," Kai chuckles from behind me, "because that would be way too much crazy for one family."

"Is there a Pick On Hudson contest going on that I am unaware of," I sniff, "because y'all have been so rude."

"Suck it up Sally, you know we love you, sometimes you just need to be brought down a notch, or twelve," Brooks points out, "The reason the room seems small is because of your giant ass ego."

"I can't help the fact that I am a precision machine, designed for awesomeness."

"Allow me to put you out of our misery," Kai tells me, right before pinning me back to the bed and trying to smother me with a pillow. Since he's behind me and only pinning me down by the pillow, I'm able to reach back and slap him in the dick.

"Goddamnit," he grunts, loosening his grip on the pillow enough for me to wiggle out and drop onto the floor.

I turn quickly and launch back onto the bed, hitting Kai square in the chest and knocking him back on the bed.

"You might be bigger than me, but I'm totally going to kick your ass," I tell him, right before Brooks grabs me by the collar and yanks me backward off the bed and back onto the floor.

"We don't have time for this shit, you two," he admonishes, "keep it together in case they check in tonight. We have no idea what the actual plan is on their end, remember?"

"You're such a party pooper," I huff.

"Be that as it may, it's the truth. Now can I go take a shower without you dipshits creating complete havoc in here?"

"Maybe," I reply.

"Probably," Kai says.

"Oh my god," he mutters, turning away and heading into the bathroom.

 "You know, fucking with him is definitely in my top ten of fun shit to do," I tell Kai, kicking off my shoes before dropping back down on the bed and propping up pillows behind me.

"I totally agree," Kai replies, fist bumping me before tossing me the remote.

CHAPTER TWENTY-FIVE

Dmitri

All four of us stuck in this suite together is fucking weird. At least Simon got us a room big enough to spread out a little, but I'm not used to being in such close quarters with Morris and Marco. Remi I can ignore, I've been doing it for over 30 years now, but it's like I'm inherently aware of where Morris and Marco are at all times.

Even staying at the main house, sharing dinner every night, it's not the same as being stuck here. I definitely should have gone out the other night, knowing I would be in this situation. I have too much pent up and it's making me twitchy.

The swirling pheromones, excitement and adrenaline in such a small space is taking its own toll on me. I'm used to running jobs on my own or with Remi, having Marco and Morris here isn't just outside of my comfort zone, it's a downright distraction.

"Go sit out on the balcony, have a drink," Remi murmurs, dropping down on the couch next to me and handing me a beer, "maybe the fresh air will help."

"Simon said no one should leave the room."

"We're six floors up, it's bricked out on each side, no one's going to see you."

I take a few mouthfuls of the beer, "Anything better in the mini bar?"

"Probably not the best time to tie one on," he side-eyes me, "just go outside and breathe it out."

A few more swallows and I hand the empty bottle back to him, "Don't tell me what to do."

I walk across the suite and slip out onto the balcony, making sure to open the door as little as possible and not reveal the interior. The curtains are pulled on all the windows, including the balcony doors. We're probably being paranoid, but it's always better to err on the side of caution.

Our main goal is getting Mariella out of here safe, closely followed by neutralizing her father, that piece of shit, and getting our hands on at least one of those bottom feeders. Getting rid of her father will make sure that Mariella is safe, at least for the time being. Getting Petruk and Volkov will guarantee her safety and Sloane's, plus allow all of us to get a little revenge.

I brace my hands on the railing, leaning forward enough to appreciate the drop. I close my eyes and take a few deep, centering breaths. I try to find some peace, but the calm I'm looking for doesn't come from some fresh air and meditation. I need to feel leather in my hands and the sweet cries of a sub giving in to me. Feel a tight clutch around my cock, from a pussy or an ass. Even a mouth would do at this point.

I should have gone to Blur and found a partner as soon as I knew we were going to be doing this. Instead, being a dumbass, I decided to power through with the intent to spend the next few days at the club, enjoying myself. I thought I could resist my baser urges, since I've been doing it just fine at the house the last several days.

I didn't take into account that we would be in such close quarters. Every inhale is full of Marco and Morris. I rarely find myself attracted to other alphas. Given that one of the alphas in question is my boss and the other is pining for my boss, I'm totally fucked in this situation. And not in the fun way.

I hear the door click open behind me. My fingers tighten on the rail. Remi wouldn't bother me out here, he knows I'm struggling, so there's only two other options. Neither of which I'm in the state of mind to deal with.

"You're agitated," Marco says, still standing by the door.

"Yea," I reply, focusing on flexing and relaxing my fingers one by one around the rail.

"Anything I can help with?"

I laugh humorlessly, "I don't think so."

"I need you to have your head in this. We're all relying on you as part of this team. If you need to let loose then I'll do what I can to help."

I wheel around to stare at him, incredulous.

"I don't think you know what you're saying right now and I think you need to go back inside."

"I know exactly what I'm saying," he snaps, stepping away from the door and taking several more steps toward me, "You didn't go to Blur like you wanted to, you weren't able to blow off steam like you needed to. Now you're stuck here for who knows how long, not able to leave and get what you need. I'm not going to let you beat me, but if you need to fuck I'll be a willing participant. It's not like I haven't dabbled in the past."

"A willing participant," I sneer, "thanks, I'll pass."

I turn back to the railing, squeezing until my knuckles blanch. To be offered something I've been craving, in such a trivial way? Absolute bullshit.

"Dmitri-"

"Go back inside, Marco," I grit out, my jaw clenched.

"Listen," he snaps, "Maybe I don't have the best 'game' okay? It's not like I have to work for it anymore, ladies know the score. I'm 55 fucking years old, Dmitri, I don't know how to approach this shit anymore."

"You don't want me Marco. I'm not up for being a substitute right now. I just need to be left alone, let me get my head straight."

"It's not like that. Can you at least look at me?"

I take two deep breaths before turning around. I hook my hands on the rail behind me, still holding on for dear life. The pain of the railing digging into my hands is keeping me grounded.

"I know you see a lot…a lot," he stresses, "being close to us now that things are unstable. It's obvious, I think, to everyone except Morris, how much I want him. But just because I want him, doesn't mean I can't want you at the same time."

I stare at him, unblinking, not sure how to process that information. I do not need to get involved with another alpha, it'll be a dominance fight every damn day. Not to mention the alpha in question also wants to fuck my boss. This is messy.

"Just because I want to fuck you, doesn't mean I should," is all I can come up with.

"Okay, so don't fuck me. It's been awhile for me anyway," he chuckles a little, "prep would probably take too long. I can - I will gladly suck your dick, especially if it will help even you out."

"That's not really how I do things," I tell him, my cock already rock hard at the idea of having his mouth wrapped around it, "You don't suck my dick, I fuck your mouth."

"Always the one in charge, right," he asks, stepping closer.

"Always. Grab a pillow," I nod at one of the chairs on the balcony that has a decorative throw pillow on it.

"Such a gentleman," he smiles, grabbing the pillow and dropping it at my feet.

"I figure your knees should be comfortable because your throat definitely won't be."

He's tall enough that, once he kneels down, he's at the perfect height. I stroke my fingers across the top of his head a few times before gripping a handful of hair.

"Unzip my jeans and take my cock out," I order quietly.

He complies so quickly, my dick jerks in my pants. Fuck. I didn't realize how heady it would be to have such a strong alpha kneeling before me, taking every command.

"That's good. Good boy," I tell him as he squeezes my cock before tugging my jeans open enough to bring my balls out, too.

I use the grip on his hair to tug him close, "Suck my balls."

I brace one elbow on the railing and tilt my head back, reveling in the feeling of his hot mouth sucking on me. I let him continue that for a minute, the wet sounds of his sucking making my cock throb.

"Enough," I pull him away, gripping my cock with my other hand, "open."

I feed him my cock, pushing his mouth down on me until I feel the back of his throat. I look down at him, watching his eyes water as I push past the back of his mouth and into his actual throat.

I groan as I hold myself inside of him, the first tear escaping his eye and saliva starting to leak out of the corner of his mouth. I pull back enough for him to get a breath, then push forward again, this time pushing in until his nose touches my stomach.

"You are such a good boy," I mutter, "You take my cock so well. Are you ready for the next part?"

He moans around my cock, the vibration making me grunt, but I take it as acquiescence. I make sure my grip in his hair is firm and, holding his head completely still, I snap my hips forward. Thrusting in and out of his mouth, I set a brutal pace.

I watch my cock disappear between his lips, taking in his wet, reddened eyes and enjoying the obscene wet and gagging sounds he makes as I brutalize his throat. It's such a complete fantasy made reality, that it's not even going to take me that long.

"You're going to swallow every drop. I going to watch my cum fill your mouth and you're going to swallow every bit of it, fuck yeah you are," I groan, increasing my pace until my balls pulls up tight and I feel the tingle at the base of my spine.

"Open," I order, pulling my cock free and jacking it roughly.

A new scent on the breeze distracts me for a moment and I glance toward the doorway, seeing Morris outlined in the opening, Remi trying to pull him back in. I can't stop this show, though, I'm too far gone.

I make eye contact with Morris, squeezing my cock and yanking it until my cum shoots all over Marco's tongue. I groan as each pump coats his mouth.

I break eye contact with Morris to look down at Marco, mouth open, showing me my cum like a good boy.

"Swallow it, every drop."

I keep my eyes trained on his mouth, watching his throat work until he pops open his mouth again, showing me that he listened.

"Such a good, good boy you are, Marco."

I look back up, but the door is shut now. No evidence that Morris was there, even his scent is gone.

CHAPTER TWENTY-SIX

Brooks

We get the call from Simon at 10 the next morning that Mariella and her father have checked into the room. Simon confirmed via the security cameras in the hallway that they both entered the room and neither of them have left.

The next part is up to Simon. He's going to contact the front desk, report a concern that there's a gas leak in the area and all of the guests need to temporarily evacuate the building until there is confirmation it's safe.

Instead of evacuating, we'll be putting our plan into play. Morris, Marco and Dmitri will infiltrate the room while it's empty. Once she's secure and the father is dealt with, Morris and Marco will transport her to the warehouse. Remi will station himself in the bar as a look out and the rest of us will be stationed outside, waiting for Petruk or Volkov or both to show.

Hopefully we're not sitting out there all day. We debated when we thought they would come for the girl and ultimately decided that the likelihood was they would show up as close to check in as possible. That's why it was imperative that we were here first.

We get the notification 10 minutes later, telling us to gather in the lobby for a momentary evacuation. Hudson grabs our duffle bag and we slip out into the stairwell. Heading down to the first floor so we can exit the same way we came in last night.

"Remi is on his way to the lobby, Morris and the others are on their way to the room, Brooks and the others are heading out the employee entrance," Simon's voice comes over the comms.

We're using the same set up we had when rescuing Sloane. Simon has us all wired so he can communicate between all of us while watching the security cameras in the hotel.

"Hudson is going to drop their duffle at the car, Kai is staying at the employee entrance while Brooks makes his way to the delivery entrance," Simon intones, "and Remi just stepped off the elevator."

I climb the steps to the loading dock, plopping down and dangling my legs off the edge, doing my best to look comfortable, like I belong here. I pull out my phone and start randomly clicking and scrolling apps, like I'm just a worker on break.

"Everyone is in place, I'm going to wait 10 minutes and call back with an all clear."

Hudson joins me after a few minutes, leaning against the concrete pillars next to the loading dock and pulling out his phone, same as me. Just two guys enjoying a morning break and some crisp, fresh air.

"We have a problem," Remi's tinny voice comes through the comms, "Simon, check the bar. Back booth, under the ugly ass ballerina painting."

"Hang on, that area is dead on security. Give me a minute to redirect some cameras," Simon reports.

"What do you see, Remi," I ask quietly, glancing around to make sure we're still alone.

"I think it's Petruk, but I'm not 100% sure and he's sitting with someone that I do not recognize. I want Simon to take a look and confirm."

"Fuck," I mutter, eyeballing Hudson, "if they're already in the building, we need to head them off so they can't follow them back to the room."

"Let's not jump the gun until we hear back from Simon," Hudson replies, "Petruk isn't exactly a blend in kinda guy; gold teeth, remember? Maybe Remi's seeing things."

"Fuck, it is Petruk," Simon tells us all, "I have no fucking clue how I missed him. He's wearing a hoodie and he's got a bandana on, plus he's wearing several layers of clothes, changing his whole structure. I have no idea who he's sitting with, I'm trying to run facial recognition on him, but I can't get a totally clear shot of his face."

"Okay, listen," I say quickly, before anyone else can get on the line and freak out, "the plan doesn't change. We need to get Mariella out and get ahold of Petruk. Kai, Hudson and I are heading back to you. Assuming they're going to follow Mariella and her father back to their room, we'll head up the stairwell and cut them off before they can get to Mariella. Morris and Marco secure the girl, get her out to the warehouse, Dmitri neutralizes the father. Remi have the car pulled up to the side entrance so you're ready to transport them."

"We're good with that plan," Marco replies, "Dmitri will join you once the girl is secure."

"Agreed, we're heading to Kai now."

"Once I see you in the stairwell, I'll call in the all clear," Simon adds.

We meet Kai and start hoofing it up the stairs. It's a relatively quick trip, given the adrenaline we all have pumping right now. We figured the major confrontation would take place outside, while they were trying to enter the building, we never thought they would already be inside.

We stop at the landing, lining up against the wall, next to the door so we can move out quickly once they clear the elevator.

"Everyone's heading back to the elevators. Mariella and her father got on the one to the left and they're heading up, two other people for that floor as well. Petruk and his friend are too far back to get on this round of elevators, it will be another few minutes before they show up," Simon keeps us updated.

"As soon as they're all in their rooms, let us know and we'll exit the stairwell," I tell Simon.

"Will do."

There's a tense few minutes of silence then, "Clear to move."

We move out of the stairwell as a unit, quickly surveying the set up of the hallway. The elevators are at the opposite end, Mariella's room halfway between. There's also the hallway where the entrance to the closet, vending and freight entrance are. We cross to the hallway, gathering halfway behind the ice machine.

"Kai, wait here," I press my PTT so everyone can listen, "You and Dmitri can cover Marco and Morris while they hustle the girl out. Come out of the freight elevator at the first floor with them, but come back around to the regular elevators. Hudson and I will stand at the elevator on this floor, like we're waiting for a ride down, then keep them from getting out. Once our elevator makes it to the ground floor, you two can step in and help us."

"You think it's going to be that easy," Kai asks.

"I think Hudson and I can keep them occupied long enough until you and Dmitri can assist in securing them."

"Yeah, unless they have guns," Sloane's voice comes through the comms, "I don't like this plan."

"They're not going to fire guns inside an elevator, *tesoro*, a ricochet would be too likely to injure them as one of us. Petruk might be a thug, but he's not an idiot."

"And what about the man with him, no one even knows who it is. He might be an idiot!"

"*Cara,* it's going to be okay. We're all going to make it back to you in one piece. I know you're worried, but this has to be done," Kai tries to soothe her.

"I just can't lose any of you," she chokes out.

"Give the comms back to Simon, baby, we're going to be fine. The desire to get back to you will override everything else," Hudson croons.

There's some sniffling across the line, then Simon's back on, "Sorry, she was insistent. You guys can't leave me with her if she's going to cry, I can't stand up to that," he whispers.

I can't help but chuckle, even given the severity of the current situation, "I doubt any of us could, Si, you did fine."

"Petruk and his friend just got on the elevator, there's a guest getting off on the floor below you, but otherwise it's just them. You need to move now."

Just as Simon finishes, Dmitri comes across, "The omega's secured, we're heading out."

The closet door opens behind us, Marco stepping out first, his shirt collar stretched and torn on one side. Morris follows, a set of red, angry scratch marks down the side of his neck. Dmitri is last, his hand wrapped around the back of the girl's neck, pushing her ahead of him.

She looks sufficiently cowed at this point, but based on Marco's disheveled appearance and the scratches on Morris, she put up a decent fight first. I always knew Dmitri was a strong alpha, but if he put down a girl that Morris and Marco couldn't? That's a serious bark.

"You better keep her away from Sloane when you get to the warehouse," Kai murmurs to Marco.

"She's already in a shit mood and seeing those scratches will set her off," Hudson adds before heading out of the hallway toward the elevator.

"One sec, Hudson," I turn back to Dmitri, "You going to be able to come back with Kai or will you need to keep her secured back to the warehouse? I can't have her there if she's going to be a loose cannon."

"Oh, she's going to cooperate, aren't you," Dmitri snarls into her ear.

Mariella shudders, whining out a low, "Yes."

"You're not going to cause any problems, are you?"

She shakes her head.

"You're going to go with Morris and Marco and you're going to be a perfect little captive for them. You're going to be quiet and listen and wait for me to come and collect you, right?"

She nods, then takes a shuddering breath and whimpers out one more, "Yes."

"Good girl," he whispers in her ear before pushing her through the employee entrance.

Kai and I exchange a loaded glance before I turn on my heel and hustle to catch up to Hudson. Who knew Dmitri had all that in him?

Just as I stop next to Hudson, the elevator pings and the doors start sliding open. Before they can open all the way, Hudson and I are pushing through, each of us grabbing one of the men inside and slamming them back against the wall.

"Mudak," Petruk grunts, driving his fist into my kidney.

I grunt, pushing through the pain and land my own punch in his stomach. We grapple against the side of the elevator, struggling for dominance, throwing punches and kicks. I can hear the same happening behind me.

I decide to take the low road and bring my knee up into his dick. He lets out a wheezing breath, sagging against the wall. Taking advantage, I attempt to wrap my arm around his neck and put him in a headlock. Before I can tighten my arm, I feel a fist in my hair and I'm violently yanked away from him.

I trip and slam into the opposite wall. Petruk's friend steps over Hudson who's splayed on the floor. Smiling maniacally, blood smeared across his teeth, nose obviously broken, he launches his fist into my temple. I stumble to the side , tripping over Hudson again and dropping to the floor.

Fuck. My ears are ringing and I can't focus. I keep trying to push myself up, but can't get the coordination to do it. I can hear Simon under the ringing, but it's not clear enough to understand.

The elevator pings, the sound of gunfire breaks through the ringing. I lurch forward, covering Hudson, unsure of where the shots are coming from or where they're going. I can feel him breathing below me, thank god.

I feel someone grabbing my shoulders and I fight back instinctively, throwing my head back and grappling against the strong hands.

Instead of hurting me, though, the hands are just shaking me, then pushing me over when I won't stop fighting. I look up and see Kai standing over me, his mouth is moving, but all I can hear is this fucking ringing.

Dmitri is hauling Hudson up over his shoulders in a fireman's carry and Kaiser thrusts his hand out toward me, waving it to encourage me to take it. He yanks me to my feet, holding me tight when I stumble against him. He wraps one arm under my arms and practically drags me out of the elevator, heading toward the back of the building and the employee entrance.

Wait, I try to say, but my mouth is not cooperating with my brain. My brain isn't cooperating with my brain. Fuck.

I stumble up the stairs next to Kai, slowing us enough that he finally gives up on dragging me and hauls me over his shoulder. He takes the stairs two at a time, right behind Dmitri who doesn't seem to be breaking a sweat hauling Hudson.

"Hudson has the keys," I hear Kai say, his voice tinny and far away sounding, but at least the ringing is subsiding.

"What the fuck is happening," I manage, when Kai finally drops me to my feet next to the Q5.

"We need to get out of here, get in the car," he opens the door and pushes me in while Dmitri lays Hudson in the back.

"Is he okay," I groan as Dmitri climbs in the passenger seat, Kai driving.

"He's fine, breathing. Severe concussion, some broken fingers, maybe some facial bones, nothing fatal," Dmitri responds, "You're pretty fucking concussed, too."

"Yeah," I agree, dropping my head back onto the seat, "I'm pretty fucked up, now will someone please tell me what the hell happened? Where's Simon?"

"Comms are off, Morris and Marco made it back to the warehouse with Remi and the girl but Simon had to throw himself between Sloane and Mariella to keep her from murdering her for attacking her pops," Kai tells me.

"Hudson told Marco to keep them apart, what the hell were they thinking?"

"I'll deal with it when we get there. She's a manipulative little thing," Dmitri replies, "but didn't realize who she was dealing with. Sloane would've wiped the floor with her if Simon hadn't intervened."

"Why are we on our way back to the warehouse and why don't we have Petruk and his friend," I ask, pushing myself up into a sitting position, cradling my pounding head.

"Based on what we heard while Simon was yelling through the comms," Dmitri starts, "Petruk's friend beat the shit out of Hudson. After Hudson went down, he turned on you and landed a pretty sharp one on your temple. He pulled a gun right before the doors opened, Simon had enough time to warn us to clear out. He came out firing and dragging Petruk. They booked it through the lobby and out the front, we came in and got you two out and now we're here."

I hear shifting behind me, then Hudson groaning.

"What the fuck," he mutters, "where am I?"

"We're on our way back to the warehouse," I tell him.

"Jesus christ, that guy…" Hudson trails off.

"You still with us," I ask, half turning back toward him.

"Yeah, fucking fists of iron, man. He really fucked me up."

"Me, too brother."

"Simon called Dr. Branson," Kai tells us, "she's still a doctor at the end of the day and she's already under contract with Morris. She'll meet us at the warehouse and look you both over."

"Can she meet us in the garage? I think I'll live down there until the swelling goes down," Hudson snarks, "I don't need the ass kicking that Sloane is going to give me for this."

"We're making it back alive, that's basically what we promised. Just whine and look pathetic, she'll feel so sorry for you, she won't think about beating you" I tell him.

"I don't think that will be too hard, based on how I feel right now," Hudson coughs a few times before groaning, "Fuck, definitely broke some ribs."

"You know you don't look so great either, princess," Dmitri says, "she'll probably kick both your asses."

"Better brace yourselves, boys, we're almost there."

"When did you become such a shit driver, Kai," Hudson calls from the back, "You've hit every fucking pothole so far!"

"And I'll hit every single one on the way down to the parking garage if you don't shut the fuck up."

"I'm telling Sloane you were picking on me while I was bleeding out in the back."

"I'll tell Sloane that you take naked pictures of her while she's sleeping."

"You wouldn't dare," Hudson gasps comically before groaning in pain, "Shit, I hate broken ribs."

"I'm sure Dr. Branson will get you all taped up and Sloane will be mooning over you soon enough," I tell him, "now both of you shut up, my fucking head is splitting."

We ride the last few minutes in silence and I thank every god to ever exist because my brain feels like it's going to explode. I haven't had a concussion in almost a decade and I had forgotten how brutal it could be. The pressure inside of my skull is off the charts.

The worst part is, I know there's nothing that Dr. Branson can do for it. I'll just have to wait it out. And having Hudson whining about his injuries at the same time is not a prime recuperative environment.

I lean back, addressing Hudson, "We're recovering in our own rooms, Sloane can join us if she wants to, but you're not bogarting her time by trying to wiggle your way into staying with her."

He groans, "Low blow, dude."

"I know how shifty you are. You'll use whatever pathetic excuse you can to try to bogart her time. It's not happening."

"Fine," he scoffs, "not like I'll be able to do anything for a few days anyway."

"Alright fellas, gird your loins," Dmitri says.

I watch as we turn onto the ramp into the parking garage for the warehouse. Kai pulls the Q5 to the slot closest to the elevator. I slide out, groaning at the fluorescent lights above making my eyes burn.

"Are you gonna carry me up, big guy," Hudson asks when Dmitri opens the back hatch to let him out.

"I carry you and it's going to be over my shoulder with your face in my ass."

"I'd like that a lot more if I was up for ass play right now," Hudson quips, "but I guess I can make it up myself."

"I'll carry you if you need it, dipshit," Kai tells him grudingly.

"True story, it would probably hurt more than walking. I can't crunch up my ribs any more right now, they're fucking bad, man."

The elevator doors ping and I look around realizing that none of us were close enough to push it. I turn as they start to open and Sloane slips out between them, tears streaking her face. She sees me first.

"Oh, baby," she runs to my side, cupping my cheeks and turning my head, inspecting the side that's throbbing and sore, "he got you good. Does it hurt? Dr. Branson is upstairs waiting to check on you. Where's Hudson?"

"I'm okay, *tesoro*, just a little concussion. It hurts, but it'll heal," I hug her to me, kissing the tears off her face, "don't cry for me, I'm okay."

She sniffs several times, breaths shuddering as I rock her gently against me.

"I was so scared," she whispers against my chest.

"I know, I know, but we're all okay," I tilt her head back and look into her eyes, "we all came back to you. Go see Hudson before he starts crying like a baby that he's being left out."

She kisses me softly before turning away and heading over to Hudson, where she starts crying all over again.

"What did he do to you, *bello*?"

"Hey, little omega, you finally got it right," he whispers, pulling her up against him in spite of the pain I know he's in, "Brooks is right, we're fine. Nothing a little time won't heal."

Hudson looks to Kai who comes over and gathers Sloane up in his arms, "We have to get them upstairs, *cara*, so doc can take a look at them, okay?"

She nods before burying her face in his neck and clinging to him. He pushes the button and the doors slide open immediately, letting all of us squeeze in together. Hudson has one arm wrapped around his middle, the other braced on the railing. I'm focused on the floor, the brightness of the lights in here making me want to puke.

"She's waiting in the kitchen, says she wanted to be close to a clean water source and that it had the best lighting to stitches," her breath stutters on the last.

"I'm definitely going to need some of those," Hudson chuckles, "and I, for one, am thankful she has the best lighting for it. Don't want to ruin this masterpiece, amirite?"

"This is not a joking matter," Sloane hisses, peering over Kai's shoulder to pin Hudson with her angry eyes, "you could have brain damage!"

"My skull's too hard for that, baby."

She snarls, scrabbling at Kai's shoulder like she's going to climb right over him and fly at Hudson.

"Okay, okay, killer," Kai snaps, tugging her around and wrapping both arms around her so she's dangling off the ground, "he is injured. As much as I'd love for you to kick his ass right now, maybe let him recover a little first, okay?"

"Why do you have to antagonize her all the time," I ask.

"It's fun. I fucking love it when she's feral like that. Next time I piss her off, I'm going to make sure we're both naked first."

Sloane hisses.

Luckily the elevator slides open a few seconds later and Kai just carries her out and directly into the sitting room. He drops down on the couch with her, tucking her against him and making a cage with his body to keep her snuggled tight and contained for the moment.

Simon's standing in the kitchen with Dr. Branson.

"Jesus, Hudson…" he trails off

"Yeah, I know, too handsome for words, huh?"

"I definitely need to look at you first, Hudson. If you'll have a seat in here, please."

"Where's everyone else," Dmitri asks, stepping into the kitchen and looking around.

"They're the next level down, the entertainment wing. The gym is down there, the pool, and the movie room. I set them up in there, but let them know they could explore, whatever," Simon tells him.

"Thanks," he says before turning and heading back to the elevator.

"Alright, let's get you cleaned up, see what I'm working with here."

"Not much," I mutter, dropping into the chair next to him, "think you can make him look any better, doc?"

"I'll see what I can do."

I cross my arms on the table, dropping my head down to rest it there while she works on Hudson. The throbbing is so intense it's taking over everything. I feel like I can't concentrate on anything except the thump-thump-thump inside my skull.

I listen as Dr. Branson tells Hudson that she needs to stitch two of the lacerations on his face, but the other three are shallow enough they should heal easily on their own. Shockingly, none of the bones in his face are broken, in spite of his face being the size of a basketball.

"I'm going to use a local-"

"No," he cuts her off, "I don't need that, just stitch it, doc."

"I need you to have it. If you twitch while I'm stitching, that can cause issues with healing and scarring, especially this one close to your eye."

"I won't twitch, doc. I just don't like pharmaceuticals. Trust me, I've done this on myself plenty of times."

"I'm going to pretend you didn't tell me that, Hudson, but we'll try it your way. I'll do the one on your forehead first, if that goes okay then I'll do the one on your cheek."

"Deal."

I turn my head enough that I can watch as she starts to stitch Hudson's forehead. Holding the skin together gently with one hand and running the needle through with the other. True to his word, he doesn't twitch once. He sits quietly, eyes closed like he's meditating.

"Well. You've convinced me," Dr. Branson tells him, "as weird as this is, I'll remember it for the future."

"You're Sloane's doc, you won't have to take care of us again, Dr. Branson," I tell her, wincing when the sound of my own voice echoes back through my head.

"Something tells me this won't be the last time I'm called to do something like this. I signed the contract with Morris, I had a feeling I'd eventually be dragged into this. It's important you have a professional to take care of you when you get yourselves in trouble."

I nod back at her, not trusting that my brain will stay in one piece if I try to talk again.

"Okay, ice all that as much as possible. We'll tape your fingers and your ribs next and then I'll get some pain meds for you. In the meantime, Mr. Conti, let me take a look at you, you look like you're ready to keel over."

I let her inspect my face, gently prodding across the cheekbone and nose. She has me follow a penlight with my eyes, up and down then side to side.

"Nothing broken, just what I suspect is a monster concussion. Whoever hit you knew what he was doing. I'd say it was an impressive hit, but since he's the bad guy here, we'll just pretend it was a lucky strike. I highly doubt any kind of subdural hematoma or deeper brain damage, so I feel confident giving you some Norco to relieve your pain."

"Thanks doc, I appreciate you."

She pulls a pill bottle out of her bag, checks the label and sets it on the table.

"There's enough here for you to share. No more than two at a time, every 4-6 hours. No acetaminophen with this, but you can take ibuprofen for aches and pains. Hudson, after I tape you up you're getting an antibiotic shot. Brooks, you're good to go to bed. Take two of these," she tells me, handing me pills from a different bottle, "but wait until you're actually in bed. They hit hard."

"Maybe you should just move in with us, doc," Hudson drawls from behind her, "you can watch over Sloane and earn extra credit with all of us."

She chuckles before turning back to him, "I'm currently under contract to another employer, but I'll think about your offer."

"Come on, buddy, let's get you to bed," Kai squeezes my shoulder gently.

"I'm due for a nap anyway. I'll keep an eye on you," Sloane says, resting her head on my back as she leans over to hug me.

"Sounds like a plan," I push back from the table and stand up, "you can bring Hudson in there once he's done, too, as long as he promises to behave."

"I just want to sleep, bro, just like you. Maybe I'll wake up and all this will be gone," he chuckles, gesturing at his face.

CHAPTER TWENTY-SEVEN

Sloane

When I wake up a few hours later, squished between Brooks and Hudson, I'm scared to move, not wanting to jostle either of them. Brooks' face isn't so bad, but Hudson's whole body is discolored. He has bruises up and down both ribs, his face looks like someone kicked it around for a few hours and the stitches don't help.

Dr. Branson gave them both a whole lot of pain medication, so I know they'll stay asleep, I just don't want to hurt them any more than they already are. They probably wouldn't feel it, but it's more of a psychological thing for me.

I finally psych myself up enough to wiggle down to the end of the bed. I pop out the bottom of the covers and stand up, taking a minute to look them both over and relish the fact that they made it back here safe. And they helped rescue another vulnerable omega.

Which is what's currently on my mind. I tug my sweater back on and head out to the kitchen, hoping to find someone to give me an update on what's happening now that Petruk got away. I come around the kitchen and smile at the scene I find.

Papa and Marco are in the kitchen with Kai, working together to put dinner on. Simon and Remi are setting the table, Mariella is sitting at the island, but Dmitri isn't anywhere to be seen. I cross the kitchen and push up on my toes to give Kai a kiss.

He holds me against him with one arm, continuing to stir the sauce with the other.

"How are you feeling, *cara*," he asks, brushing his hand against my abdomen.

"I'm good, nice and refreshed," I smile at him and squeeze his hand before I pass through the kitchen, hugging papa and Marco.

I lean over and give Simon a quick kiss while he's passing plates out around the table before grabbing some glasses and moving around to each place setting.

"Did someone get wine," I ask.

"Not yet, I was telling Morris about the wine cellar. Do you want to take him down and show him, *cara*? You can pick something out for us."

"Sure," I walk over to papa, looping my arm through his and heading over to the elevator with him, "you'll love this!"

"I'm sure it's impressive, given the rest of this place."

I push the button for the bottom floor, excited to show him one of the things I love about this place. The first place that Simon and I connected. It's stupid how much it means to me.

"I'm sure you already know, you've already guessed, but I wanted to let you know. Officially. You are going to be a grandpa," I turn to him smiling, waiting to see his reaction.

"I knew it," he crows, "I knew it. I'm going to be the best *nonno, mia figlia*. I have so many plans for this little guy!"

He rubs my belly, leaning down to speak directly to it, "This is your *nonno*, young man. Be good to your mother and I can't wait to meet you."

I laugh as papa grins ear to ear.

"Have you discussed names?"

"Well, I have some ideas, but we haven't discussed them, no."

"What are you thinking," papa asks as we walk out the elevator and into the wine cellar, "Impressive," he murmurs, taking in the organization and hanging signs.

"I like Sebastian for a boy and Ophelia for a girl, I told Brooks and Hudson one day, before I even knew for sure I was pregnant, but they haven't brought it up since."

"In this case, I say it's completely up to you. You're going to carry that baby and give birth to it, you can name him whatever you want. And those are both very good names, *stellina*."

"Thank you, papa," I step into him and hug him tight.

"I should be thanking you, bringing new life into this world, making me a *nonno*. The best gift I've ever been given," he chuckles then, "I guess the wine selection is completely up to me, then?"

"Hey, just because I can't drink it doesn't mean I can't pair it!"

"You don't even know what we're cooking, how can you pair?"

"Oh fine," I laugh, "pick whatever you want, just make sure it's good. Kai's a bit of a wine snob."

"I'm sure he'll trust what I choose, he did offer to let me come down here."

"True, true. You know how happy it makes me that you all get along so well, especially given the fact that you've always been rivals."

"We all love you, Sloane. That goes a long way to bringing people together. And, unfortunately, the time you were gone gave us the opportunity to band together, spend time together, learn a lot in a short space of time."

"Nothing brings people together like a crisis," I murmur as we make our way up and down the aisles.

"And we're still mired in that crisis, though to a much lesser degree."

"Mariella," I ask.

"Mariella," he confirms.

"What are you planning on doing with her? I mean, you can't let her go home or anywhere, really, that she's been before. I mean, she needs to be protected until Volkov is dealt with."

"I agree, it's just a matter of getting everyone else to agree."

"No, it's not," I tell him, "you're the boss, be bossy."

He laughs, patting my hand still tucked into his arm, "If only it were that simple, *stellina*. She rubs Dmitri the wrong way, Remi finds it funny but I'm not sure it will be conducive to have her in the house, especially since Remi and Dmitri are two of the only people we're 100% sure of right now."

"Dmitri? He's usually so…stoic. I didn't think anything really rattled him. I mean, you can confine her to a guest suite, it's not like a prison cell. You could put her up at one of your properties with guards, too."

"I want to keep her close. I don't want to have gone through rescuing her and then have something happen to her that I could have prevented."

"Dmitri and Remi need to stay at the house, papa. Your safety comes first."

"I agree," he tells me, stopping to pull two bottles of Pinot Rosa off the shelf.

"Are you making fish?"

"Chicken with velouté sauce, risotto, and ciabatta. Does that pass muster, ma'am?"

"Yes, sir," I laugh as we swing around and make our way back to the elevator.

"I've already talked to Dmitri about it and he agrees that she should stay at the compound, in spite of the fact that she makes him uncomfortable. He says he can handle it."

"Then why are we even having this discussion?"

"Dmitri has certain…predilections. I'm concerned that putting him under extra stress will lead him to indulge more often and maybe lead to other issues."

"If he says he's okay with it, I would trust him. He's a grown man, papa."

"I know, I know. I just want to do what's best for all of my people."

"I know you do, because you're a good man," I squeeze his arm, pushing the call button for the elevator, "but again, if he says he's okay, then let him deal with it. Check in with him regularly to make sure he's okay, but trust that he knows how to take care of himself."

"I love you, my girl, always with the best advice."

I rest my head on his shoulder as we step into the elevator and ride back up with the wine.

When we step off, I hear Hudson's voice coming from the kitchen. He's leaning against the island, holding a bag of frozen peas on his face, telling everyone in the room about how his superior swimmers were definitely the ones to impregnate me.

"Hudson Pietro Alfera, you will shut your mouth right now if you know what's good for you," I screech, wishing I could slap my hands over his mouth, but not wanting to cause him any more pain.

"Oh, hey, baby," he pulls the bag of peas away long enough to smile at me, the action grotesquely stretching his already swollen lips, "I was just letting the rest of the group know that I knocked you up."

"Shut up or I will punch you in the nuts," I hiss, gently poking a finger into his chest to show I mean business.

"Kai said you were walking your dad down to the wine cellar, I figured you already told him! Did I ruin the surprise? I'm sorry."

"You didn't ruin - I don't want you telling everyone…I mean, just don't say it like that. God. Just tell them I'm pregnant without mentioning anything about swimmers or baby batter or whatever other horrifying thing you were telling them!"

"Oh, okay," he tells me, turning back to the room, "Sloane's pregnant."

"I swear you misunderstand me on purpose. You think you're cute, but you're not. You're in trouble," I wag my finger at him, stepping around the island to sit down at the table next to Brooks.

"How are you feeling," I grasp his hand gently, kissing his fingers instead of his black and blue face.

"Better, *tesoro*, whatever pills Branson gave me were pretty good. I'm still a little loopy, but the smell of food brought me out here. And the fact that a certain omega was missing from my bed," he squeezes my fingers, leaning in to kiss me lightly.

"I didn't want to wake you, either of you. I figured the more sleep the better," I glance my fingers over his temple and cheek, "I just want you to feel better."

"I feel much better now," he pulls me into his lap, "and I'm not as damaged as that crazy asshole."

"I'm amazed he's even standing," I admit, "he looks like shit."

"He takes a lickin and keeps on tickin, huh," Remi jokes, sitting across the table. Someone expanded the table, adding two extra leaves so all of us would have space to sit.

"Says the guy who hung out in the bar all morning, then drove the getaway car," I say, rolling my eyes at him.

"Whoa, whoa there, I had a very important job, thank you. If you remember correctly, I'm the one who spotted Petruk in the bar to begin with."

"Okay, I'll give you that," I tell him begrudgingly, "but you still weren't exactly in danger. Papa and Marco took more damage than you and they dealt with a girl!"

"Hey, I take offense to that," Mariella says, sitting next to Remi, "I'm no push over."

"Clearly," I growl, still struggling with my protective instincts, "Sorry, didn't mean to let that slip."

"It's okay, I get it. I mean, I wouldn't care if someone fucked up my dad - clearly, since I'm sitting at the table with the people who offed him - but I understand why you would be upset that I hurt someone you loved."

I look at her for a second, "I'm not really sure what to say to that. Although…I guess…I get it. I mean, Iris is a horrible stain on the earth, I couldn't care less what happens to her, so yeah."

"Iris your mom," Mariella asks as Kai, Marco and papa start putting platters of food on the table.

"Something like that," I tell her, sliding back into my chair and grabbing the risotto. Before spooning some out for Brooks then taking some for myself.

The chair on my other side scrapes back and Hudson drops down into it, still holding the peas to his face.

"Will you feed me, little omega?"

"You are not an invalid and I'm still mad at you," I tell him, but still spoon some risotto before passing it to Simon on Hudson's other side.

Dmitri steps in from the balcony, nose red from the cold, and sits at the far end of the table, as far away from Mariella as he can get. We work on passing the dishes around, piling food on our plates and making small talk while we enjoy a nice dinner together.

Brooks reaches for the bottle of wine and I slap his hand, "No drinking with that medication."

"Ouch, so mean," he admonishes.

"You should know better than to push my buttons right now," I retort.

"I just wanted to make a toast to my beautiful omega," he smiles, taking my hand.

"Don't try to cute your way out of it. No excuses."

"But I have something very important. Since we're all here together, the entire family. Well, plus Mariella, but we'll just call her a material witness -"

"She'll be sticking around for a while anyway, according to Marco. Gotta keep her safe from Volkov, until we manage to hunt the little prick down," Hudson interrupts to add his two cents, like usual.

"Hudson, shut the fuck up," Brooks tells him without breaking eye contact with me.

I smile, feeling the love flowing down the bond, his nervousness and excitement.

"My beautiful, perfect little omega. I knew you were it for me that first night. I knew you were meant to be with us, a part of our lives, the center of our pack. The road to where we are now has been filled with ups and downs and a whole lot of crazy shit, but we're still here together at the end of it. I know I don't have to give you the words, because you can feel my love for you every second of every day, but for those in this room that can't feel it, I want to tell you."

He stops for a moment, grasping each of my hands and kissing them gently before holding them against his chest.

"I love you more than I thought was possible to love another human being. Every single day of my life starts and ends with you. Your smile, your heart, your love. You are so very perfect for us and we will spend every day of the rest of our lives making sure we are worthy of you, if you'll have us."

He lets go of one of my hands, reaching into his pocket to pull out a small black box. My breath hitches.

"Will you marry us," he flips the box open with one hand.

Nestled inside the black velvet is a gorgeous emerald cut solitaire diamond ring. Each corner is lined with two baguettes. Ruby for Brooks, peridot for Hudson. Extremely apropos that their birthstones would be Christmas colors. The other corners are citrine for Kaiser and amethyst for Simon.

It's so perfect. My heart is overflowing.

"What do you say, *cara*," Kai rests his hand on my shoulder, standing next to me now, with Simon at his side. I was so focused on Brooks and his beautiful speech that I didn't even notice them coming to stand beside me.

"Say yes, little omega, you know you want to," Hudson says, sliding his hand up to massage the back of my neck.

"God yes," I laugh, "Of course, yes. I can't say yes enough."

My laughter turns to tears as Brooks slides that beautiful ring onto my finger, sealing the promise between us. Forever.

Epilogue

Simon

It's been almost a week since we rescued Mariella and I haven't found shit when it comes to Volkov or his plans. It's like he and his men dropped off the face of the earth, but I know that's not the case. We've disrespected him twice now. There's no way he's not planning some kind of revenge.

I'm sure that revenge is going to somehow involve Sloane and Mariella, so we've been hypervigilant whenever we have to leave the warehouse. I don't think Morris lets Mariella leave the compound at all. She's barely allowed out of the main house and usually, it's just to go to the gym or pool.

Sloane and Mariella talk regularly. Everyone thought it would be helpful for Mariella to have a woman, a friend to talk to, but usually it just turns into a bitch fest. Sloane bitching about us and Mariella bitching about them. None of us can win at this point.

I push myself away from my desk, before standing and stretching gently. I'm still not allowed to do yoga, or anything extra physical really, but they finally let me come back down to the basement and work when I need to. Trying to research on a laptop is the worst. I need all my screens.

Sloane's still worried about me, so she limits my time down here. Not like I can get into much trouble or hurt myself, since I spend all my time sitting, but I don't want to do anything to rock the boat. We're finally at a good place, all of us.

I press the elevator button and check my watch. Sloane wanted me to meet her in the movie room so we could watch some movie on Netflix and then take a nap. We'll probably end up falling asleep there like usual, though. The chaises are so damn comfortable and once we're cuddling together under one of her fuzzy blankets, it's like straight melatonin to the brain.

I step off the elevator and head left toward the movie room. The gym and pool are to the right, so it's always a little humid down here, too. The pool is strictly salt water, operating on a chlorine generator to convert salt to chlorine. Keeps the pool just as clean but without the chemicals or the harsh smell.

"Hey there, beautiful girl," I call out, entering the movie room, "fancy meeting you here."

"Well hello, my handsome beta, so glad you could join me," she smiles, taking my hand and tugging me toward the two chaises she's pushed together in the middle of the room.

"So tell me, what kind of masterpiece are we watching today?"

"Oh, it's a really good one. One of my favorites, actually!"

I try really hard not to laugh. Sloane's favorites are some of the cheesiest movies on the planet and I have no idea what she's about to subject me to.

"I can't wait, but first," I cup her cheeks, sliding my hands back into her hair and dropping my mouth to hers. I spend a few moments exploring her mouth, nibbling at her lips and just enjoying her presence before turning and directing her back to the chaises.

We sit down and get comfortable, adjusting the pillows and blanket until we're snuggled in nice and tight. She reaches back for the remote, smiling at me, her eyes sparkling as she turns the TV on and selects Netflix.

"Are you ready for this? Because it's seriously, so funny."

"I am definitely ready to laugh. What's in the queue?"

"Jack and Jill! Arguably one of Sandler's best movies," she starts and I can't help but laugh. Her love for cheesy Adam Sandler movies knows no bounds.

"I've heard of it, yeah," I laugh, tucking an arm around her and pulling her close, "but I don't care what you pick, as long as we get to watch it together."

"You know, it would be nice to watch but it's even better as background noise," Sloane murmurs, pressing against my side and sliding her hand down my stomach and then up under my shirt to brush across the waistband of my sweats.

"Background for what, baby," I whisper as she leans close, pressing her lips to mine.

She slides her tongue into my mouth at the same moment she slides her hand down my pants. I groan against her mouth as she grips my rapidly hardening cock.

"It's been over two weeks since your surgery," she tells me, her lips whispering across mine with every word, her hand working my cock, "and I want your cock inside of me."

"Shit," I whisper, dick jerking in her hand.

"Would you like that?"

"Yes, very much," I groan when she drops her mouth to my neck, sucking and biting her way down to my shoulder.

"Good, that's good," she murmurs, sliding over to straddle my lap and pulling her shirt off, revealing her perfect tits.

They've gotten larger in the past two weeks, her nipples darker. Not a huge difference, but just enough to notice.

Her dusky nipples are hard and begging for attention. I slide my hands up to cup them, stroking my thumbs across each one.

She moans softly, rocking her pussy right over my hard cock. I tug her waist, pulling her toward me until she's leaning forward, arms braced on the back of the chaise behind me. I suck her left nipple into my mouth, biting the peak and flicking my tongue over it while twisting and plucking the right one.

We've had a few more sessions since the first, learning each other and what we like. All leading to this moment now, when I'm recovered enough to be inside her.

She loves nipple play, but it makes her horny and restless. She has no patience when I just want to spend all day tasting these perfect breasts and ripe little nipples. Even now, she's whimpering and grinding down on me, searching for release.

"So impatient," I murmur against her breast, "do you need to cum, beautiful?"

I lick her nipple slowly before switching to the other one. I slide my hand into her leggings, pleased to find she's not wearing panties, her little pussy soaked with slick. Knowing what she likes now, I circle her clit a few times before sliding two fingers inside of her.

She drops her head back and moans, riding my fingers as I use my thumb to stroke her clit. I reach up with my other hand, twisting and plucking her nipples while she chases an orgasm on my hand.

"Oh, I want you inside of me, not your fingers," she whimpers, still moving against my hand.

"Cum for me first, then you can take me," I tell her, increasing the pressure of my thumb on her clit, rubbing tight rough circles as I feel her pussy clenching around my fingers.

I hook my fingers forward, putting pressure on her g-spot, then bring my other hand down so I can use three fingers to stroke hard against her clit. I keep the pressure on her clit even as she rides my fingers.

I ease the pressure when she tosses her head back and screams, slick leaking around my fingers and soaking both of us. I slide three fingers in my mouth, relishing in the feeling of her pussy throbbing around my other two.

My cock twitches as I taste her, imagining her tight little cunt squeezing my dick like that. God, I hope I can last. At least I gave her one first.

She rises up off my fingers, sliding off my lap so she can strip off her leggings. I slide to the edge of the chaise, lifting my ass enough to pull my sweats off. I toss my t-shirt down on the floor next to hers.

This is only the second time I've managed to be naked in front of her, but I think it's the most important time. I want to feel her against me as we come together. The initial redness has receded anyway and the scar continues to look better everyday. Sloane got me a special cream to use on it once I told her how self conscious it made me.

"I love you, Simon," she tells me, sliding her arms over my shoulders and lowering herself down onto me, trapping my cock against her wet lips.

"I love you, Sloane," I groan as she slides her slick coated pussy back and forth across the top of my cock.

"Lay back," she whispers in my ear, pushing gently on my shoulders until I'm laying back across the chaise, feet planted on the floor.

She rises above me like a goddess, her long hair loose around her shoulders, curtaining her body. She adjusts her knees next to my hips, reaching between us to position my dick at her opening before sinking down slowly.

I hiss as the heat of her pussy engulfs me, groaning when I'm finally seated all the way inside of her. I can feel her slick rolling off my balls and I desperately search my mind for anything else to think about.

I start working my way through the Von Neumann architecture model, starting with the processing unit and moving to the arithmetic logic unit, the processor registers and control unit.

"What are you thinking about," Sloane murmurs, rubbing her thumb between my eyebrows, "because you are clearly not with me."

She rolls her hips a few times, "Come back to me, Simon."

"I can't," I pant, "I'm…I need to think about…the instruction register and program counter."

"Simon, look at me," she chuckles, stroking her fingers down my cheek.

I blink open my eyes. Big mistake. She's leaning forward enough that her breasts are right in my face, her hard little nipples begging to be sucked.

"Look at my face, Simon," she chuckles, still rocking slowly on top of me.

"Baby, you feel too fucking good, I can't…I'm already struggling," I croak.

"Hey, hey. We talked about this, remember? It's okay, just stay with me. I'd rather have you with me in this moment than trying to make yourself last longer. You're supposed to enjoy this, too, you know," she whispers against my lips, plucking a gentle kiss before rolling her hips quickly.

"Fuck," I groan, "you're killing me."

"But what a great way to go, right," Kai's voice rumbles from behind me.

My head snaps back, seeing him standing at the other side of the chaise. Albeit, I'm seeing him upside down, but he's definitely there.

"Fuck, this is gonna be alot harder for me than I thought," Kai groans, gripping his cock through his jeans.

"You can join in next time, I promise," Sloane tells him, rocking against me, "but this is ours. You can watch, but you can't touch."

"Why," I groan as she starts to ride me slowly, "oh fuck, baby. Oh, shit. Why…are you here?"

"I'm going to fuck you," Sloane pants, "he's going to bite you. Now just enjoy the ride, okay?"

Sloane leans over, bracing one arm next to me and sliding the other down between us. She starts really riding my dick, sliding up and down on my cock while she rubs her sweet little clit. I reach up and grab each breast in hand, twisting and tugging her nipples until she's mewling above me.

I feel her pussy clench around me, pulsing as she cries out. The new sensation does me in, my cock exploding inside of her. My whole body tightens as my dick spasms.

Kai pushes my head to the side and sinks his teeth into my neck, biting until I feel a drop of blood roll down the back of my neck. The pain quickly turns into pleasure, my cock throbbing back to life.

"Ooooh," Sloane moans and I can feel it, inside of me. I can feel her desire and her love, just as sure as I can feel her hot little pussy clamped around my dick. I feel Kai's desire and longing, a hint of jealousy as Sloane starts to ride me once more.

"This definitely counts as next time," Kai says, standing and yanking off his clothes, almost tripping when he tugs his jeans off, "and I am not just watching this time."

"Yes, please," I respond, reaching back to wrap my hand around his cock, "just remember that the two of you have to do all the work."

"I'm okay with that," Sloane mutters, snapping her hips against mine, riding me fast and dirty, while Kai drops down onto the chaise to feed me his dick, "just lay there like a good boy and take it."

"Yes, ma'am," I tell her, just as Kai pushes into my mouth.

We spend the next hour enjoying each other in every way possible, before Hudson and Brooks finally give in and show up. The rest of the night is a hot, slick soaked dream that will live on as one of the best moments of my life.

Perfect Little Captive: Book One

Book one features the beginning of the story of Morris, Marco, Dmitri, Remi and Mariella. It will be released in June of 2023.

They killed my father and kidnapped me. They told me a story about how my father traded me to get his gambling debts wiped out. That a human trafficker is coming for me. That I'm not safe.

Now they're holding me captive in a giant compound outside the city, but how can I trust them when they're keeping secrets from each other. There's dissension in the ranks and I don't know where the cards will fall.

Am I safe here? Or would I be safer on my own? Take my savings and disappear? Or take a chance on the broken men trying so hard to make me feel safe?

Printed in Great Britain
by Amazon